"Bless you, Arrah." Mami squeezes my hand and heads for the door. "The merchants in the East Market are putting on a street fair tomorrow night, now that things are back to normal. You should come."

I fiddle with my hands. "Things don't feel anything like normal."

"The night may be long, child," Mami says, "but morning always comes."

Once she leaves, I press my back against the door. For the first time in a long while, I can see a glimpse of a future for myself. I will make good on my promise to my father. I will not only be strong for him, but I will use the chieftains' gift to help others.

Their sacrifice will not be in vain.

THE KINGDOM OF SOULS TRILOGY

Kingdom of Souls
Reaper of Souls
Master of Souls

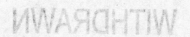

REAPER
OF
SOULS

RENA BARRON

An Imprint of HarperCollinsPublishers

HarperTeen is an imprint of HarperCollins Publishers.

Reaper of Souls
Copyright © 2021 by Rena Barron
Map by Maxime Plasse

Library of Congress Control Number: 2020949380
ISBN 978-0-06-287099-5

Typography by Jenna Stempel-Lobell
21 22 23 24 25 PC/LSCH 10 9 8 7 6 5 4 3 2 1
❖
First paperback edition, 2022

To the storytellers and dreamers, this book is dedicated to you . . .

. . . and to my family

PART I

PART I

PROLOGUE
DIMMA

I will start my story at the beginning, the middle, and the end. For I have lived a thousand lives and died a thousand deaths, and every time I die, I relive the same memory. The last moments of my first life, when I was Dimma: god, girl, wife, mother, traitor, monster. The unspeakable act that set the end of the world into motion. The start of the war between the gods and my beloved Daho.

I sit upon a throne of polished bone inlaid with gold and jewels that is at once grotesque and beautiful. I am high above the floor, at the top of the stairs that Daho built for me to watch the heavens. At this hour, when my brother Re'Mec rules, I am bathed in his sunlight through the amethyst sky dome above.

I hold my child. He is a small spark vibrating against my palm, tiny and precious. He has his father's heart and my stolen gift of immortality. He tells me that he loves me through our secret language. But my vessel betrays my intentions. I can't stop crying. He is the flaw in the Supreme Cataclysm's design, the part of me that my brethren want to destroy. I squeeze my eyes shut, shuddering.

A cloak of darkness bleeds into the chamber, swallowing the sunshine and the sounds of the battle. One of my siblings has slipped past Daho and his army and broken through my defenses. I let out a deep, tired sigh.

So many will die because of my decisions. My sister Koré once told me that a god's love is a dangerous thing. I know that now. I don't want to die, but I deserve my fate.

"Oh, Dimma." Fram's anguished dual voices cut through me. "What have you done?"

When I open my eyes, Fram stands before me in their two forms, twins of light and dark, life and death, chaos and calm. I realize almost immediately that I have lost a slice of time—there is a hole in my memories, a piece cut out. I look down at my clenched fist, the hand that only a moment ago held my child. My fingers tremble as they unfold, one by one, and reveal an empty palm.

The amethyst ceiling cracks with my rage and rains down in shards that tear into my flesh. The walls weep my tears. "Where is he?" I demand. "Where is my son?"

"I am sorry, sister," Fram says as their shadows cup my face. They brush away my tears, and I am flooded with relief that it is Fram who came to steal my life, not Koré or Re'Mec. Of all my siblings, they understand me best. "You shouldn't have been the one to do it. That is cruelty that I do not wish upon anyone."

"I killed him?" I ask, drawing the only possible conclusion. I shrink against the throne, gutted and hollow. I've done something unforgivable. "I killed my son."

I remember every single moment of my first life, except this one.

I'd cradled my child in my hands and then . . . he was gone. Some acts are too horrible to remember—some deeds too painful to keep.

Tears spill from Fram's eyes, too. "Re'Mec and Koré will end the war only when both you and the child are dead. They will spare Daho and his people if you agree to our terms."

I stare down at my hands again. I can't live with what I've done—I can't face Daho. I cannot tell him that I've killed our son. "Do it," I say. "Before I change my mind."

Fram strikes me with ribbons of light. They cut into my chest and rip out the part of me connected to the Supreme Cataclysm—my immortality. My soul withers as their shadows brush away the last of the tears on my empty vessel's face. Even I cannot free myself from the clutches of the god of life and death. But as I've said, this is not the end of my story.

It is also the beginning.

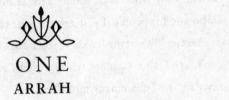

ONE
ARRAH

Sparks of magic drift through the inn walls, chased by moonlight and shadows. It's the hour of *ösana*, the sliver of time between night and day when magic is most potent. I clench my teeth as the sparks burrow underneath my skin, adding to my strength. Twenty-gods, they burn, but I can't let go. I can't fail again—I've already lost so much.

I clutch the arms of my chair, swallowing down the bile on my tongue as the last sparks melt. The chieftains' *kas* stir inside me, spilling lifetimes of memories and wisdom. With their sacrifice and gift, I have more magic than I could ever dream of. It has to be enough to save Sukar.

"It will work," Essnai says, giving me one of Sukar's sickles. The steel flashes in the dim light of the bedchamber and Zu symbols vibrate against the blade. The worn wood of the hilt feels odd in my hand, like I'm taking something personal without permission.

Still, I find a smile for Essnai as she props her back against the wall to watch the ritual. I'm glad that she's here with me. While we

tend to Sukar, Rudjek and the others have gone ahead to the Kingdom to carry news of the battle at Heka's Temple. Fadyi and Raëke,
two of his craven guardians, stayed behind, though they've kept
their distance as I prepared for the ritual. I don't linger on Rudjek's
absence. I can't let that distract me—not now, even if I want nothing
more than to be with him. Essnai isn't bemoaning Kira's absence.
Though I have caught her more than once staring longingly toward
the east, in the direction of home.

Sukar's ragged breathing and the crackle of the candle flames
fill the silence in the chamber. He looks so small in the bed, tucked
underneath the tavern's dingy quilt. He hasn't woken since the
battle—since I almost killed him. Guilt gnaws at my belly, one of a
tangle of emotions that cut deep whenever I let my guard down.

Koré attempted to heal Sukar before we left the tribal lands, but
she didn't wait to see if he was getting better. The moon orisha's
priority is the box that holds the Demon King's soul, except she has
no clue where she hid it. She erased her memories to keep it safe from
my sister. It makes me uneasy that his soul is still out there somewhere, but he can't escape now—not with the tribal people dead.
With Heka, the god of the tribal lands, gone, there's no one left with
enough magic to free him. And my mother and sister can do no more
harm. I snatch my mind back from those thoughts, too, for they cut
the deepest of all.

The sun orisha, Re'Mec, had left before his twin. Not that he's
ever shown much concern for mortal life. He's chasing the Demon
King's dagger, which Shezmu, my sister's demon father, stole in the
aftermath of the battle.

"The orishas got what they wanted out of us," I say, my gaze pinned on Sukar's gaunt face. Maybe I expected too much from them after all that we've sacrificed to help clean up their mess. "Now, they've gone back to playing gods."

"Doing what they do best," Essnai says, but with no malice in her voice.

Sukar hasn't opened his eyes in seventeen days. I keep replaying the moment in my mind. How Efiya raised her sword over his head. How I flung his body through the air with my magic. How he crashed into the stone column at the Temple and didn't get up. I only wanted to save my friend, but I almost killed him. I'm the reason he hasn't awakened.

I suck in a deep breath as I lean closer to Sukar. I have the knowledge and magic of the five tribal chieftains inside me. Icarata of Tribe Mulani, U'metu of Tribe Kes, Beka of Tribe Zu, Töra Eké of Tribe Litho. And my grandmother Mnekka of Tribe Aatiri. The Litho chieftain is the most talented healer of the five, but his method requires that I merge my *ka* with Sukar's. Dozens died before he perfected the practice. I can't risk making a mistake. The Kes chieftain's method requires three sacrifices over three days at the start of the new moon.

Sukar would want me to honor his traditions, so I have chosen a ritual relying on scrivener magic from Tribe Zu. For this, I need Beka. He stirs inside me like leaves rustling in the wind as his knowledge pours into my mind. I don't even have to ask—his *ka* is waiting for me to call upon it. I once knew every ritual scroll in my father's shop by heart, but they'd been useless when I had no way to conjure their power. Now I have magic's secrets at my fingertips.

I come to my feet with Sukar's sickle in my hand. "I'm ready."

"After this, you will rest," Essnai says, leaving no room to refuse. "You look tired."

"Yes, Mama Essnai," I relent.

She clucks her tongue at me, and it almost feels like old times.

I move to the table where the bowl of ink sits between three candles and a bone with one end sharpened to a needle point. The Zu chieftain's shadow stretches against the wall. Beka was a bit taller than me, and his *ado*, the horned headpiece, gave him yet more height. His *ka* still wears a ruby mask with onyx trim around the eyes—the mask of his station as Zu chieftain.

It needs your blood, Beka whispers in a hoarse voice only I can hear, and it sends chills through me. The chieftains rarely speak, and when they do, I'm almost grateful it's never more than a few words.

I slice the sickle across my palm and let the blood drip into the mixture of ink and herbs. Smoke curls up from the bowl. By the time I've put the blade aside, the cut has healed, leaving the smell of warm iron in the air. It isn't something that I have to think about; my new magic acts on instinct. I hadn't expected that. I still have so much to learn.

In the days since the battle, Sukar's hair has grown in, and Essnai shaved some off for the ritual. I add a pinch of it to the ink. I take the bowl and needle and sit on the edge of the bed. Beads of sweat trickle down Sukar's forehead as the smoke fills the room. Beka sends me images of the symbols for strength, healing, and fortification. My cheeks warm as a fourth symbol appears in my mind. Two bodies intertwined—the fertility symbol. It seems that Beka has a sense of humor.

"I bestow strength upon you in the name of the father and mother of the tribal lands." I dip the needle into the ink. "Let Heka guide you through the dark."

I push back the sheet from Sukar's bare chest, revealing a dozen or so tattoos barren of magic. His skin is smooth and warm to the touch. If he were awake, he'd most definitely have a sharp remark. I miss his ability to make light of a dire situation.

Magic pulses in my blood as my palm brushes across his hip bone. I begin the long and tedious process of etching a reaper. It will become a twin to the one above his other hip to give him strength. Each prick of the needle against Sukar's flesh draws a bead of blood. "Take courage, son of Tribe Zu."

I tap out two more tattoos—matching antlers on his wrists imbued with healing magic. A *yul* with three branches in the crook of his elbow to reinforce his previous tattoos. When the *yul* is completed, his body pulses with light, and I smile.

"What's happening?" Essnai asks from her perch against the wall.

"His tattoos are glowing again," I explain, knowing that she can't see the magic.

Essnai lets out a sigh of relief, but Sukar doesn't move. We wait for a half bell while the light fades from his tattoos, bit by bit, stealing our hope with it. Essnai casts a desperate look at me to do something when I tell her that the tattoos have nearly gone dark. I reach toward the *yul*, intending to infuse it with more magic, but pain shoots through my fingers. The needle slips from my hand, and the shadow of the Zu chieftain disappears. My fingers twist and bend in impossible ways. I snatch my hand away and cradle it against my chest. I realize my mistake almost immediately. I cannot give the tattoo more magic than it can handle at once.

Essnai kneels in front of me. "Are you okay?"

The last of the light fades from Sukar's tattoos.

"It should've worked," I breathe. "I have to try something else."

Essnai takes my hand between her palms as the pain subsides. "Try again at your father's shop after you've gotten some rest. We're less than a day's journey from Tamar, and Sukar will hold on that long—he's too stubborn to die."

"I don't need rest," I say. "I'm fine."

"You almost ascended into death mere weeks ago," Essnai counters. "Give it time." She lets go of my hand, her eyes betraying her disappointment. "I'll see about getting us some food."

When she opens the door, the noise from the tavern rushes into the chamber. We're two levels up, but we might as well be on the ground floor with all the patrons filling their bellies with beer.

I put the bone needle and the blood medicine aside, and settle back in the chair. I close my eyes and massage my forehead. Did I miss something? Grandmother would make me recall the steps of a ritual in painstaking detail. I remember her sitting cross-legged with her white locs in a crown. She was always patient with me. Thinking of her adds to my resolve—maybe Essnai is right, and I just need more rest before I try a second time.

A sharp, burning smell makes me open my eyes again. Smoke curls up from Sukar's new tattoos, and ash flakes from his skin. He inhales another ragged breath, and it takes a beat too long for me to realize that he never lets it out.

"Sukar," I whisper as I rush to his side. "No, no, no."

His body convulses against the bed as his face twists in pain. I hold him, not sure what else I can do. Dread untangles from the emotions buried inside me. I'd gone over the Zu ritual in my head for days. I can't have messed this up, too.

Essnai steps into the chamber with two bowls in her arms. "The kitchen only had stale bread and cold—" She falters upon seeing Sukar shaking, then drops the meal on a table. She rushes to his other side. "What happened?"

"I don't know," I say, but then I notice the faintest light coming from his tattoos, growing brighter and stronger. My shoulders sag in relief as Sukar's whole body starts to glow. "He's . . . I think he's coming around."

Sukar's face screws up into a deep frown, and Essnai laughs, her voice a sharp note. He tries and fails to speak, then Essnai shushes him and presses a cup of water from his bedside to his lips.

When he finally comes to his senses, he croaks out, "Why do I feel like I've ascended into death and come back?"

I smile as I squeeze his hand. He's going to be okay. "Because you have."

TWO
ARRAH

Sukar squints against the candlelight as tentacles of ink spread out from the *kaheri*—the star tattoo at the center of his chest. It grows crooked branches that reach his collarbone and roots that wind down his belly. The reconfiguration is a good sign. The tree shows strength. His body has enough magic to help him recover. When his eyes finally come into focus, he grimaces.

Essnai gives him a playful slap on the cheek. "Don't ever scare us like that again."

I expect Sukar to say something witty or sharp, but his red-rimmed eyes glisten with unshed tears. Beads of sweat streak down his forehead as he groans, "What did I miss?"

"Efiya caught you off guard—I suppose you were daydreaming on the battlefield or something," Essnai tells him, flicking her wrist. To which Sukar wrinkles his nose at her. "Arrah used her magic to fling you out of the way of Efiya's killing blow. Had she not, we'd be performing a Zu burial rite for you right now."

Sukar flinches—the movement almost imperceptible. He strains to adjust his position, and Essnai helps him sit with his back against the wall. "Did we win?"

I nod, biting back the phantom pain in my side where Efiya stabbed me. I can't bring myself to say that I killed my sister. That I both loved and despised her. That I pitied her and hated her. That I could never forgive her for what she did to our parents, to the tribes, to Rudjek. That I failed her. Maybe if I would've tried harder, taught her better, I could've saved her, too.

"Efiya's dead," I say, and then shift the conversation back to him. "Sorry for almost killing you."

Sukar stares at me, his eyes wide. I desperately want him to crack a joke like he always does, but he only massages his temples.

Essnai pats his arm. "You'll get over it—she fixed you."

"Let me get this right." Sukar cocks an eyebrow—a hint of a smile finally stretching across his sharp cheekbones. "Arrah almost killed me, and I should be grateful that she saved my life."

I'm relieved that he's found his sense of humor, but it doesn't wash away the guilt that aches inside me—the regrets, the mistakes, the pain. I've missed the husky sound of his voice and the three of us teasing each other. I should take this moment as a promise that one day things will be all right again, but I can't just smile and pretend that the wounds in my mind aren't still bleeding.

Essnai shrugs. "Well, you are alive."

"Did you really break every bone in my body?" Sukar asks me, incredulous.

"I'm afraid so," I say, glancing away.

He inches his fingers toward mine. I look up again, and a little of his old spark is back. He squeezes my hand, and he shrugs. "Like Essnai said, I am alive."

I bite my lip. "And now you have three new tattoos to show off."

"Please tell me you did not use scrivener magic." Sukar groans again as he searches his body for the new ink. "For Heka's sake, if you've given me ugly tattoos, I swear . . ."

"I did an adequate job," I say, defending myself.

Sukar opens his mouth, his gaze roaming between Essnai and me, weighing his next words. "How are you still alive?" he asks, his voice cautious. "My uncle said that wielding the Demon King's dagger would kill you."

I exchange a look with Essnai. She and Rudjek had wondered the same in the days after the battle. I could remember Efiya bleeding on the Temple floor, reaching for me, then nothing at all until the dream. A winged beast with a jackal head had swept down from the sky and stolen me away from the world. It was only a dream, not a vision, not a shadow of what's to come. I had to believe that. I could channel Grandmother's gift to find out, but I couldn't bring myself to do it. There was that moment before the dream—a slice of midnight sky, serenity, a brief feeling of letting go. I cling to that shred of peace instead of reliving a memory I am glad to have forgotten. "I may have died for a little while."

"Your magic brought you back?" Sukar asks, his eyes twinkling with curiosity.

My magic. I'll never get used to feeling it teeming under my skin in a warm embrace.

"That or the orisha of life and death." I clear my throat. "Koré thinks they helped me."

"Fram?" Sukar rubs his chin. "That's an interesting choice for a god that deals in death."

A feeling of uncertainty edges at the back of my mind, urging me to let it go. I'm alive. It doesn't matter how or why. I survived despite everything. I have a second chance and the magic to help fix some of the havoc my family wreaked on the world.

"You both need some sleep." Essnai settles in the chair beside Sukar's bed, then she raises an eyebrow at me when I don't move. "Scat!"

"Good to know things haven't changed," Sukar says in a lazy drawl. "You're still a tyrant."

Essnai looks quite satisfied with herself, and I don't have the energy to argue with her. Magic takes from all, and my bones ache like I've been on the losing side of a street fight. But it's a small price to pay for healing Sukar. I bid my friends good night and slip into the narrow corridor. I'm assaulted by the cloying smells of tobacco and stale beer, and a flurry of laughter floating up the stairs. I encounter a patron from the tavern who fumbles with his key before half falling into his room.

Once I'm in my chamber, I lie in bed and stare up at the cracked ceiling in the dark. I'm tired, but I'm restless. I don't know what tomorrow will bring. I have nothing to go back to in Tamar. I can't stand the idea of living in the villa again and seeing the Mulani dancers my mother painted prancing along the wall. Or my father's abandoned garden. After failing to save the tribes, I don't know if I can stomach more devastation. The city had been in ruins when we left, whole neighborhoods burned to the ground. I wish I could believe that time heals all wounds, but it's never that simple.

There's still the matter of my banishment. Has Rudjek been able to convince his father to change his mind, or will soldiers be waiting to arrest me? If everyone knows that my mother and sister were behind the demon attacks, they might think I had something to do with them, too. Do they know the tribes are gone, cut down by my sister's hand, the people slaughtered?

I reach for my magic, desperate for a way to lessen the pain. The chieftains' memories rush in at once and drown out my thoughts. I sink into the noise and weep until there are no more tears inside me. When I am on the edge of sleep, one of the chieftains' memories washes out the others. There is a boy shrouded in shadows sitting beside a frozen lake with his knees drawn to his chest. He's whispering something too low for me to hear, and his voice is the calm of melting snow. I strain to catch his words, but they fade around the edges until they are only faint impressions that lure me into sleep.

In the morning, Sukar is still weak and complains of a headache, but he insists upon walking. Even with Essnai's staff to support his weight, he stumbles twice by the time we are down the stairs and through the scatter of new patrons. They mingle with the night owls who've been drinking well past sunup with no end in sight.

"Perhaps I should go easy on the wine," Sukar says when he stumbles a third time.

"Hmm," Essnai replies, playing along. "Where would you be without your wonderful friends to take care of you?"

Droves of people wander the streets as the eye of Re'Mec climbs across the sky. They pace along the hardened, cracked dirt with donkeys and carts on their way to trade and sell. The air smells of dung, hay, and blood. The blood is from a butcher pushing a cart that leaks from the bottom, leaving a trail in his wake. It reminds me of the battlefield and how close we'd come to losing everything.

The cravens' anti-magic tingles against my skin before I spot them near our wagon. Fadyi nods in our direction as Raëke runs her hand through one of the horses' manes. Fadyi passes for human at first glance with a shock of black curls and his hair shaved on the sides. His face is someone's idea of what a Tamaran should look like—rich brown skin, dark eyes, sharp features. With my magic, only I can see that his skin is always in flux, rearranging itself, working to hold his shape. Raëke's impersonation of a human is almost as good except her eyes are too large and she often forgets to blink.

I haven't gotten used to how their anti-magic scrapes against my skin like a sudden shadow on a cloudless day. My magic feels on alert in their presence, thrashing and coiling inside me. Restless. The way it reacts to the cravens is a constant warning that Rudjek and I can never be together. We can never touch, never kiss, never find comfort in each other's arms. I push down the knot in my belly. We'd left so much unsaid, and I owe him an apology for being so awful after Efiya hurt him. I don't deserve his forgiveness.

"You've been carting me around like a sack of grain?" Sukar asks, leaning on the staff.

"And what of it?" Essnai returns his question with one of her own.

Sukar rolls his eyes. "I suppose it's better than dragging me through the dirt."

"Oh, we did that, too," I add, forcing a smile, "until we could find a wagon."

"Some friends you are." Sukar waves me off, but he looks grateful. "I suppose I'll take the wagon since you went through so much trouble."

My nerves are on edge most of the day, as we trek through well-worn farmlands and dirt roads. Sukar, Essnai, and I have walked this path often with my father, journeying to and from the tribal lands. We'd traveled with a caravan of more than a hundred families, heading to the Blood Moon Festival. I dig my nails into my palms, determined to keep it together. I hold on to my father's last words.

Little Priestess, I need you to be strong a little longer.

It's hard to be strong when I will never hear another one of his stories or see his smile.

When we're on a stretch of road alone, Raëke shifts into a sunbird. The transformation is almost immediate. Her body becomes gray liquid that shrinks to take a blank shape. The details start to come together—wings, black feathers, beady eyes, a beak. Her underbelly is bright yellow and her long tail, iridescent. The cravens' anti-magic may feel overwhelming, but it's also extraordinary. Raëke lets out a high-pitched chirp, then takes to the sky to carry news to Rudjek that we will be arriving soon.

The rest of the way, Essnai and Fadyi fill Sukar in on everything he missed at the end of the battle while I stay quiet. They tell him that Shezmu and some of the demons escaped after stealing the Demon King's dagger. Every time I think of it, my blood goes cold. I keep telling myself that we've stopped Efiya, and Shezmu can't release the Demon King without her. But the demons can still do so much harm on their own. It's only a matter of time before Re'Mec and the other orishas hunt them down, if they haven't already.

"And what of the tribes?" Sukar asks, his voice breaking.

"We searched each of them," Fadyi says, lowering his gaze. "There were no survivors."

The cravens found the remains of the tribal people picked over by scavenger birds, and Koré burned the bodies out of respect. I'm ashamed to admit it, but I'm glad I didn't have to see the tribes that way. I was too weak to help with the search.

I couldn't stand to see my cousins Nenii and Semma, who'd always been so kind to me, or Great-Aunt Zee with her snide remarks. They didn't deserve to die like that—cut down and left to rot in the sun. I swallow my tears, holding on to my last memories of them. Nenii flirting with a Kes boy at the Blood Moon Festival. Semma sashaying in her beaded kaftan. Great-Aunt Zee laughing while the five tribes danced and celebrated as one.

The conversation falls silent as we come upon a single crowded road that leads into the city from the west. It sits in the shadow of the Almighty Palace and the watchtowers stationed along the cliffs. Ahead of us, there is a checkpoint that hadn't been there before and a long line of caravans.

Red-clad gendars in silver breastplates shout orders. "Those with horses, mules, and caged animals to the left. Everyone else to the right!"

"This is new," Sukar says from his perch in the wagon bed.

He doesn't seem concerned about the checkpoint, but then again, he has no reason to be. I'm nervous that Rudjek hasn't been able to clear my name—that at any moment one of the gendars will execute me on sight. We move to the left line. A scribe at its head records names and reasons for visiting the city. Meanwhile, the gendars search everything. "Let me see your eyes," a soldier demands of the woman in front of us traveling with a mule weighed down with sacks of grain.

"See my what?" the woman asks, flustered.

"Your eyes," the soldier repeats in a slow, mocking tone.

The woman tilts her head up, and the gendar stares down at her. "All clear," he says after a pause.

I don't know what the gendars' orders are, but they seem specific.

When it's our turn, the scribe asks for my name. I could lie, but I don't. I won't hide who I am. "Arrah N'yar."

"From where?" the scribe asks.

"From the city," I say. "I'm Tamaran."

"Hmm, name sounds Aatiri or Kes," the scribe remarks. "Where do you reside?"

I can't go back to the villa, so I give him the address of my father's shop.

"Show me your eyes," the gendar working alongside the scribe says.

As I tilt my head up to him, I ask, "What are you looking for?"

The man stares into my eyes intently, searching. "Demons."

I shudder at his admission. "Are there still demons in the city?"

"No, and we'd like to keep it that way," the gendar says. "It's all in the eyes."

He's right, I realize. Months ago, the sun orisha, Re'Mec, disguised as the Temple scribe Tam, said that all demons had glowing green eyes. It was the mark of their race. Even when they possessed others, their eyes changed to some shade of green. I'd seen it for myself the first time my sister raised a hand to the sky and caught a demon's *ka*. She'd put his soul in a stray cat, then later in the body of a fisherman from Kefu. His eyes had been the same eerie glowing jade in both of his *vessels* before I ended his life.

After we pass the checkpoint, we pour into the crowded city. It's so congested that we move at a snail's pace. Most people head toward the East Market and the docks, where they can set up free trade, but we stay to the west. Once we arrive at my father's shop, I'll find some concoction to help Sukar with his headache.

The third afternoon bells toll as we reach the pristine cobblestones of the West Market. Attendants bustle back and forth with baskets of food, textiles, and supplies. Some wear silk elaras, embroidered and jeweled, almost as fancy as the families they serve. Others don modest, rough-woven tunics with no personal effects. They all bear one thing in common: their employers' crests, sewn on sleeves or shirttails. Never higher, so no one mistakes them above their station.

Head attendants command troupes of apprentices nipping at their heels as they carry out their duties. Even if I've never liked the idea of parading around with attendants, I'm relieved to see the market back to normal. When we'd left for the tribal lands, it was all but abandoned.

At the courtyard near the coliseum, our progress slows to a halt. Tension chokes the perfumed air, and it's too crowded to move. There are more scholars, scribes, and families of import than I've ever seen in the market at once. People of high stations hardly ever come to the markets unless there's an assembly in session. These people swarm around like a hive of angry bees.

I catch snatches of conversations. "Traitor." "Liar." "Heretic."

"We won't stand for this disrespect," says a man in a green elara with double rings on each of his fingers. "We have been patient long enough!" My eyes travel to his crest—a ram's head—the emblem of the royal family and homage to the sun god, Re'Mec. A *Sukkara*, here—in the market and not inside a fancy litter?

I can hardly believe who's causing all the fuss. It's Prince Derane—uncle to the new Almighty One, Tyrek Sukkara. He's surrounded by others from the royal family and flanked by a dozen guards. Second Son Tyrek became the Almighty One after his father's and brother's deaths. Once he took the throne, he let the demons run amok in the city and kill countless Tamarans.

A woman in a scribe's robe almost runs straight into me, too busy gossiping to watch where she's going. When she glances up, she stops in her tracks. "It's her!" the woman shouts, backing away. "The *owahyat* who set the demons upon us."

She flings the word like an insult, and I flinch. My heart aches for Ty, our matron, and Nezi, our porter—both former women of the streets, abused by *Ka*-Priest Ren Eké. He wouldn't have gotten away with hurting so many women if not for people like this scribe who thought them less. Nezi gave her soul over to a demon, and I haven't seen Ty since I left the villa in Kefu.

"Watch your tongue, scribe," Essnai warns, "or I'll relieve you of it."

"That's not the *Ka*-Priestess, fool," someone else says. "That's her daughter."

"The one who set the demons free?" asks another, distressed.

"No, that one is dead," comes the answer.

I guess I no longer have to worry about what people know of my mother's and sister's crimes. They got the gist of it. Before long, we're surrounded by people pointing and sneering, and I bite back a curse. The voices from the crowd rise to a deafening chorus. As the mob presses in closer, the magic stirs inside me, and the chieftains' *kas* come alive.

Burn them. The Kes chieftain's voice drowns out the crowd. He's gifted me with the power to call firestorms. And my fingers ache as clouds swell in the sky over the market. Some of the patrons take note and back away, but most are too furious to notice. *Bring them to their knees*.

I don't want to hurt these people, but I won't let them hurt me, either. Grandmother's words cut through the rage rushing through my body. *Speak your truth, Little Priestess*. "I had nothing to do with bringing the demons back," I say, finding my voice.

"Keep your lies, girl," someone snaps.

Essnai points her staff at a balding man easing closer with a kobachi knife in his hand. "Another step and I'll shatter every bone in your arm." He spits at her feet but heeds her warning.

Sukar climbs from the wagon and hunches over with his sickles in his hands. "I've been itching for another fight."

People in gray tunics push through the angry crowd. A woman in the sheer white headscarf favored among those who've chosen Koré as their patron god leads them. I recognize Emere, the head of the Temple attendants.

"Leave her be!" Emere shouts. She and her companions form a line between us and the mob. "The Temple will not let harm come to this girl."

"We're supposed to listen to you?" someone screams. "A Temple loyalist who sat back while *that girl's* mother killed our children?"

My heart leaps in my chest, remembering the night my mother sacrificed Kofi and the others to Shezmu. She'd done it so that he could beget a child strong enough to free the Demon King. My friend died so Efiya could be born, and I'd been too weak to save him. My knees almost give out, but Essnai leans against my side and her reassuring presence gives me strength.

"I make no excuses for the vile things the *Ka*-Priestess did," Emere says. "Nor do I make excuses for her predecessor, *Ka*-Priest Ren Eké. So many people knew of his perversions and kept his secrets for decades."

"Let the Almighty One be the judge of her," someone else yells.

"Acting Almighty One," Prince Derane corrects, "until I reclaim my birthright."

"You conspired with Tyrek to cheat your way to the throne," comes another voice.

"How dare you!" Prince Derane says, pressing a hand over his heart to show offense.

The crowd throws around so many accusations that I can't keep track of them.

The gong rings atop the coliseum and a contingent of gendars marches into the courtyard. I go still as the first brush of anti-magic pricks against my skin. But the feeling pales in comparison to the wild hope that flares inside me at the sight of Rudjek.

He makes his way through the crowd on horseback with Kira and Majka riding on his heels. All three wear fancy elaras of fitted tunics and matching pants. Majka in royal blue, Kira in black, and

Rudjek in white and gold silks, the Vizier's colors. His elara is even more beautiful than the one he wore at his Coming of Age Ceremony. A flush of warmth creeps into my cheeks. It's only been a few weeks since we last saw each other, but, oh, how I've missed him.

Rudjek's obsidian eyes find me and seem to say that things will be okay—that I only have to trust him. His horse stops abruptly, and he frowns, looking decidedly annoyed. I bite back a smile at seeing him so out of his element. Kira leans close to him and mumbles something. Rudjek nods as he tightens his grip on the reins and nudges the horse. This time the horse walks forward until the three of them reach the center of the crowd. I notice, then, that Rudjek's horse is bedecked in a white garment with his family's crest, a lion's head, stitched in gold thread.

"I am Majka of House Kelu," Majka addresses the crowd first. He wears the crest of a leopard pinned to his collar. "I am here to attest that Arrah N'yar saved our country from a great evil."

Kira's gilded plume crest glimmers in the sunlight. "I am Kira Ny—daughter of Guildmaster Ny of House Ny." She adds her voice. "I second that Arrah is the only reason any of you are alive."

"And I am Rudjek Omari, of House Omari," Rudjek says, his deep timbre projecting over the crowd with ease. "Your Crown Prince."

I can't believe what I'm hearing. Crown Prince? I feel like I've fallen out of one nightmare into another one.

"I am a descendant of the sun god like my Sukkara cousins," Rudjek continues. His horse takes an impromptu side step and almost butts into Kira. Rudjek clears his throat. "Magic and charms cannot influence my mind or my words." He holds on to the horse's reins tightly—his other hand squeezing his shotel so hard that his knuckles are pale. "So hear my words now. I, too, attest that Arrah put an end to Efiya's tyranny and the demon threat. She saved us all."

The crowd deflates upon hearing Rudjek's decree, but I am breathless. I can't stop staring at him, realizing what this must mean. His father, Vizier Suran Omari, has seized control of the Kingdom.

THREE
RUDJEK

Let it be known that I, Rudjek Omari, survived the cravens, a demon army, and meddling gods only to be bested by a horse. But how could I deprive the people of seeing their Crown Prince? Now that I've made a show of proclaiming Arrah's innocence, I can't dismount without making a fool of myself.

It's hard to keep my composure when my thighs are burning like a blazing inferno, but the mob has stopped advancing. Arrah stands between Sukar and Essnai. I ignore the sting of her magic, which feels like needles poking into my spine. She's dusty from the road, but she still looks like she could snap her fingers and bring this pathetic mob to its knees. I have half a mind to encourage her. She quirks an eyebrow like she knows that I'm thinking of something wicked, but I keep my expression neutral. I need these people to accept my authority without question.

"No harm shall come to Arrah N'yar," I declare. "Be thankful that she saved our Kingdom and go back to your lives."

I'm prepared for the crowd to reject me and call me a fraud. I am a fraud—I have no illusion about that, though I'll be the best fraud they've ever seen. By no stroke of luck, they do heed me—their *acting* Crown Prince. I'd be lying if I said that I couldn't believe my father arrested Tyrek Sukkara and seized the Kingdom. I'm only surprised that he didn't do it sooner. I want no part in his political posturing, but I have no choice but to play his game for now.

"Well, if it isn't the wayward son," sneers a voice from the thinning mob. The gendars part to reveal Prince Derane looking like a complete ass in his opulent jewels. "Returned from the dead twice now."

I flourish a half bow. "It is good to see you, too, cousin."

Behind him, Jahla slips from her place disguised among the Temple loyalists. A lock of her silver hair falls from beneath her gray hood as she leans close to Arrah to deliver a message for me. I squeeze the pommel on the saddle, annoyed to no end that I can't go to her myself, but this is not the place nor the time. Not with Prince Derane riling people up.

"Talk some sense into Suran before this goes too far," Prince Derane says, like I have a shred of influence over my father.

The Temple loyalists fuss over Sukar and pull him into their ranks. I'm surprised to see him alive, considering his poor state in the tribal lands. Arrah had vowed to heal him—and she'd finally done it. I bite back my contempt in knowing the same magic that saved Sukar could kill me.

Arrah and Essnai head in the opposite direction with the cravens—Jahla and Raëke. Fadyi remains hidden in the crowd, watching out for me. Now that Arrah's safe, I turn my attention back to Derane, who's in the middle of a tirade. "Perhaps we should speak in private, cousin."

Derane Sukkara throws back his head and laughs. "I'm done with talking in private. Your father would have me cower at his feet and beg for my throne, but I will not stand for it."

I ward off a yawn, bored. If Derane had any power, he would've already raised an army to take back the Kingdom. The news of his little outburst will get back to my father and only make things worse, and I haven't more time to waste here. I nudge my horse to leave. "I am sure things will work out for the best."

Prince Derane grimaces as another Sukkara whispers something in his ear. At that, he storms off with his family and attendants trailing behind him.

"We should've taken litters." Majka sits astride his horse, writhing like a worm on a hook. "It would've made for a more striking entrance." He brushes a hand across his messy curls and a few girls near the edge of the crowd giggle. It's not my imagination that they're greedily eyeing all three of us—Kira, Majka, and me. Majka waves at them, and one actually squeals.

I clear my throat and glance away from our admirers. "It's important for people to see me as one of them. Not some pretend *royal* hiding behind a curtain."

"I suppose," Majka grumbles, "but I could do without the flies."

Kira blows out an exaggerated sigh, making it a point to show her distaste. She is the picture of respectability in the saddle, her back arched, her shoulders squared, though her light skin is flushed in the heat. "Well, we know one thing for sure," she says, her tone cutting.

"Neither of you will be winning a prize for horsemanship. That's what you get for skipping lessons with your riding scribes."

A gendar pushes through the ranks and interrupts our bickering. "Crown Prince," the soldier addresses me in a brisk voice, "your father summons you to the palace at once."

With the fourth afternoon bells striking on top of the coliseum, I shove down my frustration. I'd planned to see Arrah after this debacle, but I can't ignore my father. "That didn't take long."

"Good." Majka shoos away a fly buzzing in his face. "We can finally take a litter."

I don't answer the soldier as we set off for the Almighty Palace. With a few hours in the saddle under my belt, my legs finally adjust to the horse. It's a subtle shift, nothing visible to the naked eye—but I can feel my body changing to relieve my discomfort. After a moment or two, the soreness in my thighs and backside dissipates. I cannot shift my appearance like the cravens, but this new part of me—this anti-magic—does have a way of making itself known. It's been like that since my awakening in the Dark Forest—the night Jahla killed me, and I became something else.

We dismount at the bottom of the mountain, underneath where the Almighty Palace looms above the city, and gendars take our horses. The only way up is by litter and a sophisticated pulley system. I was still a little runt, no more than seven or eight, the first time I visited the palace. An attendant had hauled me into a litter next to my older brother. Jemi spent the entire time pointing out buildings in Tamar as we soared over the city.

That was years before he and our brother Uran volunteered for the Rite of Passage—before they returned home broken men. I still resent Father for sending Jemi away after the altercation in the market that left a merchant dead. He needed his family, and Father abandoned him.

I shake off thoughts of the past as two gendars lead us to a golden litter with edges that curve into ram's horns. "Sorry for getting you both into this mess," I tell my friends.

"No, you're not." Kira slips onto the red velvet seat and slides to the far side. "You have a talent for trouble."

Majka leans back against the plush cushion next to her. "That mob was lucky they didn't piss Arrah off, or we'd have a bloodbath on our hands."

"That's not funny," Kira scolds him.

"It wasn't meant to be," says Majka.

I shut my eyes as the litter lifts from the ground and ascends the mountain. I *had* felt a spike in Arrah's magic when the crowd closed around her. She would've been well within her rights to defend herself.

I'd seen the devastation of her wielding magic firsthand at the sacred Gaer tree when those spineless thugs had thought us an easy mark. She picked up a handful of dirt and tossed it in one of their faces. It had melted the flesh from the man's bones. *Gods.* Again, when she'd struck the shotani down with lightning on the way to the tribal lands. And I could never forget the demon at the Almighty Temple. By the time I found the two of them, there was nothing left of his body, only ashes.

"Your father is not going to be happy when he hears of your stunt today," Majka says as our litter pitches to a stop on top of the mountain. "I wonder how you'll weasel your way out of trouble this time."

"When is he ever happy about anything?"

The captain of the guards opens our litter door. Two dozen gendars stand at attention, forming a path to the palace's steps behind him. They are in red elaras and silver armor, a shotel on each of their hips—two per soldier. "I'm here to escort you to the Almighty One, Crown Prince—" Captain Dakte curses when he sees Kira and Majka. "Why are you out of uniform?"

"I requested a favor of them that required it," I answer on their behalf.

Captain Dakte is up in years, silver haired, brown skinned, and broad shouldered, an officer who'd climbed the ranks. "That's quite unfortunate," he says disapprovingly.

I have no patience for his incessant nagging today as Kira, Majka, and I climb from the litter. The Almighty Palace sits at the center of the mountain, crowned by a gold dome and surrounded by four towers, with ivory walls trimmed in vibrant blue stone. The Sukkaras still live at the palace alongside our Omari cousins who've taken up residence. Contrary to what Prince Derane thinks, my father has no intention of ever giving up the throne.

The palace grounds are elaborate, with endless gardens and ponds. A lion roars from one of the stables. Tyrek's father, Jerek Sukkara, had liked parading them around in the city on occasion. A dog bounds across my path. It's Fadyi—he insists that at least one of my craven guardians is close by at all times. He must have turned himself into a bird and flown from the coliseum here before taking the dog's form.

As we cross the gardens and enter the grand tower, attendants stop and bow. They're worse than the attendants at our old villa who averted their eyes when my parents were around. I don't like this place—or how everyone treats me like I'm a goose egg balanced on a stick. Majka and Kira leave me to change back into their uniforms.

Captain Dakte leads the way to a private chamber, and two gendars push open the doors. I walk in with my hands on my hips. I will not cower in front of my father. My parents sit at a low table, having afternoon tea. Father studies a scroll splayed out next to a platter of sweets while my mother stares contemplatively through the windows into the gardens.

Neither acknowledges me in front of the guards, but my mother climbs to her feet once they leave. She clasps my hands and offers me a warm smile. "Join us for tea, son." As always, her quiet voice disarms me, and I almost forget that I am here for a scolding.

"Of course, Adé," I say, using the Delenian term of endearment. Then I turn to my father. "You summoned me?"

The *acting* Almighty One looks up from his scroll and lets out a frustrated sigh. It would be an understatement to say that I resemble my father—his impressive height, eyes the color of a moonless night, the Omari high cheeks and prominent jaw. The only notable difference is that his skin is darker, while mine is a shade between his and Adé's light brown, and I inherited my mother's distinct northern traits. "I've gotten word that the *Ka*-Priestess's daughter has arrived in the city via the western checkpoint."

Straight to business, then. Right. I remove my shotels and take a seat on a cushion at the table. Adé pours me a cup of tea, and I nod to show her my thanks. An attendant rushes into the salon with a bowl of warm water for me to wash my hands. I wait until she leaves before speaking. "I trust that our agreement still stands. Arrah is free to move about the Kingdom."

"I said that I would lift her banishment *if* she caused no trouble." Father clutches the scroll in his fist. "According to this report, she nearly started a riot in the West Market. It was no happenstance that you were there, gallivanting around like a fool, to come to her rescue."

"Only the second part of that statement is true." I add a pinch of cinnamon to my tea. "I was indeed gallivanting around the city, making a fool of myself for her."

Father grits his teeth, but Adé speaks up in her gentle, quiet way, her words placating. "Stop antagonizing each other, lest you leave a door open for the Sukkaras to win back the throne. We can all agree that no one wants that. Derane Sukkara cares more about his indulgences than he does the Kingdom."

Ah, my mother's Delenian princess side rears its head. Her tactics aren't as obvious as Father's, but she wants the throne as much as he does.

"Speaking of Derane Sukkara." I clear my throat. "He was the one who nearly started the riot in the West Market, rallying his supporters to win back the throne. You should worry about him before he does something drastic."

Ignoring me, Father remarks, "The girl should be easier to handle than her mother."

"She doesn't need handling," I say, my voice low.

When I brought him the news of the *Ka*-Priestess's death, my father showed contempt for a brief moment, then pretended not to care. It had infuriated me how he turned to the next order of business in the same breath. He was more interested to learn the fate of the tribes, since it meant no more trade with the Kingdom. That's why I've kept the news about our craven lineage a secret. He'd just find a way to exploit it to his advantage. Best he not know.

Father glances at the dregs at the bottom of his teacup, his brows furrowed together. "I did not summon you without reason. We have bigger problems to discuss. The Guard patrolling the East Market reported four people murdered this morning. A witness saw the culprits—two demons."

My hand slips, and hot tea spills on my fingers before I regain control. I squeeze my eyes shut, and Efiya's there, lurking in my mind. She's wearing Arrah's face as she climbs into the furs. My belly burns like someone's twisting a knife inside me. I hear the echo of her words when she stopped time on the battlefield. Words that I have never repeated to anyone.

"Are you okay, son?" My mother's soothing voice brings me back to the here and now.

"Yes, of course." I put down the tea. "The news caught me off guard."

"We need to take care of the problem before word spreads across the city," Father says, getting straight to the point. "Derane will try to use it to strengthen his position."

Some of the demons had escaped after the battle, but I never thought them brave enough to come back to the Kingdom. It worries me that they've appeared upon Arrah's return. That can't be a coincidence. She killed their mistress—could they be out for revenge? "I have the most experience with the demons. Let me hunt them down."

Adé pauses, cradling her teacup. "There's no need to put yourself at undue risk, son."

"For once, I agree with Rudjek." Father picks up a new scroll and a quill from his pile beside the table. "It will serve our cause to have the Crown Prince about the city to win the people's hearts. I will send some gendars to assist you. You're not to go anywhere outside the palace grounds at any time without them—do you understand?"

"I prefer to pick my own guards," I say, keeping my tone even for the sake of peace.

"It's not up for discussion," Father snaps, but Adé catches his eye. My mother's expression is neutral, some might even call it benign, but I know better. A faint tapestry of veins presses against her skin along her forehead. They stand out more when she is of ill-temper—like right now.

Father turns his attention back to me. If his looks could cut, I'd already have a dozen slashes across my chest. "We'll choose your guards together," he concedes, his voice bristling with resignation. I give him a winning smile. "Take care of the demon problem and keep that tribal witch under control while she's in my city."

FOUR

ARRAH

My father's shop is on a quiet street in the West Market. I smooth my hand across the door, my fingers catching on the chipped yellow paint and splintered wood. It looks like someone's taken an ax to it, but my father's magic kept them out. It lingers even now, a faint rustling in the wind, a hum, an unfinished song. The whole building pulses with it.

Before I had the chieftains' gifts, I could only see magic, floating in the air in little colorful sparks. This is something entirely different. I can sense the flavor of my father's magic, his unique impression. I wrap myself in the feeling of it, knowing that each time I walk into the shop, it will greet me with open arms.

Essnai pats me on the shoulder and sets off for the East Market. At this time of day, her mother and siblings will be hard at work, measuring patrons for the next batch of sheaths. I imagine them showering Essnai with hugs and kisses as they push a dress into her arms that needs her keen eye.

"Would you like one of us to stay with you?" Jahla asks from beneath her gray Temple hood. I'm still surprised by how well she blended in with them. "It may be some time before Rudjek can come."

I shake my head as I step forward in a daze. I want to be alone.

"We should make sure it's safe first," Raëke suggests.

I place my hand on the latch, and magic tingles against my palm as the door gives. I smile to myself, remembering a morning when I was very young and visiting my father's shop. "The door will always open for you, Little Priestess," Oshhe said, lifting me onto his hip.

"Will it open for Arti, too?" I asked.

"What did I say about calling your mother by her name?"

"She doesn't like it when I call her Mama."

My father drew in a deep breath and kissed my forehead. "To answer your question, no, the shop will only open for you and me when it's locked. One day when I'm too old to run it, it will be yours."

Even then, my father had done so much to make up for the distance between my mother and me. This shop has always been my safe place, and now it will be my home. I always dreamed of working with my father, not crushing herbs or cleaning bones, but doing *real* magic. I'd heal people of their ailments, but I'd make frivolous things, too, like hair color for Essnai. I never thought any part of that dream would come true until now.

The door creaks open as Oshhe's promise echoes in my mind. Hints of thyme and lavender and lemongrass underpin the stale air. "I'll be okay here," I tell Jahla and Raëke.

"We'll stay close," Jahla says as I step across the threshold.

I thank them and shut the door behind me. The strap from my sack slides from my shoulder and drops to the floor, kicking up a fury of dust. The jars of oil set about the shop flare to life, and sparks of magic in brilliant colors rise from the shelves. I imagine my father sitting on the empty cushion at the back of the shop, sipping tea, waiting for me to join him. But that part of my dream will never come true—it will always be wishful thinking.

I move through the shelves, taking stock of the pots of dried flowers and herbs, the animal bones, and the charms. Except for the dust, the shop's the same as it was the night I first traded my years for magic. In the little room at the back, the pot I used to brew the blood medicine sits where I left it.

With a few changes, I can turn the room into an apartment. Rudjek won't be happy with my decision to live here, and neither will Essnai and Sukar. Rudjek, the new *Crown Prince*. His father has everything he's ever dreamed of now—control of the throne and no more Arti to oppose him. Rudjek looked uncomfortable with the crowd's undivided attention. *Gods*. He also looked the part— unwavering in his authority, beautiful, and charming. I wondered for days what I would say when I saw him again—what I would do. With this news, it feels like we have yet another thing to keep us apart.

I take to dusting the shop to push aside my thoughts. Magic flounces around in a frenzy as I wipe down jars and pots and bones. I'm halfway through the task when it occurs to me that more sparks have floated through the shop's walls. It crowds the air, vibrating with energy, pulsing with light, singing a silent song. "Why is it coming here?"

I hold my hand out, and a ruby spark leaps onto my palm. I stumble back, almost bumping into a shelf. I didn't call the magic, not like when I was healing Sukar. I only wanted to touch it. I look to the chieftains for an answer, and they draw me into a memory of the sacred circle at the Blood Moon Festival. The rolling beats of the djembe drums move through me, and I twist and leap, the magic in the night air shadowing my every step. The leaders of the tribes—the *edam*—danced at the start of the festival. I see it now through the Kes chieftain's eyes.

I thought they had called the magic that night, but, no, it willingly came to them like it's coming to *me* now. I smile as more magic dances around the shop like an instrument awaiting a player. We could make beautiful music together—music to heal, bring rain to crops, and build something new. The possibilities are endless. I lose track of time as I put away the items from my traveling sack. It's near nightfall when there's a knock at the door. A rush of excitement sets my nerves on edge. *Gods.* I have to pull myself together.

On the way to answer, I stop by the mirror and startle at my reflection. I hardly recognize myself. The face staring back at me is gaunt, with sunken cheeks and eyes rimmed in dark lines. My braids are fraying with the first signs of gray sprouting at my roots. I poke my tongue into the gap where my tooth fell out after I summoned my ancestors in an attempt to stop Efiya. I can take away these scars with the chieftains' magic, but I wouldn't have the reminder of what I'd lost—my father, my grandmother, my whole world. Magic can't erase the past or bring my family back. I won't put on a more pleasant face. This is who I am now.

The knock comes again, and I grimace, feeling self-conscious. I open the door, but it's not Rudjek. A round woman stands with her hands on her hips. It's Chima's mother—a friend of my father.

"Mami!" I say, hiding my disappointment.

She bustles into the shop, and I catch a glimpse of Raëke and Jahla behind her, their looks questioning. I raise a hand to let them know it's okay. "I came as soon as I heard," Mami says, her eyes bloodshot from crying. "I'm so sorry, Arrah. May your father's soul become one with the mother and the father."

I wrap my arms around my shoulders—pushing back the sobs that threaten to burst from my chest. I don't tell her that my father can never ascend because Efiya ate his soul. "If not for Arti, he'd still be here."

Mami glances at a shelf of charms, her gaze roaming across the trinkets. "Despite the bad your mother did in the end, she wasn't always like that. She opened the orphanage, educated the poor, and fed the hungry."

"Spare me the speech, Mami." I temper the anger in my voice. "I do not need reminding of my mother's deeds, good or bad."

Mami clicks her tongue and removes a bag from across her shoulder. "Never mind that. I brought you something to eat." She sets bowls and food wrapped in cloth on an empty shelf, and I catch a whiff of tomato, onion, and cumin. "I was hoping that you'd come stay with us—no reason for you to go back to that big villa alone. I have grandchildren your age . . . and Chima thinks of you as a daughter."

I force a smile, thankful for her offer. "I have a place to stay."

Mami's face creases in heavy lines like she's got something else on her mind. "Some folks are planning to go to the tribal lands and search for survivors."

"There's no one left," I whisper as a shiver racks through me.

"We've all heard the stories, child." She places a reassuring hand on my arm. "People are hurting. They need to see for themselves that the tribes are really gone."

Mami offers a gap-toothed smile that reminds me of Grandmother, and I notice an odd vibration in her touch—an uneven, unsteady beat. It takes me a moment to understand what's happening. Through the chieftains' magic, I'm hearing the rhythm of her heart. It sounds all wrong. "How long have you been ill?" I ask, realizing at once.

"Just old age." Mami shoos off my concerns. "Your father used to help with the pain."

I frown. "Did he?"

"Why are you so surprised?" She narrows her eyes. "Oshhe saw more people with failing health than rich patrons looking to cheat old age, girl."

"You exaggerate, Mami," I say. "I would know if my father had healed so many people."

Mami gets that look—one that says she is about to set me straight. "Your father would see patrons from the East Market from sunup to midday, and he never asked for a single coin. You would've been in lessons during that time."

I shake my head. It isn't that I don't want to believe her, but my father had never mentioned it before. "Why didn't he ever tell me?"

"One who milks his neighbor's goat does not do it for glory," Mami says, reciting a tribal proverb. "To truly help, one does not need recognition in return."

I glance around the shop at the magic fluttering like butterfly wings and take comfort in her words. In her own way, she's given me another gift to remember my father by and hold close to my heart. "Come back in a day or two once I've reopened the shop," I tell her. "I may be able to help with your pain."

"Bless you, Arrah." Mami squeezes my hand and heads for the door. "The merchants in the East Market are putting on a street fair tomorrow night, now that things are back to normal. You should come."

I fiddle with my hands. "Things don't feel anything like normal."

"The night may be long, child," Mami says, "but morning always comes."

Once she leaves, I press my back against the door. For the first time in a long while, I can see a glimpse of a future for myself. I will make good on my promise to my father. I will not only be strong for him, but I will use the chieftains' gift to help others. Their sacrifice will not be in vain.

THE UNNAMED ORISHA: DIMMA

In one beginning, I crawl out of the bowels of an inferno. Let's call this my birth.

In another beginning, I exist in eternal darkness. Let's call this my death.

Between those moments, my sister Koré brings me to the top of a mountain in Ilora. She found the snow and ice soothing after her birth, so she leaves me alone with my thoughts.

I observe everything. The rustling of the wind, the rising and setting of the sun. Snow falling, ice melting. The restless churning of this world and all the worlds in the universe. The roar of the Supreme Cataclysm. The cycle of mortal life.

I am thinking of these things when a boy with silver wings falls from the sky and cracks my frozen lake. Fractures blossom around his still form and stretch across the ice. It happens at the exact moment my brother's light pierces through the clouds at daybreak. The feverish voice in the boy's head—in his dreams—calls him Daho.

The boy's pain spreads across my soul and snaps my full awareness to him. I understand pain—it's the one thing that the Supreme
Cataclysm taught its children. For my making was two sparks
slammed together, then shredded and twisted and molded. I remember every moment of the pain that left me writhing in the inferno.
Pain that forced me to crawl out of the darkness at the end of the
tunnel . . . to be born. His pain is different—it is much worse. It is
hollow and all-consuming and deep. It wraps his soul in a cloak of
shadows.

I search the folds of his mind and absorb his memories. His
people—demons—are my sister Koré's first creations, *her children*.
His family ruled over Jiiek, which covers most of Ilora, before a man
with a scar across his face killed them. He escaped, but the man and
his supporters hunt him even now.

The boy opens his eyes, and they are pools of lush evergreen that
glow in the sunlight. I see myself through them. I am a shapeless fog
hovering over the ice. He is dying. It's a concept that I do not yet
understand. It is a condition of being mortal. The boy is mortal. I
am not.

I reshape myself into a physical body. I could appear as any of my
brethren's creations, but he only knows of his race and two others—
endoyans and humans. I choose to become an endoyan—a cousin of
the demon people, without their wings, but sharing their diaphanous
skin, different from humans' opaqueness.

I see this new body through his perception. He is silver, and I am
brown. His eyes are light; mine are dark. His hair is slick with mud
and ice while mine stands up in a tapestry of coils.

"Dimma," he croaks, blinking back tears.

The word means both *beautiful* and *deadly* in his language. He thinks that I am both.

The boy's injuries are broken strings. Strings I can pull and bend. His soul teeters on his frozen blue lips—a mist the same color as the fog rising from the ice. I have an unexplainable urge to touch his soul, and do so with the hand I have created for myself. It pulses against my fingertips, and warmth spreads up my arm.

Am I dead? the boy asks through the cosmic strings that connect us.

Yes and no, I tell him. *You are on the cusp of ascension.*

His soul shudders against my hand—resigned, tired, regretful. Life and death are mortal constraints. Beyond that, there is infinite existence. Energy cannot be created or destroyed, but it can change. Ascension is a cosmic compulsion to return to the Supreme Cataclysm to be unmade and made anew.

I'm scared, the boy says. *I don't want to die.*

Convinced by his words, I push his soul back into his parted lips, and his vessel expands as he inhales a breath. I do the same, learning from him how to mimic mortal life in that way. His crooked and broken wing trembles while the rest of his body writhes in pain. I put my hands in the hollow space between where his wings meet his shoulders.

The boy screams. The raw sound of his voice disturbs the peace of my frozen lake. His pain flows through the strings that connect us, and I jerk away. Mending the strings of his life isn't as easy as I thought it would be. I must proceed with caution.

I lift him in my arms and hold him against my chest. The cracked ice beneath my bare feet gives way to the water beneath, and the fog grows thicker to support our weight. As I carry him, his pain lessens, and he loses consciousness.

I focus on the snow, where I often ponder my existence. A shimmer of light sparks and grows, shaped by my will and his memories of safety and comfort. It isn't the cavernous palace that sits high above Jiiek that he thinks of returning to one day. In his dreams, he's in a little wooden house tucked in a forest that borders the palace grounds. The place where he used to watch his father, covered in sawdust, carve and paint figurines.

I remake the house by reordering the space around me—the same as I've done with my body. A room to wash. A hearth to keep him warm. A bed to rest. A table covered in miniature beasts, carving tools, and wood chips.

While Daho sleeps, I stand in front of the window, looking at my frozen lake. It is no longer pristine, as it was before Daho came. Something is comforting about the change.

Shadows gather beside me at the window and take a shape that resembles a mortal body. I recognize the new presence as one of my brethren. His name is Iben. "This moment is the beginning of the end," comes his voice, at once eager and grave. "I thought it would be more . . . *dramatic*."

"The end?" I echo.

"I couldn't stay away," he confesses. "I had to see this for myself."

"I don't understand."

"No, you wouldn't." Iben pats my shoulder, and I experience two strange sensations—frustration and confusion. "Only I can travel the threads of time, and I must keep its secrets."

Here's what I do understand about time. It intersects with the physical world. Every decision and indecision creates a possible future. Some decisions have far-reaching implications, and others are less significant. "You would not be here if this moment was not important," I conclude.

"You are correct, sister," Iben says. "For now, it is only important to know that this is the beginning of the end, and you are the catalyst."

FIVE
ARRAH

Smoke curls from the chimney of the little wooden house with snow on the roof. A white curtain flutters at the single window. My breath aches in my chest as I watch the two people inside. They sit at a table facing each other, as stiff as statues, but I can't tell if they're friends or adversaries. Their body language somehow suggests both. The curtain keeps getting tangled in the wind, so I can't see them well, but it is unmistakable that one has *wings*. I stumble back from the house.

I wake with a start, drenched in sweat. It takes a moment to remember that I fell asleep on the pillows in the open salon where my father used to serve tea. I'm beneath an old blanket and shivering as if the cold from my dream has seeped into the shop.

I wash at the pump in the back room, which draws from one of the communal wells that connect the buildings of the West Market. The cold water feels good against my skin, and the dream fades away. I'm bursting with purpose as I go over the things I'll need to reopen the shop. The biggest concern is finding space to grow herbs for blood medicine. I could use my father's garden at our old villa, if it's still standing, but that would be my last choice.

I clench my fists as I look to the empty shelves along the back wall that once held my father's scrolls. Arti had made him burn them, so I wouldn't find a ritual to stand against her. Soon I'll be able to build a collection of my own. Once I convert the storage room into an apartment, it won't take much time to get everything else ready. But I can't do any of these things if Rudjek hasn't convinced his father to reverse my banishment. I could be getting my hopes up for nothing.

It's midmorning when there's a knock on the door. I know who it is before I cross the shop. Rudjek's anti-magic is a gush of warm air that almost steals my breath away. My magic responds to the danger of it like a viper curling up inside me ready to strike, but I don't care. It's been weeks since we've spent time together alone—much longer since that private moment beneath Heka's Temple. His soft lips pressing against mine, his hand finding the curve of my waist.

I am most definitely blushing by the time I open the door. He's standing there with a twinkle in his dark eyes, his wild curls tamed for once. He's wearing a gendar's red elara, his tunic embroidered with a golden lion's head stitched across his chest.

Rudjek smooths a finger along one of the silver clasps pinned to his collar and clears his throat. "Apparently I'm an honorary commandant in the Almighty Army now. I have so many titles that it takes two lines to sign my name." He pauses and gives me a crooked smile. "May I come in?"

He looks so good—and he smells like the heavens. "Only if you promise to stop rambling."

Kira, Majka, and another ten gendars fan out in front of the shop. I'm not surprised that Fadyi and Jahla have slipped into the gendar ranks, posing as soldiers. I wonder how long they'll remain with Rudjek now that we've stopped my sister.

"Why so many guards for a boy who slays demons with the ease of cutting bread?" I ask, closing the door behind him.

"Not my idea," he groans as he looks around. "My father is nothing but persistent."

"And quite ambitious," I mumble under my breath.

"Quite," Rudjek says, "but he did lift your banishment."

"He did?" I laugh and, without thinking, take a step closer to him. Then I stop. I can't make a mistake like that again. "Sorry." I catch another glimpse of myself in the mirror—and regret my decision to keep my scars from trading my years.

"Wait!" Rudjek fumbles with the hem of his tunic and reaches into his pocket. "I think I found a solution . . . well, not a solution, but a way to cheat until we get this figured out."

"You're rambling again." I cross my arms, but it's good to hear the familiar timbre of his voice after all the time we've been apart. "What are you going on about?"

"These." Rudjek dangles a pair of red leather gloves that match his uniform. When I woke after almost dying, he'd been able to hold my hand while wearing gloves. "There's only one way to find out if they still work."

"Oh," I gasp, realizing that he intends to touch me—that I want him to.

Rudjek pulls on the gloves and moves cautiously until the tips of his fingers brush my cheek. He pauses at that, his eyes intent, his attention seemingly turning inward. I do the same, checking my magic's response. Nothing so far. No sign of it coiling tighter with his touch, but, gods, my ache for him only grows in intensity. I tilt my chin up and lean in closer. "I've missed you," Rudjek says, his voice quiet. The longing threaded between his words makes me forget about my missing tooth and gray hairs. He could have any girl he wants, but he's here with me.

I close my eyes, and he presses his gloved hand full against my face, no longer just testing the waters. "I've missed you, too." I want nothing more than to sink into his arms—to feel his embrace like that stolen kiss in the tomb. Something about that memory snags at the back of my mind, but it flits away. Compared to his real touch, the leather feels cold against my skin. This is almost worse than not touching at all. I press my lips against his palm and pull away. "Would you like some tea?"

"Yes," he says, trying to make it sound effortless, but his voice is wrought with tension. "I would love tea if it's not too much trouble."

I hear his emphasis on *tea* and remember the last time we were in the shop together. I'd offered him tea then, and he blushed, saying that in his mother's home country, Delene, offering tea in certain situations was an invitation for something else. I want so badly for it to be an invitation and a promise now, but the bitter truth of our predicament burns inside me.

I force down my thoughts. "When has it ever been trouble making tea?"

Rudjek shrugs and his shoulders relax like the weight of the world lifts from his back, even if it's only for a moment. "How are you holding up?"

"I was about to ask you the same." I gesture to the shelves as we move to the salon. "Last time you set foot in the shop, the magic made you sick."

"I'm stronger now," he says as I put the kettle on the brazier.

I smile at that—it's a sad, pathetic smile. I know that without seeing my face. Rudjek removes his gloves, slipping them into his trousers, and puts his shotels aside. "I'm glad for that." We both know that's a lie, but he doesn't call me on it.

It feels nice to have a moment alone, but I find myself at a loss for words. Rudjek clears his throat again as we settle into an awkward silence at the low table in the salon. I reach for the jar of tea at the same time he shifts on his pillow. My fingers brush against the back of his hand. It happens then, in the span of a breath, a sharp awareness, my magic rising to the surface, an instinct to strike. The sickening churn of my stomach as his anti-magic assaults my senses. Rudjek jerks his hand away.

Neither of us acknowledges what almost happened—what *will* happen if we tempt fate. Shifting my position away from him, I scoop dried mint leaves into his cup. He looks like he has something on his mind, and I have things I need to say, too. "I've decided to reopen the shop," I blurt out. "I'm going to continue my father's work—without the rich patrons wasting their coins on their vanity." Though, come to think of it, those wealthy patrons might be the reason my father could afford to help the less fortunate.

"That's a brilliant idea," Rudjek says, his eyes bright.

I pour water into our cups. "I'm going to convert the storage room into an apartment."

He cringes at that. "You're not joking, are you?"

I shake my head before taking a sip of tea.

"I assumed that you wouldn't want to stay at your parents' old villa, but there are ample apartments in the city. We have whole empty wings at the Almighty Palace." He lets his words hang in the air like he's waiting for me to answer. When I don't, he sighs. "If that's not enough space, you can stay in my old apartment at the Omari estate—there's only staff for upkeep now. You'll have the place to yourself." He glances at his hands. "I would rest easier knowing that you're someplace safe."

"I am someplace safe," I counter.

Rudjek quirks his eyebrows. "Someplace safe and near me."

"And how will your father take that?" I ask. "Last I recall, he still hates me."

Rudjek blows across the top of his tea, and I can't stop thinking about our fleeting moment in the tomb beneath Heka's Temple. He once told me that I smelled sweet and intoxicating . . . like something forbidden. The irony of how his words have come back to haunt us isn't lost on me.

He glances away and avoids my question. "Speaking of my father—he's holding my cousin Tyrek's trial tomorrow for his crimes against the Kingdom. You might want to stay clear of the coliseum."

"I'm surprised the Vizier—excuse me—the *Almighty One* waited this long." I stare at my tea. "I thought he would execute his predecessor immediately."

"*Acting* Almighty One for now. The guildmasters must take a vote before he's confirmed," Rudjek corrects me. "The Sukkaras are powerful, and Tyrek's mother is from a highly respected family, the Ohakims. Her brother is the Guildmaster of Labor. My father would be a fool to move in haste, considering their political ties."

I think of Sukar's uncle, Barasa, the Zu seer. He was Sukar's only family left, and Tyrek Sukkara had him executed along with the other seers. And if the rumors were true, Tyrek sided with my sister and willingly did her bidding. I don't care what happens to him, but it irks me to no end that Suran Omari will keep the throne. I have no doubts about that. "How are you adjusting to your new position as *acting* Crown Prince?"

"I am . . . adjusting best I can." Rudjek's gaze drifts in my direction again, and he flinches. I know why, and my heart sinks. "How are you, really?"

I squirm on the pillow. I can't bring myself to lie and say that I'm well, but I also don't want him to worry. We've both done enough of that. "I'm coping."

His eyes flit back and forth between the wall and me. When he catches me staring, he says, "Sorry, it's just . . . you know."

"Rudjek . . . I owe you an apology." I work up the nerve to broach the subject of my sister. "I don't expect you to forgive me, but—"

"Apology for what?" He looks amused by my words, and that makes this harder.

It comes out wrong—my words jumbled together, my voice trembling. "Before, when . . . when Efiya tried to have her way with you." I wring my hands, unable to be still. "I mean when she pretended to be me . . . when she tricked you." All traces of amusement slip from his face. "I messed up, Rudjek."

His features smooth out, replaced by the mask he wears in public, the one meant to reassure, to disguise.

"Are you okay talking about this?" I realize too late that he might not be. "Because we don't have to if . . ."

"I want to," Rudjek says, his voice raspy like his throat has suddenly gone dry. "We need to put this behind us."

I push myself to continue—not quite knowing if I'm making sense. "When I saw you with Efiya, I saw her. The way she's always looked to me."

"I saw you. Down to the little mole over your left eyebrow." When he looks at me this time he doesn't flinch.

"I know that now," I say, my belly twisting with anguish. "She did such a vile thing." I swallow hard and finally get the words out. "And I blamed you for not knowing that she wasn't me." My voice is desperate now, and I fight back the tears choking my throat. "I was wrong, Rudjek, and I'm sorry."

"I should've known." He rubs his hand across his eyes. "Re'Mec warned me, after the chieftains had bound themselves to you, that we could never be together." His mask slips and his obsidian eyes burn, his pain shining through. "She didn't smell like you. Deep down, I knew something wasn't right, but I was caught in the moment."

"You can't blame yourself." I shake my head. "You know that, don't you?"

"Yes." Rudjek nods. "Just as you must know that you're not responsible for Efiya's actions."

"But . . . ," I say, ready to prove him wrong.

"No *buts*." Rudjek lifts a hand. "I don't want this to stand between us."

"Me either." I can't help but wonder what Efiya whispered in his ear on the battlefield, but I won't ask. It's not my place. If he wants to tell me, he will.

A knock on the door interrupts our conversation, and we both come to our feet. I brush wrinkles from my tunic, and Rudjek gives me a sheepish smile. "I can't stay." He pulls on his sword belt. "I've got official Kingdom business to attend to, but let's meet tomorrow at twelfth bells in our *secret place*." He says it like we're kids again, sneaking out against our parents' wishes. I miss those days.

I cock my head. "Official Kingdom business, eh?"

"I . . . ," Rudjek splutters as he shifts his hands to the hilts of his shotels; then, he lets them fall at his sides. He doesn't seem to know what to do with them. "I'll be spending most of the day meeting my adoring fans." He laughs at that, but he's anxious. I smile back even though I know he's lying to me. What I want to know is why.

SIX
ARRAH

After Rudjek leaves, I set out to peruse the East Market, uneasy about how our conversation ended. Why was he so nervous when I asked him about his official Kingdom business? Without intending to, instead of going east, I end up at my family's old villa. I peer through the wrought-iron gate and soak up the sight of it. The earth-toned walls, the tan shingles, the three sides enclosing a private courtyard. The gardens blossoming with lilies and irises and hibiscuses. Birds chirp in the trees. It's exactly as we left it. The porter's station sits empty, where Nezi would lean against the wall, rubbing her scarred hands.

I am surprised that the Vizier hasn't destroyed the villa, or a mob hasn't vandalized it. The reason why becomes apparent when I touch the gate. A storm roars in my ears as my mother's magic flares to life like a sleeping giant stirring. I stumble back as sparks rise from the grass and lace together into a dome that surrounds the gardens.

Arti must've warded the villa. She probably did it to annoy Suran Omari. I imagine how mad he would've been to discover that he couldn't even touch it. It serves him right for the villa to stand as a reminder of his despicable actions.

Both my parents had thought to use protection spells, be it for different reasons. The lock on the gate clicks, and it creeps open. I turn away from the villa, and my mother's magic teems at my back, threatening to consume everything in its path.

I have half a mind to take down her ward, to shred it to pieces. The knowledge is within me; I know I can do it, but I won't. Let this be a reminder to me, too, to never take my magic for granted, to never use it for the wrong reason. I'll never be like her—I won't let my magic turn me into a monster. I take one step away and falter. The gate opened for me. I blink back tears, remembering Arti's desperate plea on the battlefield. She had offered to die in my place. Whatever my mother's plan might've been, I don't believe she ever intended for Efiya and me to be enemies.

I touch my chest, where she'd carved the Demon King's mark, the serpent. The scar's gone now, but I can still trace where it had once been. In her own twisted way, she'd done it to protect me. "Be brave."

I turn around to face the villa and stalk through the gate, which creaks closed behind me. The moment is surreal, as a lifetime of memories flood back into my mind. I push them aside—I'm not here to reminisce. I round the gardens to the kitchen entry, which is closest to my old room. The air inside is cool and smells like honey and coconut—*like my mother*. Candles come alive as I head into the corridor. The dancers on the wall prance, leap, and twist to keep pace with me. Good to know they're still in a mood to celebrate.

When I step into the room, the echo of thunder draws me back to that awful night. Lightning struck outside my window, and a torrent of rain slapped against the roof. My mother stood in shadows with the dagger she used to carve the serpent into my chest. The memory feels so real that a whimper escapes my lips. *I've given you a gift*, she said.

I cross the room quickly, not intending to stay long. I sigh when my eyes land on the altar coated in thick dust. The necklace of teeth my father gave me at Imebyé lies between three clay dolls. Feeling immense relief, I brush off the dust and slip it around my neck.

Someone clears their throat behind me, and my heart leaps in my chest. I know that voice, but it can't be. When I turn around, a plump woman stands in the doorway. Even in the dim light, I can see her eyes—the warm brown of copper coins. Not green. I don't feel any magic from her, either. It's really her—no tricks, no demon.

"Ty?" I take a reluctant step toward her. The last time I saw the matron of our house was at the villa in Kefu when I tried to convince her to run away with Terra and me. I had assumed the worst, but I should've known that Arti would protect her. "Are you okay?"

Ty nods as she steps into the room. She looks much the same as when we still had some semblance of a normal life, and I'm relieved. She touches the wall, then cocks her head to the side and frowns at me with surprise and hope in her eyes.

"I'm not staying." I clutch the charm around my neck. "I only came for this." Ty looks away, her face dropping in disappointment. "I'm glad you're here." When she doesn't respond, I blurt out, "I'm sorry about Nezi."

Ty taps her chest twice and turns her palm to face the ceiling. *It was her choice.*

I shake with anger that she could give me such a flippant answer. Ty and Nezi had both sided with Arti and supported her vile actions. "It was my mother's choice to do awful things in the name of revenge, too. For Heka's sake, Ty, we lost everything—our family, the tribes. So many innocent people died in her bid to bring the Kingdom to its knees. Was it worth it in the end?" I clasp my hand over my mouth to bury my sobs.

Ty looks at me, unblinking, for a long time as she thinks on it. I expect her to be dismissive, but instead, she shakes her head. *No.*

I draw in a breath to calm myself and wipe away the beads of sweat on my forehead. Ty will be safe at the villa. She can live without fear. "I have to go," I say, as if it's an apology. I can't stand to stay here any longer. "I'll be at my father's shop if you'd like to visit me sometime, but I won't be coming back here."

Ty nods, then she holds up a finger. *Wait.*

"What is it?" I ask, but she turns on her heel and scurries out of the room. When she returns, she hands me a small pouch that I recognize as belonging to my father. I take it and feel the weight of coins. "You're giving me money?"

She nods.

"You should keep it." I shove the pouch back at her. "I've got the shop now."

Ty makes a cradle with her arm. *I have plenty.*

As matron of our house, she must have access to Arti and Osh-he's wealth, but I don't ask. I accept her offer and take the coins. I can use the money to buy things for the shop. "Thank you."

Ty smiles and presses her hand to her heart.

I return the gesture. *I love you, too.*

I pocket the purse as Ty slips back into the shadows. She was never one for goodbyes. I leave the villa after that, and it hurts not to look back. I head down the cobblestones, crossing the point where the pavement turns to dirt. I walk through rows of modest homes to arrive at the East Market. The smells and noises assail my senses at once, and I smile.

A donkey kicks up a cloud of dust as a man rings a bell, announcing his wagon of fresh eggs and goat milk. Merchants shout over each other to attract patrons to their wares. One gives out samples of kebabs simmered in a spicy tomato broth.

"Authentic Estherian silk scarves!" shouts another merchant. "Look your best at only forty-five copper coins."

Most people don't recognize me, and hardly anyone cuts their eyes in my direction. It's nice to be back in my old routine, moving with the flow of the market, blending in with the crowd. The money immediately comes in handy. I barter with several merchants and put down deposits for a bed and some new clothes.

I finish haggling over the price of a dresser at sunset. I'm ready to call it a day when a troupe of dancers in shimmering dresses dips around me, bells draped around their hips. I'd forgotten about the street fair tonight, and before I can slip away, I get caught up in a crowd. The energy is infectious as musicians crop up on every corner. The music is a mix of bold, shattering beats, strings, and percussion, one song rolling into the next.

A whistling sound fills the air, pops, then a rainbow of sparks bursts over the crowd. The colors blend in with the magic already flowing in the night sky, and the effect is a canopy of brilliant light. I can sense magic around me, too, in some of the people of tribal descent. Most of it is faint and fleeting as onlookers bump into me.

Bystanders hold each other and mourn the tribes. They weep and rock side to side. Some sway to the music as tears streak down their cheeks. At first, I think it's a mistake to be here—that their anguish will overwhelm me—but I find comfort in our shared grief.

I walk through a group of dancers wearing Zu masks, turning in wild circles around each other. Most of the masks are fake, and the symbols on them don't make any sense, but one stops me in my tracks. It pulses with white light as the boy wearing it braces his fists on his waist and shakes his hips.

His eyes lock with my own, and he points to his chest. I shake my head, but it's too late. He struts over to me, fire dancing in his gray eyes. "Dance with me, pretty girl?" he says, his voice heavy with drink.

The mask pulses with light from each of its symbols. I frown, realizing from Beka's memories that it's a warrior mask—not one of the imitations sold in the market. A crow with outstretched wings covers the forehead with three small suns along the brow. Tiger stripes mark both cheeks. The mask hums with a name; it's a whisper in my ear that drowns out the noise from the celebration. *Rassa.*

"You're not *Rassa*, are you?" I ask, hesitant, not wanting to assume, but no Zu warrior would disrespect his mask by wearing it for a street fair.

The boy laughs. "I can be Rassa tonight if you're into that sort of thing."

"How did you get that mask?" I ask, ignoring him.

"It's quite striking, isn't it?" the boy answers. "I bought it from a merchant."

I have an almost uncontrollable urge to snatch it off his face, but I force my hands to stay still. It's a show of disrespect to wear another warrior's mask, or even touch it without permission. How could a merchant in Tamar come to possess a real Zu mask? Had someone raided the tribe after the battle and stolen from the dead? I wouldn't put it past some of the scavengers in the market, who'd sell their own arm if it'd return a big enough profit.

The light of the mask pulses brighter when the boy leans close to me and asks, "You want to get out of here?"

I force a smile. "Can I see your mask?"

"Ah, now we're getting somewhere," the boy says, reaching up to untie the mask. He goes on, but I don't hear him as he hands it over.

When I touch the mask, I can feel its magic vibrating against my palm. A Zu's mask is more than a show of prowess; it's a story-keeper and holds impressions of its owner's memories. "Can I have it?" I look up at the boy, who frowns at me. "I'll pay you for it."

"Why do you want this mask when there're plenty in the market?" he asks.

It wouldn't be worth my time to explain it to him. "I like *your* mask," I say with a false smile. "I'll give you a silver coin for it."

"A silver coin for a useless mask?" The boy laughs again.

"I take it that we have a deal?"

The boy shrugs, and I reach into my pouch. He accepts the coin and raises an eyebrow, expectantly. Before he says something else absurd, I slip into the crowd.

Once I'm back at the shop, I sit in the salon with my legs crossed and the mask in my lap. I clear my mind and focus on the magic vibrating inside it, listening for the whisper of its story. I draw myself deeper until all I hear is the throb of the mask like a heartbeat. Flashes of images fill my vision. So many come at once that I almost sever my connection, but I brace myself and sink into Rassa's memories.

I'm in another place—on the edge of a Zu encampment. I stand in a line of tattooed and masked warriors armed with sickles. The cool mountain breeze sends chills down my spine, and I dig my fingers underneath my mask to scratch my face. I hadn't had time to sand down the inside before we heard of the demon attack near the Temple, so it keeps itching.

My initiation into the warrior caste was supposed to happen at the first snowfall of Osesé. Had I gone through the initiation, I would be with the warriors who left two days ago to fight the demons in the foothills.

"We are the last line," says our commander as he paces back and forth in front of us. His voice echoes across the mountain; it puts fire in my bones. "We must give the rest of the tribe as much time as possible to escape before the demons arrive. Heka willing, our ancestors will join us in battle. We will die as warriors!"

I see the tail end of the group fleeing from the mountain, disappearing around a ridge. Even if I die today, my mother and little brother will live. I have to believe that we'll buy them enough time, but the demons appear at the foot of our village moments later. There are so many that I can't see the end of them. My older brother squeezes my shoulder. We will fight to the end together.

The mask slips from my trembling hands, and the memory fades. It lands with a heavy thump on the floor. I dig my nails into my knees. Rassa saw hundreds of Zu fleeing their tribe before the battle. Does this mean . . . does this mean that there are survivors out there somewhere? My heart races as I snatch up the mask and come to my feet. Some of the tribal people found a way to escape my sister's wrath.

SEVEN
RUDJEK

How many lies will I tell before I'm no better than an alley rat scratching the bottom of an empty barrel? One, two, three, four, until my tongue bleeds. What's one more in a sea of lies when I have good reason? Arrah doesn't need to know there are demons still in the city preying upon poor Tamarans. They're my responsibility now. And it's in everyone's best interest if she stays far away from those foul creatures.

I can't shake the feeling that they're either out for revenge or here because of her magic. She was strong enough to kill their mistress and survive the Demon King's dagger—that has to mean something to them. Arrah is the only person left alive who could release the Demon King. Do they mean to coerce her into doing it? So far, thankfully, the cravens have reported no signs of any demons near her.

Dust stings my eyes as we stroll through the crowds of the East Market. My guards keep the merchants at bay, while Majka and Kira pass out silver coins to desperate hands. The coins were my father's idea to win favor. That's the advantage he has over our Sukkara cousins. They think mingling on any level with the common people is below their station. I have no doubt that's how my father found it so easy to seize power.

I wave and smile at the people yelling my name from behind a wall of soldiers. It irks me that my father wouldn't let me leave the palace without them. How quickly he's forgotten that I won the swords competition in the arena three years in a row. *Twenty-gods*, I helped defeat an entire demon army. I didn't train this hard for so long to be a stage prop in a commandant's uniform.

When I was a boy, people would hardly look at me, but I made it my business to catch their eye. It always seemed to put them at ease—especially when they saw my family crest. Now they only look upon me in desperation as we move through the market with purpose. Since the first report of demon activity, two more people died during the street fair last night. Both attacks were in isolated areas. The demons had to know that under most circumstances, the City Guard wouldn't bat an eye at the poor dying. But these aren't normal circumstances, and my father is a cautious man. The Guard paid money to keep the incidents quiet, but it's only a matter of time before the news spreads.

"Bless you, Crown Prince," says a woman wearing a wreath of daisies around her neck.

"We are thankful for the Almighty One's kindness," interjects another, fooled by my father's false generosity.

"Be well," I reply, but my attention is elsewhere.

An awareness pricks at the back of my neck and stretches down my spine. A rush of anger fills my belly. I can feel all magic—even the occasional magic that floats in the sky. Ah, but demon magic has the strongest pull and the foulest smell. I grit my teeth against my urge to draw my shotels here in front of all these people. That little weasel of a god Re'Mec made cravens this way—so we could help the orishas suss the demons out.

My target stands on the edge of the crowd wearing the skin of a Tamaran merchant. He's a stout man with broad shoulders and hair in cornrows. I curse under my breath as the tingling at the base of my skull becomes a dull ache.

"We need to take a detour," I say calmly as every muscle in my body coils tight in anticipation. "Take a right after the cassava merchant."

The three gendars leading our procession do as told without question. Fadyi and Jahla move closer to me. Taking their cue, Majka and Kira do the same. A faint glimmer catches my eye, and I look up to see Raëke crouched on the edge of a roof. She looks too comfortable for one teetering on a shingle.

I can't kill the demon in front of my father's men. If I'm injured during the fight, my body will heal immediately. It was the first thing that Fadyi taught me, but I haven't learned how to control it. My father can't find out what I can do—or how it's possible. Instead, in the thicket of the crowd, I duck out of formation and take Fadyi with me. "The rest of you continue on your tour through the market. This will only take a moment."

"Crown Prince," says Captain Dakte, that usual bitter edge to his voice, "I would advise against this course of action."

"My father bade me to hunt down the demons discreetly, so let me." I'm still annoyed that he's my second-in-command. Father refused to relent when I argued against choosing him. "Do you wish to disobey the Almighty One's orders, Captain Dakte?"

He doesn't answer, so I consider the matter closed. Raëke, now leaning against a merchant's stall, tosses me a dark cloak, her too-big eyes a little off-center. I wink at her, eager to fight, but I must keep my head about me. The demons aren't to be underestimated. I was overconfident at Heka's Temple, and it cost the craven twins, Ezaric and Tzaric, their lives.

I catch the cloak, and in moments it's across my back and the hood is over my head. It feels as rough as a burlap sack and scratches my skin, but it covers my elara so that I can better blend in with the crowd. My father would never approve of me breaking protocol, but, then again, he wouldn't approve of anything I do. Might as well live up to his expectations.

Raëke stays behind to make sure no innocent people stumble in my way. Neither Majka nor Kira looks too happy with me for leaving them with the other gendars. I slip down the alley following the demon while Fadyi circles around to block his path. I am alone except for a white cat scuttling across the rooftops, keeping pace with me. That would be Jahla. Even when the cravens shift, I can tell them apart. It does help that Jahla seems quite fond of her white hair, although in her natural form, she has no hair at all. I'm glad I didn't inherit that trait. I'm rather fond of my gorgeous curls.

I catch the demon's saccharine scent again halfway down the alley. It reminds me of Efiya—that memory is a stubborn scar that refuses to heal. Mud splashes on my pants, but I hardly notice. The alleyway smells of fish guts and piss and decay. Not for the first time,

I wish that I could transform into a faster creature. Something that has four legs instead of two—or sprout a pair of powerful wings.

When I step out of one alley into another, I'm not surprised to find the demon waiting for me. He's smoking a tobacco pipe with his eyes closed, his back against a wall, savoring the taste. The dank air smells like cloves and cinnamon, but the decay is strongest here. The shacks are crowded so close together that the eaves block out the sun. When I see the first body, I curse—then I see them all lined up against the rotting walls. Dead Tamarans sprawled out in muck, their faces bloated and discolored. One, two, ten, a dozen. Two dozen. How could no one have seen this massacre? *Twenty-gods.* Did he do this alone? I push down my rage. First, I need answers, then I will make him pay for what he's done.

"Hello," I say, tightening my hands on my shotels.

The demon doesn't open his eyes as he takes another puff from his pipe. There's a tattoo of a disk on his left cheek. It's a sign that the original owner of his body was a devout follower of Kekiyé, the orisha of gratitude. I grimace. I still have no love for the gods, especially those who conveniently decided to sit out the battle at Heka's Temple.

When he finally opens his eyes, there's where the similarity to a Tamaran ends. His eyes are green, but not like those of some Yöomi or Northerners. His irises glow with an iridescent light. "Business or pleasure, boy?" he asks.

My jaw flexes before I can stop myself. It isn't because he doesn't seem to recognize who I am. It's the arrogance in his voice, so assured that he has nothing to fear. He wears a straight sword at his side, not that he needs it. "Both," I answer with a cutting smile.

The demon takes a closer look at me, his gaze lingering on my swords, the cloak, and the finer clothes beneath it. His eyes go wide as he sees beyond my disguise, beyond the flesh. He sees the part of me that awakened after death.

"Filthy beast." He spits on the ground. "You're far from home, craven."

As I draw my shotels, the metal grates against the leather sheaths, the sound echoing in the alley. "Not as far as you think."

The demon charges at me in a blur of shifting colors. His mouth stretches wide enough that I can see down his throat into the blackness inside. All the tension in my body from a moment ago melts away. I am ready for him. When he is within arm's reach, I crouch and spin both shotels in an arc that tears into his belly at two separate points. He stumbles back, his hands pressed against the blood gushing from his wounds.

"You little bastard," he barks. "You're going to regret that."

I laugh, unimpressed by his threat. "Tell me where the rest of your demon friends are, and I'll let you live." Perhaps he knows it's a lie by how unfeeling my voice has become. My instinct is to kill—to destroy the filth that invaded my land, tortured my people. The ones who helped Efiya destroy the five tribes—and a part of Arrah with them.

"Why would I do that?" The demon smiles as he pulls out his sword. His wounds heal before my eyes, and he straightens himself back up. Two more demons step into the alley behind him. Both wear the gray smocks and rubber boots of dockworkers, and they draw their swords, too. I sense another two at my back—five in total. Good. Now it's a fair fight.

The cat poises to leap from the rooftop, and a black-and-gray eagle lands on a garbage bin. I shake my head almost imperceptibly to my guardians—my friends—to tell them to hold off. I must take these demons on my own; I need to be stronger. The eagle—Fadyi—cries out a sharp shriek of disapproval but does as I've asked.

"Oh, you don't have to tell me." I shrug. "You demons are quite predictable. Where there's one, there's always a nest of you nearby . . . rather like rats."

"I tire of you, boy," the merchant demon snarls.

"And I of you," I say as all five attack at once.

I spin my shotels, slicing two across their chests, but the other three dance out of my way. One of the dockworkers' blades bites into my shoulder. I yelp in pain as the filth of his magic enters my blood. I whirl my other arm around and decapitate the man. His head lands in a puddle of dank alley water that darkens with his blood. Let him get up from that. I bite back the pang of satisfaction I get from killing him. I can't let myself become tainted by their bloodlust. The fire in my shoulder fades, and the pain dies as my body heals.

There used to be a running joke among the gendars that the Almighty Kingdom had no enemies bold enough to strike. My whole life, I'd foolishly thought it true, until the demons disabused me of that notion.

That joke blurs in my mind as I become something else. I am one with my shotels. I only see flashes. The clash of swords, the crunch of bones, the ease with which flesh splits and bleeds. When it's over, my pulse is throbbing in my ears. I have a gash in my side, deeper than the first cut. It will take more time to heal. My shotels drip blood, and my breath comes out hard and loud. I retreat to a corner inside myself where I can hide from these egregious acts.

The white cat and the black-and-gray eagle are gone. Now Jahla and Fadyi stand in the alley, peering upon me in the shadows. Jahla's ice-white hair and pale face remind me of the Northerners from Galke. Fadyi looks more like a Tamaran than I do.

"You can't keep losing yourself in the fight like that," Fadyi says, ignoring the last demon gasping for air at my feet. "You lose too much precision with little gain in return."

"Well," I bite back, "I got the job done, didn't I?"

"While expending more energy than needed," Jahla points out, unimpressed.

I sheath my shotels and squat beside the demon who'd been pretending to be a merchant. With so much blood loss and no souls to feed on, he won't be able to hold on to his stolen body. "I warned you it would be easier to answer my questions from the start." I grab his chin and turn his face to me. "Where are the other demons, and why are you in Tamar?"

The demon coughs, and blood coats his lips. His eyes roll into the back of his head. "Piss off," he spits.

I dig my fingers into one of his wounds. The stink of his fading magic makes my stomach turn, but I ignore it. The demon yelps, his whole body trembling. "Efiya is dead," I say, sensing that I don't have much time left to get answers. "Are you here for Arrah?"

The demon smiles, his teeth rimmed in rot. "We don't need her for what's to come. Shezmu will open the gate and reunite our forces, and then we'll destroy your pathetic world for good. You can do nothing to stop it."

My shoulders stiffen as I glance up at Jahla and Fadyi, who both look stricken by the news. I never paid much attention to my history scribe, but I do remember that the demons come from another world. But hadn't the orishas destroyed that world long ago? "What gate?"

He coughs again and closes his eyes. "Wouldn't you like to know."

"Tell me, and I'll spare your life," I demand, shaking him.

The demon wheezes and exhales. His body falls still, and I let it drop to the ground. A faint gray smoke lifts from his lips and dissipates. I'm not strong enough to destroy his soul, but he's at least back in a bodiless state and harmless for the time being.

"Did you know about this gate?" I ask, peering up at Fadyi again.

He casts an unsure glance at Jahla. "I only know that during the war with the demons, the orishas severed the connection between worlds."

"Let me get this straight." Dread wrenches through my gut. "We foiled the demons' plot to free their king, but apparently that wasn't enough to stop them. Now they're planning to open this gate, reunite their army, and destroy our world." I pause to let the news sink in. "They don't know when to quit, do they?"

EIGHT
ARRAH

I rush out of the shop at the crack of dawn, on my way to the Almighty Temple. I would've gone sooner, but I didn't think Sukar would be happy with me waking him up in the dead of night. I clutch the mask close in a burlap sack over my shoulder. I need my friend to tell me that I'm not delusional—that I haven't fallen into some magic-induced fever dream. I need him to tell me that the impressions from the mask are real.

I can't let myself believe it—not yet. Sweat pours down my forehead, and my tunic sticks to my skin as I weave through the busy West Market. I dip out of the way of a man pushing a barrel after almost walking straight into him.

Soon I'm clear of the crowd and climbing the precipice to the Almighty Temple. I think about my journey to the Temple after Efiya killed the *edam*. The city had been gloomy in the half light and littered with the ashes of whole neighborhoods. Now most of the debris has been cleared away, leaving gaping wounds. But Tamar has already started to heal. From here I can see the markets bursting at the seams, the boats choking the docks, the coliseum. A giggling boy pushes past me on the way to the Temple, running with his sister on his heels. Their parents follow, calling for them to slow down.

At the top of the precipice, two attendants in gray robes greet patrons with warm smiles. I take in the five gray stone buildings connected by a half-moon ingress. On the southernmost point stands the Hall of Orishas. Next to it sits the Forum, where the scribes teach the holy script, and the Archive that houses the city's records. The seers' quarters, the kitchens, and attendant barracks make up the rest of the Temple.

Children play in the gardens while their parents congregate in the courtyard. Some people head to the Hall of Orishas to make offerings and pray. It's a far cry from the days when thousands of patrons visited the Temple. Not that I blame those who don't come anymore—not after my mother's deeds.

"Have you seen Sukar?" I ask an attendant as she sweeps across the courtyard.

When she looks up and sees me, she dips her head. "Hello, Arrah." She says my name with a kind of reverence that makes me uncomfortable. "I last saw Attendant Sukar in the vegetable garden."

I thank her, and the woman lingers as if eager for me to ask another question. Even for a Temple attendant, she's acting strangely.

I leave the courtyard and the public gardens, heading for the barracks at the north side of the Temple. I slip behind a thicket of vines, where the noise from only a moment ago feels like it's a world away. Sukar's kneeling in front of a row of greens, pulling up weeds, shirtless. His deep brown skin glistens with sweat and clumps of dirt. He stops for a moment, braces his hands on his lower back, and stretches. My insides twist as I remember how he slammed into the pillar and slumped to the ground on the battlefield. I almost killed him—my own friend.

"Are you going to stand there and watch me, or say something?" He turns to face me with one eyebrow raised. "I felt your magic as soon as you passed through the gates."

"You look well." My gaze travels to the tree that had inked across his chest after I healed him. It extends down his belly and disappears beneath his trousers. At the center of the tree lies the *kaheri*—a star that connects him to Heka.

With Beka's knowledge inside me, I can't resist taking stock of his other tattoos. The *ayame*, twin leaves on each of his forearms, give him courage. The *lofa*—a bird with its wings spread to reflect upon the past and look to the future—sits upon his left forearm. The *hortiti* or war horn, a symbol of vengeance and justice, on his right. On his neck, the *pa'soni*, the flame to bind him to his ancestors and draw their protection. My gaze lingers on the twin antlers that I tattooed on his wrist, imbued with the magic to heal. "I see that my poor drawing skills didn't kill you after all."

"A stroke of luck," Sukar says with none of his usual playfulness. He studies my face, his eyes searching, then he brushes the dirt off his hands. "In truth, I wouldn't be here if not for you. . . . I was sure that I wouldn't wake again."

I look at the pile of weeds he's pulled from the ground. "I never pegged you for a gardener."

"Ah, did you think I spent all my time at the Temple answering to my uncle's every whim?" He flashes me a sly grin and wipes sweat from his forehead. The raised tiger stripes on his cheeks glow. "I do have quite the green thumb, and Emere put me to work. . . ."

A dull ache edges between my eyes as Sukar drones on about Emere. I massage my forehead, willing the pain to go away. I take one step forward and sway on my feet. The world tilts, and my legs give out.

Sukar lunges forward and catches me in his arms. "I've got you," he says, his tattoos glowing. It feels nice to be close to him—to know that my touch won't hurt him. He's leaner than Rudjek, his chest narrower, his skin hot from the sun. I shouldn't compare them. One is my friend, and one I wish could be more. "Are you okay?"

"Yes," I answer a little too quickly as I pull away.

He narrows his eyes. "You're a horrible liar."

"I'm feeling a little tired," I admit, my mind foggy.

"Let's go inside." Sukar guides me toward the Temple. "It's mighty hot out today."

We step beneath the shade of the vestibule. Out of the reach of the sun, the air is cool and damp. Magic flutters in the corridor, almost as much as at the shop. Something flickers in and out of the corners of my eyes—faint impressions of generations of people passing through the Temple. Not ghosts—echoes of memories. Grandmother's presence brushes against my mind. This is her gift: the magic to peer across time. "I wish you could see this," I tell Sukar.

He glances around the hall. "I can sense magic here, but I don't know what it's doing."

"It's replaying memories," I breathe.

Sukar frowns as we walk past attendants, some real and some

only echoes. We reach the door to one of the guest apartments and move into the salon. I drop into a chair, still massaging my forehead, while he slips into a tunic.

"Tell me what's wrong." He kneels in front of me with a cup of water. Only a few days ago, Essnai and I were taking care of him, and now he's returning the favor. "Are you unwell because you healed me?"

I shake my head and take a sip from the cup, thankful to have something to occupy the awkward silence that falls between us. I only jokingly thought I was in a magic-induced fever dream, but now I have to wonder if it's true. I don't know why my magic showed me the impressions in the corridor. "I've brought something that I'd like you to take a look at." I squeeze the cup between my hands until the wood pinches into my palm. "I think it might be important."

"Arrah, what are you talking about?" Sukar asks, looking increasingly worried.

"A mask." I shove the sack at him. "I found a Zu mask."

He frowns. "What do you mean, found—did you buy a mask?"

"Just take a look at it, please," I insist, flustered.

"Okay." Sukar unstrings the sack and slips the mask out. He studies the glowing symbols, unblinking. "For Heka's sake." His hands shake. "How did you get this?"

"I got it from a boy at the street fair last night," I say, and when Sukar quirks an eyebrow, I add, "That part isn't important."

"Burning fires, it *is* important." His voice rises. "This is a warrior's mask, not some knockoff from the East Market."

I slump in the chair, my head spinning. This whole conversation has gone in the wrong direction. "Let me start at the beginning," I say, then explain to him how I came by the mask. "The boy said that he'd bought it from a merchant. Who knows if that's true or not, but, Sukar, when I touch it, I can see the warrior's last memories."

Sukar looks down at the mask again. "I'm afraid that this *ben'ik* does not possess your gifts. I see only that the symbols are glowing—nothing more."

I shove down my disappointment. Sukar's magic is from his tattoos. He has no natural affinity for it—the way I never had before the chieftains' sacrifice. Still, I hoped that he'd have some sense of awareness or some connection with the scrivener magic. I want him to tell me that what I saw was real—that I haven't lost my mind and I'm not a fool for believing there's a chance.

"Something about this memory is important?" he asks hesitantly.

"The tribal people—they're not all gone," I say, breathless. "I held the mask most of the night. I hardly got any sleep over it. In Rassa's memory—the boy who owned the mask—the Zu tribe split up before the demons attacked. Some people escaped."

"Escaped?" Sukar repeats, his doubt evident.

"Yes," I say, the lack of sleep catching up with me.

"How is that possible?" Sukar shakes his head. "The cravens searched the tribal lands after they found the tribes destroyed. There were no survivors."

"No one survived the battle, yes, but some people got away before it started." I smile through my tears as he puts the mask aside.

Sukar squeezes his eyes shut for a brief moment. "Can you find them?"

"Yes," I answer, sure of it. "I don't know where they are, but if I go to the ridge in the mountains, I can pick up their trail."

Sukar breaks into a big grin, his chestnut eyes bright. "Well then, this more than makes up for you almost killing me and giving me three ugly tattoos."

"You're an ungrateful brat." I struggle to keep a straight face.

"I know." He clasps my hand between his own. "They're really alive."

Triumph fills my belly with heat as I consider what this means. How did Tribe Zu trick the demons? Had people from the other tribes fled before the demons arrived, too? If there are survivors, then I'm not the only one—I'm not the last witchdoctor. The tribal lands will heal, too, just like the Almighty Kingdom.

Only yesterday, I had grand plans to reopen my father's shop, but that will have to wait for now. It won't take more than a couple of months, maybe, to search for the missing tribal people. "We're going to find them," I vow, more to myself than to Sukar.

PART II

PART II

THE UNNAMED ORISHA: DIMMA

I often wonder how I can remember every moment of my many lives, yet not remember the exact moment I fell in love with Daho. Time may be linear, but it's a fickle thing that toys with even the likes of my kind. I believe, then, that the moment I seek is not one but many stretched across time.

The first moment happens when Daho finally breaks his silence. He spends days after our first brief conversation lost in the fragments of his memories. His thoughts are a tangle of roots that I cannot decipher, but eventually the knots unravel.

I sit completely still on the edge of the lake. If I were bound to the limitations of my physical body, it would've succumbed to the elements days ago. But it would be a falsehood to let my vessel wither—and I am already pretending to be a thing that I am not. For the first time, I consider the difference between having a vessel and simply existing as part of the universe. In this body, I am my own world.

"You are very strange," Daho says, coming to stand beside me. He stares across the lake with a blanket wrapped around his shoulders, and I wonder what he sees. "You're not really endoyan. No one could withstand this cold for days on end in your flimsy clothes."

"There are many names for what I am," I say, "but they are all meaningless."

"I have to call you something," Daho insists. Underneath his words, his intentions pour out like a silent song. *You are Dimma, beautiful and terrifying. You are my salvation; you are death.*

That name again. It's beginning to grow on me—the way he thinks of it with such trepidation. It has taken on a new meaning for him. "You may call me Dimma, but I am not terrifying, nor am I death."

"You can read my thoughts?" he asks, as if that is unusual.

Even though my skin is cold, a subtle warmth flushes into my face. I touch my cheeks, fascinated by this change. "Yes."

"You can't go poking around in people's heads," Daho groans.

"Why?" I ask, confused when his mind is open.

"It's an invasion of privacy." He shudders and glances over his shoulder. "This explains how that cabin looks exactly like my father's old workshop. You gleaned it from my mind."

"How would I know that you want to call me Dimma if not from your thoughts?"

Daho's cheeks deepen in color. "People share what they want through words."

"Words on their own seem to lack . . . *color*," I say. "What about listening to the meaning underneath your words? Is that an invasion of privacy?"

Daho groans again. "I would very much appreciate it if you don't do that either, okay?"

"Okay," I echo him. I am fascinated by the limitations of mortality and its rules, but I will stay my curiosity.

Daho digs his tattered shoes into the snow. "Thank you for saving my life." He hesitates—his voice coarse and tense. "Can you bring my parents back from death, too? Like you did for me?"

There is hope woven between his words—and I already know that my answer will disappoint him. "There are many states of death, but it is not final until the soul joins with the creator. And final death is only the beginning of rebirth."

"Please," Daho begs.

I search the realms for a trace of the souls that bear his mark—that show some kinship. There are some, but they are distant in relation. Had his parents' souls lingered, even without a body, I could make them new vessels. But there is nothing left but impressions, echoes of what they once were. "I can't."

Daho sits down in the snow next to me. Faint black veins show through his diaphanous skin. Tears run down his cheeks, and I know that I have made a mistake. I underestimated his bond with his parents. This is another thing for which I lack context. I have never felt a bond with anyone.

"I am sorry, Daho." His name rolls around my mouth, full on my tongue. *Daho*. Da-o. Silent *h*. *Daho*.

He draws in a sharp breath, his shoulders trembling. "My uncle raided the royal palace and killed my parents—he cut them down like dogs."

I open my mouth to speak again and pause. I'm still getting used to words, and I can't think of any that will reassure him. It would be so much easier for him to share my thoughts.

Daho wipes his face with the blanket. "I don't have anyone without them—I am alone."

I turn back to staring at the lake, an uneasiness settling in my vessel. "I have always been alone."

"Always?" he says. "What about your parents?"

I tell him about the Supreme Cataclysm, and Koré bringing me here, to which he asks, "She just left you by yourself?" His glowing eyes widen. When I nod, he sighs. "I was hardly ever alone until the servants in the palace helped me escape the slaughter. I ran until I couldn't go any farther, then I flew."

"How long have you been running?" I ask, curious.

"I don't know . . . a few months now." He shrugs. "In truth, my uncle may still be searching for me." His eyes meet mine. "How old are you?"

"Age is a mortal construct," I say. "I can't age."

Daho bites his lip, pushing back a fresh crop of tears. "I'm almost seventeen, but I bet you already knew that."

I nod, but to elaborate on how I know is too complicated for words.

He draws his knees to his chest and hugs his legs. "My uncle will kill me if I show my face in Jiiek again, but I will go back once I'm stronger. I must avenge my parents. If I don't, I will die without honor."

"You could stay here for a while," I say. "Until you're stronger."

He glances at me through silver lashes. "Thank you."

"You can keep calling me Dimma," I say, suddenly glad that he can't read the intention beneath my words—the longing. "I would very much like that."

Daho laughs. His voice echoes across the frozen lake, and I feel a strange sensation in my chest. I do not know why he's laughing, but I would do anything to make him laugh again. That was the moment I vowed neither of us would ever be alone again.

NINE
ARRAH

The Zu mask hums with magic that clings to my fingers like finely spun gossamer. I've been too wrapped up in the news about the tribal people to notice that Sukar has brought me to a familiar guest apartment. He, Essnai, and I used to come here to hide from our lessons.

As a favorite attendant, he's always had his own bedchamber while the others lived in communal quarters. But his room is nothing like this one. He had a narrow bunk, a dressing table, and a dozen Zu masks decorating the walls. That room smelled like sweet perfume—everything ordered and in its place. This apartment is dusty, with crates stacked along one wall.

I take in the silver-and-blue engravings on the bedposts, dulled with time, and the gold-trimmed dresser. The floor is covered in gray marble with a faint outline of a sundial that spans most of the room. I reach underneath the cushion on the chair and run my fingers across the three names carved in the wood. *Sukar. Essnai. Arrah.*

I cringe as the memories from so many years ago come rushing back in. "You brought me *here* of all places?"

Sukar looks around, his nose wrinkled. "I don't like the decor, either. It's rather old-fashioned. But when I got back, Emere had boxed up my things and moved someone else into my room."

I stare at him in disbelief, heat burning down my neck. "I'm not talking about the decor," I shoot back. "We once hid in here from our lessons, and you asked if you could . . ." I squirm in the chair, remembering the thrill of the moment. He asked if he could kiss Essnai and me. "Never mind—it doesn't matter."

A knock sounds at the door, and Sukar sighs. "Go away, Emere."

I frown and whisper, "How do you know it's her?"

Sukar smacks his forehead. "She's been asking about you since we got back."

"Why?" I remember how weird the attendant in the courtyard had acted when I was looking for Sukar. Now I'm thinking that she went straight to tell Emere I was here.

"Sukar, I'd like a word with Arrah?" the head attendant says from the other side of the apartment door. Her voice always rises so that her every phrase sounds like a question.

"For Heka's sake, Emere," Sukar groans. "Not now."

"What have I told you about invoking Heka's name in the orishas' holy place?" she presses.

"What do you want, Emere?" I sound too much like a petulant child. She's only six years older than us, but even when we were younger, she was such a nag.

"It's important that I speak with you," she repeats.

Sukar looks to me for confirmation, and I nod. He shakes his head as he crosses the room and lets her in. She enters with a pleasant yet reserved smile. Her gray robe pales in comparison to the richness of her brown skin, her high cheekbones, and her small mouth. She wears silver crescent moon earrings and a sheer white headscarf. "I'm sorry to disturb you." Emere bows to me. "I wouldn't have if it wasn't of grave importance."

The melodrama I expected, but averting her eyes and bowing . . . "What are you doing?"

"Showing respect, of course," Emere says. "Sukar told me that you carry the souls of the chieftains."

"What's this about?" I cut my eyes to Sukar, who only shrugs. He'd conveniently forgotten to mention the part about him gossiping with Emere.

"The Almighty One will be putting Tyrek Sukkara on trial for his crimes this afternoon."

Rudjek's already told me this, and I don't see what it has to do with me. "Yes?"

"A lot has happened in your absence." Emere paces around the room with her hands clasped against the small of her back. "The Almighty One has spoken at length about disbanding the Temple leadership. He doesn't plan to seek out suitable candidates to fill the seers' positions. Gods, I don't know if there *are* suitable replacements after what happened to the tribes. How are we going to run the Temple without seers—who's going to keep the balance of power in check?" Emere glances away. "Your mother . . ."

I grit my teeth as her words ring in my ears, digging up my doubt. *I won't be like her.*

"She resisted Suran Omari's attempts to limit the Temple's power for years," Emere says. "He's always wanted complete control over the Kingdom."

I understand now why the mob in the West Market angrily called Emere and the others *Temple loyalists*. If Suran wants to limit the Temple, he'd have plenty of support to discredit those who oppose him. He won't stop until he has the whole Kingdom under his thumb. I clutch the arms of my chair. I can't say that I'm surprised, but I never thought he'd go so far. "Have you talked to any of the people of tribal lineage in the city? Some of them may be willing to serve the Temple and stand against Suran Omari."

"We need a gifted leader to stand against the Almighty One," Emere says, distressed, as she comes to rest in front of me. "We need someone who can remind Tamarans that magic has done a lot of good for our great city. The seers have ended countless famines, treated the sick, and tempered the seasons to keep our crops plentiful. The charlatans in the markets can't do that."

She stands still, her lips parted, on the verge of saying more. "No." I answer the question before she asks. My voice is a sharp note of pent-up anger threatening to burst free.

Sukar leans against one of the bedposts with his arms crossed, his face unreadable. Had he known of her plans to ask me to join the Almighty Temple?

"We need *you*, Arrah," Emere begs. "With the tribes gone, you are undoubtedly the most suited to the role of *Ka*-Priestess. You already have the favor of Crown Prince Rudjek, from what I saw in the West Market the other day."

My head throbs. I can't believe what she's asking. She wants me to be my mother's successor. She wants me to be *Ka*-Priestess of the Almighty Kingdom.

"Suran Omari's planning to claim the tribal lands," adds Emere, desperate.

Sukar straightens at that. He glances at the mask, then at me, his eyebrows raised. I shake my head. We need to be sure about what I saw in Rassa's memory before we tell Emere—especially if what she says is true. The nerve of Suran Omari to think that he can just take the tribal lands. He has no respect for all the people who died. It's business as usual for him. Trades to make. Land to steal.

"Where did you hear that?" I ask Emere.

"Prince Derane Sukkara," she answers. "He thought it information the Temple could use against Suran Omari." Emere draws in a ragged breath. "Now you know why we need your help."

"Let it go, Emere," Sukar says, his voice sympathetic. "She already said no."

Emere's eyes brim with unshed tears, but she brushes them away with the back of her sleeve. She clears her throat and lifts her chin. "I understand." She smiles and, on her way to the door, pauses to pat my shoulder. "I know I ask too much, and I'm sorry for that." I have no words for her, so I squeeze her hand before she lets herself out.

When she's gone, Sukar drops onto the bed. "I should've warned you. She's been at it for days, going on about you taking your mother's place."

I massage my forehead. "I have to go."

"Why don't you stay a little longer?" Sukar offers. "That way, you can avoid the trial altogether."

"I can't," I say, thinking about my promise to meet Rudjek by the Serpent River. "I'll come back soon so we can make plans to leave for the tribal lands."

I bypass the heart of the West Market along the quieter streets, headed for the Serpent River. The bells strike the thirteenth hour, and I curse. I'm late. My forearms tingle before I spot Rudjek up ahead on the path. There's something off about his gait—he's favoring his right side. His guards are with him, but he holds up one hand to tell them to fall back as he crosses the space between us. Kira and Majka mumble to each other, their conversation almost inaudible. For once, even Fadyi and Jahla look on edge. Another guard, the oldest of the bunch, with gray hair, watches me like a hawk.

Rudjek stops within arm's reach of me. "I waited for you at the river."

I pinch the bridge of my nose. "Sorry—I lost track of time at the Temple."

"How is Sukar?" Rudjek asks after clearing his throat.

"Much better," I say, anxious to tell him about the tribal people and ask if his father really means to claim their lands. But I can't do that with his guards so near and risk them taking news back to Suran Omari. I frown, noticing that Rudjek's elara is a tad snug. One of his guards wears a bloodstained uniform that's too big, with a lion's head stitched across the chest. It's not a far stretch to believe that he and Rudjek have switched tunics. "What happened?"

Rudjek scratches the back of his neck, but it doesn't cover the nervous energy radiating from him. "I got into a little disagreement."

I cross my arms. "So little that one of your guards couldn't handle it?"

Rudjek opens his mouth, his dark eyes darting away from my face. "It got ugly," he admits, all pretense gone. He stumbles over his next words. "There's a lot of tension among some circles in the city right now . . . people with grudges and scores to settle." He presses his arm close against his side—a flash of pain etching across his face. When he catches me looking, his features smooth out; his mask slips into place.

"Emere asked me to speak for the Temple at Tyrek Sukkara's trial," I tell him.

"She is more than capable of speaking herself," Rudjek says, his voice brittle. "You've been through enough."

"You've been through as much, yet . . ." I gesture to his uniform.

The gong rings in the West Market, and the lingering echo sets my teeth on edge. It's the first call to gather the assembly for the trial. I can't get Emere's disappointed face and her words out of my head. *I know I ask too much.* Does she truly not understand that I could never step into my mother's role or be her replacement? I could never be that for her or for the Kingdom, but I also can't let Suran go unchecked.

The guard with the gray hair strolls forward. "We must leave soon before we're late for the trial, Commandant."

"Don't mind Captain Dakte," Rudjek says with his back still to the soldier. "He means to spy on my every move and report to my father."

"I'm here to protect the Almighty One's interests," the man says, resentful. "Shall we go?"

"After I finish the conversation you so rudely interrupted," Rudjek snaps at him.

Captain Dakte lets out an exasperated breath. The gendars stare between the two of them as if waiting for the next move in a game. With a man like that around, I'm glad that Rudjek has loyal friends with him.

"I'll come to the assembly with you," I blurt out against my better judgment. "In case Emere does need my support."

"It's your decision." Rudjek gives me a look like he knows I'm not telling the whole truth, but then again, neither is he. "For my part, I want nothing more than to have you by my side."

There's weight in his words that even the most oblivious person in the world could understand. I want him by my side, too, but this is nothing like when he pledged to help me find the child snatcher. How can we be there for each other when my magic and his anti-magic stand between us?

I decide against telling Rudjek about the Zu mask—until I'm sure Suran Omari can't use the information to his advantage. I smile to reassure him, all while feeling like I'm falling into the same pit of vipers that destroyed my mother.

TEN
ARRAH

Rudjek keeps casting nervous glances at everyone we pass as if he expects more trouble. He says nothing more about his earlier *disagreement*, but it isn't hard to figure out. His father has many enemies; some poor fools must have thought him an easy target.

We walk toward the crowded part of the West Market with a gap between us that could fit a whole person. He clenches and unclenches his hands, the leather gloves creaking. My magic is restless with him so near, and it itches underneath my skin. Along with the headache, it's hard to concentrate. I want to go to our secret spot by the river and dream together. I want to be reckless and kiss him right here in front of everyone, but I also want to retreat from his anti-magic.

"Dare I ask what you're thinking?" His midnight eyes burn with longing.

"Things wholly inappropriate in this moment," I say, my voice pitched low.

Rudjek laughs, and the sound is pure music to my heart. With all that's happened, it makes me feel less alone in the world—less afraid. When did this boy become so important to me? It's such an impossible question to answer. I've loved him in one way or another for so long that it doesn't matter.

I eye the pendant dangling around his neck. "Remember the first time you showed me your family crest?"

"I told you that it protected me against magic," Rudjek muses, a dreamy look in his eyes. "To which you asked in the snottiest tone, 'Will it stop us from being friends once I have magic?'"

I glare at him for making me sound like a brat. "You offered to throw the pendant into the river so that it wouldn't stand in the way of our friendship."

"I still wish I could, but I'd have to throw myself in the river with it." Rudjek runs his hand absently across the craven bone crest. "We'll find a way to be together, Arrah. A clever man only needs one stone to kill two birds."

I smile, finding it ironic that he's quoting a tribal proverb to me. I should take strength from Rudjek's resolve, but I'm losing hope.

We come upon dozens of Temple loyalists in gray robes standing near the coliseum walls. They swat the ground with sticks to show their disapproval. People shout at them to go home, but the loyalists repeat three lines:

"Magic is the language of the gods."

"Magic connects us to the divine."

"Magic is a blessed gift."

"Magic is a gift and a curse," I whisper.

"Is that her?" a person asks when their eyes lock with mine. "Is that the new *Ka*-Priestess with the Crown Prince?"

"It's a sign from the orishas," someone else yells in relief, and my stomach falls to my knees. It's enough to make me turn on my heel and flee the scene, but I don't. I will hear this trial out, and I will make sure Suran Omari knows that I stand between him and the tribal lands.

Rudjek groans something under his breath, but his mask never slips. Murmurs rise through the market as word of our arrival spreads. Sweat trickles down my back, and I dig my nails into my palms. I don't want to be the voice of the Temple—I don't want people depending on me. I don't want to fail them like I failed my father.

"Twenty-gods," Majka curses, his eyes bright with admiration. I follow his gaze to Jahla, who had slipped away before we reached the market to *change*. Now she's entering the coliseum, wearing a white sheath fitted through the bust and hips. Her silver locks flow in waves down her back. Raëke is with her, dressed in a jeweled tunic and wide-leg pants. If they're in disguises to hide among the crowd, then Rudjek is expecting more trouble. "She is magnificent."

"Careful, Majka," Kira says at his side. "She looks like more than you can handle."

"Is that a challenge?" He laughs. "I love challenges."

My cheeks warm at the thought of myself in my dusty tunic compared to all the people in fancy garb. Not so long ago, laborers had carried Arti and me into the coliseum in a litter. My mother had timed our arrival to spoil Suran Omari's plans. My sheath had been so lovely that day, but I hadn't appreciated it.

"What are we going to do with the tribes gone?" asks a teary-eyed woman with slender veins along her temples, talking to a friend. She looks to be of Kes descent or Delenian like Rudjek's mother.

"What will the Kingdom do when there's another drought or a famine? Who's going to help us if all the witchdoctors are gone?"

"Can you stop thinking about yourself for once?" her friend says, glaring at her. "They're gone—every single one of them. It's horrible."

I cringe as the gong rings the third and final time. Some two thousand people fill the circular benches that face each other. The coliseum's mosaic ceiling shrouds them in a prism of flitting shadows. I recognize many of their faces from the days my mother stood against Suran Omari at past assemblies. Beyond them, the two-tiered stage looms over the crowd. Arti and the seers used to sit on one side of the first tier, the Vizier and his guildmasters on the other side. Now there are six empty high-backed chairs in the middle of the tier.

The royal family once occupied a gilded box on the second tier, high above the first. The late Almighty One, Jerek Sukkara, and his sons, Crown Prince Darnek and Second Son Tyrek. Tyrek, who had looked upon the rivalry between Rudjek's father and my mother with keen interest. Now there's only shadows and cobwebs and the echo of memories in the royal family's place.

Two gendars in full body armor drag Tyrek from a private room behind the first tier. They force him to his knees, and his head dips between his sunken shoulders. His exquisite blue elara trimmed in silver does nothing to hide the bruises on his gaunt face or the cuts on his rough-shaven head. I can hardly stand to look at him, knowing that he chose to side with my sister. He seized his chance to take the throne while letting the demons prey upon the city.

"How dare you put a Sukkara on his knees," shouts Prince

Derane from his perch on the highest bench in the audience. A dozen Sukkaras with their ram's head pendants and fine clothes surround him. With Tyrek's arrest, he should be on the second tier—he should be Almighty One. "It is a show of disrespect to the gods themselves."

"You are mistaken, Prince Derane," says a voice that silences the coliseum. Suran Omari enters the stage from the hidden door, followed by his four guildmasters. He glides across the tier in a white-and-gold elara that shimmers as he moves. Bile burns a trail of fire up my throat, and my magic coils tight underneath my skin. I push down an urge to burn him where he stands. "Even those of us with divine ties to the gods must learn to subjugate ourselves before the eyes of justice."

"Were you interested in justice, I would be in your place," Prince Derane says, rallying the crowd. The coliseum falls into chaos as Suran Omari and the guildmasters move to take their seats.

After not seeing Suran since the day he banished my family, I'd almost forgotten how much Rudjek looks like him. The resemblance is jarring. His once chiseled jaw has gone slack with age, but Rudjek has his angular face, haunting dark eyes, and thick eyebrows. Suran is tall, too, broad shouldered, though he's soft around the waist. He keeps his hair cropped so short you can hardly tell that it's curly like his son's. I bite back my anger—why should he get to be alive, healthy, and well, while my father suffered to the end of his days?

Rudjek leans close to me and says, "I have to join them."

I nod, and he strolls forward, the trepidation gone and the swagger back in his step. Kira points out the place reserved for his guards. I move to sit with them, which starts an uproar among the loyalists who had been quiet when Prince Derane spoke.

Once the crowd quiets again, Emere stands up from her spot among the loyalists. She looks formidable with her head high and her shoulders back. "I volunteer to speak for the Temple," she announces. "We talk about showing respect to the orishas, but no one speaks for them today."

"Oh, yes, we should have a representative from the Temple, on that we can agree." Suran waves for her to join them on the first tier as Rudjek settles in the chair to his right. Suran's voice is deceptively friendly. When Emere puts one foot on the steps to climb up to the tier, he clears his throat. "There is one matter to clarify. One cannot be the voice of the gods unless the gods speak to them." He turns a cold, biting smile on Emere. "Do they speak to you, child?"

Emere freezes on the steps, her face twisted in panic. "No." Her fire from only a moment ago cools to embers.

"It seems to me that the gods have spoken with their silence." Suran sighs. "For too long, we've displeased them by embracing magic, and now we must make amends for our insolence. Lord Re'Mec warned us in the holy script that magic would be the end of mortal kind, and see how it has brought so much death upon us."

I clench my fists on my lap as several people agree and call for Emere to take a seat. She glances at me on her way back to the bench, her eyes begging, but I look away. It was a mistake coming here. Suran Omari is impossible to reason with—there's no point in trying. Yet I can't let him get away with disrespecting Emere and the Temple. He's gotten away with too much already. My legs tremble as I come to my feet. I don't know why I'm doing this, or what I hope to gain.

"I can stand for the Temple," I say, pushing back my doubts.

"The gods speak to me." Several people at the assembly can attest to this—Rudjek, Majka, Kira, and the cravens.

All eyes turn to me. People whisper, some laugh, and others cheer. I feel like a caged animal waiting to perform tricks at a street fair, but I've committed to this course.

"Arrah N'yar—daughter of *Ka*-Priestess Arti, traitor and murderer of children." Suran leans forward, his eyes burning with disdain. "I thought you'd still be mourning the loss of your entire family."

I will not let Suran Omari provoke me. "The Kingdom would be laid to waste had I not stopped my sister with magic, and I carry the souls of the five chieftains. Who better to speak for the Temple?"

"Hasn't your family done enough?" someone shouts. "The Kingdom doesn't need your kind anymore."

Suran raises a hand, a look of satisfaction on his parted lips. "I will allow her to speak for the Temple if she wishes." His voice has an edge to it that makes me think I'm walking into a trap.

I swallow my nerves as I approach the stairs leading up to the first tier. I expect Suran to pull another trick when I start to climb, but he holds his tongue. People gawk at me—some with hate and some with hope in their eyes. I cross my arms like the gesture can shield me from them. I catch Tyrek staring at me, too, still on his knees, his shoulders slumped. His eyes are hollow black pits. I force myself to look away.

"We are most thankful to have this child speak on behalf of the orishas if it is their will," Suran says. "You don't mind standing, do you? We seem to be short on chairs."

I can almost feel his hatred buzzing under his skin. I remind myself that although he has craven blood, he hasn't died and re-turned; his heritage is dormant. He is no threat to me. "I'm quite fine." *Fine as long as I stay far away from you.*

"That simply won't do." Rudjek abruptly comes to his feet. He beckons for two gendars, who rush from the shadows at the rear of the stage. "Take her my chair."

The smile slips from Suran's face as Rudjek moves to stand at his side while the gendars bring the chair to me. He turns back to address the crowd. "We have gathered today with great purpose. It brings me no joy to see my cousin fall to such tragedy and betrayal. We have pored over the evidence and corroborated the witnesses' stories." Suran takes a deep breath like he has a heavy heart.

The audience jeers and slings insults at the disgraced prince on his knees. For his part, Tyrek doesn't even flinch.

"To ensure that this trial is fair and just, I will put the matter to a vote," Suran continues. "Each of the guildmasters, the Temple, and I will give our vote to determine the final verdict." He waves to the open double doors where twelve men in all black with straight swords at their waists rush inside the coliseum, carrying a litter. They place it on the ground, and the crowd whispers to each other. Rudjek casts a confused look my way.

Three people climb from the litter—a man and two veiled women. The woman in front lifts the delicate fabric of her veil with practiced grace. Her diaphanous brown skin stands out against her red braids pinned up in a bun. The woman in the middle wears white silks trimmed in gold—the Omari family's colors—but she doesn't remove her veil. The man is in black with a straight sword at his waist and stands close to her.

"I asked for a delegation from Galke to serve as a neutral party to this matter," Suran explains. "They have heard the facts in the case against Second Son Tyrek."

"This is preposterous," Prince Derane shouts as the delegation climbs the first tier. "You've brought outsiders to rule on my nephew's fate?"

"Of course not," Suran says. "The Galke delegation is only here to bear witness."

"I am Prefect Clopa," the one who removed her veil says. "I am the adviser to Princess Veeka." She nods to the woman in the white-and-gold silks. "It is our honor to lend aid to our allies."

Suran turns on a charming smile that makes him look too much like Rudjek for comfort. "We are most thankful."

The delegation passes me without a glance. Prefect Clopa moves to stand on Suran's left, between him and the Master of Arms. The woman in the white-and-gold silks takes a place to Rudjek's right. The Galke man remains to the side, not far from me, but his eyes never leave the princess as he rests his hand on the hilt of his sword.

"For the record of this assembly, I will read the charges against Second Son Tyrek Sukkara." Suran pauses as an attendant hurries forward to hand him a scroll the length of his forearm. He clears his throat and begins. "The charges are as follows: Conspiring and carrying out the murder of the Almighty One, Jerek Sukkara, your father. Conspiring and carrying out the murder of Crown Prince Darnek Sukkara, your brother." Suran drones through a list of names that includes the seers, gendars, and attendants. "Conspiring to kill anyone who opposed you—myself included. Desecrating sacred orisha statues. Allowing demons to terrorize our city, costing the lives of three thousand citizens. The complete destruction of the five tribes . . ."

I go still when he mentions the tribes. Thirty thousand tribal people had attended the Blood Moon Festival months ago. How many escaped before the demons attacked? Will there be enough to help me stop Suran from claiming their lands for the Kingdom's profit?

When he finishes listing Tyrek's crimes, the audience roars with anger. People curse and fling insults; and some jump out of their seats, shaking their fists and spitting. Tyrek drops his head and his whole body trembles. I don't allow myself to think of the torture he's endured. I only want to get this over with and go search for the survivors in the tribal lands.

"Well, Second Son Tyrek, do you have anything to say for yourself?" Suran asks.

Tyrek lifts his chin, and even in his diminished state, he bears a look of defiance at odds with his predicament. "Should I repeat the speech my jailers forced me to commit to memory, or should I improvise?"

If he had hoped to get under Suran Omari's skin, his words miss their mark. Suran gives him a sympathetic smile. "Try starting with the truth. This is your only chance to earn back a shred of dignity before it's too late."

"As I've told you countless times before, Efiya made me hurt people." Tyrek squeezes his eyes shut and jabs a finger against his temple. "She was in my mind—*she* controlled my every action."

My heart pounds against my chest. Is he saying what I think he is? It can't be.

Tyrek opens his eyes again. "But that isn't what you want to hear, correct? You want half-truths."

I sit forward, grasping the chair, dread flooding my chest. Magic flares inside me again, and I want to strike Tyrek down. I want to put an end to this nightmare. He is the last loose end.

"Enough lies, boy," Suran snaps. "Let the vote begin."

My sister turned children into *ndzumbis* to have playmates. She made a child cut off his finger and smile while doing it. If what he's saying is true . . . if Efiya forced him to commit treason . . . to kill his own family . . . I inhale a sharp breath.

The guildmaster to the far left of the tier, a gaunt-faced man with a neatly trimmed beard—Tyrek's uncle on his mother's side—casts the first vote. "I, Guildmaster Ohakim of the Laborers' Guild, vote guilty." There is no hesitation in his voice as he condemns his nephew.

Next to him, Suran's twin sister, General Solar, wears a face of indifference. "As head of the Military Guild, I also vote guilty."

Kira's father, Master Ny of the Scribes' Guild, sitting to the right of Princess Veeka and Rudjek, votes next. He's a prudish man of Estherian lineage, with porcelain skin and bone-straight hair like his daughter's, who has a reputation for his moderate views. "I vote to postpone the trial until we can investigate his new claims." His vote sends a flurry of whispers through the coliseum.

"I second the vote to postpone," adds the Master of the Scholars. She is the oldest of the guildmasters, with snow-white curls against her dark skin. She yawns like she's unimpressed by the heckling from the crowd. She, along with the other guildmasters, looks to Suran, and he turns to me.

"What say you, the voice of the Temple?" Suran asks, his question laced with sarcasm.

"He . . ." I lick my dry lips and look around the assembly. So many faces peer at me from the shadows—people who deserve justice and closure. Everyone seems to be holding their breath, waiting on my answer. I don't want this burden, but it's mine to bear. "He may be telling the truth about my sister. I vote to postpone."

The crowd erupts again as Tyrek breaks down into uncontrollable sobs. My belly twists in knots, and I immediately wish that I could take back my words.

Suran Omari raises his hand, his face riddled with false concern, and I know that I have played into his trap. The crowd falls silent so he can speak. "Surely Tyrek's claims can't be true," he muses. "The Sukkaras—and the Omaris, for that matter—are protected from magic. Perhaps the voice of the Temple can give us an explanation."

I shrink under the sudden weight on my shoulders. Suran Omari's black eyes shine with glee. He's outmaneuvered me, and I'm a fool not to see it coming. This trial isn't only about Tyrek's guilt or innocence. Suran wants to prove that magic is dangerous. He wants to erase its influence—that's why he'd tried to discredit the Temple loyalists.

"We're waiting," Suran presses. "Is there a way that Second Son Tyrek could be telling the truth?"

"Yes," I hiss, and my voice is raw. "My sister was powerful enough to turn people into *ndzumbis* to command at her will. Even the craven bones the royal family wears would not have protected them."

"I understand that your mother possessed that talent as well," Suran says, leading. "Can you also put another person under your control?"

"I don't know." I shake my head, but that's a lie. "I wouldn't do it if I could."

"Ah, I see." Suran clucks his tongue. "It seems that the orishas have been right all along. Magic is dangerous in the hands of mortal kind. Let us all bear witness to the corruption that magic has brought upon our citizens." Suran gives me a sidelong glance, his expression triumphant. I've walked right into his carefully laid trap. "To protect the Kingdom, I hereby ban all unauthorized use of magic until further notice."

ELEVEN
RUDJEK

People in the audience yell, curse, and spit at the line of guards standing between them and the stage. The noise echoes in the coliseum, creating pure pandemonium, and my father lets it play out. He counted on this reaction. He *can't* ban magic. The tribes may be gone, but there are enough people here in Tamar who still possess it in small amounts. *Gods, Arrah.* She's gone completely still, her eyes two golden orbs of fire. Her skin practically glows, and her magic feels like the serrated edge of a tobachi knife cutting me deep.

"You forget yourself, *Vizier*," Prince Derane shouts over the crowd, using my father's official title. Vizier of the Almighty Kingdom, second to the Almighty One before my father seized control. "You are only *acting* Almighty One. You have no authority to ban magic. The Sukkaras will stand with the Temple against you."

"Fair enough, Prince Derane." Father holds up his hand in a peace offering, but I don't buy it for one moment. He's got something else up his sleeve. "We will table the conversation about the dangers of magic for the next assembly meeting."

I grit my teeth as sweat trickles down my back. My eyes land on Fadyi, Jahla, and Raëke. They've managed to work their way up to the front of the first tier. I follow their intent stares; all three watch Arrah, waiting for her next move. They can't really think that she'd use magic here. As they draw closer to her, the stabbing pain in my gut relents. Arrah deflates, sinking in the chair, looking miserable. Her magic subsides, and I relax a little.

"You see now, don't you?" Father leans close to me. Although his face is calm, his words hum with animosity. "This is why I've long warned you about her kind. Those with magic will always sow discord."

"Arrah isn't your enemy," I say, my voice hoarse. "Why can't you understand that? She's not like her mother or her sister."

Princess Veeka clears her throat from behind me, and I tense. My father would've only invited the Galke delegation to drum up more support for his bid to keep the throne. It takes a moment for me to remember my manners. I've moved closer to my father and inadvertently turned my back to the princess, an act of disrespect in the North.

"My apologies, Princess." I adjust my position so she's in my line of vision.

"Not to worry, Crown Prince," Princess Veeka says. "I'm not as old-fashioned as most in my family, nor do I expect anyone outside Galke to know every single one of our customs."

I meet her eyes, which are an iridescent violet beneath her sheer veil. "That's good to know."

"I'm intrigued by Second Son Tyrek's claims," Princess Veeka remarks.

"As am I," Father says, but he's lying through his teeth. He must have known what Tyrek would say. He'd planned to use it as a reason to further his agenda against magic. "This new information is certainly worth investigating."

New information, my ass. I don't know what exactly my father is playing at this time, but I know it'll be something else I won't like.

"Did Efiya bewitch him into doing her bidding or not?" shouts someone from the audience.

Arrah's eyes shine with unshed tears. "It's possible, but I can't say for sure."

My fingers twitch in my gloves, and I want so badly to go to her if only to let her know that she isn't alone.

"Is there any way to corroborate his story?" asks Guildmaster Ny to Princess Veeka's right.

"She can," Tyrek cries out, angling his body toward Arrah. "Please help me . . . please show them the truth."

Arrah looks to me, her eyes begging. I shake my head, not bothering to be subtle about it. She doesn't have to do this. It doesn't matter if he's guilty or not. People will still want blood. If it's not his, then it'll be hers.

"I'll try," she says, her voice small.

My father signals the end of the session, and the gong rings to make it official. "I will postpone judgment until we can get to the bottom of this new development. We will adjourn for now."

The solution seems to appease the crowd—and I ease out a sigh of relief. As soon as my father dismisses the assembly, I cross the tier to Arrah. "You don't have to get involved with this mess."

"I can't let someone else take the blame for my sister's deeds," she says, choking back tears. "You know that, don't you? I can't."

No point in arguing with her when she's like this. She's more stubborn than a mule with his head up his ass. "I know."

"Have her brought to the palace tomorrow." My father croaks out the order, then turns to the Galke delegation. "It would be my pleasure to give you a tour of our beautiful city."

I'm sure it would be his pleasure. I can see him now spending the entire tour securing Galke's full support. He'll already have Delene on his side through Adé. With both, the Sukkaras won't have a chance against him if the guildmasters confirm his appointment.

"I need to get out of here," Arrah groans.

"Let me accompany you to your father's shop," I offer as the loyalists congregate at the foot of the first tier, waiting for her. "We haven't spent much time together since you've been back." Never mind that she's only been in Tamar a couple of days.

She massages her forehead. "I'd best deal with Emere and the others on my own. Will I see you tomorrow at the palace?"

"Of course," I say, eager. "I'll make sure we run the entire staff through drills to prepare for your arrival." She doesn't even scoff at my poor attempt at humor. Nothing I say could make this day less of a disaster.

She comes to her feet, finally cracking a shadow of a smile. "Until tomorrow, Crown Prince."

"Raëke will stay near you in the West Market," I say, thinking about the demons in the alley. "In case anyone gets any ideas."

"Thank you." Arrah passes so close her magic brushes against my skin. It's only a tickle, an insatiable itch, an urge to react. Part of me wants to take her into my arms—to drown her in kisses—but the anti-magic pulls me away. The feeling only abates when she's gone. *Burning fires*. I'm relieved to be free of it.

When I enter into the wing of the palace reserved for the Crown Prince, I'm second-guessing myself. I should have left Fadyi or Jahla to help Raëke guard Arrah against the demons. Or maybe stationed half the City Guard at her doorstep. I can't stop thinking about the demon in the alley and the two dozen people he'd killed without regard.

The five of us—Fadyi, Jahla, Majka, Kira, and me—enter a salon that belonged to Crown Prince Darnek. The palace is the only place I'm allowed to roam without guards, so I send the others away. I'm glad to be rid of Captain Dakte for the time being.

The salon is eccentric and not at all to my taste. Swathes of white gossamer drape from the ceiling like spiderwebs that I have to keep pushing out of my face. I bump into one of the dozen couches and stumble over piles of pillows. None of which is half as absurd as the stage in one of the corners. Like his father and uncle, my Sukkara cousin loved his indulgences.

"I sealed off the attendants' passageways in your wing of the palace last night," Jahla says, headed straight for the window. She's still in the white sheath. "There's no way in or out, and no way for your father to spy on you here."

Majka dramatically clutches at his chest. "I hope you made sure the passageways were empty first. I'd hate it if some poor soul got stuck inside."

"Of course." Jahla grimaces. "Do you take me for a fool?"

"That was a joke," Majka grumbles under his breath.

Jahla waves like he's a gnat buzzing around her ear and turns to peer out the window. Before our eyes, her clothes change from her fitted sheath to a loose white elara. I have to remind myself that she isn't wearing clothes at all—she's only creating an illusion for our benefit. Though the thought that she's naked makes me avert my eyes.

Majka nudges my shoulder. "I don't think she likes me."

"Stop messing around, will you." I unbuckle my sword belt and drop my shotels on the nearest couch. I miss the weight of them almost immediately. "We need to figure out if the demons can open this gate."

"Can't you put in a good word for me, though?" Majka whispers. "I'm your most loyal friend, and I deserve that much from you."

"You do realize that she can hear your every word." I glance at Jahla's back. "Those superior craven senses, remember?"

"Oh, good." Majka lets out a sigh. "I do love an awkward courtship."

Jahla scoffs at the window, but she doesn't acknowledge Majka otherwise.

"I read about the gate in my advanced history lessons." Kira perches on the edge of a couch and pulls a dagger from a hidden sheath in her uniform. "Iben, the orisha of time, built it," she explains. "He bent the distance between two points to connect one world to the next. Some scholars believe that he connected them all."

"Not every world," comes a drawling voice. I whirl around to find Re'Mec, the sun god, lying on his side on the stage, cloaked in shadows. I groan at the sight of him. After the demons and that mockery of a trial, the last thing I want to deal with is a pompous god in need of attention. "Iben was a dreamer. He would cut a door to a world, then he'd linger for centuries on end, getting to know it."

Re'Mec climbs to his feet, his movements languid, his shadows writhing like a pit of vipers. As he crosses the salon, they settle around him in a blanket of fog. I blink as the edges of my vision blur. My eyelids droop, my mind slows. My knees suddenly go weak, and I can't stop staring at Re'Mec as his shadows bleed across the floor, creeping closer to me. He is without a doubt captivating.

"It's a thing of glory to behold your god, isn't it?" Re'Mec snaps me out of my daze. His body shifts into that of his persona Tam—a golden-haired, brown-skinned boy in a black elara.

I shake the cobwebs from my head and bite back the insult on the tip of my tongue. I don't have time for his little games. "So let me get this straight. The demons wouldn't have come here if the orishas hadn't connected our two worlds through this gate. Meaning the war that almost destroyed our world five thousand years ago was your fault."

"Well, if you put it that way, yes," Re'Mec says. "Koré's first children, the demons, lived on a world we call Ilora. They were the first of any of our children to discover the gate and figure out how to use it. The demons and their endoyan cousins, who they called their familiars, formed a trade relationship with Zöran, your world. All was well until one of my sisters—you know her as the Unnamed orisha—made the demons immortal. They became insufferable after that."

"I don't get it," Majka interrupts. "If you're all-powerful, why do you need this gate to travel from one world to the next?"

"Because the universe is vast, even for a god, and it keeps expanding," Kira answers as if it should be obvious.

"It's not expanding anymore." Re'Mec glowers, his lips turned down. "When my sister stole immortality from the Supreme Cataclysm, she upset the balance. Now the Supreme Cataclysm does not create—it only destroys, and the universe is finite."

"The gate, Re'Mec," I press him. "We don't care about the orisha origin story."

Some part of me mourns Tam—his snark, his absurd lies, his stories. Though he and Re'Mec have the same personality, it will never be the same between us.

"I'll get to that soon," Re'Mec says, "but first, you need to understand history. We were born with the same need to create as the Supreme Cataclysm, but the space around it was unstable. We needed distance, so Iben cut a path to the edge of the universe, where we built Ilora, Zöran, and countless other worlds."

"You're saying that the gate existed before mortal life?" I ask.

"No"—Kira frowns—"he's saying that life exists *because* of the gate."

Re'Mec winks at her. "Smart girl."

I sift through the plethora of new information fighting for space in my mind. "The demon in the alley said that Shezmu is planning to reunite the demon army and destroy Zöran. Does he have the power to control the gate? And if he does, why hasn't he opened it already?"

"Shezmu killed Iben and ate his soul, so, yes, he can control the gate," Re'Mec explains. "As far as why he hasn't opened it, I assume he has some grander scheme in mind. Shezmu was always a good strategist. He'll open the gate at the opportune moment."

"Burning fires," Kira swears. "The demons ate the souls of gods, too?"

Re'Mec looks miserable as he nods confirmation. "Most of them died from indigestion, but some, like Shezmu, did not."

Majka laughs, but then abruptly stops when we all glare at him. "What?"

I shove down the sinking feeling in the pit of my stomach. What chance do we stand against an army that can bring gods to their knees? I push the thought away—it doesn't matter how powerful the demons are. They aren't infallible. They must have a weakness, or they'll make a mistake. "Why haven't you killed Shezmu yourself?"

"He's hiding from me," Re'Mec says, his voice low and resentful.

"What about the box with the Demon King's soul?" Fadyi asks, leaning against the wall next to the door. He and Jahla have positioned themselves near the only exits in the salon, ever the watchful guardians. "Has the moon orisha found it?"

"No." Re'Mec narrows his eyes, his tone icy. "She has hundreds of worlds to search, and without the gate, that is not an easy task even for our kind. Speaking metaphorically, my sister is quick-footed, but the universe is vast. Think of it as looking for a blade of grass in the entirety of Zöran. It will take time."

Majka stares at the sun orisha in disbelief. "How can she not know where it is?"

"My sister erased her memories of where she hid the box in case her encounter with Efiya went bad." Re'Mec's anger sends waves of heat through the salon, and Majka scrunches up his nose like he smells something rank.

"So Koré doesn't have access to the gate, but Shezmu does," I say as the puzzle pieces start to click together. "The box is not on our world, or else Koré would've found it already. It stands to reason that Shezmu has kept the gate closed to slow down her search, but it has to be more than that. Shezmu must be using the gate to look for the Demon King's soul himself. Perhaps he won't attack until he is sure that his master is safe from the orishas."

"Shezmu is strong, but he can't free the Demon King even if he does find the box." Re'Mec brushes off the idea, but his voice is tense. "My twin sister is quite talented in her own right, and Iben's gift would be no match for her power. The Demon King's soul will stay imprisoned as long as you keep Arrah in line. She's the wild card in this game. She has Heka's magic—and his magic has proven itself to be unpredictable."

"What does Arrah have to do with any of this?" I scoff at his accusation, though I remember that moment in the coliseum when her magic had felt like hot knives. "The last time I checked, she's the only one of us who lost everything to save the world. She's done nothing for you to cast such doubt on her."

"How quickly you forget," the sun god snaps. "Her mother hadn't done anything, either, until she sacrificed children to wake a demon. Her sister destroyed thousands of people in a matter of months. Let's just say that her family has a particular propensity for ruination. Arrah has more magic now than any mortal before her—she is a very dangerous creature, even if you haven't figured that out yet."

Fadyi and Jahla exchange a meaningful glance like they're in agreement. I should've told Arrah about the demons in the city. She deserves to know the truth, and contrary to what Re'Mec might think, she would never use her magic for the wrong reasons. "We have more important things to worry about than Arrah at the moment," I say, annoyed at the lot of them. "How many demons are left in Ilora? We need to know what to expect if they attack."

"As far as I recall, ten thousand, give or take a few hundred." Re'Mec shrugs. "You can expect total annihilation if Shezmu opens the gate. The demons here are weak from five thousand years of imprisonment. The ones in Ilora will have no such limitations. They will make the ones you faced in the tribal lands look like amateurs."

"As far as you *recall*? From five millennia ago?" Kira says, flinching at his words. "There have to be millions of them now."

"I'm positive that their population hasn't changed in that time," Re'Mec corrects her. "They no longer have the ability to bear offspring, or your world would be overrun in days, instead of, say, a year."

"Where is the gate?" I groan. This keeps getting worse, and I fear what will become of the Almighty Kingdom if Shezmu opens the gate. The massacre in the alley will be nothing compared to the havoc he will unleash upon our world if we don't stop him. "Assuming that Shezmu is searching for the Demon King's soul right now, then he'll have to come back through it. We can set a trap for him."

"If it were that simple, we wouldn't be having this conversation," Re'Mec says, his voice devoid of its usual humor. "If Shezmu has full control over the gate, he'll be able to open it anywhere he chooses."

TWELVE
ARRAH

The Temple loyalists shove people out of my path. I am at once grateful and disturbed as they slap away stray hands reaching out to touch me. People shout *to* and *at* me, their voices a chorus of chaos that makes my head throb. Arti would never have had to ask people to make space for her—she would've made her own way. She wouldn't have let Suran Omari make a fool of her, either.

"He won't get away with outlawing magic," Emere says, keeping pace with me while the loyalists fan out around us in the West Market. "The Sukkaras aren't the only devout followers of the Temple with influence. We'll gather support."

My sandals scrape against the cobblestones as I head for my father's shop. Today was a painful reminder that people like Suran Omari will always distrust magic. If he succeeds in banning it, where will that leave me—how will I run the shop? I don't want to give up, but I don't want to become the target of his agenda—though it might be too late for that. "Be careful with him, Emere," I warn her. "He will do anything to get what he wants—my mother knew that best."

Emere puts a hand on my shoulder. "You may want no part of the life of a seer, but it suits your temperament to help those in need. If you do change your mind, you always know where to find me."

"Goodbye, Emere," I say, and I leave her and the rest of the loyalists behind. If anything, after this debacle, I have even more reason to stay away from the Temple and Kingdom politics.

I don't know how Arti stood toe to toe with Suran Omari and always looked so unbothered by him. He irks me to no end. I'm already dreading seeing him at the Almighty Palace tomorrow, but I push that out of my mind. I don't have time for Suran's games. I must tell Essnai about the Zu mask, so we can plan for the journey back to the tribal lands with Sukar. As much as I hate to admit it, Rudjek can't come with us. His anti-magic might hinder our search, and it's not as if his father would let him anyway. Whether I like it or not, he *is* the Crown Prince of the Almighty Kingdom and that comes before all else.

It's hard to temper the flame growing inside me—knowing there's still a chance some of the tribal people are alive. Only months ago, I was an outsider without magic in the tribes, and now I am an outsider in Tamar with it. I have to believe that one day the tribes will come together for another Blood Moon and that I will be with them. Even if Heka never comes back to the tribal lands, the people will pick up the pieces of their lives and start again.

I'm almost in front of the shop when Chima and a man in a dusty teal kaftan—one of the charlatans from the East Market—approach the door. They both hold on to one of Mami's arms. Her brown skin is slick with sweat, and she's clutching her chest. "How long has she been like this?" I ask, rushing over to meet them.

"Thank Heka," Chima says upon seeing me. "Since this morning—I came to fetch you earlier, but you were already out."

"Let's get her inside." I open the door quickly. "Put her on the pallet."

"Can you help her?" Chima asks, his eyes rimmed with tears. "Is it too late?"

"I'll try." I kneel at Mami's side. She writhes in pain, her eyes screwed shut while she murmurs nonsense. I press a hand above her heart, and my magic wakes under my skin. I reach for a memory from the Litho chieftain that allows me to find what ails her heart. Flashes of flesh and blood and bone fill my head. I clench my teeth to push back my headache and the dizziness that nearly overcomes me.

Broken, the Litho chieftain whispers in my ear in his harsh voice.

He means that her heart is failing—she's dying. I rush through the chieftains' memories again, looking for a ritual to direct my magic. The Mulani chieftain knows a blood medicine that restores organs, but it takes two days to brew. Grandmother's method needs two witchdoctors to perform, and I don't think the charlatan will be of any use. The magic I sense from him is too faint. The Kes chieftain's technique involves cutting open Mami's chest. I could use Beka's scrivener magic, but I haven't the time to prepare the ink.

"Stop hesitating, girl—do something," the charlatan demands from behind me.

"I'm . . . I'm trying to think of a ritual that'll help." I pause. "Give me a moment."

"You can do it without a ritual," the charlatan insists.

"It's too risky." I shake my head. "I need to channel the magic."

"If you don't do something soon," he says, "she will die."

"Arrah, please," Chima begs.

I climb up from the floor—the charlatan is right. There isn't much time, but I must protect Mami in case things go wrong. I grab sulfur and salt and make a circle around her like my father used to do for his sick patrons. "Stay out of the circle," I tell Chima and the charlatan. The powder looks plain compared to the rituals in the chieftains' memories, but it will work all the same. It will keep her soul from ascending into death.

I kneel beside Mami again, listening to her ragged breathing and the echo of her broken heartbeat. She's unconscious now, which is for the best. I'm counting on the Litho chieftain's traditions, and I don't trust his work to *not* be painful, for both Mami and me.

I reach for the aimless magic in the shop, and it gathers in my palms until the colors blend into white light. It burns my skin, but I push back the pain and begin to stretch and braid the light into a rope that tethers Mami to me. With the Litho chieftain's knowledge, I can grow her a new heart out of magic, but it must be a copy of my own.

Chima paces out of my line of sight. "What are you doing?"

"She's building a bridge between herself and your mother," answers the charlatan for me.

Chima stops abruptly. "Is that good?"

"It's . . ." The charlatan stutters. "It's beautiful."

"Shh," I hiss. "I need to concentrate."

I press one end of the rope to my chest and the other end to Mami's. The connection is immediate—it feels like a rush of water against my face, almost like drowning. I gasp to catch my breath as the sound of two heartbeats echoes in my ears. One is a murmur, and one is fast and steady. I squeeze my eyes shut against the pain building in my chest and the splitting headache.

The shape of Mami's heart appears in shadows and lights behind my eyes. I replace her old heart bit by bit with magic that reshapes into flesh and blood. Sweat trickles down my forehead. I work as fast as I can, weaving and braiding, but Mami stops breathing.

"No!" Chima cries out, and I can hear a scuffle behind me.

I push faster, harder, until something snaps that sounds like breaking bone. Mami's *ka* shakes loose from her body. It's a shapeless gray thing that tugs at the tether between us. I slip into darkness—and I hear a great roaring, a rattle, a call. It pulls at me, beckoning, compelling. I want to fall into it—let it swallow me whole.

I realize that I'm ascending into death, pulled by the tether tied to Mami. But the sulfur and salt keep the both of us from going farther. The five tribes call death a crossing into the kingdom of souls to join with the mother and father—Heka. But this feels more like Re'Mec's story of the Supreme Cataclysm—the great creator and destroyer.

"You've finally come home, my love," hums a smooth voice laced with honey. His breath is warm against my neck, and I sigh in relief. My mind falls to Rudjek, but, no. Rudjek's voice is a rumble in his chest, still stuck between boy and man. This voice is young, too, but ancient and tender in a way that raises a deep longing within me.

Something about the way it curls around my thoughts reminds me of the serpent that Arti carved into my chest. The magic that wielded my hand when I killed the men by the sacred Gaer tree. The magic that almost seduced me in Kefu. The Demon King.

"No," I whisper, and my breath comes out in wisps of smoke.

In a rush, I remember the night Rudjek and I explored the tomb underneath Heka's Temple. We'd climbed down the ladder, waded through the bones, and found the Demon King's dagger. But a blank spot in my memory from that night splutters and stretches with new images.

I desperately reach for my magic, but it's too late. I thought the nightmare was over with Efiya and Arti gone, and the Demon King still in his prison. How could I be such a fool—how could I *not* know he'd turn to me next? I let myself forget the danger of having too much magic. *Burning fires*. The Demon King's found a way into my mind when no one else ever has. Shielding my thoughts had been my only true gift before I received the chieftains' magic. Now he's taken that from me.

I try to resist the pull of another new memory—one that reeks of the tomb and plays out in fits and starts. I sit in front of a frozen lake beside a boy with silver wings tucked against his back. His face is so beautiful in profile that I can only bear to look at him from the corners of my eyes. *Gods*. This can't be happening.

"Who are you?" I say, my voice trembling, but I know the answer.

"You remember nothing?" His voice is a purr, a lullaby, sweet music.

I can't answer—I can't let myself. I won't like the answer.

"I am Daho."

I don't care what he's calling himself now.

"I—I know this place," I stutter, unable to break from the sequence of the memory.

"This is our place," Daho tells me.

"No," I whisper, shaking my head. "This is a trick."

"Fram stole your memories," he sighs, "but they'll come back in time."

"I won't let you play games with me like you did with my mother." I grit my teeth. "I don't know how you broke into my mind, but I'm not like Arti or Efiya. I won't do your bidding."

"I'm not in your mind, *Dimma*," he says. "You're in mine."

As I hear the name, a sharp pain slices through my head as suns and moons flash before my eyes. They chase each other across the sky so fast that they're a blur of never-ending fire and ice. My head feels like it will split in two. I squeeze my forehead between my palms, but the pain cuts deeper.

"Are you okay, child?" A frantic voice drags me from the memory.

When I open my eyes, my vision is muddy. I blink until the world comes into focus. I stare up at three worried faces. Mami is among them. It was her voice that brought me back. Chima clutches an amulet of the orisha Kiva, with his crooked eyes and bulbous nose. The charlatan murmurs a prayer.

My stomach churns, and bile burns in my throat. I can't trust the memory. The mind can be too easily molded and reshaped like I've just done with Mami's heart. I'd thought myself better than my mother—that I'm different—but I've fallen into the same trap. The Demon King wants to manipulate me so I'll free him from his prison, and I won't let him.

"You've got a strange look in your eyes, girl," the charlatan says, fanning himself. "Perhaps the chieftains made a mistake giving you their magic." His voice reeks of an unspoken accusation.

Mami and Chima help me to my feet. He's right again—it was

a mistake. The chieftains had to know this could happen—that it *would* happen. I am the only one left with enough magic for the Demon King to reach. "Had they not given her their magic," Mami says in my defense, "none of us would be standing here alive today."

"Her mother got that look sometimes, too," the charlatan counters. "Mark my words—"

"Leave." I croak out a harsh command that stirs up the aimless magic in the shop. It flutters wildly around the shelves as if my anger has suddenly given it purpose.

The charlatan stumbles back, his kaftan rustling in his haste.

"You heard her." Mami waves at him dismissively. "Get out."

The charlatan offers an apology before he turns on his heel and flees the shop.

Heat creeps up my neck as the memory by the frozen lake replays in my mind. I swallow hard and disguise my trembling hands by brushing wrinkles from my tunic.

"It's not my place to ask, Arrah," Chima says, "but did you have a vision?"

He and Mami both look to me, their eyes anxious—him clutching his amulet and Mami wringing her hands. I can't let anyone know, not even Rudjek. I have to figure out how to shield my mind from the Demon King. "No." It's a painful lie, but I see no other choice. "The ritual took more effort than I expected."

"Bless you, child, for giving me another chance to live." Mami squeezes my hand. Once she and Chima leave, I rush to lock the shop and press my back against the door.

I'm not in your mind, Dimma. You're in mine.

I immediately think of the Unnamed orisha with the serpents coiled around her arms. The orisha who betrayed her brethren for the Demon King—she's his *ama*, his love. "She's Dimma."

Why is he calling me her name?

She is not *me*—I am not *her*.

"I know who I am," I whisper in the empty shop.

THE UNNAMED ORISHA: DIMMA

Everything in the universe will die. My brethren and I are the only constant. We are an extension of the Supreme Cataclysm. But what happens when the constant changes? You already know the answer.

Even though I saw Daho almost die, nothing could prepare me for the rabbit. "It's my pleasure, dear Dimma," Daho says, "to introduce you to real food. No more wild berries."

I smile at him. It happens without conscious thought. I don't quite understand why, but it makes me feel warm inside. But my smile slips when I see that he's holding one of the small furry creatures from the mountain, limp in his hand. I come to my feet beside the frozen lake.

"I would've preferred a chicken," he says, "but a rabbit will do."

"What have you done?" I know this rabbit, the way I know every single creature on my mountain. "You took its life."

Daho frowns, his eyes searching my face. "Did I do something wrong?"

My vision blurs with tears. "It was mortal—it won't come back."

"We all die one day . . . well, not you, but the rest of us." Daho stares down at the rabbit and inhales a deep breath. "I'm sorry."

His words connect two missing pieces in my mind. One day Daho will return to the Supreme Cataclysm and be remade into something *not him*. That thing will not have his smile, his laugh, his face, his soul. I don't want that to happen, but it's the nature of mortality. How can I know this to be true and still not accept it?

"I'll bury it," Daho says, his voice full of anguish. "I can't eat it, knowing what it meant to you."

"Give it to me," I say, and Daho does so without hesitation.

I cradle the rabbit in my arms until his fur, flesh, and bone change into tiny sparks of light. They hold on to the shape of a rabbit for a moment, then the sparks drift apart, scattering over the mountain.

"Dimma," Daho says, his eyes wide. "That was beautiful."

Later that night, we're in the cabin, and Daho's stomach is growling as he curls up on the bed. "I can make food," I decide after some thought, "but I need to understand it better."

Daho taps his head. "I can show you."

I take a peek inside his mind, careful only to skim the surface of his memories. I create a meal of roasted chicken, rosemary potatoes, curried green beans, and plum juice. Daho stumbles out of bed, his mouth open, his eyes wide. Although he tells me that the meal is delightful, I haven't come to any conclusion about the taste. "How many times do you chew after each bite? Do you eat first, then drink, or drink first, then eat?"

He bursts into laughter and takes a gulp of the plum juice. "It depends on the food and how hungry or thirsty you are." He wipes his mouth, his eyes brightening. "Next time, I'll cook for you."

I raise an eyebrow, and he laughs again. "Don't give me that look! I used to sneak into the kitchens at night and practice with our head chef. I'm quite good at it; I can teach you."

When we're done eating, Daho cleans up and settles on the bed. He wraps the blanket around himself. "Why don't you sleep in the cabin with me?" His skin flushes violet as he glances away. "I mean sleep in the cabin. . . . You never stay at night."

I smile at him. "I'd like to stay sometimes."

"Come sit with me." He pats the bed beside him. "I'll tell you about Jiiek."

I climb into bed with him, and his voice is majestic as he tells me the first of many stories. Each night he tells me a new story, and I start to imagine myself eating cake, swimming in a river, soaring in the sky. We go from sitting together, to lying side by side, to lying face-to-face, to him holding me.

I lie on his chest, listening to the steady rhythm of his heartbeat as his fingers tangle in my hair. "I would very much like to kiss you," Daho says, his voice husky, after finishing another story.

I sit up to look at him. "Like the demon boy and endoyan girl in your story?"

"Am I that obvious?" he says, his color deepening.

"Yes."

Daho props his back against the wall. "Can I tell you a secret, Dimma?" When I nod, he confesses, "I'm afraid that one day my stories will bore you, and you'll send me away."

"I could never send you away." I don't tell him about the fear that's been on my mind since the white rabbit. "Show me how to kiss."

He rubs the back of his neck. "I've never kissed anyone before, either."

"We can learn together," I say, hopeful.

Daho leans close to me and cups my face in his hands. His skin is warm and smooth and delightful. I press my lips against his palm, feeling his heat intertwine with mine. The moment stretches out, unfurling across time, second by second. As my anticipation builds, sparks of light twist around our bodies. Every inch of me aches with longing. I lean forward, meeting his lips, and our teeth bump together.

"We need practice," Daho whispers against my mouth.

"Lots," I say, pressing in closer to him.

THIRTEEN
ARRAH

I spend all night poring through the chieftains' memories, trying to find a way to shield my mind from the Demon King. I search my father's shelves, pulling down boxes of bones and dried herbs and animal parts. Myrrh oil, white ox bones, black copra skin, wormwood, honey brush, ragweed.

Sweat stings my eyes as I get down on my knees on the floor to sort them into piles. I have the ingredients to perform six of the twelve rituals that the chieftains know to protect one's mind. The other six rituals involve my ancestors' bones, and I have no way of completing them.

What the charlatan said was true. I can perform complex magic without rituals, but is that how the Demon King broke into my mind? Rituals help to hone magic, to refine its intentions. Magic without them, especially complex magic, is more unpredictable.

Of the six rituals, I start on the laborious task to prepare three. A bone charm of animal teeth, set in a precise order. A sachet of crushed herbs that I must keep with me at all times. A blood medicine that needs three days to complete and that I must take every day. I brew enough to cover the trip to and from the tribal lands, until I'll be able to make more.

I work well into the morning, my fingers raw from crushing herbs and bones and brewing. My arms are shaking with fatigue by the time I put the second bone charm around my neck and stuff the sachet into my pocket. I can only hope that they'll work against the Demon King.

Essnai arrives at eighth morning bells with sweet bread and fried plantains and a sack across her shoulder. She wisps into the shop in a gold cropped top and billowy black trousers, her hair dyed the color of corn silk. A dozen bracelets jangle on each of her arms, an exact match to her crimson lipstick. How she manages to look so radiant this early in the morning baffles me. We eat in silence, and my headache dulls with each bite. I almost feel like myself again, except I will never be only myself, not with the Demon King in my mind.

Essnai takes a sip of her tea. "You look like you haven't slept in days."

"I haven't." I stare at the crumbs of sweet bread. I think about the frozen lake, the brisk wind that bit against my skin, the clean air that ached in my chest.

"With good reason, I'm sure," Essnai says, quirking an eyebrow.

In the memory, the boy shifts his position, and his wings brush against my side. "Yes."

"Is there something you want to tell me?" Essnai asks, her question blunt.

I snap out of the memory with a start and almost knock over my tea. "What?"

Essnai frowns and puts aside her cup. "Sukar told me about the Zu mask, that you're planning to go look for the tribal people. But that's not what's on your mind, is it? Did something happen with Rudjek?"

I let out a shaky breath and rub my tired eyes. Did I really think that I could keep this a secret from my friends? I need to tell someone—I need to know that I'm going to be okay. "I heard him last night," I confess, and Essnai's frown deepens.

"*Him?*" she asks in a tone that says she already knows who.

"Yes," I whisper. "Him."

"Oh, Arrah." Her voice chokes up. "What can be done?"

I tell her about the blood medicine, show her the bone charm and the sachet. "One of the rituals has to work, and if not one alone, all three together." I squeeze my eyes shut for a moment, my heart racing. "I won't let this get in the way of finding the surviving tribal people, but if I lose control—"

"Don't even say it," Essnai interrupts me. "You won't give in to him."

"Even still, if . . ."

She narrows her eyes, her face dead serious. "Sukar and I will keep you in line."

I sigh, clutching the bone charm. "I hope so."

"Do you want to talk about it?" Her gaze drifts to my hand. "What did he say?"

"He called me Dimma." The name rings in my ears and sets my teeth on edge. It makes no sense. "Best I can tell, it's the Unnamed orisha's real name—his um, *ama.*" The memory by the frozen lake feels too personal to share, so I keep it for myself.

Essnai studies my face like she can sense the doubt brewing in my mind. "You already know you can't believe anything he says. He'll try to trick you, but you're smarter than that." She stares intently into my eyes. "You will beat him."

I hold her words close like they are another shield of protection against the Demon King. I don't know what I would do without her, Sukar, and Rudjek. "Right." I nod once, then change the subject. "We should leave for the tribal lands soon."

"Good—I've been itching to get out of the city." Essnai bounces up from the floor. She doesn't miss a beat as she grabs her sack and pulls out a red-and-gold sheath. "But first, Kira told me about your appointment at the palace today, so I brought something for you to wear. Can you get the wrinkles out?"

"How am I supposed to do that?" I ask, cocking my head to the side.

Essnai holds out the sheath. "Magic, of course."

I cross my arms, though I can't keep a straight face. "Do you expect me to use magic for something so frivolous?"

"Don't be such a disapproving auntie," Essnai says. "Have a little fun."

Not for the first time since receiving the chieftains' gift, I hesitate. Even though I suspect performing complex magic without a ritual opened my mind to the Demon King, I still don't know for sure. Will it happen the next time I call upon magic for any reason? I should have enough protection with the bone charm and the sachet, but I still worry. What if I can't keep him out? I can't *not* wield magic—it's a part of me now, and I don't want to give it up. Impulsively, I flick my wrist and conjure a wind that blows away the wrinkles in the sheath. I whisper a silent thank you to the chieftains when nothing else happens.

Essnai smiles. "Leave your hair to me."

Soon she's sitting on a stool with me on the floor as she unravels my braids one by one. Her fingers comb through my strands, untangling the knots. I close my eyes and forget about the Demon King, if only for a moment.

When the midday bells ring, Majka and Kira arrive to escort us to the palace. Kira takes her *ama*'s hand and brings it to her mouth. "I dare not ruin lips as sweet and beautiful as yours."

Essnai leans close to Kira and whispers, "They're yours to ruin."

"Can we ruin lips another day?" Majka clears his throat. "We're on a tight schedule."

Once we're at the bottom of the mountain beneath the palace, we climb into a litter. The rope creaks as we ascend, and the Almighty Palace comes into view. It looms over Tamar—white walls trimmed in mother-of-pearl and lapis lazuli, four towers and a gilded dome roof.

Rudjek stands in the courtyard between two lines of attendants. He's wearing a blue elara with gold accents. "You look lovely," he tells me as Majka, Kira, and Essnai slip around us and head for the palace.

"As do you," I reply, my cheeks warm.

Rudjek smiles. "I'll show you the gardens after this business with Tyrek."

I glance to the ground, my mind wandering back to the memory of the Demon King. His words ring in my ears like a lullaby. *I am*

Daho. This is our place. I push aside my treacherous thoughts. "I'd like that."

"Rudjek, son," his mother, Serre, says from the palace steps. She wears a white kaba with long sleeves and a skirt that spreads around her feet like a blooming flower. "Bring Arrah to the throne room."

Rudjek's father has always been clear about his feelings toward me, but his mother is harder to read. Her white veil is sheer enough that I can see her dark eyes, yet they reveal nothing beyond her aloof expression.

"Are there any protocols I should be aware of?" I ask as we enter the cool palace with too wide halls and too high ceilings. It doesn't feel like a place that anyone would live in. Attendants flutter about their business, lowering their heads as we pass them. "I'm sure your father would be glad for me to make a fool of myself."

Rudjek winces by my side. "This is an informal inquiry, so consider it a casual affair—no need for pretenses and court pleasantries."

"Oh good," I say. "I had no intention of bowing before your father."

Rudjek gives me a conspiratorial smile. "Nor should you."

We exit one wing of the palace and cross a courtyard. Soon we arrive at a grand hall with towering stained glass windows. Inside, the Sukkara family surrounds Prince Derane. The Galke delegation—Prefect Clopa, Princess Veeka, and their male companion—are here, too, but they keep to themselves. Both women have their veils peeled back, and Princess Veeka is much younger than I expected. Much prettier, too. Her skin is amber, a shade akin to Rudjek's, though she has straight black hair and eyes the color of lavender. On one wall stands a line of Kingdom soldiers in red and, across from them, soldiers from Galke in black. They are so still that they almost blend into the decor.

"That's Princess Veeka," Rudjek says, his voice low. "From Galke."

I resist the urge to say "I know" as my attention shifts to Tyrek's mother, Queen Estelle. *Former queen.* She stands in a semicircle with her family, the Ohakims, one of the most powerful families in the Kingdom. I haven't seen the queen in years, and she's even more beautiful than I remember. Her dark skin shimmers with flecks of gold across her high cheekbones and broad nose. Her shoulders are straight and strong, her chin tilted up in a way that makes her look ethereal.

I nudge my tongue against my gums, finding the empty spot, and again regret not using magic to grow a new tooth. I am so out of place among these people, but this is Rudjek's future. Unless something changes, he will be their—*our*—king one day. Where do I fit in his new life? His advisers will say that a king cannot be with someone he can't touch, who can't bear him heirs. Rudjek believes that we will find a way to overcome the aversion between his anti-magic and my magic, but I'm less sure.

"As the, um . . . Crown Prince, I must join my family for the proceedings." Rudjek rubs the back of his neck, looking embarrassed. "It's a silly palace tradition."

I inhale a shaky breath. "I hope this is over soon."

"Me, too," he says before he moves to stand to the right of the empty throne while his mother sits to the left.

Suran Omari enters the room from the balcony with his guild-masters on his heels. It's hard to think of him as the Almighty One.

It's even harder to be this close to him and not wring his neck. "I see the voice of the Temple has arrived." Suran settles on the throne between his wife and son. "How fortunate."

The guildmasters stand in a small group to the left of the throne. The Master of Arms, Rudjek's aunt. The Master of Scribes, Kira's father. The Master of Scholars; and the Master of Laborers, Tyrek's uncle.

Two gendars push Tyrek Sukkara into the chamber, and he stumbles over his shackled feet. His eyes are those of a desperate boy who knows that no matter what, his life as he knew it is over. Queen Estelle's face breaks when she sees her son, but she doesn't utter a single word. Guildmaster Ohakim appears indifferent. Could he truly not care about his nephew's fate, or is he pretending to appease Suran Omari? He doesn't make eye contact with Queen Estelle, who gives him a scathing look.

"We are here to examine Second Son Tyrek's claims of innocence," Suran says. "We will hear his side of the story, and the voice of the Temple will give her opinion on the matter." Suran flourishes his hand lazily at Tyrek like the whole affair is no more than a petty dispute. "Go on, then. Tell us."

"I already told you." Tyrek's voice is icy, and Prefect Clopa and Princess Veeka cast glances at each other. "I was on a hunting expedition with my brother in the desert." He licks his cracked lips and digs his nails into his arm. "I was taking a respite on a ridge high above a plateau of jagged rocks when . . . when *she* came. I tried to call the guards, but before I could, she was in my thoughts. She made me kill my brother."

I swallow hard as sweat prickles against my forehead. The throne room feels too small, the air too thin. I resist the urge to clutch my protective charm again. I should've prepared something to help with Tyrek, but I'd been too focused on myself.

"Young Priestess," Queen Estelle addresses me. "Does my son tell the truth?" There is so much desperation and hope muddled in her voice that it breaks my heart.

"I would need to see into his mind to answer that," I say.

"Do it." Tyrek holds his arms wide in an offering. "I have nothing to hide."

I step forward to where he is kneeling. The Galke and Kingdom guards standing along the walls ease their hands close to their swords. I don't doubt that Suran Omari has ordered them to be on alert in my presence. The throne room falls silent as everyone waits. They all stare at me—the Galke delegates, the Sukkaras, the Omaris, the guildmasters, my friends, Rudjek.

I call upon Grandmother's knowledge. Each time she read minds had been like peeling back the curtains into a new, strange world. Every mind had its particular temperament. I cast my consciousness out to Tyrek and sense his eagerness to let me explore his thoughts. Before I lose my nerve, I plunge into his mind. A scream burns in my chest, and the roots of my teeth ache as his memories unfurl and threaten to split open my skull.

I am sitting on the edge of the cliff with Darnek. He's complaining that I've dragged him away from his charming companions in his tent. I hate that we hardly ever spend any time together, just the two of us, not the Crown Prince and *his shadow*.

I'm sorry, I say, but the words are only in my mind. The witch won't give me the smallest semblance of control. I am wearing my family crest, the ram's head made of craven bone, and a wristlet for good measure. They're supposed to protect me from magic, but she's too strong.

"Why so somber, brother?" Darnek slaps me on the back. "Loosen up and live a little!"

"Kill him," Efiya whispers in my ear.

I scream inside my head, but I do her bidding without hesitation. I'm glad to do it—I want to please her. I shove my brother hard in the chest, and his eyes go wide.

"Ty-rek," Darnek stutters. "What—"

Tears blur my vision as I shove him again, and he tumbles over the edge, his body breaking on the rocks below. When it's done, I try to throw myself over the cliff, too, but Efiya doesn't allow that.

I move the memory forward like paging through an ancient tome. I'm in my father's bathhouse. He's in the pool with one of his play-things. Flickers of firelight dance across the mosaic stone floors. The room is rich in golds and reds and browns. Rubies and black opals and emeralds embellish the walls. My father spends most of his free time here.

"You're so pretty," he says, nibbling on his companion's earlobe.

She's another Mulani girl—maybe Darnek's age—nineteen or so. She bears a resemblance to the *Ka*-Priestess. His concubines always do. The golden eyes, the wild curls, the curves. An infectious laugh bubbles up from her throat and it's obviously fake, yet he doesn't seem to notice or care.

The bathhouse is empty save for my father's two most trusted attendants, whom I've already killed. I stare down at the knife in my hand. Efiya is in my mind even now. She's controlling my thoughts—making me believe these are *my* actions, when they're hers. My father and the Mulani girl are too busy to pay me any mind. I walk to the edge of the pool and kneel next to them.

"Twenty-gods, boy," Father curses when he catches sight of me. "Go away! Can't you see I'm busy?"

The Mulani girl giggles with her hands clasped over her mouth. She climbs out of the water and lies down on the mosaic tiles, and then her body falls still. Efiya stops the girl's heart without me lifting a finger. She dies peacefully.

"What did she ever see in you?" I climb into the water fully clothed. It's my voice, but Efiya's words. "She despises you now, but she loved you once."

"Did your mother put you up to this . . . ? Are you conspiring to take my throne?" he snaps.

When he says *your mother,* he's thinking of his wife, but I'm thinking of the *Ka*-Priestess. Efiya's mother. I wade in the water, drawing closer to him as he backs away.

"Guards!" he calls. When they don't answer, he looks over his shoulder and sees them dead on the floor. "Tyrek, what are you doing, son?" His voice is quiet, gentle even, and something stirs within me.

"Killing you," I say.

"Guards!" he screams again.

I raise the knife from underneath the water and slit his throat. Father chokes as blood gushes between his fingers. He claws at his wound until it vanishes. I make him whole again. I won't let him die that easily. I will take all night to kill him.

I pull myself from Tyrek's memories. My head is throbbing again, and I clench my teeth. I wish that I could erase the new images from my mind—that I could forget them. But I know that they will be with me until the day I die. "He's . . . he's telling the truth."

There is a collective gasp in the room. I sway on shaky legs as the onlookers break into arguments. The magic has spent my energy, and Rudjek helps me to a chaise near one of the balconies. "What can I do?" he asks.

"Space," I breathe as his anti-magic burns against my skin.

Rudjek's face falls as he moves away. By the time he does, Essnai slips into the throne room amidst a flurry of attendants rushing to serve refreshments to the flustered dignitaries. She kneels at my side and presses a wet cloth against my forehead. I'm tired, but more than anything else, I am relieved that the Demon King didn't break into my mind again. It could be that I didn't draw as much magic as I'd done to heal Mami, or that my charms are working against him.

"The boy is clearly unstable." Suran looks down his nose at Tyrek. "Spoiled by the filth of magic."

"Unstable?" Tyrek laughs, his eyes wild. "I'll show you unstable." He grabs a dagger sheathed at one of his guards' waists and leaps for Suran. Soldiers rush at Tyrek, and I jump to my feet. Magic uncurls beneath my skin as I draw on the Mulani chieftain's strength. The magic twines around the soldiers' throats, and they fall to their knees, choking. Tyrek laughs again as the dagger slips from his hand and clanks against the floor. The room falls into chaos with people shouting and fleeing.

I see the horror of what I've done. The soldiers, from both the Kingdom and Galke, claw at their throats, gasping for air. How easy it would be to let them die. To take them over the edge like the Litho chieftain used to do to those who opposed him.

"Arrah!" Rudjek shouts as he steps into my path. His anti-magic mutes my magic, and the soldiers fall to the ground, sucking in ragged breaths.

"He *wants* you to kill him," I whisper. "Don't you see that?" *Don't you see that he's suffering under the guilt of what my sister made him do?*

Suran looks at me with a cutting smile, and I realize I've only given him one more reason to ban magic in the Kingdom. He's always two steps ahead of me. I wonder if he gets any sleep at night for all the scheming he must do in his spare time.

Prince Derane takes a glass of wine from a servant's tray. "By the Almighty One's own admission, my nephew is unstable, but the blame lies with the tribal witch who ruined him." He swirls his wine, and it sloshes around in the glass. A hint of a smile crosses his lips. "Surely you don't mean to execute him now, with this new information to consider."

For Suran's part, he only sits back on his throne, his face smug. "Of course not," he says. "I hereby drop all charges against Tyrek Sukkara, on the honor of the voice of the Temple." Queen Estelle gasps, and several people express their surprise. I wait, seeing the gleam in Suran's eyes. "However, for the crime of attempting to murder your king only a moment ago, Second Son Tyrek, you are hereby banished from the Kingdom. May your path never cross mine again, or your life with be forfeit."

Another murmur of hushed conversation blankets the room. Most people seem to agree with the banishment.

"Now that's settled," Rudjek's mother announces. "We have much to celebrate. Arrah, please join us tonight along with our honored guests from Galke for the evening meal. You have done the Kingdom a great service today. Sukkaras and Omaris owe you our gratitude."

"If it's all the same to you, I'll take my leave," I say.

"Nonsense, young Priestess," Prince Derane insists. "You saved my nephew. At the very least, we must break bread together."

I nod my agreement, knowing that they won't relent. I can make it through one meal. "Is there a place I can rest?"

When Rudjek steps toward me, his father takes a sudden interest in my well-being. "An attendant can take her to a salon. We have business with the Galke delegation to see to before the evening meal."

"I'll take you," Kira says, with Essnai at her side.

I stumble out of the room, too many voices buzzing in my ears, too many sounds, too much pain. But one voice rises above the rest and stops me cold in my tracks.

Dimma, the Demon King pleads. *Please don't shut me out.*

FOURTEEN
ARRAH

The bone charm vibrates against my neck, and the teeth knock into each other. I keep it together until Kira and Essnai lead me into a private salon. Then I fumble to get the sachet of herbs from a hidden pocket in my sheath. As soon as I squeeze it in my hand, it crumbles to ashes. It shouldn't be possible, but the Demon King has obliterated the protection charm. I reach for the bone charm, my mind racing through the chieftains' memories again. There has to be another way to keep him out.

"Twenty-gods," Kira swears, her hand easing to one of her blades. "What was that?"

"It's nothing," Essnai answers quckly.

"That doesn't look like nothing," Kira observes, relaxing her hand.

Essnai grabs my shoulders. "Breathe."

I stare into my friend's calm face, drawing strength from her. Essnai's right—she's always right. *Breathe.* I close my eyes and think of Rudjek and me lying beside the river. Rudjek kissing me in the tomb. Rudjek's hands toying with my hair. I don't know when it happens exactly, but eventually, at some point, as I take shelter in these memories, the bone charm falls still and the Demon King is no longer with me. I exhale, feeling tired and hollowed out. "I'm okay," I say to convince myself.

Kira looks between Essnai and me as if she knows that we have a secret, but she doesn't ask. I rest in the salon with them, regaining some semblance of composure. Essnai and Kira sit on a chaise across from me. They make small talk for a while, but I'm too distracted to add to the conversation.

"Some of my cousins are visiting from Estheria," Kira tells Essnai excitedly. "They're dying to meet you. One is a dressmaker, too, and he almost fainted when my sisters showed off some of your beautiful designs. Do you think you can come to an evening meal soon? My mother has been quite put out that you haven't visited since you got back."

Essnai smile as she plays with her *ama*'s long braid. I don't think she's told her of our plans to return to the tribal lands yet, and I doubt that Kira will be happy about it. "Every time I visit, one of your sisters sweet-talks me into making her a new sheath."

"I promise I'll keep you safe from their greedy little paws," Kira says with a laugh.

"Speaking of greedy." Essnai whispers something that makes Kira's cheeks flush.

"That's quite scandalous," Kira replies with a conspiratorial raise of her eyebrow. "I do most certainly approve."

Soon I'm beckoned for the evening meal while Essnai and Kira stay behind. I miss the comfort of their presence as an attendant walks me down the palace corridor and into the dining hall. I'm shown my place at the opposite end of the table from Rudjek. Princess Veeka leans close to him as he recounts the story of how he won a three-way fight in his father's arena.

Suran Omari is at the head of the table with his wife, his left hand intertwined with hers, a glass of wine in the other. Serre chats with the Master of Scholars, while the guildmasters to her left talk among themselves. To Suran's right, Rudjek sits next to Princess Veeka and the Galke delegation.

"My opponents didn't take me seriously from the start," Rudjek says. "Between the two of them, they had some thirty years of experience. One had fought in an incursion on our east bank in his youth. They thought that their impressive résumés would intimidate me, I suppose. Their mistake."

"How could they not take *you* seriously?" Princess Veeka laughs. "You're so imposing."

I'm not surprised that Rudjek's parents arranged for me to sit as far from him as possible. But it still hurts to see Princess Veeka at his side. The mood is more somber among the Sukkaras and their Omari cousins on this end of the long table. Queen Estelle has left an empty seat next to her to mourn her husband and son.

Prince Derane sits next to me, his breath reeking of onion. "You've hardly touched your meal, young Priestess. Shall I have the attendants fetch something more to your taste?"

"The food is fine," I say.

"I wish you would reconsider your position about the Temple."

He doesn't bother hiding that he's been talking to Emere. "We need a strong leader—someone who can keep Suran in check."

"I'm a bit young to be a seer, don't you think?" I ask, lacing my voice with sarcasm.

"Your mother was nineteen when she apprenticed to *Ka*-Priest Ren Eké," says Prince Derane.

"Look what that got her," I reply, trying to keep my emotions under control.

Prince Derane's rings clank against his glass as he gulps down wine. "You have a biting tongue, Arrah. We need that fire to restore the Almighty Temple to its true glory."

The Galkian princess's shrill voice drags my attention away from our conversation. "I've been dying to see more of Tamar."

Rudjek clears his throat and casts a glance in my direction. "I thought my father gave you a tour yesterday."

"I wasn't able to attend." Princess Veeka pouts. "I wasn't feeling well."

"I'm sure my son can give your highness a proper tour," Suran says before Rudjek can refuse.

Prince Derane snaps his fingers in front of my face. "Where's your mind, girl?"

Princess Veeka brushes her hand against Rudjek's, and his body tenses. She smiles up at him as he reaches for his wine. "What are you hiding beneath those gloves, Prince Rudjek?" she asks, a shy grin on her lips. "It's much too warm in the Kingdom for such extra clothing."

He takes a sip of wine and coughs. "I thought gloves were

fashionable in the Northern states."

"Quite," Princess Veeka says, "but what would I see if I took off yours?"

My magic writhes in irritation underneath my skin as the people closest to Rudjek and the princess share secret glances. I bite down on my lip, doing my best to ignore them and utterly failing.

Rudjek quirks an eyebrow. "Some things are best left to the imagination, don't you think?"

Is she flirting with him, and, more important, is he flirting back? I curse under my breath as Suran looks between his son and Princess Veeka, his eyes calculating. I'm a fool not to have seen this coming. Wasn't this his plan all those months ago—to pair Rudjek with a princess from the North?

Princess Veeka scoops up her glass. "I wager ten gold coins that one of your hands is disfigured."

Prefect Clopa gasps, and Serre looks mortified. I don't need to understand Northern etiquette to know the princess has overstepped. She only smiles and lifts her wine to her lips, quite pleased with herself. My fingers twitch, and her glass shatters, spraying wine on her face and purple sheath.

Princess Veeka lurches to her feet so fast that her chair hits the floor—the sound echoing in the room. The conversations at the table fall silent as people turn to stare at the princess. Tears fill her eyes, and I sink back in my seat, my face hot with shame.

"Are you okay?" Rudjek stands, too, and takes her shaking hands to calm her.

"I'm sorry," she apologizes. "You must think me quite clumsy."

"You have nothing to be sorry for," Suran Omari assures her. "The fault is our own for serving you with flawed glassware. You have my sincerest apology. I will personally ensure that the attendant who served you will be severely punished."

I sink even lower in my chair. I can't let someone else take the blame for my mistake. I'll have to tell Rudjek the truth, if he hasn't already guessed what happened. I shouldn't have lost control like that.

"That is kind of you," Prefect Clopa says, coming to her feet. "If you will excuse us—we shall retire for the night."

"Until tomorrow." Princess Veeka smiles at Rudjek. "Don't forget my tour."

Rudjek waits until she and her delegation depart to sit down again. It isn't my imagination that he avoids looking in my direction.

"I love a petty quarrel." Prince Derane adjusts the rings on his left hand. His accusation is apparent. He knows that I broke the princess's glass. "Like mother, like daughter."

"Excuse me." I push my chair back. "I need some fresh air."

I don't wait for a reply from Prince Derane as I rush pass attendants pouring fresh rounds of wine. I don't know if I'm angrier at what I did or the fact that he compared me to my mother.

I stumble down the corridor and stop to rest in an alcove with a window overlooking the courtyard. Princess Veeka's giggles echo against the stone walls. "He's quite handsome, isn't he?" she says. "A little aloof, but I think that adds to his appeal."

"Princess, control yourself," Prefect Clopa chides her, their voices growing distant. "Your mother would be quite disappointed in your behavior tonight."

"My mother is a third wife," the princess says, her voice sharp, "and I don't intend to be."

Not wanting to hear more, I slip out of the alcove and head back to the salon where I left Essnai and Kira. But they're entwined in a passionate kiss, and I dare not interrupt them. Oh, but how it makes me ache for a moment of my own with Rudjek, a moment I will never have.

With my luck, I'll run into Majka next, entangled with some new lover in another room. I push ahead until I find a set of doors to the gardens. The warm night air smells of lilac and jasmine, and I'm relieved to find that the courtyard is empty. I slump on a bench and close my eyes. But whatever peace I'd hoped for whisks away with the sting of approaching anti-magic.

"Tell me you didn't break Princess Veeka's glass," Rudjek demands.

He steps into the garden with his arms crossed, keeping his distance. The shadows from the trees hide his expression, but his anger rolls off his body in waves. When I don't answer, he groans and sits on the bench, leaving a wide space between us.

I glance down at my hands. "I don't know what came over me."

"You almost killed those soldiers earlier." Rudjek sighs, deflating beside me. "My father will use that as another tool to discredit magic. You're making it easy for him."

"I'm leaving tomorrow." My words tumble out without preamble, nothing to soften the blow. Even if Sukar and Essnai can't leave immediately, I'll go ahead without them. I can't wait to find the tribal people—not with the Demon King still in my head. I can't risk what could happen if our connection grows stronger.

"What?" Rudjek splutters, surprised. "What do you mean leaving?"

I dig my elbows into my knees, fighting back tears. "I don't have a choice."

"Arrah," Rudjek says, "look at me, please."

I don't—I can't look him in the eye with this secret weighing on my chest. "Essnai, Sukar, and I are going to the tribal lands for a little while. We think there may be survivors."

"There aren't any survivors," he says, his voice apprehensive. "The cravens searched for days."

I want to tell him about the Zu mask and the vision, but it's not my only reason for wanting to leave the city. I spring to my feet and pace in circles. "You wouldn't understand."

"What are you not telling me?" He inhales a sharp breath, shifting his position on the bench. When I don't answer, he stares out into the dark, his expression resigned.

"Prince Derane compared me to my mother tonight." I wrap my arms around my shoulders. "He was right. I am like her."

Rudjek stands, too, and I hate how his anti-magic is always so suffocating. "You made a mistake," he argues. "Everyone makes mistakes."

"Was it a mistake?" I ask, the truth clear before my eyes for the first time. "All the little mistakes will add up until one day I'm no different from her. You don't understand. . . . I wanted to hurt Princess Veeka. I was jealous and being petty."

Rudjek touches my arm—his glove and the fabric of my sheath the only barrier between his anti-magic and my magic. "Arrah." My name is a plea in his deep timbre, an offering. "You have no reason to be jealous of her. You must know how I feel about you."

I close my eyes and imagine myself leaning against his chest—him kissing my neck, his teeth teasing my ear. Instead, I go still and his arm falls limp to his sides. His eyes are darker than the shadows pooling in the gardens.

"What happens if we can never find a way to be together?" I don't mean to come off so hostile, but I'm tired of pretending that things will work themselves out. "What then?"

Rudjek stares across my shoulder. "I . . . I don't have the answer to that." He grimaces and meets my gaze again. "But I don't want to give up on us, okay?"

"I don't want to give up, either," I say, the fire burning out of me. Does he hear the doubt in my voice? We may not have a choice. I ease out a breath, bracing myself for my next words. "I can hear him now."

Rudjek takes a step back, shaking his head, his beautiful face transformed by anguish. "I don't understand."

I force a bitter laugh. "What is there not to understand?"

"Is the Demon King free of his prison?" Rudjek asks, reaching to rest his hands on shotels that aren't there. He settles for his hips. "Is he in the Kingdom—in the city?"

I massage the dull ache between my eyes. "I don't think so. He wouldn't be trying to reach my mind if he were free. That's why he needs me—I'm the only one left with enough magic to release him from Koré's box."

"But you won't," Rudjek says, his voice hopeful.

Arti told me that she served the Demon King because she wanted revenge on Suran Omari and Jerek Sukkara. But would the results be the same if she hadn't wanted to go along with his agenda? Would he have controlled her anyway, like Efiya did Tyrek? Could I keep him out my entire life, or would he destroy charm after charm until I succumbed to him?

Rudjek glances away, and he looks like there's something on the tip of his tongue. "I can't come with you to the tribal lands." He pauses, weighing his words. "I didn't want to worry you, but there are demons still in the city . . . nothing I can't handle with my guardians."

"Is that it?" Not that a few demons are easy, but it's better than the likes of what we've had to face in recent months.

Rudjek laughs, but he's holding something back. "Isn't it enough?"

"Do you need my—"

"Given your current situation," Rudjek remarks, "I think we should keep you far away from the demons."

My current situation. "Right."

He flashes me a pained smile. "Promise me you'll stay safe."

I smile back. "Only if you promise me that you won't run off and marry Princess Veeka."

"Of that, you can be sure," Rudjek says, a twinkle in his eyes.

We settle on the bench in the garden again, our shoulders close but never touching. It's our last night together for the foreseeable future, and the moment guts me. Is this all we can ever have of each other, while I'm stuck spending the rest of my life fighting the Demon King in my head? Silent tears slip down my cheeks as we watch the moths driven by instinct to the torch flames hanging about the garden. Rudjek inches his fingers closer to my hand, but I draw away from him. It will never be enough.

FIFTEEN
RUDJEK

My dagger pierces the heart of the Serpent River on the map against the wall. I have an urge to pound my fist into the hilt and drive it deeper, but that'll do nothing to assuage my frustration. I pace the salon, eyeballing the map from north to south, east to west. I keep thinking there's something I'm missing—some small detail hidden beneath the ink. "I can't accept that there's no way to figure out where Shezmu will open the gate or when," I say. "He must have some plan."

"Hmm." Re'Mec lounges on a couch with his legs crossed at the ankles. "Now that you've had that ridiculous gossamer ripped down, this room isn't half bad. Still, I'd suggest you get a decorator to give it some flair."

I glare at the sun god, who's staring up at the ceiling while wrapping a frilly tassel around his finger. "Why are you here, Re'Mec, if you're not helping?"

"I am helping," he says, his voice a long drawl. "I'm here for moral support while my brethren keep an eye out for any suspicious demon activity."

"Isn't any demon activity suspicious?" Majka asks.

Re'Mec yawns, stretching his arms over his head. "True."

Kira hunches over a table with scrolls splayed out in front of her. Majka is next to her, spearing a candied apple with a dagger. Fadyi sits cross-legged against a wall, avoiding the couches altogether. At Re'Mec's request, Raëke has left for the Dark Forest to warn the cravens about the gate, and Jahla is out prowling the city for signs of more demons.

"We don't have time to speculate about Shezmu's next move. We need to find him and put an end to whatever it is he's planning." I bite my tongue as I turn back to the map. I haven't told anyone about my last conversation with Arrah three nights ago. I don't trust Re'Mec not to kill her if he thinks she's a threat. No one needs to know about her connection with the Demon King—not until there is a reason. "Show me all the places where demons have been sighted since the battle."

Re'Mec grunts as black holes burn across the map—several in every major city and continent. Delene, Fyaran, Zeknor, and Galke, the city-states of the North. Kefu, Estheria, and Yöom on the east coast. The Almighty Kingdom. The barren tribal lands to the west. Even the less populous Ghujiek and Siihi in the south. I yank my knife from the wall. "They've scattered everywhere except the Dark Forest."

"I think we can safely rule out the forest and the surrounding valley," Fadyi says. "Our forces are strong enough to protect the land and to neutralize their magic."

I study the map again. "The demons would encounter less opposition if they opened the gate in Ghujiek or Siihi. The biggest drawback is that you can't travel to and from the islands most of the year. The seas are too treacherous, with storms in the warmer months and ice in the winter." I grimace when my gaze falls on the tribal lands, where Arrah is heading right now. That last night together in the gardens had been painful. I couldn't find the right words to comfort her. *Gods.* She'd even flinched when I tried to touch her. "There could be survivors in the tribal lands. I would assume, though, that the demons would go someplace more populated so they'd have souls readily available." *If they're after Arrah, then that's another story.*

"They don't need souls to survive." Kira stares at the scroll in her hand. "One of the early scribes said of the demons, 'They hunger for souls, but it is not souls they seek. Souls are a balm to a wound that will not heal.'"

"Lynis was a foolish scribe," Re'Mec spits, "always hiding in his room, writing things that he should not. But he wasn't wrong in his conclusion. The demons are immortal regardless, but souls give them certain powers, including the ability to hide."

I frown, noting the burn spots on the map. "They want us to see them." When Re'Mec grumbles affirmation, I cross the room to where he's lying with his eyes closed. He looks so small on the couch, so childish, carefree. Half the time, I wonder if this is all just a game for him. "You created the cravens . . . you created *us* to be hounds to track down the demons for you."

The sun god opens his eyes, and they're the color of a brooding sky before a storm—the color of pain and grief, of regret. They're the color of what he wants me to see, and I'm not in the mood for his crap. "To put it in terms you'll understand, Rudjek"—he sits up—"I sense everything in the universe at the same time—a grain of sand, a dying star, the air you're breathing right now. Every single thing. For me, finding Shezmu is akin to searching for an ant in a mound of many. That he is immortal only makes it impossible, for he is good at hiding. I needed to create a people who have an aversion to magic to be able to sense the demons."

"And use us to fight your war," I counter, disgusted with him.

"There would be no one left to fight for if I had not made you," Re'Mec admits with a sigh. "I did what I thought was best at the time."

"Rudjek, you may be onto something. . . . Maybe they *do* want us to see them," adds Kira, returning to the matter at hand. "If the demons can hide from the gods, then they're making it a point to show themselves. It's like they're hiding in plain sight."

I freeze at her words. Plain sight. Could it be that simple? I look at the map again. "Re'Mec, how many demons fled after the battle?"

"A little over three hundred," he says.

I count the dots on the map. Only fifty. "These sightings are a distraction to keep the orishas busy while Shezmu makes his next move. He must be setting up a camp with the bulk of the demons elsewhere."

Majka tosses a handful of almonds into his mouth. "There are thousands of towns they could hide in."

"Thousands of towns, but not impossible to figure out which one," I insist.

There's a knock on the door, and two gendars push into the salon without waiting for an answer. My father strolls forward, and Kira and Majka scramble to their feet, their backs straight. Fadyi follows their lead.

Father peers around the room, his face hard. "Why did you summon me here, Rudjek?"

I cut my eyes in Re'Mec's direction, but he's conveniently disappeared. I clear my throat. "We have a bigger problem than the demons in Tamar," I tell my father and catch him up on the news about Shezmu. "I need your resources to help determine where the demons intend to open the gate."

"You seem to have resources of your own already, to have uncovered so much about the demons." Father smiles, his eyes narrowing as he meets my gaze again. "You are coming into your own, son, as I knew you would."

It's the first bit of praise my father's given me in a long time. I don't know how to take it, so I do what he expects and ignore it. "I need detailed maps of every city and town across Zöran and reports on any clusters of unusual activity."

"It will be done," Father agrees without hesitation. "I have eyes everywhere."

"One more thing," I say, and my father raises his eyebrows. "I need an army."

Moonlight pours through the curtains in the dead of night. The palace is peaceful, but it'll never feel like our villa. I can't get used to the curves of the ceilings, the cold drafts, and the way these sheets smell as I try and fail to fall asleep. It's nothing like the comfort of home—no memories to grasp on to.

My father had been more agreeable than I expected. He'd understood the demon threat all too well, and given me the army I asked for—five hundred soldiers. I've trained for this all my life, but I'd never thought I'd be commanding troops before my eighteenth birthday. Now we just need to figure out where Shezmu will open the gate. It still bothers me that we have no clue how to find him. He might not even be in our world if he's still searching for Koré's box. Either way, he'll be back. Arrah's here, and she's the only one who can free his master. He'll come for her soon enough if I don't find a way to stop him first.

I roll onto my back and cross my arms behind my head. I wonder where Arrah is now, what she's doing. Is she okay? I have to believe that if something were wrong, I'd know, but it's only wishful thinking. When I finally fall asleep, I dream about touching her, kissing her—doing more than kissing her.

I'm having the most delightfully inappropriate dream when something pricks at my awareness. I open my eyes. The room is pitch-dark and ice-cold. Another warning tingles at the back of my neck. *Danger. Move. Go.* I force myself to stay completely still. I can't act—not without understanding the situation. I squint against the bleeding darkness. There's no sound, not even the whisper of wind wafting in from the antechamber, yet I know I'm not alone.

I blink once, and my vision adjusts to the dark. Shadows blacker than night slither on the walls and the floor. Are those the wayward shadows—the Familiars that Arrah has talked about? She called them bad omens. Wherever they went, death soon followed. But no one without magic could see them, and they couldn't interact with our world. How is it possible that they're visible to me now, and why are they in my bedchamber?

I bolt up in bed, and sharp pain shoots up my legs. One of the wayward shadows is burning through my sheet. They can't do that—this shouldn't be possible. I throw off the sheet and reach for my scabbard as another shadow lands on my arm. It sears through my skin like butter sizzling in a hot pan. I snatch my arm back, shocked. Mangled, burned flesh and angry welts run from my shoulder down to my wrist.

"You little piece of—" I bite back a curse.

I can already feel my legs start to heal. The pain lessens with each moment. I rip off the part of the sheet that hasn't burned and wrap it around my hand. As the Familiars close in around me, I leap from the bed and hit the floor hard.

I go for my scabbard again. "I could use some help here!"

Cradling my burned arm against my side, I pull a shotel from the scabbard and slice at one of the shadows. I don't expect it to work, but when the sword cuts through it, the Familiar falls to the floor in two pieces. It slows down for a mere moment as the two halves melt back together and attack again.

I slice through another and another until one lands on my back and brings me to my knees. I scream at the same time someone bursts into my bedchamber. Two human-shaped shadows rush through the door, screeching and cutting. Fadyi and Jahla. Fadyi rips the wayward shadow off my back, and with it, my skin. I fall forward on my face.

I notice, then, that the Familiars don't attack my guardians. They keep coming for me, but Fadyi is ready for them. His shadow form grows until he blankets the entire chamber. He sprouts hundreds of

tentacles and lashes out at the Familiars. He shreds them into ribbons, but the Familiars don't die from that, either. He does make
them think twice, though, for they slither through the gaps in the
door and flee into the night.

"They're gone," Jahla says, out of breath, from behind me.

I wince, trying and failing to get to my feet. "They shouldn't be
able to attack people."

"Well, they attacked you." She kneels at my side and presses her
hand against my back. The pain dulls as she pours her anti-magic
into me. It feels like cool water washing over my skin.

"Thank you," I say as she and Fadyi help me to my feet.

"This is our fault." Fadyi lowers his eyes. "We've been so preoc-
cupied with the demons that we haven't been training you. You're
only part craven, Rudjek, which means you're more susceptible to
attacks. Once you fully understand your anti-magic, you'll be able to
anticipate the enemy."

"It's not your fault that I couldn't heal myself fast enough." I
drop onto the bed. "And it's not like I was expecting to be set on fire
tonight."

"No, but it is our fault that you haven't been able to shift your
form," Fadyi says. "If you could, you would've avoided being burned
to start with."

I look back and forth between Fadyi and Jahla, surprised that
they haven't figured it out already. I would laugh if I weren't still
in pain. "Don't you see? Re'Mec said that the demons called their
endoyan cousins their *familiars*. That's what these wayward shadows are—and somehow with the demons back they've gained the

ability to interact with our world." I pause, staring at the charred sheets. "The demons must've sent the Familiars to attack because we're onto something, and they're scared."

I leave out the other little thing I noticed. The demons seem particularly interested in killing me.

SIXTEEN
ARRAH

We reach Ejun, a town in the foothills of the Barat Mountains, at sunset. It's a welcome sight after three days of riding through farmlands and manured fields. People fill the streets, and we dismount near the center of town. Sukar almost falls face-first in the mud and dung, and Essnai and I barely do better. My thighs and back hurt from riding, and my legs wobble. We thought it would be faster to take horses, but I'm second-guessing that decision now.

"Heka, mother and father," Sukar moans, "spare me the antics of this wretched beast sent to torture me to the end of my days."

"What I wouldn't give for a hot bath right now," Essnai says.

I breathe in the fresh mountain air as we pass buildings with mud-brick walls and thatched roofs. We come upon a crowd standing around an elevated platform where a man holds up a caged hen. People shout bids at him as I dig through my saddlebag to retrieve the blood medicine.

Even though I've only heard the Demon King's voice when conjuring more complex magic, it's best not to tempt fate. I haven't used my magic since the palace, but I won't be able to avoid it when we're closer to Tribe Zu. I'll need it to pick up the survivors' trail. I hope that the bone charm, along with the daily dose of blood medicine, will be enough to keep him out. I can't forget how the sachet of herbs had turned to ashes in the palm of my hand. If this doesn't work, I don't know what I'll do.

The jug of blood medicine is too awkward to turn up to my mouth, so I keep my nightly dose in a small flask. I grimace when the medicine hits my tongue. It tastes metallic, underscored by a rot that nearly makes me gag. It burns on the way down, but as long as it keeps the Demon King out of my mind, I'll endure it for the rest of my life.

"Tell me you brought some herbs to ease our troubles," Sukar begs as we head toward a tavern with rooms for rent. It's so decrepit that it looks like it'll fall over in a strong wind. "Please."

"Nothing a little sleep can't cure," I say as two drunk men stumble across our path.

Smoke wafts into our faces as we step inside the dimly lit tavern. Patrons sit at low tables, their faces shrouded in shadows while dancers sway their hips to the music. Four musicians play a high-spirited melody on the bala, djembe, shekere, and udu. The floor hums under our feet to the beat, while cheers and laughter spill from every corner. The energy in the tavern reminds me of the excitement on the first night of the Blood Moon Festival.

"What's that I smell in the air?" Sukar says, breaking the spell. "Beer, sweat, and vomit."

Some patrons take notice of us as we search for an empty table. A man with an ashy face in a tattered tunic grabs at Essnai, and she smacks him on his knuckles with her staff. He draws back his hand, holding it close to his chest. "Feisty one, aren't you?" He smiles, his greedy eyes roaming where they should not. "So pretty."

"Next time," Essnai growls, "I'll break every bone in your hand."

"And when she's done," Sukar adds, "I'll break every bone in your face."

The man looks at the three of us and doubles over laughing. "And you, little Mulani girl"—he turns to me—"what part will you break? I'm dying to know."

I take one step closer to him, the blood boiling in my veins. The chieftains tell me how I could hurt him, but there's a dismissive edge to their voices. This man isn't worth my time. Still, I can't stop myself from answering, "I'll break everything else for good measure."

The man laughs again as we push past him. Sukar spots a table, and we take it before someone else does. It reeks of unwashed skin, and the pillows on the floor are damp. An attendant comes to greet us—a girl no older than we are, wearing a brown apron over a dark cotton sheath. "What's your pleasure?" Her eyes are on Sukar, who gives her a polite smile and turns his attention to the dancers.

"We'd like hot meals, and a room for the night," I answer as a fight breaks out at another table.

"Eighteen bronze coins for three meals," she says, seemingly oblivious to the ruckus. "A silver coin for a room."

I root around in the money pouch, and my fingers bump into something else before I count out the coins to pay. The attendant smiles and disappears into the crowd. The music slows as the beats stretch into a long tempo, low and steady.

The dancers gather in a corner, with their backs to us. Patrons catcall, begging for them to dance again, while some jeer at the interruption, yelling obscenities. The tavern descends into a chorus of complaints until they back away from their corner, rolling their hips and shoulders as they do a slow turn. The dancers shimmer in the half-light and ease into a rhythm to match the music.

The attendant returns with our meals and mugs of beer, and a key for a room. Essnai and Sukar dig into their stew, but my appetite fades as I catch a whiff of gamey meat in the broth. It's hard to tell with the tomato and chili and peanuts, but it could be goat. I push the bowl aside.

"It tastes better than it smells." Essnai takes another bite.

Sukar scoffs and sniffs his beer. "That's not saying much."

A man at a table cheers when a dancer drops into his lap. He leans against the woman and whispers in her ear as he runs a hand up her leg. There's an exchange of coins.

"Move along," someone shouts at another table across the room. There's a frantic, familiar edge to the voice.

My heart leaps at the sight of Second Son Tyrek, drowning himself in drink. He waves off a man who asks to share his table. It's been days since Essnai and I saw him at the palace, and his face looks no less gaunt. Beneath the bruises, he has his mother's ethereal beauty, broad nose, and large eyes. His intent expression reminds me of when he watched the debates at the assembly with keen interest.

"*Eefu kawa*," Essnai curses in Aatiri. *Son of a coward.* "What's he doing here?"

Sukar eases one hand toward his sickle, his attention on the disgraced prince.

I don't have a drop of sympathy for what happened to Jerek Sukkara. He should've stood up for Arti all those years ago. He was her *ama*, but he let Suran Omari give her over to the depravity of *Ka*-Priest Ren Eké. But I do feel sorry for what happened to Tyrek and his brother, and all the people who died by my sister's hand. "We don't have to like him"—I put aside my untouched stew—"but he is innocent."

"So he says," Sukar grumbles, his eyes cold.

"So I say," I insist. "Is my word not enough?"

Sukar's jaw twitches in annoyance. "Of course your word is enough, but I don't trust him."

"Neither do I," says Essnai.

Tyrek climbs to his feet and spills beer on a patron at the table next to him. The man curses, but instead of apologizing, Tyrek only laughs and stumbles away. He's halfway across the tavern, heading in our direction, when the patron grabs him by the shoulder.

"You owe me an apology," the man spits, his words slurred by drink. "Didn't your *owahyat* of a mama teach you any matters?"

It's meant as an insult, but Tyrek only smiles at the man's slight. "Friend, are you sure it's an apology you want, or something else?" He takes another gulp from his beer, swaying on his feet. "Perhaps you should come up to my room later."

The patron jabs a knee into Tyrek's belly, which makes him double over and vomit on the floor. Some of it splashes on the men at the nearest table. I cringe as people laugh, but the men at the table take offense. They jump to their feet in outrage and pull their daggers. "You're going to regret that," one growls. "I ought to gut you where you stand."

"Should we do something?" I ask, but Essnai and Sukar both shake their heads. It would be a mistake for me to use magic if not absolutely necessary, so I don't move, either.

"Do you intend to use those knives or stand there looking like fools?" Tyrek taunts the men. "I don't have all night for you to decide."

"Your mouth is too smart for your own good, pretty boy," says the man who kneed him in the stomach. "This might be the night it gets you killed."

"That's the idea," Tyrek says, his voice bored. The man catches him with a hard punch across the jaw. The prince falls flat on his back in his own vomit. The tavern bursts into laughter, and the men with the daggers return to their table.

"So, does this mean I'll see you later?" Tyrek groans, but the patron slips back into the shadows.

"It couldn't have happened to a more deserving royal brat," Sukar snorts.

I sink back against the wall as Tyrek drags himself to his feet, vomit smeared on his elara. He tugs at the bottom of his tunic, as if straightening it will make him look less a fool. He blows a kiss to the man who punched him and bows to the two who threatened to gut him. Then he turns on his heel and heads for our table. Predictably, Sukar reaches for his sickles. I put a hand on my friend's arm—feeling the tattoo there wiggle on his skin in anticipation of a fight. He lets out a groan as he picks up his mug of beer instead.

"Ar-rah," Tyrek stutters over my name as he gives me a crooked smile. "Some interesting gossip made it to my ears while I was still at the palace."

I tense. He can't know my secret. "Why are you here, Second Son Tyrek?"

He presses his fingers to his lips. "Just Tyrek now. I don't deserve titles."

"You mean you were stripped of your titles," Sukar murmurs.

"That, too." Tyrek shrugs. "May I have a word with you, Arrah?"

I'm reluctant to say yes, but I don't think he'll go away if I say no. When I nod, he squats beside me. He smells atrocious, and I clench my stomach to keep from being sick. "I have many friends in the palace." He pitches his voice low. "One such friend overheard a conversation between you and the new Crown Prince in the gardens."

So he does know. Fine. I swallow my nerves. Had he sought to reveal my secret to Suran Omari, I'd be rotting in prison already or worse off, dead. I turn my back to Sukar and Essnai to keep our conversation private. "What do you want?"

"To help." Tyrek flourishes his hand like it should be obvious. "I know what it's like to act against one's will—to do another's bidding." He pauses for a moment, his gaze flitting away. "I'm the *only* one who knows what you're going through right now."

My friends might see a drunk, fallen prince covered in vomit, but I see the longing in his eyes, the sorrow. He's lost everything—his friends, his family, and now his country.

"If the Demon King is as powerful as Efiya, he'll get what he wants sooner or later," Tyrek says. "Your magic won't protect you." His eyes are sad and resolute, like I'm already a lost soul. "Let me help you."

"How can you help me?" I ask, a bitter edge to my voice.

"I thought that death was the only way to break free of Efiya's control," Tyrek says. "Then I found out that she could change her appearance, so even if I died, she could continue to torment my people in my name if she so chose." He leans a little closer, his breath on my ear. His next words are slippery, eager. "You have an advantage over me. The Demon King is still in his prison, and he needs your magic to free him. That is his greatest weapon against you, and it's also your greatest weapon against him."

I hate that he's summed up my predicament so completely. If not for my magic, I wouldn't have the Demon King in my head—yet it's my magic I must rely on to keep him out. A shudder racks my body. The blood medicine and charm will work—they have to. "What are you proposing?"

Tyrek draws back and meets my eyes, his smile wicked. "I'm here to kill you."

Magic rises to the surface of my skin at his threat, but I push it down. He's half-drunk and powerless with or without his titles. "Why would I let you do that?"

"Please don't take offense." Tyrek holds up his hands. "I'm offering to help you should you need it."

He might be right, I realize, though part of me recoils at the idea. Essnai and Sukar will try to keep me in line, but would they hesitate if my death was the only way to stop the Demon King? A split second could be the difference between saving the world and unleashing chaos. I can't put my friends in that position.

"If you want to help, then I need you to promise me . . ." I can't bring myself to finish my sentence. I don't particularly like or trust Tyrek, but he does understand in a way that no one else can.

"Say no more." Tyrek touches his hand to his forehead and dips his head in the Aatiri tradition. "I will not hesitate when the time comes."

"*If* the time comes."

"We all tell ourselves what we need to hear to survive another day," he says as he comes to his feet. "Thank you for giving me a purpose again."

PART III

PART II

THE UNNAMED ORISHA: DIMMA

I remember the pitch of Daho's voice, the way it ebbed and flowed like the wind that howls on the mountain. Every night, he would tell me a story. The best were the ones of us traveling across Ilora looking for adventure. We sought lost treasure, flew in a sandstorm, raced on the backs of giant turtles. Tonight, he tells the story of a young prince lost at sea until a maiden rescues him.

Daho lies on his side with his head propped on his elbow, and there's such light in his eyes that I can't look away. He brushes his fingers across my cheek, down my neck, along my collarbone, sending a warm thrill through me. When we're this close, I notice changes in his body, too, though I do not call attention to them.

"Do you want to see the world?" I ask, considering. "We can explore every corner of it together."

"The world is fine and all, but I want you . . . and to see Jiiek again." His voice lingers on *you*, heavy and raw, yearning. It puts words to my own feelings. I want him, too, in ways I do not fully understand. He hasn't talked about going home since those first days we were together. "I doubt that anyone I knew is still alive."

"Why go back if you have no one?"

"I don't know." He frowns. "I guess I'm homesick."

"Isn't this your home, too?" I ask, hesitant, afraid that he will reject this idea.

"Oh, yes," Daho says, his voice bright, "and you are my family."

He leans over to kiss me, and I press my finger to his lips. "I don't want to lose you."

"You won't," he breathes against me.

But that isn't true. He is mortal. All mortals die.

When Daho falls asleep, I shed my body, so its constraints do not bind me. It feels good to be free of it. The parts that make up the whole of me stretch across the frozen lake and the mountain. I have a single goal: cure Daho of his mortality. Without a physical presence, I can cover many worlds in my search in a shorter time.

I start at the bottom of the mountain, which overlooks the farmlands on the outskirts of an endoyan city. A scattering of lights pushes back the night, and the people wrap themselves in furs against the cold. I find a forge with fires and an endoyan shoves dead bodies into slots in the walls. In another room, an endoyan scoops ashes into a jar and closes the lid. I stretch my consciousness across the land, finding thousands of people with ashes. Some spread them in the wind, some pour them in lakes or oceans, and some keep them in their dwellings.

I travel to the edges of Jiiek, feeling guilty that I am here without Daho. The night is almost as bright as day, full of lights and endless sounds. The endoyan city had been flat, but here the dwellings reach into the sky. The people don't burn their dead; they collect their useful parts and bury the rest in the ground. Sometimes they grow new body parts, which extends the lives of the demons. It still isn't enough to save Daho.

Iben's gate is a circle of energy that sparks and spins, moving in and out of time. It is and isn't there. Time does not exist in the space inside it, yet I can feel its pull, its call, its tethers reaching into my soul. There is a sprawling city built around the gate, of both endoyan and demon design. The city is the center of Ilora's trade with Zöran. The mortals have not yet learned how to adjust the frequencies of the gate to visit other worlds.

"Isn't it beautiful?" Iben says, his voice a whisper on the wind. "Without it, there would be no mortal life. Do you understand, Dimma?"

I understand through the vibrations of the universe. The Supreme Cataclysm continuously destroys and remakes everything close to it. Only my brethren and I can survive that chaos unchanged. That's why Koré, Re'Mec, and the others made these worlds so far away from the Supreme Cataclysm to seed life. "Why must they die?"

"The child is not his parent." Iben's form shimmers into a shape with wings sitting on top of the gate. "We are of the Supreme Cataclysm—it is our parent, but we are not the embodiment of it. We have limits. We cannot create immortality."

My frustration quivers across the sky and land. The ground beneath me cracks, trees split, the molten rocks in the center of the world grow hotter.

"If you keep doing that, you will destroy this world."

"I . . . I don't understand," I say. "I didn't mean to do that."

"Our intentions and emotions manifest in mysterious ways," Iben explains. "You've changed the shape of this world with one small slip." He looks up as it begins to rain—droplets that fall in heavy sheets. "It's fortunate that you've done no real damage."

"When you came to the cabin, you said that you were there to see the beginning of the end." I bury my desperation deep to keep it contained, and it burns inside me. "What did you mean?"

"I am the guardian of time and its secrets," Iben answers. "If I went around telling everything I know, then I would be a rotten guardian, wouldn't I?"

"You'll never do anything to influence the possible futures you see." As soon as I convey that thought, something else more terrible occurs to me. "You're not here by coincidence; you knew that I would seek the gate."

Iben's shimmering body dims with anguish, but his pain doesn't spread across the land like mine. "Sometimes our nature brings us joy, and sometimes it brings us pain." He shifts his position so that his wings spread to their full width. "Nothing I say tonight will have any effect on the future."

Knowing that I will get no answers from him, I bid my brother good night and pass through the gate. Inside it is a void of space and time with endless threads into many worlds. I don't know where to start, but I push forward into one, determined and restless.

I visit two dozen worlds, searching for some sign. On each of them, life has a beginning and an end. It is finite. I'm tired when

I finally return to Ilora and slip back into my physical form. The weight of my anguish almost brings me to my knees as I lean against the cabin, feeling the cold for the first time. I will search again for a cure for death. I will search to the end of time.

SEVENTEEN
ARRAH

We trudge through the narrowest path of the Barat Mountains pass with the wind howling in our ears. With a week on the road behind us, the snowcapped summit ahead promises rest and the start of our descent. Icy mud splashes against my ankles and slips into my boots. I walk alongside my horse, holding the reins with one hand and rubbing his shoulder to keep him calm. The cold air aches in my lungs, but the peace of the mountain gives me some solace.

Sukar walks ahead of me, Tyrek behind, and Essnai brings up the rear. Neither Sukar nor Essnai were particularly happy when I invited Tyrek to travel with us. They say it's a mistake to trust a Sukkara, but they don't know about the deal I made with him.

The last time we trekked across the mountains, I'd been sure that I was on my way to die. One of the craven twins, Tzaric or Ezaric, had told stories to lighten the mood. Somehow I defied the odds and survived. I thought my path was clear for the first time in my life, but the ritual with Mami changed everything. Now I'm anxious to search for the tribal people, and my confidence has all but withered.

We clear the path and set up camp below the line of snow, where the ground is still dry. While we tie up our horses, a group of travelers crests the north side of the trail, on their way from the tribal lands. They look weary and tired, and when Sukar asks them if they met any survivors, they shake their heads. I notice their bulging saddlebags and suspect that is how the Zu mask ended up in the East Market. People like them have been raiding the tribes and stealing from the dead.

"It doesn't mean anything," I say after the travelers are gone. "None of them have magic, so they couldn't possibly track down the survivors if they don't want to be found."

Sukar nods as he gathers twigs and leaves for a fire, but he's clearly disappointed at the news. We all are.

Tyrek clutches his extravagant fur cloak tight to him, warding off the biting cold. "Wouldn't it be faster to use magic?"

I unpack my bedroll and kick off my frozen boots. Faster, yes, but is it worth the risk? It's been more than a week now since I called upon magic or sought knowledge from the chieftains. "I can't."

"Come again?" Tyrek cocks his head, a sarcastic smile on his lips. "So, you can peer inside my mind but not do something so trivial?"

"No one asked you," Sukar snaps at him.

"It's a valid question." Tyrek blows on his cupped hands. "Is that why you haven't"—he taps one of his perfectly straight teeth—"fixed that?"

Sukar hurls a rock at Tyrek, and Essnai deflects it with her staff. "You behave," she tells Sukar before glaring at Tyrek, "and you shut it."

I glance away, my face burning with embarrassment. I hadn't felt the Demon King's presence when I called wind for Essnai or when I broke Princess Veeka's glass. Starting a fire should be just as simple—nothing like growing a new heart or reliving someone else's memories. "I'll do it," I blurt out, already regretting my decision.

"Are you sure?" Essnai asks.

Sukar bares his teeth at Tyrek. "You have nothing to prove to the likes of *him*."

"Yes, I do," I whisper. "I will never know if the blood medicine works if I don't start testing it."

I give Tyrek a meaningful look, and he catches on. *If I lose control, you know what to do.* He eases his hand toward the dagger at his waist and angles his body so Essnai and Sukar can't see it. He gives me a nod as if to say he's ready. It's only then that I remember I haven't actually taken my nightly dose of blood medicine.

I turn my awareness inward, my mind tuned into the hum beneath my heartbeat. My skin tingles as the magic wakes like a sleeping mammoth, unfurling, stretching, seeking. I raise my hands and sparks light on my fingertips, hues of silver and blue and black. I stare at them for a moment, afraid, anxious, and relieved when nothing happens, then I flick my wrist. The sparks hop to the pile of sticks and the fire ignites.

The whole thing is . . . *uneventful.* Oh, but how wonderful it feels to wield magic again, like I've been missing a vital part of myself for the past week. Soon the fire is large enough to give us heat and a place to cook. The moment passes, but my friends and Tyrek wait. After a while, I smile, shaking my head to let them know that I don't hear the Demon King's voice. I'm filled with newfound hope. Not missing a beat, Essnai tosses yams on the edge of the fire. Sukar removes his boots, and Tyrek's hand falls from the hilt of his dagger.

Later, when the moon is high, Tyrek takes a swig from his wineskin, the fire reflecting in his dark eyes. "My family never cared for magic, but I've always loved it. When I was a child, it was popular among the Sukkara children—Darnek, my cousins, and me. My father would have charlatans brought from the East Market to entertain us. They'd do all kinds of tricks—make things disappear, turn their faces green, levitate."

"Wasteful," Essnai murmurs, a blanket wrapped around her shoulders.

Sukar snorts, then laughs. "No more wasteful than getting your hair magically colored."

"That is completely different," Essnai says dismissively as she turns over the yams. "Magic doesn't damage hair like dyes, so it's worth it."

"Ah, I see." Sukar rakes a hand across his shaved head. "I wouldn't know."

Tyrek peers at me from across the fire, oblivious to Sukar and Essnai teasing each other. "I never knew why my family feared magic until Efiya."

We all go still at the mention of my sister's name. The pain and regret in Tyrek's eyes are unmistakable. He'd have to live with those memories for the rest of his life. "I did what I could to stop her," I say, apologetic. "She was so strong."

Tyrek takes another pull from his wineskin. "I know."

Sukar digs in his bag and removes a Zu drum encircled with a net of cowrie shells. He taps out a slow beat at first. Each thump sends a haunting hum echoing against the mountain.

"For what it's worth," Tyrek says after a long silence, "I am sorry for my part in everything." He doesn't address any of us in particular.

"How about you share some of that wine," says Essnai. "The rest of us are thirsty, too."

Tyrek perks up at that. "Oh, if it's a drink you want, I packed plenty for my travels." He walks over to his saddlebags, nestled against a tree, and removes two more wineskins.

I shake my head in disbelief. "Did you bring any *real* supplies?"

"I didn't think that far ahead." He grins, his smile genuine for the first time since the tavern.

He hands one of the wineskins to Essnai and one to me. I take a swallow, and the wine is deceptively sweet and benign. "Sukar," I call before tossing the skin over to him.

He catches it with one hand and pours a bit on the ground. "A drink for the dead."

"Let me play," I say, reaching for the drum.

"I hope your playing is better than your tattooing skills," Sukar teases as he turns over the drum. I poke out my tongue at him—the ungrateful brat that he is—then smooth my hand across the lambskin, tugged tight against the wood base. The Zu chieftain had a liking for music, and my fingers itch with an overwhelming need to play. Beka's memories pour into my mind—the way his hands flew across the drum, the way he felt the music in his bones. "I might know a song." I tap once with my wrist, twice with my palm, then fall into an easy rhythm with a fast tempo. *Tap. Tap. Slap. Tap Tap. Slap. Tap Tap. Roll.*

"Will you do me the honor?" Sukar asks, reaching for Essnai's hand.

She drags herself to her feet. "Why not."

I watch as they move to the beat, swaying their hips, twisting and shaking in perfect sync. Essnai's a good dancer, but Sukar has a natural grace. His body flows with ease. He slides one hand on Essnai's waist and slowly circles her, his brown eyes warm in the firelight.

"Interesting," Tyrek says, startling me. I'd been so caught up in the dance that I hadn't noticed he'd moved to sit beside me. "I thought that you and my Omari cousin were together from the way he acted with you at the palace."

"Excuse me?" I miss a beat on the drum and earn myself a scathing look from Sukar. Tyrek has a lot of nerve to comment about something that's none of his business.

Tyrek glances at Sukar again. "Just an observation."

"What are you insinuating?" I ask, growing impatient.

"Nothing at all." Tyrek gulps down another swig from his wineskin. "It's not like any Sukkara or Omari ever marries for love anyway. We only marry for political gain."

His last words catch me completely off guard, and my hand falters on the drum. I miss several beats. When I start up again, my mind is elsewhere. I've tried not to think about Rudjek taking Princess Veeka on tours of Tamar and sharing meals with her. He doesn't have to worry about wearing gloves or fear what will happen if they touch. I hold on to my memories of him, but even they aren't enough to soothe away my doubt.

My thoughts cut short as something whizzes past my ear. Sukar clutches his arm, and blood runs down his elbow. It takes too long for me to put the pieces together as the presence of anti-magic sears across my senses. I start to come to my feet when a sharp pain splits through me. I gasp, choking. A metal taste. Blood. I look down and stare at the tip of a jagged bone poking out of my chest. Black veins stretch from the wound. My body convulses, and the pain—gods, it burns like a raging fire.

The world spins, and my *ka* strains against my body. It's like before with Mami, but so much worst. The tether between my body and soul pulls taut and starts to fray. The chieftains' strength holds me together, if only by their sheer will. Tyrek jumps to his feet, the wineskin forgotten. Sukar's face twists in horror. Essnai cuts across my sight with her staff in tow as men in black elaras sweep into our camp.

Darkness blankets my eyes, and the sounds around me grow faint. "Sleep," coo twin voices, so gentle that I almost give in to them. I fight against the urge, but the lull is so strong. "Let go, Dimma." My eyes snap open. I know their voices—it's not the chieftains, not the Demon King. It's Fram, the orisha of life and death. Why do I know their voices? A memory shakes loose like a butterfly opening its wings for the first time. They called me *Dimma*.

Do you still love him?

And what of the craven?

I snap out of the memory to find Essnai and Sukar fighting off assassins. Sukar's tattoos and sickles aren't glowing. The anti-magic is blocking his protection spells. That doesn't stop him or Essnai from cutting down assassin after assassin. Someone else moves in and out of the shadows, attacking the assassins from behind. I can't see their face as I gasp for air.

Someone pulls the craven bone from my chest and turns me on my back. I stare up at a man in a black elara, his face covered in thick dark hair. He lifts my head to expose my bare throat. I struggle to move, to fight, to save myself, but my body feels like heavy stone. Magic rushes into the wound in my chest, filling it with warmth and light, sealing it, repairing it. As the assassin brings the jagged bone down on my throat, Tyrek strikes. He runs the man through with his sword. Blood splashes in my face.

Tyrek ducks out of the way of another assassin and almost trips over the dead man next to me. The new attacker swipes his sword at the prince and misses. Tyrek uses the opportunity to plunge his shotel in the man's belly.

More assassins charge him as the pull of ascension sweeps through me. My body isn't healing fast enough to hold my *ka*. I begin to drift up again, but the chieftains surround me. They grab my arms, my back, my shoulders, to keep me rooted in place. He is here, too—his presence a soothing song, his soul calling to mine, and it feels like he's always been with me. . . .

Grandmother's spirit materializes in front of me, her gray hair in that familiar crown. A twinkle in her dark eyes. "You must resist, Little Priestess." Even as magic repairs my body, the call of death is so strong. I'm so tired. I want to rest—I want to sleep. I want the pain to go away.

Sukar and Essnai keep fighting as Tyrek drags the dead assassin and the craven dagger away from me. The magic burrows deeper into my flesh, leaving a trail of pure agony in its wake. It repairs my torn skin and makes blood to replace what was lost. This hurts worse than the dagger—and more than once, I scream through the pain. As I draw in a ragged breath after it's done, Tyrek kneels beside me. "They win if you die."

My lips form the word *who*, but I am struck by the desperation in his voice. I should mean nothing to him. He offered to kill me only days ago, but, then again, I'm the only one who truly knows the havoc my sister wreaked on his mind. I am the only one who understands the guilt he lives with every day.

"Get away from her!" Sukar shoves Tyrek aside. "Arrah, you're going to be okay." His hands tremble as he cups my face, and his touch is warm, so gentle.

Essnai kneels opposite him, pressing a cloth to my wound. "Get some water." Tyrek stumbles away, doing as she asked. "Heka, heal her."

I inhale another sharp breath in exhaustion. "I . . . I'm okay."

Tyrek returns with a waterskin, and Essnai pours some into my mouth. When she checks my wound, it's almost healed. She swears and looks up with tears in her eyes. "That's quite the trick." She smooths a hand across my skin. "You're not allowed to die today, tomorrow, the next day, or ever."

I look over her shoulder to where Tyrek stands, meeting his gaze. "You saved my life."

The prince gives me a lazy grin and flops to the ground, clutching a wound on his side. "Consider my debt to you repaid."

EIGHTEEN
ARRAH

The air burns with the stench of anti-magic, blood, and bile. Essnai and Sukar help me to my feet, and I close my eyes until my head stops spinning. My chest still aches, but it's bearable. For these men to be here, someone besides Tyrek's "friend" must have overheard my conversation with Rudjek. Both Essnai and Sukar look bleak as they search the assassins for clues. Tyrek presses a cloth against the wound on his side, his hand trembling. If it weren't for his quick thinking, I would be dead right now.

"Let me help you with that," I say.

Tyrek grumbles as he comes closer. "It's just a scrape."

While he holds the rag against the wound, I tie a strap of cloth around his waist to keep it in place. "Thank you for saving me."

Tyrek stares at me through a fan of dark lashes. "You did the same for me not so long ago."

Remembering his words from earlier, I pitch my voice low as I ask, "Who wins if I die?"

He pulls down his bloody tunic and glances at the dead bodies.

"The person who sent these assassins, Efiya, the demons, the whole cast of bad actors out to ruin your day." He shrugs like it's no big deal, but he's still shaking. "They're all the enemies, aren't they?"

"Add the Sukkaras to that list." Essnai holds up five chains covered in blood, with craven bone crests dangling from them. "These are all ram's heads—the mark of your family."

"That's impossible." Tyrek crosses the space between them to see for himself. "No Sukkara would move against us without the head of the house's blessing. Uncle Derane may be . . . boisterous, but he's no fool. He wouldn't do something like this."

Prince Derane tried to convince me to help him build support against Suran Omari to win back the throne. Was he so offended that I refused that he would send assassins? I don't know him well enough to say, but I wouldn't put it past him. Except how would killing me help his agenda?

"Where's your family crest?" I realize that Tyrek hasn't been wearing it.

"Suran Omari took it." Tyrek looks down at his bloodstained hands. "He seized my accounts and everything in the royal coffers. Craven bone included."

Essnai fishes out the bone dagger the assassin had attacked me with, then she thrusts it in Tyrek's face. "Did you know about this?"

The prince grimaces as he shakes his head. "No . . . I wasn't even sure that craven bone really worked against magic until now. It didn't work against Efiya."

"This one's still alive." Sukar kneels beside an assassin coughing up blood. "Who sent you?"

"Piss off," the man spits.

"That's not the right answer," I say, magic rising in my blood. There is a hiccup, a hesitation. My power is exhausted from healing my wound, but I call more magic from the night sky. Hundreds of sparks rush from every direction like fireflies coming to roost on my skin. The magic gives me more strength and fuels my anger. It sears against my flesh, but I ignore the pain.

Sukar glances up as it happens, his eyes glowing from the light. I know he can't see the magic, but he can feel it. It makes me long for the times we traveled to the tribal lands for the Blood Moon. The celebrations, the dances, the hope that magic would come to me. "You're full of surprises, aren't you?" he breathes. "I've never felt anyone take so much at once."

"I have a few more tricks." The assassin's limp body rises from the ground. Blood gushes from a wound across his stomach, and he groans in anguish. The cut is deep, but not so deep that he wouldn't die a slow, painful death. Something dark crawls from the bowels of my mind, and all I can think about is revenge. My heart thunders in anticipation.

"Who sent you?" I ask, the chieftains' voices eerily overlaying my own. It's a horrible sound, even to my ears. Tyrek backs away, and Essnai and Sukar tense as I stand face-to-face with my would-be killer. "You'll tell me, or I'll make your death last for as long as I see fit."

"Do your worst!" the man barks at me. *"Owahyat!"*

He has the same hatred and fear in his eyes as the mob who called my mother and me worse when Suran Omari banished my family. There will always be people like him who despise me because of magic. More assassins waiting in the shadows to strike. When will it end?

I take a breath, and against my better judgment, I press my hand to the man's wound.

"Don't touch me, tribal witch," the assassin yells as his skin begins to knit beneath my fingers. He gasps for air in surprise, his eyes wide. When I let go, he stands on his own again.

"Is that better?" I ask, thinking that maybe we can do this another way.

The man stares down at his stomach, stained with blood, his fingers tracing an invisible scar.

"I don't want to hurt you," I say, my voice returning to normal as the chieftains' *kas* settle. "Tell us what we want to know."

The man meets my gaze again, his eyes burning with rage. His lips tremble like he's struggling to get the words out.

Then he spits in my face.

"That was rather pointless," Tyrek muses.

I hold up my hand, palm flat to the sky. Curls of magic bleed from my fingertips until it hones into a knife as black as night. I've given him a fair chance—more than he deserves. He makes to step back, but my magic holds him in place. I drag the dagger across where his wound had been on his belly. It's only a light touch, barely grazing his skin, but the magic cuts him deep. I hold my breath as his wound tears open, gushing with fresh blood.

"The Almighty One!" he screams, straining against my magic to no avail. "He sent us to kill you and Second Son Tyrek."

"That coward," Tyrek groans, his eyes wide. "Can't say I'm surprised."

It takes a moment for the truth to sink in. Rudjek's father sent assassins to kill me. Ruining Arti's life all those years ago hadn't been enough for him. He's a menace, a canker. Prince Derane and the loyalists were right. He mustn't be allowed to rule—not without oversight from the Temple.

Sukar rests his hands on his sickles. "Are there more assassins on our trail? Who else knows that Suran Omari sent you? How often do you report back to him, and by what means?"

"It's just us, and no one else knew," the man blurts out. "We're supposed to send a message back to the palace after we kill the witch and the prince."

I let go of my hold on the assassin, and he bends over onto his hands and knees, blood dripping from his wound. There is a subtle shift in his energy, and a cloak of shadows wraps around him. "He's lying." I dig the dagger into his shoulder to loosen his tongue.

"There's a camp not far from here with another thirty men," the assassin confesses through gritted teeth.

"What are we going to do?" Tyrek asks, looking down at the man.

"We take the camp by surprise," Sukar suggests, "and cut the snake's head off now."

"Too risky," Essnai says. "Besides the obvious chance of getting hurt, we can't let this set us back from looking for the tribal people. With Arrah's . . ." She glances at Tyrek. I can imagine what she wants to say. *Her affliction, her problem, her little secret.* "We do not have time on our side."

I heal the would-be assassin again. "Stand up."

The man's eyes brim with hate. Suran will never give up—not until he gets what he wants: me out of his way. As I take a step back, the assassin draws a blade to my throat. The movement is so quick that I barely have time to react. I seize his hand with my magic, and he drops the knife. I reach for Beka's scrivener gift and combine it with the Kes chieftain's intimate knowledge of souls. This time I don't need ink and a needle; instead, I forge a symbol with magic: two glowing serpents intertwined. The symbols for binding. I narrow my focus and trace the symbol in the air with the dagger. The magic becomes tangible, visible for all to behold.

"What is that?" Tyrek whispers, staring at the symbols.

"Arrah," Sukar says, his voice cautious. "Don't."

Sukar's plea is a distant echo lost in the maelstrom of my mind. I must send a message to Suran Omari and everyone like him. I will not live in fear and let them destroy my life, not after surviving Efiya and Arti, after losing my father. The symbol careens into the assassin's chest, and he screams as it burns into his flesh like hot iron put to cowhide. Smoke billows up from his skin.

"Gods." Tyrek fumbles with the blade at his side. He launches for me, his moves clumsy but quick. He aims for my heart, making good on his promise. But I stay his hand with a flick of my wrist. He grits his teeth, fighting against my hold on him.

Someone else grabs my arm and spins me around. I blink a few times to see it's Essnai. She's yelling at me, but I only hear the beat of the assassin's heart, and the chains forging inside his mind—chains that bind him to me. Essnai slaps me hard. "What have you done!" When I don't answer, she slaps me again. Harder. Her hand stings against my face, dragging me out of a daze.

The assassin drops to his knees, convulsing. His eyes roll into the back of his head. My hold on Tyrek falters. "Mistress," the would-be assassin coos as he looks up at me. "I am yours to command."

I stumble back, and a scream tears from my lungs. Sukar takes me into his arms. "Shhh," he whispers. I frown at him, confused. Why is he comforting me? "It isn't your fault."

"How is this not her fault?" Tyrek demands.

"Don't you see that the Demon King made her do it!" Sukar bites back in my defense, and I burn with shame.

Essnai crosses her arms, glancing between the assassin and me. "Did he make you turn this man into a *ndzumbi*?"

My heart pounds against my chest. The answer is worse than that. "No."

"I need a moment." Tyrek stumbles away from camp.

"This isn't a good time for people to be going off alone," Sukar calls after him. Tyrek keeps walking.

I pull away from Sukar and step back in the opposite direction.

"Arrah," he says, but Essnai puts a hand on his shoulder to stop him from following me. The assassin climbs to his feet, and Sukar turns his attention to the man. I walk away, but I can hear the assassin struggling as my friends hold him back.

When I'm out of his line of sight, the assassin screams my name, his voice echoing against the mountain. I send a command through our bond, and he falls silent. I stumble on rocks and tree roots in the dark as I move farther from camp. Shadows melt around me; cold creeps inside my soul. The wind whips the tears from my cheeks. I keep seeing the disappointment in Essnai's eyes, Tyrek's fear, Sukar's denial.

What I've done is unforgivable. I am no better than Arti or Efiya. I'm something worse.

NINETEEN
RUDJEK

A welcome perk of my craven heritage is that I need less sleep. I spend my days and nights with Fadyi and Jahla poring over the reports and maps from my father's spies. Tonight Kira and Majka are with us, hunched over scrolls sprawled across the floor. An attendant pushes into the salon at midnight to bring another round of tea and spiced bread.

Jahla reaches for a plate, and Majka scrambles to his knees to grab it for her. "Allow me," he says with a winning smile.

She hardly notices his gesture, but Fadyi glances at them, his expression unreadable.

I return to my pile of shipping manifests and skim through the extensive lists of cargo and crew. Every record has an addendum from my father's spies of black market items. Ivory, red powder, cursed trinkets. Delenian poisons. Weapons. *Twenty-gods*. I reel when I see manifests of people sold in the warmongering northern state, Fyaran. Most of them are Yöomi from the nomadic lands to the east of the Serpent River. How can the Kingdom turn our backs on this atrocity and the countless others listed in these pages? I realize, not for the first time, that I don't know enough about how the world works—or my own country, for that matter.

One manifest, of a Fyaran ship lost at sea ten days ago, lists a crew complement of forty-five and a hundred and thirty-two Yöomi. The ship sailed from Yöom via the strait between Galke and Estheria and disappeared near Zeknor. In ordinary times, a ship lost at sea in that region isn't unheard of, but these aren't ordinary times. "Who has the weather charts for the Northern city-states?"

"I've got them." Kira waves a fistful of scrolls at me.

"What was the weather like around ten days ago?" I ask.

Kira shuffles through a dozen scrolls before she finds an answer. "No storms reported, clear skies."

"A ship of a hundred and seventy-seven people was lost in the Great Sea. It happened somewhere between Zeknor and Galke." I frown, flipping through accounts of other ships that sailed the day before and the day after. "It might be nothing, but it doesn't sit right with me."

"This is interesting." Majka clears his throat and glances at Jahla. "Abezer, a town in Zeknor, started rerouting ships to neighboring ports around the same time."

"That can't be a coincidence." I push aside the manifests and snatch up a detailed map of Zeknor. I draw my finger across the paper until I pinpoint Abezer between two rocky shores. The nearest towns are three days away on horseback. "It's isolated." I look up from the map. "And the ports are small enough that no one would raise concerns about redirected ships." I come to my feet, every muscle in my body firing. "Re'Mec!" I call for the sun god.

He appears in a cloud of shifting shadows perched on the back of a couch. "Am I wrong to think that you're starting to enjoy my company again, Rudjek?"

"Don't fool yourself," I say dismissively. "I need you to check on a town in the north called Abezer." I grimace, remembering how my last five hunches haven't panned out. "I have a good feeling about this one."

Re'Mec smiles. "Admit it. You like having a god as your little errand boy."

"Get on with it, will you," I grumble, not-so-secretly glad for his help. "We haven't the time for games."

The sun god's eyes change from sky blue to stormy gray and back to blue again. It happens so fast that one could easily miss it. "It's empty."

"What do you mean empty?" I ask obtusely.

"I can't sense a single soul," Re'Mec says.

"How did we not see this before now?" I bite back a curse. "The demons never invaded the North. Let my mother tell it, the Northerners don't even believe that the demons are back. It's the perfect place to hide."

I could laugh. After searching through manifests, maps, and reports for days, we've found Shezmu and the bulk of his demons. I'm sure of that, but I'm less sure of what to expect when we arrive in the port town.

"We have our answer." I stare at the sun god. "Now we need a ship."

Belowdecks, the ship smells like urine and vomit, and the air has a greasy texture that sticks to my skin. When I close my eyes, my other senses sharpen into knives. I hear rats gnawing in the bowels, the sway of the sea, and . . . intimate interactions I wish I could leave unheard. I groan in annoyance and rattle the shackles on my hands and feet to drown out the other sounds.

I open my eyes again, and they immediately adjust to the dark. "Is there ever a time on this ship someone's not bedding someone else?"

"Your senses are quite improved, Rudjek." Fadyi paces the cargo hold, pointedly ignoring my question. "Though, you have yet to heal the cut on your leg or free yourself from bondage."

"Go easier on me," I say through gritted teeth. "I'm a baby craven—haven't even seen my first birth day. Would you expect a baby to crawl out of the womb on his own?"

Fadyi clasps his hands behind his back. "Cravens can walk and fly within moments of birth."

I cock an eyebrow at him, but he shows no sign that he's joking. I groan again. It's easier to be a human, with our dull senses, slow healing, and lack of shape-shifting . . . but I'm not human anymore. With all that's happened, I haven't had time to consider what that means.

"Why do I still appear human?" I ask, my mouth and throat parched. "Shouldn't I have changed to be more like . . ." My voice falters. To be more like the monsters from the fairy tales, with tree bark skin, horned noses, and deadly claws. More like the monsters that Oshin Omari had supposedly killed in a glorious battle. "I don't mean to offend."

"Physical appearances are irrelevant to us." Fadyi smiles, and the skin crinkles around his eyes. "Cravens are whatever we want to be:

a tree, a frog, a whale. This beard gives you the impression of author-ity. My kind eyes portray a sense of trustworthiness. But these are only projections. The version of ourselves from your stories is how we have chosen to appear to humans to keep them out of our forest."

"You became the monsters they feared." I bite my lip. "But if Re'Mec created cravens to fight the demons *alongside* humans, what happened? We were once allies."

"Would you believe me if I told you that humans are greedy and have a knack for taking more than they need to survive?" Fadyi asks.

I don't think long before answering, "Sounds about right."

"Once the gate between worlds closed, and the war was over, we retreated to the Dark Forest." Fadyi leans against a barrel of grain. "There, our people lived in peace until Oshin Omari attacked."

Oshin Omari, celebrated hero, craven slayer, the stuff of legends. The man who I thought was my ancestor turned out to be a drunk who got himself killed. Someone should pen a play on that—it'll be a hit among the royals and common folk alike. We'll call it *Oshin Omari: The Rise and Fall of a Drunken Fool*. It'll be a parody for the ages. "Tell me about my real ancestor—the man who took Oshin's place."

Fadyi looks to my wound, almost healed now, and nods as though satisfied. "Caster of the Eldest Clan. His mother, Cassa, was our leader when Oshin Omari and the Kingdom invaded the Aloo Valley. The stories say Caster was brave, kind, honest, and a bit bois-terous at times."

"So, he was nothing like me, eh?" I bite back the pain as I struggle to pull my hands through the shackles. I vaguely remember Re'Mec telling me about Caster and the clans when I woke from my human death. Those first days, I drifted in and out of consciousness, my mind foggy. The sun orisha first made the cravens by pulling energy from his own body and altering it to be the opposite of him. Anti-magic. The first two craven he named Elder and Eldest. He made many cravens after them, but Elder and Eldest ruled their people together.

"Like most from the Eldest clan, Caster could see glimpses of the future," Fadyi explains. "He foresaw that his bloodline would one day father a king of craven and human lineage to unite our people."

"Come again?" I stop struggling against my chains. "You do know I'm not a king."

"You're the son and chosen heir of the Almighty One, aren't you?" Fadyi says nonchalantly, as if it should be obvious.

"You're forgetting the fact that my father shouldn't be on the throne," I say. "Prince Derane will likely start a civil war to get it back."

Fadyi inhales a deep breath, making it a point to be noisy. "Your chains, Rudjek."

I redouble my efforts to slide my hands from the metal cuffs latched on my wrists and ankles. The muscles in my arms and shoulders burn, and the chains have rubbed my skin raw. Did Caster feel nervous strolling into Oshin's camp, or facing the Almighty One for the first time wearing Oshin's face? He faked his way through court, and no one was the wiser. Maybe that's what I have to do—fake it as commandant until I figure out what I'm doing. I can't let my battalion see their leader look like a fool.

"Did he . . ." I stare intently at nothing as a bone cracks in my left wrist. Sharp pain rages through my hand. I grit my teeth and snatch my limp hand from the cuff. "Did Caster see a queen by my side in his vision?" I'm getting ahead of myself, but I want to know if he saw Arrah with me.

Fadyi pushes himself off the barrel as I free my second hand. "I don't recall the mention of a queen in the stories."

Not the answer I was hoping for, but it doesn't mean anything. I refuse to believe that her magic and my anti-magic will be between us forever. Once this mess is over with the demons, we'll have more time to figure things out. I'm just glad that Arrah's safe in the tribal lands, far away from Shezmu and the demons. I work out the pins in the cuffs around my ankles, then slip back into my shoes and wriggle my fingers at Fadyi. "All free."

"Next time, do it without injuring yourself." He shakes his head. "You must take your training seriously, Rudjek. The demons will target you if they think you're weak."

"I am, my friend." I pat Fadyi on the shoulder. "I'll do better next time."

"See that you do," he lectures me, like one of my old scribes.

I slip out of the cargo hold into a narrow passageway, and I catch a whiff of something burning in the galley. Fadyi and I pass soldiers belowdecks who stop and press themselves against the wall when they see me. I'm nervous about our impending arrival in the North. "This is all too convenient, isn't it? Shezmu and his army pick a town in Zeknor to hide in plain sight. A country that has a shaky relationship with the Kingdom, and we're arriving with five hundred gendars? It seems like an obvious trap. One misstep, and we'll find ourselves with the Zeknorians at our throat."

"Let us hope that the Zeknorians are reasonable," Fadyi says from behind me.

I squeeze my wrist, feeling the ghost of the pain from only moments ago. What other option do we have if the demon army is in Zeknor? We can't wait to ask for a formal invitation—not when Shezmu could decide to open the gate at any moment.

As soon as we climb above deck, the burning smell grows stronger, and I wrinkle my nose. Gendars shout as Majka and Jahla face off against each other—him with one of his shotels and her with two long knives. Majka grins as he gives her a flourishing bow. Then they spar, blade against blade, circling each other like hungry vultures. Jahla dips low, sweeping her knife a breath from his stomach. Majka dramatically swipes the back of his hand across his forehead, and when Jahla attempts to sidestep him, he lurches forward and pins her to his chest.

"Yield!" Majka says, out of breath.

On the surface, they are unevenly matched. Majka is a head taller than Jahla and twice her weight. He's got a wicked swing, but she is quick, nimble, and deadly. Months ago, when I'd gone in search of Arrah, led astray by false information, Jahla had been the one to best me. I traveled to the Aloo Valley by boat and found the abandoned camp outside the Dark Forest. It smelled like Arrah—sweet and intoxicating.

Perhaps it had been part desperation and part audacity that led me to charge into the forest, intent on rescuing her. Within moments the cravens had surrounded me in their nightmarish form: bark skin, ivory horns, razor-sharp claws, and for good measure, eyes of blackest night.

Five stepped forward from various places in the circle. Later I would find out it was Fadyi, Jahla, Raëke, and the twins, Ezaric and Tzaric. They formed a smaller circle and bent on one knee, their heads bowed. It baffled me then, and of course, I thought, *Well, yes, I am the descendant of the great Oshin Omari, craven slayer.* But then they'd attacked, the five of them at once—shotels against claws. Twenty-gods, I shudder to remember how quick they were—blurs of bone and bark. Still, I held my own for a time until Jahla parried one of my blows, dropped into a crouch, and clawed out my guts.

Now she tilts her head up and leans in closer to Majka, her teeth bared. He gazes down at her hungrily, and she knees him in a compromising place. He hunches over, groaning, while the men cheer and exchange coins. "Ouch," he whines as she sheathes her knives and pats him on the back. "That hurt."

"You're not the worst-looking man I've beaten." Jahla smiles down at him. "And you lasted much longer than the others."

"Oh, that's a relief," Majka croaks out. "Considering that I have but a scrap of dignity left."

Fadyi looks between Jahla and Majka, amused. "Does he know that she can smell his intentions toward her? His odor has been quite obvious for some time."

"I think Majka knows." I watch as the two of them lean against the hull, laughing. "You don't approve?"

"I don't *disapprove*," he says with an uncharacteristic shrug. "I find the dance of courtship curious, though it's not something of personal interest to me." Fadyi glances around the deck. "It's been quite tiresome to keep fending off would-be suitors since we started the voyage. Humans are . . . needy."

"*Needy* is a quaint way of putting it." I rub the back of my neck, embarrassed. "Say the word, and I will make sure it stops." I may not be able to ever repay him, Jahla, and Raëke for sticking by my side since the Dark Forest, but at least I can keep my soldiers in check.

"I might take you up on that offer." Fadyi's attention shifts to Captain Dakte, who's headed straight for us.

I bite back my irritation and keep my face neutral. "Crown Prince," says my appointed second in command as he reaches us. I swear he goes out of his way to annoy me.

"Commandant," I correct him, projecting my voice so others will hear. "Address me as such."

"My apologies, Commandant." He gives me a little bow. "The crew has spotted land—we're almost off the coast of Abezer."

"Good—"

"Not good," Captain Dakte says. "The town is on fire."

I peer across his shoulder to see smoke rising in the distance. The smell from earlier hadn't been from the galley. It was Abezer burning. Fadyi nods like he'd been waiting for me to figure it out on my own. I *would* have eventually guessed it, if I'd been paying more attention.

Behind him, Kira clings to the crow's nest on the highest point of the ship with a spyglass pressed to her eye. "No movement on the ground."

"Stay outside firing range," Captain Dakte shouts. "Gendars at the ready."

I push through soldiers hastily putting on breastplates and helmets and strapping on their scabbards. When I reach the bow, I don't need a spyglass to see the coast. Abezer is mostly a pile of charred buildings and smothering ashes. There's no sign of life, people or otherwise. "The trap."

"We should take the ship up the coast and find another place to disembark," Captain Dakte advises, following me. "The last thing we need is the Zeknorians thinking that the Kingdom is responsible for this."

"No." I stare at the black smoke curling up from the town. "That would be a mistake."

"With all due respect, Commandant," Captain Dakte says, his voice stiffer than usual, "your title is honorary. You have no field experience. I know how to handle this situation."

I grip the railing along the bow, my nails digging into the wood. "Yet I'm the one who's fought a demon army and won."

Captain Dakte's fingers twitch at his sides. "What are your orders, Commandant?"

"We need to tread carefully." I stare at the port town again. "A show of force is not the answer. You and I will take a third of the men ashore by boat to investigate the situation."

"Yes, Commandant," Dakte says, turning on his heel.

Soon I'm beneath layers of armor with my faceplate shoved back as the men row boats toward the shore. I ordered Majka, Kira, and Jahla to stay behind in case the demons send a ship from behind the cliffs and attack. The frigid air chills me to the bone as the boats slosh through sheets of ice floating in the bay. It seems to take hours to navigate the empty harbor and disembark.

"Send out scouts," I tell Captain Dakte, who barks the order to his second. The scouts spread across the town, but I already know what they'll find. The acrid smell of charred flesh twists in my stomach as we march from the docks. We cross an empty market of rotten fruit, maggot-covered meat, and moldy bread dusted in snow. Fadyi is with me, and he and I exchange a look, following where the strongest scent of death leads. We discover a field of half-burned bodies in an open stretch of land on the edge of town.

Captain Dakte kneels and takes a fistful of dirt, letting it sprinkle back to the ground. "Mother Nana, god of earth, have mercy on these poor bastards' souls."

"They don't believe in gods, you know." Re'Mec appears out of thin air, yet not one of the gendars seems to notice when it happens. He's wearing a gray robe, looking like an ordinary human.

"You should've stayed on the ship, scribe." Captain Dakte grimaces, fooled by his appearance. "I fear we've walked into a bad situation about to get worse."

Across the field of broken bodies, soldiers crest a slope, marching straight for us. The Zeknorians are tall and wide shouldered, and wear fur-lined armor and broadswords. Many have bushy beards— some coarse, some curly, some straight. They possess the sort of ashen skin that can only be seen on people who get little sun year-round. Just beyond the dead, archers drop to one knee and nock their arrows. Behind them, soldiers drag forward shields large enough to protect the front line. Another third of their forces ride horses draped in chain mail. I immediately regret disembarking the ship without our full complement.

"Formation!" Captain Dakte commands. The gendars shift

behind us, outnumbered three to one.

"Hold for my word," I bark when the men begin to draw their shotels. Maybe I'm a fool for thinking that we can still come out of this without a bloodbath, but I have to try. The Kingdom isn't going to war with Zeknor under my command—not if I can help it.

I inhale, and the sting of rot and decay burns my nose and overwhelms my senses. It makes my stomach queasy. Even after seeing so much death, I will never get used to it, nor do I want to. "We'll make them see reason." I rest my hands on my shotels and step forward to address them.

"Let me handle this," Captain Dakte says, moving up alongside me. "This is not your expertise. . . . We can't afford to make another mistake here."

I can almost feel the gendars' sharp gazes cutting into my back. I'm supposed to be their leader, to give them direction—and I led them straight into the path of the Zeknorian army. "What do you propose?" I ask at the same time Re'Mec pushes himself through the gendar ranks and steps forward.

"We come in peace, barbarians," Re'Mec says in the Northern common tongue as he raises his hands. The words are clipped, direct, and efficient. He delivers them as a native speaker would. Growing up, Adé made sure that my brothers and I learned the trade language of the North. *Barbarians* is not a term of endearment. "We mean you no harm." There is so much contempt in his voice that it oozes from each word.

"Stand down, scribe," Captain Dakte spits through gritted teeth. Ignoring him, Re'Mec opens his arms wide and offers the

Zeknorians an earnest smile. "We come with the grace and blessings of the gods, who, though you have forsaken them, still watch over the lot of you on occasion."

"And why would we care about the Kingdom's false gods?" comes an answer from a man on a horse as white as the snowcapped mountains behind them.

Re'Mec scoffs and switches to Tamaran. "I don't know why I even bother."

Captain Dakte loses his last shred of patience and pushes Re'Mec aside. "We don't know what transpired here—"

Before the words are entirely out of his mouth, an arrow cuts through the air—one of the Zeknorian archers has let off a shot. I react without thinking, and time shifts around me, rippling like torrid waves. Everything slows down. The arrow inches its way closer and closer, straight for Captain Dakte's heart. I can smell the sickly sweet poison on it.

"It will pierce his armor and kill him," Re'Mec says, looking particularly bored. "Let him die. His very presence undermines your authority."

"And start a war?" I pull my shotels. "You can be awfully cynical at times."

Re'Mec shrugs. "I've been called worse."

When the arrow is close, I deflect it with my sword. The wood splinters at impact, and shards scatter. Captain Dakte ducks out of the way of the debris and pulls his shotels.

"That was a very bad idea." I project my voice across the field. "Do you really want to die today?"

The man on the white horse trots forward a bit more, his sword in hand—further showing that he is in command. I let the question linger in the air between us. He is the one I must convince to stand down. "If we were here to do harm," I say, "why would we linger in a decimated town?"

"Who is to say why the Kingdom does anything?" the man shouts back in accented Tamaran. "Especially if the rumors are true."

"What rumors would those be?" I can take a guess, but it's best to keep him talking.

"That your *Ka*-Priestess and her army single-handedly brought the Kingdom to its knees," the man says. "That doesn't bode well for a country that prides itself on its military prowess."

"I wouldn't say single-handedly," Re'Mec grumbles. "She had help."

"That's the thing about rumors, isn't it?" I smile. "They are full of half-truths and lies. The trouble that has befallen our lands is the same one that destroyed this coastal town. The demons are back."

Laughter and curses rise from the Zeknorian army, followed by a torrent of insults. Their leader raises one hand to silence them. "You expect us to believe that ghosts from the past did this?"

I seed my voice with as much arrogance as I can muster. "I expect you to have some common sense before you commit yourself to a war on two fronts."

Captain Dakte stiffens beside me. "Don't push him too much."

It's a gamble, but one worth the risk. My political and strategy scribes always said that Zeknorians weren't ones for politeness. I don't put much stake in generalizations, but I won't win over this

Zeknorian with small talk. He needs to be made to see reason.

"It's good that our arrow didn't strike your man." The Zeknorian sheaths his sword. "The smallest scratch would be deadly."

"Good indeed," I say, sweat trickling down my back. I glance over at Captain Dakte, who stares at the tear in my uniform, above the elbow, where a splinter from the arrow scraped my skin.

TWENTY
ARRAH

I tell myself that I can face what I've done, that I'm sorry. Neither is a lie, and neither is quite true. The first morning light settles across the mountains as I finally stumble back to camp. I stare at the dead assassins and the bloody ground through a haze. Someone's rolled them onto their stomachs, and I'm relieved not to have to look into their hollow eyes.

I go straight for my saddlebag to take the dose of blood medicine I missed last night, but I stop short. The contents of the bag lie scattered on the ground, the jar broken, the blood medicine long soaked into the soil. Fighting off panic, I clutch the bone charm around my neck.

Sukar and Essnai glance up at me from where they're packing the last of our things. They've cleaned the blood from their faces, but it's everywhere else. I can't read either of their expressions. I don't want to know what they're thinking. "We need to leave," Essnai says, her voice weary. "The horses are dead, so we'll walk." I can't bear to look at her, so I keep my gaze elsewhere.

Tyrek sits on the ground next to his sack, skinning the bark from a twig with a small knife. "What are we going to do about our *ndzumbi*?"

"Can you undo the curse?" Sukar asks, hopeful.

"I'm a hypocrite for saying it, but should she?" Tyrek questions, climbing to his feet. "What happens when he is free to go back to warn his camp?"

"I hate to agree, but . . ." Essnai rubs her eyes. She and Sukar both look exhausted. I should've never asked them to come. Even if I didn't expect anything like this, I knew there would be risks. "We need to get them off our trail."

I force myself to look at the assassin, lying on the ground, bound and gagged. His body tenses under my gaze, and I bite the inside of my cheek hard enough to draw blood. As I close the distance between us, I wonder if the man has a family waiting back home. I kneel and untie the binding on his hands, my fingers brushing against his calloused palms. He is a person, and I have stolen him. I am the monster stalking the night now, not Arti.

"I will release you," I say as the man rolls over to peer up at me. The morning light gives his eyes an amber hue with specks of emerald. They shine with eagerness for my command. "You only need to complete one task for me first."

The man nods feverishly, ready to do anything I ask. "Tell the others that you were the sole survivor of the attack. You heard our plans to search the caves of Tribe Aatiri for an artifact that will destroy the Kingdom. Take some of our things with you and leave them for the other assassins to find in the caves."

Tyrek strokes his chin. "Suran Omari doesn't know who he's up against. Our little Arrah has a devious streak."

Ignoring him, I say, "Once you search the caves, convince the others that we must already be on the way back to the Kingdom. Do your best to stall them."

"Yes, mistress," the man answers, breathless, after I release his gag. "I will do as you wish."

He collects items from around camp: a bowl, a headscarf, a dagger, the shards of the broken jar. Once he's done, he leaves without glancing back and begins down the south slope of the mountain, toward the assassins' camp. I scoop up my bloody cloak and slip it over my shoulders. I'm too exhausted to attempt to clean it. "That should buy us time to get to Tribe Zu without the assassins on our trail."

We head north. Time is a tricky thing when you're trapped in your head, a prisoner of your thoughts. We walk without rest for hours, and hours turn into a full day. I reach for the chieftains' memories, and they flood me with an overwhelming sense of guilt and shame to add to my own. I feel the Zu and Kes chieftains' disapproval the deepest for twisting their magic.

Töra Eké, the Litho chieftain, is the only one of the five who is indifferent. I don't expect better from a man who took pleasure in disposing of all who opposed him. My cousin Icarata of the Mulani bombards me with images of angry flames, her meaning clear. I will burn for what I've done.

"I had no choice," I hiss under my breath at them.

Every moment is a choice, child, Grandmother replies.

Of course, she would speak first. I'm bitter that she is only a memory, a fragment, a ghost. I wish she could sit me down in her tent and tell me that everything will be okay. That we'll find the tribal people who fled from my sister, safe and sound. That my mistakes do not define me. That I can live up to the expectations that she and the chieftains bestowed upon me.

I cannot trust myself with their gift—not after last night. I thought that I would be better than Arti and Efiya, that I could use magic for good. *You've got a strange look in your eyes, girl*, the charlatan had remarked at my father's shop. *Perhaps the chieftains made a mistake giving you their magic.* For Heka's sake, he'd seen something wrong with me even then. He'd known. Breaking Veeka's glass had been petty, yes, but turning the assassin into a *ndzumbi* was vicious and cruel. I will never forgive myself for it, yet I can't promise that I won't do worse if it means we can find the tribal people. I won't let anyone stand in my way.

I dig through the chieftains' memories for the answer to a question I don't want to ask. Is there a way to unbind their *kas* from mine? When I catch a glimpse of a single incantation shared across each of their memories, I shy away from the details. After we've found the tribal people, it wouldn't be so bad to give up my magic, would it? I'd be a *ben'ik* again—magicless—no different from my friends. Nothing would stand between Rudjek and me being together. I wouldn't have to fear touching him, and I would have the Demon King out of my mind. I wouldn't hurt anyone else.

The Demon King has to know that I would never release him upon the world. His demons have already caused so much pain and suffering. Yet I am curious why he thinks that calling me by his *ama*'s name will win some sympathy. *It isn't the Demon King we need to worry about,* my mother warned me. *It's your sister.* What had he said to win Arti over to his side?

We leave behind the Barat Mountains at dusk and find a place to set up camp. Tyrek pulls out his wineskin, and Essnai and Sukar argue about which of them is the better cook.

"You can't be serious after that bird stew," Sukar says, grimacing.

"That recipe has been in my family for generations," Essnai counters. "Everyone loves it."

Sukar laughs as he pokes at the campfire. "How unfortunate."

Essnai clucks her tongue. "You clearly have no taste."

I don't have the heart to tell them that they're both quite awful at cooking, though Sukar is slightly better. While they argue, I go to wash at a stream away from camp. Magic that feels like a raging storm pricks against my awareness. My shoulders go stiff, and I let out a frustrated sigh. I rise to my feet and turn around to face her.

"Did you miss me?" Koré says, her dark skin iridescent in the moonlight, her voice high-pitched. "I've missed you."

I stumble back when I see what she's carrying—the box with the Demon King's soul. The holy script carved into the wood, all that's left of the orishas who sacrificed themselves to trap him, glows. *She found it.* I'm relieved that the box is safely in her possession again, but I'm nervous that it's so close to me. Especially now that I don't have the blood medicine to help block the Demon King from reaching my mind.

"Why are you here?" All this time, she hasn't bothered to visit, not after I gave up everything in the fight against my sister. She used me like a piece on a game board and discarded me when she lost interest.

"Don't look so hurt, Arrah." Koré offers me a smile. Strands of silver light weave between her waist-length braids, and she looks majestic. Her elara is a flame against the night, changing from fire red to amber as she moves. "I would've come sooner, but as you can see"—she gestures at the box—"I have my hands full with this trickster."

The Demon King's presence stirs inside my mind like a snake coiling tighter, and there's fear, so much fear. I ache with it. Why would Koré bring the box here, knowing that I am the only one left with enough magic to free him? "How did you find it?"

"I followed some rather subtle clues I left behind to lead me back to it," Koré says with a devious smile. "I'd hidden the box in a volcano on a world close to Zöran. I've heard from my brother that Shezmu has been searching, too, but I beat him to it."

I don't press her for more, lest she become suspicious of why I want to know. I hug my shoulders, pushing down the fear crawling across my skin like ants marching to certain death. If the orisha sees me trembling in the half light, she says nothing of it. She sits on the box, and I have a mind to snatch her right off and wipe that smug smile from her face.

The Demon King's thoughts teeter at the edge of my own, and I clutch the charm around my neck. It was a mistake for Koré to bring the box here—it's only strengthened our connection. Before, I could only hear him if I used complex magic, but that's changed. His fear seeps into my mind now, and it's so heavy that I'm drowning. But his fear isn't for himself; it's for me.

She is not to be trusted, he whispers.

I flinch at his warning and catch Koré staring at me with one eyebrow raised. "Is there something the matter with you?"

I abandon clutching the bone charm, convinced that Koré will find me out at any moment and cut me down where I stand. "Why are you here now after all this time?" I ask, and it comes out harsher than I intended.

"I felt the tug of your magic." Koré props her elbows on her knees. Her words hang in the air between us, and I realize that I'd been thinking about the Demon King before she came. Did my magic draw him here? I am rarely impressed by mortals, especially ones not of my making, but I am impressed by you, Arrah." Koré pauses, her eyes pools of milky light. "My brethren and I owe you a great deal. I'm here to repay that debt if you'll let me."

I shift on my heels. She speaks of the Demon King being a trickster, but I've seen the same from her and her brother. Always twisting the truth to get what they want—omitting the details. I can't help but wonder what she has up her sleeve now. "And here I thought I was just a pawn in your game against the Demon King."

She narrows her eyes at me and slips on another devious smile. "You're nobody's mule. Always remember that." She stands again and picks up the box.

"Who is Dimma?" I know the moment the words leave my mouth it's a mistake. Streaks of crimson bleed across the moon. I stumble when Koré suddenly appears nose to nose with me, blood pooling in the whites of her eyes, too.

"How do you know that name?" she demands. "We do not speak it aloud."

"Efiya told me," I lie. "I didn't get a chance to ask you about her before you left."

Koré blinks, the blood leaving her eyes as her anger abates. "She was our sister." The moon orisha clutches the box tighter under her arm. "She fell in love with Daho and almost destroyed the universe."

I don't miss the irony of it—how Dimma and Daho had almost destroyed the universe, and Rudjek and I can't touch without nearly destroying each other. It all sounds like one of the gods' idea of a cruel joke.

"I loved my sister, and we killed her." Koré sighs, her shoulders hunching. "You'd understand that better than most."

"Yes." I don't trust myself to say more.

"We'll talk again after I'm done with this business in the North," she says. "Remember my offer. It still stands should you think of a suitable way for me to repay you."

"What business in the North?"

"I thought you knew," Koré says. "Your craven and my brother tracked down Shezmu and the rest of the demon army."

I frown, unnerved by the news. If Rudjek has already reached the North, he must've left right after we did. I swallow the lump in my throat. "Is Rudjek okay?"

Koré gives me a look of indifference. "I assume so. The battle has not yet begun."

At that, darkness melts around Koré, obscuring her body until she's gone. My hand trembles as I wipe sweat from my forehead. I pace in front of the stream, not knowing what to do with myself. Rudjek is preparing to go into battle again. I should be at his side, unless . . . unless he didn't want me there. He'd been reluctant to tell me about the demons in the city—he'd hidden the news for days. Had he also known that Shezmu and his army were in the North that night in the gardens at the Almighty Palace?

I sink to my knees beside the stream and splash cool water on my face as if I can wash away my doubt. I stare at myself through the ripples in the water and moonlight. I can feel the Demon King's presence still, even though I'm not conjuring magic and with the box gone. Any hope I had that our connection would lessen once Koré left fades away.

"I won't help you," I say, glaring at the water.

Let me show you the truth, Dimma.

His voice is a desperate plea, shards of broken glass put back together wrong. My body goes rigid, taut as a fraying rope before it snaps. The Demon King's patience threads through the silence. He could show me whatever he wants, but he waits for my permission. I can't shake the curiosity flowing through me. How could two people falling in love almost destroy the universe as Koré said? I shouldn't, but I nod anyway. I need to know why he thinks that I am Dimma.

On the surface of the stream, the water swells until my reflection settles into a new face. A girl with golden-brown skin, faint veins along her temples, dark eyes, tangled curls. Her wide nose slopes into an elegant arch, meeting full lips stretched over pointed teeth. I've seen this girl in my dreams, through the window of a cabin on a mountain. She sits at a small table across from a boy. She laughs with him. She climbs into his lap as his fingers explore the maze of her hair.

I scramble backward, dragging myself away from the reflection in the water. That girl isn't me, and she is very much dead. Koré said so. "She's gone!" I scream into the night. "Don't you see that? Let her go."

They will hurt you if they find out who you are.

He means Koré, Re'Mec, and the other orishas. If they think for one moment that I am Dimma, they will strike me down. Showing me her image doesn't explain why *he* thinks I'm her. It proves nothing, aside from the fact that he's been influencing my dreams. But I sense no deceit from the Demon King. He'd protected me from the men by the sacred Gaer tree because he believes that I'm his *ama*? I wrap my arms around my knees and draw them to my chest. I can't let myself speculate about this now, when we're so close to Tribe Zu. "Stay out of my way."

Without the blood medicine, I can't block the Demon King, so I do the next best thing. I focus on Rudjek. I daydream about *him* playing with my hair, me climbing into *his* lap, *his* hands around my waist. I take the memory of Daho and Dimma and make it about Rudjek and me. It's a nasty move, but I don't care. To my satisfaction, the Demon King recoils from my mind, but not before he whispers one last warning.

Fram won't bring you back if you die again. Be careful, Dimma.

THE UNNAMED ORISHA: DIMMA

I'd seen countless deaths on countless worlds and still hadn't found a cure for Daho's mortality. I grow resentful of the Supreme Cataclysm's compulsion to create and destroy. It's the reason Daho will die one day. Not ready to give up, I visit a world called Uthura. I sit on the roof above a city, watching its people wading through blankets of mist. Twin voices curl around me in a cool embrace that tastes of inevitability. "You seem to have an affinity for death, Dimma."

They are light and dark, night and day, chaos and order, the sweetness of a first breath and the moment of death. One half of them glows, and shadows swathe the other, together shaping symmetry. They tell me their name and nature in the shift of the wind around us: Fram, the custodian of life and death. Koré is writhing energy, the calm before the storm, the storm itself. Iben is secrecy. I would soon learn that Re'Mec is heat and rage and nurture. Of the four, there is something in Fram that calls to me most, a kinship, a likeness.

"Why are they not immortal like us?" I ask as two bodies materialize beside me, four legs dangling over the ledge. I don't mean only the Uthurans; I mean all mortal kind. I asked Iben a similar question, but perhaps Fram is more suited to answer it.

"Death is our gift to them," Fram says. "Our offspring will never have our immortality, but they have an advantage over us. They will bear children of their flesh. We can only shape what the Supreme Cataclysm creates into some semblance of our image—they are only a shadow of who we are."

"It seems more like a curse to me," I say.

"You've fallen in love with a mortal, have you?" Fram asks pointedly.

I think of Daho's lips against mine, the curve of his back, his laughter. "How do you know?"

"None of our kind ever cares about death until it affects someone they love," Fram answers.

"Are the Uthurans your children?" I ask, hiding from the truth in their words.

Fram falls still, their voices silent for a long pause. "My children are too dangerous for the mortal world, so I keep them inside me."

The Uthurans in the city below perform a ceremony to honor twelve people who died in an accident. They place their dead in a circle on a platform. Their heads form the inner ring of the circle, and their appendages form the outer. Twelve Uthurans lean to touch the deceased. They close their eyes, and energy begins to hum around the people on the platforms. Soon the dead Uthurans' bodies start to flake away, like burned leaves careening on a breeze. They fade until there is nothing left but their souls. Gray mists rise from the platforms and float to the living. They open their mouths, their jaws stretching, and they eat the souls.

I startle beside Fram—surprised and confused. "This is death for the Uthurans?"

"Death and an extension of life," Fram says, indifferent, as if the act isn't extraordinary. "When someone dies an unnatural death, their soul holds their unused years. The Uthurans have found a way to absorb those years and add to their own life by eating souls."

Excitement buzzes through my body. This is the closest thing that I've seen to immortality in any mortal world. It isn't a cure for death, but it could extend Daho's life until I find one.

"I wouldn't do that," Fram says, reading my thoughts. "The results may not be what you expect."

I close my mind to them, the way Iben had always closed his mind to me. He had his secrets, and I will have my own. My brethren won't approve of my plan. They are too complacent in the way things have always been, but I can change them. I can give Daho a chance.

"It's only a thought," I say, pretending to let it pass.

"Cherish your love for Daho while you can and hold your memories of him close when he's gone," Fram advises.

I peer into every city, town, and village of Uthura, learning about their death. "Yes," I say, letting go of my physical body as I prepare to travel through the gate. "I hope that we have many more conversations throughout our long, stagnant lives."

Fram laughs at that, the sounds like stars colliding. "I have a feeling that we will."

When I am back with Daho in our little cabin, he holds me tight against his chest. I'm lost in a kiss when we receive visitors. I pull away from him, breathless. The two souls taste of day and night, summer and winter, and chaos.

"Is anyone home?" Re'Mec asks in *kociti*, the demon language. His voice is playful, but there is something dangerous underneath the surface. Daho tenses at my side, and his apprehension is a reminder of how small he is, how very fragile, very mortal.

"It's okay," I reassure him.

I cross the room and open the door, coming face-to-face with my brother Re'Mec for the first time. He and Koré wear human vessels.

"Hello, Dimma." Re'Mec grins as he steps into the cabin, eyes roaming until they land on Daho. "You've found a little plaything, I see. One of Koré's children, no less." My brother sniffs the air. "Ah, he's seen a few more sunrises than you, but he is still a babe."

"You have learned much in such a short time," Koré says, circling me. She pays no mind to Daho. "Emulating mortal kind and limiting yourself to their rules of life. I am impressed."

Re'Mec pokes his finger into a bowl of half-eaten stew. "Tell me, Dimma, have you discovered your nature? What is your purpose in life?"

"I don't know," I whisper.

Re'Mec shrugs. "It took me two millennia to find mine."

"Why have you come here?" I ask as Re'Mec licks the stew from his finger.

To give you some advice, he says, his voice projecting in my mind so Daho won't hear. *Fram told us about your mission to find a cure for mortality.*

Be careful, little sister, Koré says, joining Re'Mec. *A god's love is a dangerous thing.* There is a warning in her voice and regret. I *once made the mistake of loving a mortal too much, and they paid the price.*

I won't let Daho die, I say.

You will try to save him and fail, Koré says.

Re'Mec pats the top of my head. *You'll find another lover after he's gone, then another and another. That's the way of our kind.*

Take care, Dimma, Koré says as they disappear into the space between time.

My brethren thought their warning would be enough to stop me, but it only fueled my desire to prove them wrong.

TWENTY-ONE
ARRAH

Heavy fog creeps across the tribal lands as we head south toward Tribe Zu. The fog is usual for this time of the year, but it's still frustrating that we can't see more than a few steps ahead of us. I reach for the chieftains' magic despite their disapproval after I turned the assassin into a *ndzumbi*. I'm afraid they will reject me, but, like an old friend, the magic comes at once. I can still do some good, but now I worry that I will make another mistake, or the Demon King will use it against me.

I need Grandmother's gift to see across the threads of time to find out what happened to the survivors. Of the five chieftains, she is still disappointed in me. I've dishonored her memory, and for that, I am even more ashamed. She doesn't speak, but I imagine her sitting in her tent, an eyebrow raised in expectation. *Do better.*

In her memories, I see a new way to peer into the past. It isn't like when my *ka* traveled through time to Rudjek's death in the Dark Forest. My heart aches, remembering him, broken and alone. He'd cracked a joke even on the edge of death. *Here lies Rudjek Omari,* he'd said. *The one to put an end to the Omari legacy.* I miss his humor. I miss him.

My mind homes in on the threads of time, invisible to all but the most talented witchdoctors. Thousands of faint white lines fill the air and weave through my friends and me like we are of no consequence. I catch echoes of memories trapped in the land. Impressions take shape in the early morning haze—the curve of a bloody mouth, an arm dangling from its socket, a mangled leg. I'm witnessing the remnants of a battle.

Essnai touches my arm, and I jump, my skin crawling. "You okay?"

I grip the strap of my burlap sack harder. My gaze roams from one apparition to another, each one more gruesome than the last. The question is so simple, but I have a mind to tell her all the ways I'm not okay. I failed to save the *edam* and the tribal people. I've killed, and I've stolen a man's soul like a thief in the night. The Demon King thinks I'm his long-dead *ama*, and maybe I've lost Rudjek's trust.

"Yes," I say, not meaning to sound so feeble.

A Litho woman melts out of the fog, her face painted white, a rawhide cloak upon her shoulders. *We're not going to make it,* she mouths, looking straight through me. A boy sucking his thumb clings to her side. *Run.* The word aches inside me. *Run.* It threatens to break free, and I clutch the strap until my hands burn. *Run.*

"You're a horrible liar." Essnai pats my shoulder. "You're not okay."

I shrug. "If you know that, then why ask?"

"To remind you that you're not alone." Her staff crunches against the ground as she walks alongside me. "We worry about you."

I press my hand to my heart, counting myself lucky and feeling undeserving of such loyal friends. I'm relieved that neither she nor Sukar has asked about the Demon King. It's like we're kids again, racing through the Hall of Orishas, pretending to be gods. That was when Sukar let the older attendants braid his hair in cornrows, before he took to shaving his head. Essnai had already been a head taller and taking staff lessons in one of the makeshift rings in the East Market. The hall was our haven, a place we could laugh until our bellies hurt and talk about our dreams.

We're pretending now—pretending that one day the world will be safe again, that we'll get our old lives back. I'm pretending that I'm not a little broken inside, a little hollow, carved out, a lot jaded. That I'm going to keep the Demon King away, that I can crush my curiosity about him. But I can't pretend that I don't see the final moments of people fleeing for their lives all around me. I let go of the memories from the battle, and the faces melt back into the fog.

"Something's wrong here." Sukar scratches his shoulder, then the side of his face. "My tattoos won't stop itching."

"You mean something's wrong *aside* from the assassins on our trail who want to take our heads back to the Kingdom?" Tyrek interjects in his lazy drawl.

"They're looking for your head, Prince," Sukar says. "I'm obliged to let them take it, too."

Tyrek wrinkles his nose and pokes out his tongue at Sukar like an insolent child. Essnai laughs, and even Sukar gives him a grudging smile.

So much magic has gathered across the foothills that along with the fog it blocks out the sunlight. Everything beyond the fog takes on a dangerous edge—the rustling of leaves, the crunch of grass underfoot, the low growls. I don't sense anything wrong, but I trust Sukar's instincts.

"It's eerie that so many people died here, and there's no sign left of them," Tyrek says.

"Re'Mec and Koré burned the bodies after the battle," Essnai tells him, her voice stricken. "I have no love for the orishas, but I respect them for putting the tribes to rest."

"Rest?" Sukar scoffs. "I doubt that the orishas sang their burial songs or properly prepared them for ascension. I hardly call that rest."

"Strange that Heka did not come to the tribal people's aid," Tyrek muses. Essnai and Sukar both go rigid, tension threading through their bodies. I hold my breath. "That he would abandon them shows how little the gods—any of them—care about us."

I don't say it aloud, but I agree with him. I'll never forgive Heka for giving Efiya the full gift of his powers, nor for standing by while she destroyed the tribes. As my anger rises, the Demon King stirs at the edges of my mind, almost like he's waiting for an invitation. His hesitation ebbs in the silence between breaths.

Tyrek stops on the trail up ahead and lets out a slew of curses that makes the three of us flinch. He stands still, his shoulders stiff, looking down. "The gods missed this one." He nods at something half-covered on the ground.

We gather around it, and Essnai pushes back the grass with her staff. Tyrek buries his nose in the crook of his elbow, and Sukar gags. It's a withered hand, leathered by the sun, plucked at by birds.

"This can't be from the battle," I say, blood rushing in my ears. "The wounds look only days old." I wonder if it's from one of the people who had left the Kingdom to search for survivors.

"It looks like someone put it here on purpose," Tyrek mumbles against his arm.

Sukar steps back and quietly retrieves his sickles. Their scrivener magic keeps them from making a sound as he does. He turns in a slow circle, his eyes sharp, his legs poised to spring into action.

"Let's keep moving," I say, on edge, too. The hand is a warning.

No one questions me as we push forward, picking up the pace to Tribe Zu. It takes all day, but we reach the foothills leading up another stretch of mountains without incident. A scatter of forts imbued with scrivener magic still stands on the outskirts of the tribe. Discarded staffs and darts and blades, broken masks, fire-scarred shields. We start our ascent on a winding path with Sukar leading the way, humming a burial chant, until he cuts off midsong. I follow his gaze to a head hanging from a tree branch, dangling from its hair.

I can't stop staring at the holes where eyes should be and the light pouring through the back of the skull. I squeeze my hands into fists, my magic aching to let loose on anyone who could be so heartless and cruel.

"The blood is fresh," Sukar says, his voice hollow.

"Does anyone else get the feeling that we're walking into an obvious trap?" Tyrek pulls his shotels, the sound echoing in the mountains. "I'm quite sure that we are."

"Shut it, Tyrek." Essnai lifts her gaze to the treetops. Her shoulders shudder as she counts the heads, each with their eyes missing.

"One for each tribe." Her voice cracks. "Zu, Litho, Aatiri, Kes, Mulani."

I drag my hands against my trousers as if I can wipe away the anger rotting my insides. Tyrek's right—it's a trap, and I can't help but think it's one especially for me. "Sukar, do you still have the mask?"

"It's in my sack," he says, peering into the surrounding woods.

Sukar stops so I can fish out the mask. I lean in close to him and loosen the drawstring. "You might just lead us to our deaths, Arrah N'yar."

Beneath his sweat, he smells like sunshine and cloves. "No one can live forever," I whisper in his ear. He lets out a little huff of disappointment.

I take the mask and peer into the Zu warrior's last memory, scanning the horizon to find the ridge where the refugees fled before the battle. I start up the trail again with the others falling in line behind me. I gather the magic from the ground, the trees, the sky, pulling it around us, into a shimmering net. The shield is not so different from the one my mother had made to protect the villa. That her protection still stands so long after her death is another testament to her gift with magic.

"I thought I was ready to die," Tyrek says, winded, "but I've changed my mind. The world would be lost without my company."

I stop at the head of a pass leading up to a ridge that curves around the mountain. The last of the sunlight washes over the forest, shifting the sky to the first signs of night. "There."

It's dark when we reach the ridge underneath the stars and full moon. I turn in circles as Tyrek leans against a tree to rest. Sukar and

Essnai keep their eyes open for trouble. "I can feel something here," I murmur.

I let go of the shield and tap into the chieftains' magic again to get a clearer picture. White light stretches out in every direction from the spot where I stand, a mess of confusing trails. *There isn't enough time,* says a man hauling two children and a baby in his arms. *Which path?* cries another. *It's too late,* someone else screams.

The memory is of the group the Zu warrior had seen fleeing before the demons attacked. They're the last to come here. "It's a crossroads." My heart drums against my chest. "The Zu created a maze of roads to trick the demons and give the survivors time to escape." I don't tell them that it's like the maze that Efiya used to trick me. "You have to walk the right path, or else the other paths will lead you in circles."

"You've found them," Essnai says, her eyes wide.

"Not yet." I inhale, and the tightness in my chest loosens a bit. "I need to figure out which path to take."

"But we're close," adds Sukar. "I count that as a win."

It's hard to temper my growing excitement, too, after two hard weeks between the assassins and the Demon King. A part of me had been afraid that we would come here and find nothing, but this is so much more than I could ever hope for. With the crossroads, we have a clear path to finding the tribal people. "Should we go tonight or wait until morning—"

"Watch out!" Tyrek pushes me aside.

Something lands with a heavy thump and rolls across the ground. I stare down in horror at the severed head at our feet—the mud-caked hair, the bloody face, the dead hazel eyes. It's the man who I turned into a *ndzumbi*. I hear it at once: the rustle of footfalls in the leaves and swords drawing from scabbards. The assassins haven't fallen for my trick, and they've come to take their revenge.

TWENTY-TWO
ARRAH

Thirty black-clad assassins slink across the mountain brush wielding straight swords and shotels. They spread out, cutting off any possible escape route. Essnai and Sukar have their weapons ready before I even think to call my magic. I don't want to hurt these people, but from the determined looks in their eyes, we may not have a choice.

Tyrek nudges my side as the assassins draw close. "Now would be the time to do something fancy with your magic."

"Clever," Sukar says, the symbols on his sickles glowing. "Let's taunt the person who's likely going to save your butt tonight."

"I'm sure you'd rather she not," Tyrek retorts. "One more person out of your way."

"Can you both stop," I snap. "This isn't the time for petty bickering. I need to think."

"There's always time for petty bickering," Tyrek says as I fling out my arm to deflect a dagger headed for his heart. He stumbles back, shaking. "I guess I see your point."

The assassins race for us, headlong, their swords raised. More daggers slice through the air, and Essnai and Sukar take turns knocking them back one by one. "Think faster!" Essnai says as one clips her staff.

Frantic, I snatch magic from the night sky. It rushes forward and burns through my skin. Angry welts rise on my hands and arms, and I can feel them on my face and neck. With the draw of magic, the Demon King surges forward into my mind, his rage and frustration mixing with my own.

I put up another shield, and the three closest assassins run straight through it. I grimace as they drop to their knees, their shotels hitting the ground. It takes all my strength not to look away. Smoke wafts up from the assassins' elaras and their skin. In mere moments they ignite in flame and fall in a heap of ashes. The other assassins slow their approach and stay well beyond the shield.

"No more have to die today," I shout to the assassins. "Leave, and we'll spare your lives."

"You'll spare our lives?" spits a man with a scar on his right cheek. He points to what's left of the assassin I turned into a *ndzumbi*. "Did you think about his life when you made him do your bidding?"

"As best I recall, you and your thugs are the ones who cut his head off," I shoot back.

"The Almighty One was right about you and your kind." The man looks down his nose at me. "You'll enslave us all if we don't put an end to you now."

"Don't say she didn't give you fair warning." Sukar lets out a deep sigh. "You had a chance to walk away."

"Give us the prince and the tribal witch," the man offers, "and we'll spare you."

Tyrek points one of his shotels at the mess of melted flesh and bone and ashes where the first assassins fell. "How about you come and get us yourself and see if you fare any better than your friends."

One of the assassins takes off his craven bone pendant of a ram's head and thrusts it into the edge of my shield. I recoil as the anti-magic brushes against my senses, and the shield dims a little. "Oh, good," the man with the scar says, his voice like stone striking stone. "I do like things the hard way."

Another assassin is kneeling to add his pendant to the edge of the barrier when an arrow plunges into his eye. A figure leaps from tree to tree, shrouded in shadows, with a bow slung across their back. I thought I'd imagined someone helping us when the scouting party attacked before. I'd dismissed it as a delusion from my injury. The assassins scatter across the ridge, ducking behind trees as the archer shoots arrow after arrow. I squint, trying to make out the archer's face, but they're too far away. One thing's for sure, they move like a skilled fighter, quick and light on their feet. But who would be hiding their identity while they help us—what could be the reason for such secrecy?

"Let down the shield." Sukar rolls his wrists, the moonlight gleaming off his sickles. He has a hungry look in his eyes like he wants nothing more than to hurt someone—to kill. The rage to strike, to fight, to do more than be afraid.

"Either now or later," Essnai says. "They'll keep coming."

"Do the two of you coordinate your bad ideas, or is it a

coincidence?" Tyrek moans, looking resentfully at them.

We have no choice but to fight. I release the shield, and the assassins descend upon the ridge in a blur of blood, pain, and death. I'm numb as I pull lightning from the sky, searing flesh and splitting skulls. When it's over, the archer's gone. I stare down at the thirty dead assassins, feeling a cold detachment as I set their remains on fire.

They deserved to die, the Demon King says in my mind.

I don't disagree.

We're bone-tired when we set up camp on the ridge amidst the assassins' ashes. With the threat behind us, I call upon magic to see across time again to study the crossroads Tribe Zu built to escape the demons.

My vision bursts into a tapestry of shadows and light woven into the memories of the last people to flee the demons. Two hundred and forty-seven had gathered along the ridge, two with the gift to see the crossroads. The group stayed back to help set traps and fortify the magic around the Zu camp. They were people who hoped that one day they'd have something to come home to.

The memories paint a gruesome story of the Zu's last stand. Broken bodies of warriors lie everywhere—the dead and the dying. A girl, no more than twelve, stands between the advancing demons and the crossroads. Tattoos shift on her ebony skin, taking a new shape as she raises her arms in an arc over her head. A circle of ashes settles on the ground about the crossroads, forming a shield. Outside it, a hundred people who'd been with the group turn back to fight the demons.

The Zu wield magic and weapons alike, slicing and cutting and severing and impaling. They open sinkholes in the ground, turn vines and trees into living, thrashing killers. Magic shaped into hyenas and lions and cheetahs stalks out of the forest to attack the demons. But these demons aren't like the ones we fought at the Temple of Heka. I stumble back as the memory plays out, dread sinking in my belly.

The demons are tall and winged, with teeth sharpened into points—like the boy from my dreams. Their magic is stronger, more refined, more sinister. Wounds to the heart and broken necks and missing heads only slow them down. One by one, their bodies remake themselves or shift into gray smoke, so weapons cannot hurt them. They tear through the Zu warriors in mere moments.

I wrap my arm around my belly, struggling to take in the memories without falling apart. Is this why the orishas couldn't stop the demons before, could only trap them in the void in Kefu? *Twenty-gods*. They wouldn't die.

An old woman grabs the girl, and her shield snuffs out like flames doused with rain. The woman pulls her away, and tears stream down both their cheeks. The girl resists as she takes in the blood and broken bodies. She sees the demons rising from the dead, sees them sprouting phantom wings.

Come, child. The woman tugs on the girl's arm. *We must join the other tribes before it's too late. We'll be stronger together*. This time the girl relents. As soon as they step onto the path, it disappears, and so do they.

The crossroads aren't only in Tribe Zu—how had I not thought of that before? Just as the *edam* banded together to help me defeat my sister, the tribes would've had a plan to evade the demons. The crossroads must be a network connecting all the tribes. That means that there *are* still people from all five tribes somewhere, hiding. They're alive. But not all—not the ones who stayed behind to protect the crossroads, not the warriors who fought. I watch in horror as the demons bind those who survived the onslaught—nearly a hundred people—and march them into the crossroads.

"No," I whisper as the last of the memories fade.

"What did you see?" Essnai asks, her voice desperate. "What is it?"

I draw in a ragged breath, tears blotting out my vision. I can't stop shaking. "Survivors from every tribe—not just Zu—escaped through the crossroads, but . . ." I can barely bring myself to say it. I don't want it to be true. "The demons entered the crossroads."

"That's not very promising news," Tyrek mutters, bleak as always.

"Then we go, too." Sukar stares into the campfire. "We can still save them."

He'll be seeing things differently once I tell them about these new demons, but for now, we need rest. We do not know what tomorrow will bring once we enter the crossroads. I curl up on my pallet, exhausted, and slip into a dream. I'm in the little cabin with Daho in the early morning. The first veins of sunlight shine against his silver skin and the flour on his cheek. He crosses the room in three steps and plants a warm kiss on my mouth that sends tingles through my body. "I made a cake," he says. "It's the first anniversary of the day you saved my life, so I figured we should celebrate."

I don't have the heart to tell him that in one year, his cells, his blood, and his soul have changed. He's one step closer to death. I smile at the lopsided cake slathered in purple buttercream. No one has ever made a cake for me. "It's beautiful."

"No, it's not." Daho laughs. "It's ugly, but it tastes good."

"I can help you live forever," I say, not sure if my plan will work. "Would you like that?"

Daho slumps in the chair at the table. "If it means I get to be with you, then yes." His gaze flits to the floor. "But first, I need to go to Jiiek to avenge my family."

The scene changes, and Daho and I sit together on the bed. I press my lips against his, catching him off guard. He breaks into a smile and pulls me into his arms. His lips are soft and warm and wild as I climb into his lap.

"Dimma," Daho breaths against my mouth. "Is this what you want?"

"I want you," I whisper. "I want you in all the ways mortals can have each other."

His teeth graze the nape of my neck, and I tremble in anticipation. "I might have a few ideas."

I wake from the dream with a start, and I bolt up on the pallet. Someone grabs my shoulders. I struggle against them, desperate to free myself. The dream lingers in my mind, the feel of his lips against mine, the touch of his silky feathers. "No," I gasp as my whole body aches for him.

"Arrah!" Essnai shouts my name. Smoke rises from her seared hands where she's touching me. I cover my mouth in horror.

"I'm sorry!"

Essnai grimaces. "I'm fine."

I take her hands into my own, tears blurring my vision. "I could've . . ." I don't finish the words as I spread magic across her palms like it's a salve. Her wounds heal.

"I'm better now." Essnai glances at Sukar, who looks worried.

Still reeling from the dream, I rush away from the camp, needing to be alone. "I'm not her," I repeat until my mouth is dry. "I'm not Dimma."

I breathe in the night air, and my lungs ache. It feels good. It feels real. I am real, and this is my life. I stop with my hands on my knees, sparks of magic circling me like a stirred-up hornets' nest.

Essnai is quiet as she steps up behind me, but I sense the calming nature of her soul. I let it wash over me, hoping that it can calm me, too. "Do you want to talk about it?"

"No." I cringe. "I want to forget."

"Okay."

"What?" I whirl around. "I hurt you, and your answer is 'okay.'"

Essnai shrugs, her face unbothered. "You said you don't want to talk about it."

We sit together in the dark, and I half bury my face against her shoulder. I'm a little kid again lost in the desert after running away from the woman who traded her years for magic at Imebyé. Essnai had found me crying that night. "He's different in my dreams than the orishas make him out to be in the stories," I confess. "How can I know what's real?"

"Have you considered that both are true?" Essnai pulls me closer, and I sag against her, knowing that in this moment I'm safe. "He was a man and a monster."

I already know it to be true, but I don't want to believe it.

"Stop trying to carry the weight of the world alone." Her voice is an anchor to my drifting boat. "Sukar and I will always be here for you. We'll help you through this thing with the Demon King when you're ready."

I pull away from Essnai, dread filling my chest. "I need you to promise me something, okay?" She cocks an eyebrow. "Promise me that if something goes wrong, you'll save yourself." Before she can protest, I add, "Run straight back to Kira. One of us should have a chance at a normal life. Heka knows that it won't be me. You both deserve to be happy."

Essnai looks away, a shadow passing across her face. "I miss her nagging me with some random historical fact and her obsession with always being right. I miss teasing her, and I miss her smile." Essnai's voice falters. "I miss her."

"Then go and be with her," I beg. "Don't waste the precious time you have."

"If things turn for the worse, I will," Essnai promises, and I know that I can take her word for it. At least she'll be safe.

The demons on the crossroads were stronger and faster than any demon we've ever fought before. I don't tell Essnai what I know to be truth. It isn't a matter of *if* things turn for the worse; it's a matter of *when*.

TWENTY-THREE
RUDJEK

One day on Zeknorian soil and I've got myself shot and poisoned. Not bad for a pretend prince playing commandant. If I thought sneaking to the docks at night with Majka and Kira had been daring, my voyage to the North had one-upped it. I'd gone from getting black eyes in alleys to almost bringing down the wrath of an army out for blood. As night falls over Zeknor, I miss the comforts of home, hot baths, copious amounts of spicy sausage, the arena. I miss Arrah and wonder if she's found the tribal people yet. Not for the first time, I regret not telling her about the demons and my plans to come North. I regret asking Kira to keep it secret from Essnai, too.

As campfires flicker in the gloom of night, Fadyi and I stand outside my tent. At my orders, Captain Dakte runs the soldiers through drills. They need to stay sharp, especially with a third of the gendars looking ashen and reeking of vomit after falling ill on the voyage. That's at least one thing that he and I agree upon. Jahla, along with Majka and Kira, left hours ago to oversee setting up a perimeter around camp.

"Are you still unwell?" Fadyi asks, glancing at the cut across my sleeve.

I attempt and fail to lift my arm. It's completely numb from shoulder to fingertip and heavy as stone. "Unwell is an understatement." I clear my throat, and my mouth feels like it's filled with desert sand. "Can you or Jahla do anything about the poison?"

"Ezaric could've drawn it out." Fadyi strokes his chin, his brow furrowed in concentration. His expression reminds me of what he said on the ship about his *kind eyes* and *authoritative beard*. "He could heal any internal ailment not to do with decay, but it takes a level of talent neither Jahla nor I have."

I swipe away the sweat gathering on my brow. "So, I'm going to die?"

Fadyi frowns like he's clueless as to how I could have come up with that conclusion. "Your best chance is to push the poison out of your blood on your own."

"Ah, of course," I grumble, like it's no big deal. "Why didn't I think of that."

"Use the means at your disposal," Fadyi says. "Humans have several methods to rid themselves of waste."

The timing is not good. The Zeknorians have been somewhat friendly since we've stopped trying to kill each other. Commander Korr gave permission for us to set up tents, though I'm rather put out that he made sure we were downwind from Abezer. Black ash from the town mixes with snow in the biting wind, coating everyone and everything. Every gust brings in the strong smell of charred wood and flesh. Like it or not, I need Korr's full support to move about in Zeknor. His complement of soldiers is equal to mine, but he could call for more if he hasn't already. "Have you gotten word from Raëke about the craven reinforcements?" I shift on my heels as an aching pain catches in my shoulder, creeping toward my chest. "Are they coming?"

"You'll be the first to know if I hear anything," Fadyi says, pulling at the hairs in his goatee. "In truth, I'm concerned that we haven't gotten word from her yet. Lord Re'Mec shouldn't have sent her off without informing us first."

I pat Fadyi on the shoulder with my good arm. "You're finally starting to see Re'Mec for the worm he is."

"Worm?" The sun god steps out of a cloud of ash. "You need to work on your limited vocabulary, Rudjek."

"And you need to stop popping up when no one's summoned you." I'm still pissed that he made the situation with the Zeknorians worse with his big mouth.

Re'Mec laughs as if delighted by the exchange of insults. He really isn't much different from his persona of Tam, except for the whole god thing. "Your reinforcements should arrive in two days with the favor of Mouran's winds. That should give you enough time to win Commander Korr's favor."

"And what of the other orishas?" I ask. "Will they bother to show up this time or stay idle while we fight your war?"

His eyes flash with angry blue flames, but I refuse to back down. "Did I hit a tender nerve, Lord Re'Mec?"

The sun god breaks into a smile, and the night sky brightens a bit even though there's no moon in sight. "Our children used to revere us and cling to our every word without challenge, but times have changed." He puts his hands on his hips as he gazes upon the camp with feigned interest, stalling to answer. "We'll have Koré's support, Mouran's, and Sisi's, who could never resist a fight."

I'm not surprised about Mouran, the sea god, who helped Arrah get back to the Kingdom all those months ago on his ship. I remember hearing about Sisi, the orisha of fire, and her short temper in my history lessons. "Is Koré back? Has she visited Arrah?"

"Yes, yes," Re'Mec mumbles under his breath. "Arrah, Tyrek, and the others are quite fine."

"Why is Tyrek with her?" I ask, and gendars gathered around a fire nearby go quiet to eavesdrop.

Re'Mec frowns. "Do I look like the tribal witch's keeper?"

"Don't call her that," I say through gritted teeth.

Re'Mec shrugs like it makes no difference to him. "Last I heard, your father sent assassins after her and Tyrek, and she destroyed them."

My whole body shakes at the news, and my blood boils. My father hasn't changed one bit. He's still the same person who had a young girl tortured. The man who sent one son away and kept the other hidden from the public out of embarrassment. How could I ever think him any better than what he's shown me? "You're sure Arrah's okay?"

"You should worry about her, but for a different reason," Re'Mec remarks. "She obliterated your father's most trained assassins with a flick of her wrist."

"And what should she have done instead?" I glare at him. "She was defending herself."

"She could've handled the situation in any number of ways," Re'Mec insists. "You must see the power imbalance—why magic is so dangerous in the hands of mortals?"

"Sounds like she's handling her magic just fine," I say, frustrated with him. I should be with Arrah. She shouldn't have to fend off my father's men with the likes of Tyrek by her side. I can't fathom what she must think of my family now. I'll be lucky if she ever talks to me again.

I have every intention of confronting my father when we return home. I already know he'll make excuses, claim that he did it for the Kingdom. Coward. He's scared of her becoming *Ka*-Priestess with the loyalists' support. But he's overplayed his hand, and I'll make sure he fails. "I need to change," I say. "Captain Dakte and I are meeting with Commander Korr in an hour."

"Do you need me to come along?" Re'Mec asks.

"Absolutely not." I enter my tent and let the curtain drop behind me.

"He's in a rather foul mood," I hear Re'Mec whisper to Fadyi on the other side.

Ignoring them, I take a bath and change into a white-and-gold elara, thinking it best to present in my princely role instead of as the commandant. Captain Dakte and I head for the Zeknorian camp on foot with six guards, Fadyi and Jahla among them. The camp is upwind of the burned city, and the air is crisp. We're greeted by two Zeknorians, one who identifies himself as Commander Korr's Second. The Second leads us into a tent that's larger than the others but half the size of my own.

"So, you claim that demons destroyed Abezer," Commander

Korr says, stoking a fire. Smoke rises through slits where the cloth gathers above it. "The monsters from your kingdom's fables."

I slip off my shoes by the entrance. "I'm afraid so."

Commander Korr looks amused and waves the iron rod in his hand. "There is no need for that, Crown Prince. We don't eat on the ground in the North."

I bite my tongue at the slight. The world spins a little, and I can't seem to find my center of balance. Commander Korr sweeps to the table at the center of the tent and gestures for us to join him. He picks up a jug and pours himself a drink, then one for Captain Dakte and me. "It's a wonder that you eat at all," I manage to say, "with the way you partake in your spirits."

"I see why Princess Veeka wrote so passionately on your behalf." Korr laughs, and that stuns me into silence. "She spoke of your father's claims that *demons* helped the *Ka*-Priestess and her daughter attack your capital city. Our king has his doubts about the validity of that information."

Captain Dakte uses my silence as a chance to interject. "Do you know Princess Veeka well?"

"She's my niece," Commander Korr says with no affection. "Her mother is my half sister—one of the Zeknorian king's bastards, same as me. Caught the eye of King Qu'setta of Galke at a social gathering and became his third wife."

"I'm grateful for Princess Veeka's kind words," I remark as Commander Korr gulps down his liquor. "I assure you we wouldn't have marched onto Zeknorian soil without good reason."

"My official position on the matter must align with our king's, you see." He pours himself another round. "My father has been itching for a war with the Kingdom since Jerek Sukkara slighted him in a trade deal. From his viewpoint, you declared war the moment you arrived on our shores."

I start to speak, but Captain Dakte cuts across me. "Do you think the Almighty One would send his heir apparent to lead an invasion of a foreign land? Come now, Commander Korr, we're both sensible men."

"Our good sense has nothing to do with war." Commander Korr grimaces. "What better way for your prince to earn his place than in a bloody battle between two formidable forces?"

I have half a mind to dismiss Captain Dakte and make him wait for me outside. He's making me look green to get the point across that my father wouldn't have sent *his heir* if the situation wasn't dire. We're *talking* to a prince; that should've tipped him off that in Zeknor, it isn't unusual for one to go into battle. I don't think it's a coincidence either that the demons chose to come to a country at odds with the Kingdom. Shezmu had counted on the petty delays of diplomacy to keep us busy and out of his way. Re'Mec said that he was clever, and I was starting to see the shape his plans had taken.

I clear my throat and redirect the conversation. "You said your official position must lie with your king. You appear to be a man who keeps himself well informed. What is your *unofficial* position?"

Captain Dakte cuts his eyes at me, looking annoyed for a moment before he hides it.

"Had we not already lost three villages before you showed up, I would've cut you down on sight," Commander Korr says. "But I believe your story about the demons. We've heard some strange reports coming out of the Kingdom. One such report said that you and a handful of others battled the demons in the tribal lands and won. An exaggeration, I'm sure."

"Then you see that it would be advantageous for us to help each other." Captain Dakte takes a sip from his cup and coughs when the liquor hits his throat.

Commander Korr watches him, carefully. Without his furs, the Zeknorian is still a large man, with thick dark hair, pale wind-burned skin, and a gold tooth. I reach for my cup, and sharp pain cuts through my chest. I bite back a wince.

"You don't look very well, Crown Prince," Commander Korr says, his eyes on me now. "Are you sure our arrow didn't hit you? Even a nick or a splinter would kill a man."

"I'm still a little ill from the voyage." I force myself to take the cup and gulp the liquor down at once. It tastes foul and burns, but I keep my face smooth under Commander Korr's scrutiny. I tell him what we know about the demons. "Shezmu killed a god named Iben and took his powers to control the gate that once connected our world to theirs. He's planning to reunite the demon army so they can lay waste to our world." As I relay this information to Korr, my gut's telling me that there's more to it. I'm missing something. Why hasn't Shezmu opened the gate and brought more demons through yet? Or *had* he and they're lying in wait to attack? But to what end?

The commander listens without comment, pouring more liquor into his mug. When he offers the same to us, Captain Dakte shakes his head while I accept another. "To be frank," he says, "I'm not sure I want to ally myself with a man who can't hold his drink and a sickly boy."

Captain Dakte tenses beside me, and I lean closer to Commander

Korr, staring him straight in the eyes. "This sickly boy fought the demons several times and won. Maybe I can teach you a thing or two before you lose another village."

Commander Korr strokes his beard. "I'll consider your offer."

"That's all we ask." I come to my feet, my head spinning. "Don't consider too long, lest your country be the first that the demons destroy."

I don't wait for him to answer. I sweep out of the tent, and Captain Dakte joins me moments later. "Have you lost your mind—storming out like that?" he asks, his voice sharp.

"Let him think about it while another village falls to the demons." I stumble, pitching forward, my breath cutting short. Captain Dakte catches my arm to keep me from falling. When I straighten myself up, he holds on to me.

"I saw that arrow scrape your arm," he says. "You're not sick from the voyage."

"You're mistaken." I laugh off his concern.

I find my way into my tent with my friends at my side. Fadyi and Majka help me to the cot in the back, and I drop onto it, my eyes drifting closed. Their voices ring in my ears, but none of the words make sense. I'm in and out of sleep, and I dream about blood and screams and death. I dream about Arrah, too. She lies on the cot with me, tucking herself against my side, her skin warm and heavenly.

She brushes my sweat-slick forehead. "You have to wake up now."

I stir on the cot and peel my eyes open. The canopy is so thick that I can't tell if it's morning yet. I sway a bit before I get my bearings. It takes only a moment for me to realize something is wrong.

I hear echoes of pain throughout the camp and catch the scent of blood on the air. I'm halfway to the tent flap when Fadyi steps inside.

"What's happened?" I say, my voice hoarse.

Fadyi holds up his hands to stop me from advancing. "Slow down, Rudjek. You've been out for two days."

"Two days?" I stumble past him, pushing the flap open. "What's he done?"

"Our scouts found the demon encampment while you were unconscious," Fadyi explains. "Captain Dakte attacked them without the Zeknorians' support. Reinforcements arrived from the Dark Forest, but I couldn't convince our craven brethren to aid the Kingdom. They will only take orders from a leader of the Elder or Eldest bloodline—from you."

My legs almost give out when I take in the camp, full of the dead and the dying, bodies strewn on cots everywhere. Captain Dakte may have destroyed our only chance to stop Shezmu from opening the gate.

TWENTY-FOUR
ARRAH

The sun rises over the Barat Mountains, bathing the forest and ridge in golden ribbons of light. I draw my knees to my chest, my magic curling around me like a blanket, but there's no warmth to be had. I sit apart from my friends, away from the crossroads, serenaded by birdsong. I'm bothered by the ease with which I killed the assassins and my numbness to the whole affair. In my heart of hearts, I know that my actions are still my own, and I can't blame the Demon King.

With my magic, I'm a danger to my friends and especially to Rudjek. I can't reconcile knowing these things and still believing that I can go back to my dream of reopening my father's shop. I can't stop hoping that Rudjek and I can beat the odds, that we don't end up another tragic story. But we're both fools thinking that things could be different.

I hear Sukar's near-silent footfalls before he crests the hill behind me. "Did you sleep up here with the frogs?" His voice is bright, and I can tell that he's come to cheer me up.

"No." It isn't exactly a lie. I didn't sleep as much as sit here all night, sulking in my misery.

Sukar thrusts a cup of mint tea into my hand and settles cross-legged beside me. "I come bearing gifts."

I cock an eyebrow at him. "You carried tea all the way here?"

"You look like you could use something stronger, but Tyrek is stingy with his wine these days," Sukar says. "Once a spoiled little prince, always a spoiled little prince."

"You're not being fair to him." I inhale the steam from the tea. It smells exactly like my father's blend, the mint and honey in the perfect proportions. "He's proven himself and his loyalty."

Sukar flourishes his hand dismissively. "Doesn't mean I can't give him a hard time."

I take a sip from the cup, letting the tea roll over my tongue and warm me from the inside. "The demons we're tracking are nothing like the ones we fought at the Temple. They're faster, stronger, more powerful. They can't be easily killed, if at all."

"If we find the tribal people, they'll add to your strength," he says. "No one's invincible."

If we find them. There is so much doubt in his voice, even if he's trying to sound strong and brave. "When we find them," I reassure him. "The demons could've consumed their souls on this ridge, but they didn't. They left a trail for me to follow."

"To what end, if the Demon King already has a connection with you?" Sukar asks, shifting on his haunches.

"I don't know," I say, "but why else would they take a hundred people alive?"

Sukar drums his fingers against his knee. "I think we're missing something."

The wind blows and whips up his smell of sunlight and cloves. I want to sink against him, the way I did with Essnai, but I can't, not like when we were younger. It doesn't feel the same. His touch is a reminder that Rudjek and I are worlds apart—his anti-magic, his future as Almighty One, his life among the Kingdom's elite. Tyrek said that no Sukkarra or Omari ever married for love—only political gain. I will never fit in that life. "I wish we knew what was happening in the North with Rudjek and the others."

Sukar stares over the ridge, tracking the path of a hawk gliding across the sky. "Rudjek is lucky to have you." His tattoos vibrate with energy, wobbling like they can't tell if he's getting ready to run or fight.

I clutch the cup hard to stop my hands from shaking.

"Arrah," he says, breathless, his eyes full of yearning. It's like I'm seeing him for the first time, vulnerable, brave, beautiful. But Sukar doesn't finish his thought, and my name is swept away in the awkward silence that follows. After a moment, he clears his throat. "Well, we better get going soon." Disappointment threads through his words.

"Yes." I climb to my feet, glad that he changed the subject. "I suspect we have some traveling yet to do, and the crossroads will be confusing to navigate from what I've seen so far."

Sukar is quiet as we descend the hill and join Essnai and Tyrek on the ridge. Once we've packed our things, I stand at the edge of the crossroads; the sunlight almost washes out the paths. "Stay close to me," I tell my friends. "One wrong step and it'll be next to impossible to find you again."

Tyrek yawns and stretches his arms. "Your pep talk could use some work."

"And your tongue could use a rest," I say, stepping onto the path.

We follow the spiraling maze for hours, walking in circles, straight lines, and loops. I keep my eyes pinned to the ground, watching the faint magic fade in and out. We take sharp turns, retrace our steps, and hack our way through thick brush. It seems nonsensical on the surface, like we are four wandering fools lost on the mountain.

I'm in awe of the talent it would take to make something so sophisticated. Had one witchdoctor built the crossroads, or had it been an effort that took many people working together? It reminds me that I could still do so much good with the chieftains' gift, if given the chance. But it's not worth the risk of keeping my magic after we find the tribal people and this ordeal with the demons is over. I hate that I don't really have a choice. The Demon King will still be with me as long as the chieftains' *kas* are tied to mine.

We follow the memories of the tribal people, herded like cattle. It's midday when we come upon a fork in the path where hundreds of impressions overlap. I stop cold.

Essnai glances around, although I know that she only sees the sun shining down on the mountain. "What's wrong?"

The memory is dark around the edges, and something hums underneath the surface. Hundreds of survivors from every tribe—Aatiri, Mulani, Kes, Litho, and Zu—gather on the path. They think they're safe until the faint white lines on the crossroads flicker in and out for a brief moment. Gray smoke converges on their position, and the demons that attacked Tribe Zu trap them. With their new prisoners in tow, the demons twist and blend the white lines to make a new path. "The demons captured many more people after they entered the crossroads," I say. This is much worse than I expected. "Then they changed the path."

"What do you mean, changed the path?" Essnai asks.

"The tribes created one path and the demons altered it." I massage my forehead. "I don't know why."

Even Tyrek looks put out by the news. "How many more people did they take?"

I watch impressions of the demons march the tribal people down the new path. "Hundreds."

"Koré told Arrah that the demons are in the North," Sukar says. "So maybe this new path is a shortcut to there."

"Are we prepared for that?" Tyrek asks, shifting on his heels.

"Prepared or not, we don't have a choice," I say.

Tyrek wrinkles his nose. "There's always a choice."

"You can choose to step off the path and disappear," Sukar suggests.

"Give it a rest, will you?" Tyrek groans. "I'm not your competition. He's in the North playing hero while you're pestering me."

Essnai glances between Sukar and me, and we both look away to keep from meeting her eyes. I can almost hear the questions working through her mind—questions I don't want to answer. Questions I can't answer without betraying my own heart. "We've already made our choice," she says. "We're going after the missing tribal people with or without you, so stop being a miserable little twit."

Tyrek blinks at her, his face confused. "Am I really a miserable little twit? Because I don't feel all that miserable these days. Maybe it's the company I'm keeping."

"From here on out, the next one to pass an insult gets left behind, okay?" I ignore their grumbles as I lead the way again, following the path where the five groups vanished.

One moment we're on the mountain, then we're near the ruins of Heka's Temple. The transition is jarring and disorienting. Both Essnai and Tyrek get sick, and we have to stop to rest, which helps with the dizziness. It happens three more times. From Heka's Temple to the reed fields along the Serpent River to the deserts of Yöom—and then to a Northern village, as Sukar suspected.

The wind and snow whip against our faces as we stand in front of an arch made of bones. It breathes magic. Sparks buzz around it like fireflies, illuminating the gaps between the bones. I don't understand how it's so solid, or how it's the only thing in the village not covered in snow. I breathe in cold air that stings my lungs.

"What is that?" Tyrek whispers, his voice almost whisked away in the howl of the wind.

"You can see it, too?" I whirl around to face him. I'm surprised and glad at once.

"Of course I can." Tyrek reaches for it. "It's like a whirlpool in the middle of the sky. I've never seen anything like it."

"Don't touch it," I snap, and he pulls away. "We don't know what it is."

"Whirlpool?" Sukar frowns, staring at it. "It's a forest."

"I see silks of all colors hanging from clotheslines flapping in the wind," Essnai says.

"So, we each see something different?" I turn around in a circle to get a good look at the village around it. We're in the middle of a courtyard, the ground icy beneath our feet. The houses are stone supported by wood beams with crooked roofs. No smoke curls up from any of the chimneys. "The tribal people aren't here. I don't feel their magic."

I face the bone arch again, a feeling of foreboding threading through my veins. I know this place. I've been through . . . *the gate* before. The memory fills in my mind in bits and pieces. A starry night, the ground trembling, a familiar voice. Some part of the gate calls to me like an old friend. "It's the gate between Zöran and Ilora—the gate between all worlds." *Ilora*. The word rolls off my tongue with ease, like I've said it countless times.

"And you think the demons took the tribal people through it?" Tyrek asks. "We don't know what's on the other side."

"It wouldn't be here if they hadn't," Essnai says.

I don't have a chance to answer as I turn my attention back to the village. I hadn't felt any magic from the houses only a moment ago, but now it chokes the air. It's nothing like the feather touch of tribal magic—it reeks of an insatiable hunger. The demons draw back the curtains in the houses as if they've just noticed us. Then I hear the creaking of doors opening. Pebbles and ice crack underfoot.

Sukar pulls his sickles. He senses the demons, too. "How many?"

"A lot," I say, my voice coming out in puffs of white mist. Among the demons, there is one with magic that feels like a thousand prying eyes crawling over my skin. It drags up my old nightmares, the night of the awful ritual. My father's mouth stretching into a gaping hole, his body convulsing against the altar. The children's souls trapped in jars. "We have to go." I back away, my heart hammering against my chest. "Shezmu's here." I don't have to say more.

Shezmu is the most powerful of the Demon King's generals, and it can be no accident the new path on the crossroads led me to him. I killed his daughter—he'll want revenge for that. But he also needs me to release his master. I'll have to face him soon enough, but right now, the tribal people are more important.

I turn to the gate. I'm not sure if the tribal people are still alive, but I'm going to find out one way or another. Essnai and Sukar tense at my sides, but neither speaks as I step through the arch, and the gate swallows me whole.

PART IV

THE UNNAMED ORISHA: DIMMA

Fram once asked me if, had another person fallen from the sky on my mountain, I would love them the same as I love Daho. I've pondered that question in the moments between my many deaths and rebirths. I still don't know the answer, but I do know that my love for Daho cast a shadow over my mortal lives. I always had trouble bonding with others—until something changed in my final life. Alas, that is the end, and we are talking about the beginning. I will tell you about my gift to Daho.

We stand on a hill overlooking the royal city of Jiiek. Demons move around us, young and old, some with wings as crooked as tree roots. Some have knots of jagged bone where wings once had been. The word *castration* bubbles to my lips, but I hold my tongue as Daho grieves for his people.

"How could this happen?" Daho asks through his tears.

I open myself to the demons' thoughts to answer that very question. The people had lived in peace for twelve generations under the

Daneers—Daho's family. There were no wars, within or without. Their nation flourished. A millennium before, their scientists had discovered cures to all known diseases. Life expectancy tripled. No one went hungry or homeless or suffered. But a growing faction believed that their people were becoming something unnatural. They wanted to return to traditional ways. When Daho's father ignored their grievances, they incited violence.

Their leader, Yaneki, killed Daho's family and punished those who opposed him. He had thousands of people beaten and stripped of their possessions. He had their wings broken or cut to remind them of their place. "The new Demon King did this."

Daho's wings flutter open in anger at himself, wide and glorious, and trembling. The tips are iridescent, and a rainbow of light dances across them. "This is my fault. I turned my back on my people."

"What are you doing, fool?" a woman yells. "Stop before someone alerts the Royal Guard."

Daho tenses and his eyes go wide in recognition. "Quiten." He whirls around to face her.

She hobbles closer on a mangled left foot that's healed wrong. Her wings are gone, leaving splintered bone in their place. Her eyes shine with unshed tears as she looks upon Daho, then glances at the people staring and pointing at him. "Come with me. It isn't safe here."

Quiten leads us through the crowded rows of shacks, and my magic spreads over the demons. It makes them forget that they ever saw us. "What are you doing here?" She frowns at me. "The Guard would behead you on sight."

"Why?" Daho asks.

"As soon as Yaneki took the throne," Quiten says, "he gave the endoyans two days to leave our lands or face death."

"But our endoyan cousins have always lived and worked in Jiiek," Daho says.

"Not always." She leads us into a house with a tin roof. "As much as I am relieved to see you alive, it isn't safe in Jiiek, my prince. If Yaneki's spies discover you're back, he'll have you executed."

"Please don't call me prince." Daho winces. "A prince doesn't allow such tragedy to befall his country."

"You will always be our prince." Quiten fidgets with her shaking hands. "No matter the lies Yaneki and his followers tell people."

Daho looks at me when he says his next words, understanding passing between us. "I'm here to take back my throne."

Quiten lets out a deep sigh as tears slide down her cheeks. "The Resistance has lost all hope that we could ever stop Yaneki—he's too powerful. No one who's stood against him has survived." She leans close to Daho and takes his hands into her own. "It can't be an accident that we found each other, Prince. I am at your command."

The next few days are a flurry of people visiting the little house. They talk and plan and plot. Daho tells them of the secret tunnel underneath the lake that leads to the palace. Some of them argue that Yaneki must have found it already, but I assure them he has not.

When we're alone at night, I lay on Daho's bare chest in a room with glass jars of food on shelves. The air smells of spices. "You don't have to fight for your kingdom. I can give it back to you with no effort on your part. Yaneki would be the only casualty."

"It's not the same," Daho says, his teeth grazing my earlobe, the sensation delightful. "I must earn my throne back, or it'll be meaningless. The only things I have left are my honor and you." He opens his mouth and lifts his tongue to remind me of the new organ I put there to prepare him for my gift. It's a simple thing, a node of flesh with a split almost invisible to the mortal eye. The Uthurans use it to eat the souls of the deceased and extend their lives. "Promise me that you'll let me do this on my own."

Daho pulls me close to his chest, and I hear the quickening of his pulse, taste his fear. "I promise I'll let you kill Yaneki on your own," I say, choosing my words with care.

Days and nights pass as I calculate the possibilities of what will happen. Soon Daho is leading seventy-two men through a dark cave by torchlight. "Most of the guards patrol the perimeter of the palace grounds," he tells them. "Once we're inside, focus on the sentries. Leave Yaneki to me."

The men ready their weapons and pour into the palace while Daho lingers behind, his eyes glowing in the dark. "Whatever happens, know that I will always love you, Dimma."

"I've always loved you and always will," I say, knowing it to be true.

Daho presses two fingers to his lips, then presses them to my mouth. "Forever."

He storms the palace with the men, and I wait in the basement as the battle stretches out into a chorus of death. I listen only to Daho's heartbeat, his breathing, the parry of his feet, the way he wields his weapon. He corners Yaneki in a library—and the man is quick as he slips a knife into Daho's chest.

Here is where I break my promise. I dissolve into my true

form—amorphous and fluid. I appear in the throne room the moment Daho collapses to his knees.

The king doesn't see me; instead he laughs at the sight of Daho dying. "Now the Daneer line has ended." He pulls the blade from Daho's chest, and my love crumples to the floor.

The king's guards file into the room and form two lines meant to stop the Resistance fighters, but there is no need. They will not make it this far. "Your death will quell any further thoughts of uprising," Yaneki says. "I should thank you for that."

I cradle Daho against my soul. He's coughing up blood now—his breath catching in his throat. "I'm sorry," he whispers.

"What did you say, boy?" Yaneki scoffs. "You're sorry?"

I send the king hurtling backward until he slams into a chair. His soldiers spring into action to help him.

A hunger awakes inside me—an insatiable need, a longing. "Let me help you."

Daho nods, the light fading from his eyes. I soothe away his pain, repair his body, give him strength. While two guards pick Yaneki up from the floor, Daho stands, too. The guards lunge at him, but I snap their necks. I take no joy in the action, and I bid them farewell as their souls return to the creator.

Yaneki gasps, his eyes wide. "What kind of witchery is this?"

"The best kind," Daho answers as the two fight again, striking and retreating.

What Daho lacks in skill, he makes up for in stamina. He is much younger than the king, who's grown round from celebrating his victory over the Daneer family. Daho slashes Yaneki across his belly.

"That was for my mother and father." Daho wipes sweat from his forehead, leaving behind blood. "This is for every single person you hurt." He plunges his sword into the man's throat. His death is quick.

"It's done," I say.

Daho squats beside Yaneki. The king's soul is fire and rage and discipline. Although it's still intact, lingering in his body, it's starting to unspool. Daho glances up at me when I retake my physical form. I sense his hesitation, and I smile to encourage him. He squeezes open the man's mouth, then opens his own. The organ beneath his tongue shivers, growing wider and wider and wider still. Golden light spills from inside it. Daho's soul. Determined, resilient, vengeful.

Yaneki's soul yanks free of his body, and as soon as Daho consumes it, I join with him. We become a tangle of three souls—Daho's, Yaneki's, and mine. My hunger to save him returns. It's so intense that I almost lose myself to it. I want to devour both their souls to keep them close to me forever, but I let go of the hunger, pushing it away. I weave together Daho's and Yaneki's souls with a part of my own, giving him my immortality and with it, my gifts.

"What have you done, Dimma!" Koré hisses as she snatches us apart.

Koré is in physical form while Re'Mec is white light and shifting shadows. He strikes with a sword that appears out of thin air. The blade is quick and precise. I scream the moment it takes Daho's head. The palace shakes, and quakes tear across Ilora, splitting the land.

Daho's broken body melts into smoke—only to reform anew, uninjured. He's curled up on the floor, shaking. "It can't be," Koré says. "It's impossible."

"Abomination." Re'Mec raises his sword to strike again, but this time Koré blocks the blow with her blade. Re'Mec melts from white light into physical form, looking annoyed and shocked that she's opposed him.

"It's done now, brother," she says, her fascination outweighing her anger. She turns to me, and her soul scrapes against my own, a warning. "Don't make me regret showing him mercy."

TWENTY-FIVE
ARRAH

The gate is a pool of black ink and veins of light that leads to endless worlds. Energy hums against our ears as the darkness peels away the fibers of our bodies bit by bit. The process isn't painful—there is no physical sensation at all. We unravel until we become pulses of sounds, the lingering echo of a song, an afterthought.

We glide like raindrops on a slanted roof, careening over the edge and landing on the other side of the gate. Whole again, head spinning, I whirl around, intending to defend us against Shezmu and his army. I blink as thick fog rolls across my vision.

"It's gone," Essnai says, her voice a whisper.

"You can call the gate back, can't you?" Tyrek asks, stepping in front of me.

I draw my gaze up from the fog to his panicked face, set in contrast against the night. His cheeks appear sharper, and his dark eyes gleam with light. The moon hangs low in the sky, the iridescent color of a seashell when the sun hits it at the perfect angle.

Sukar stares at writhing weeds that change from stark white to bloodred to white again. "This isn't Ilora."

"How could you possibly know that?" Tyrek laughs, but it doesn't cover the panic in his voice. "Why would the demons take their prisoners anywhere other than their world?"

"You don't spend your whole life an attendant in the Temple and not know the holy text." Sukar glances up at the sky. "Ilora has twin moons, one for each of Koré's first children—the endoyans and the demons."

"Does the holy text describe any other worlds besides Ilora and Zöran?" I ask. "Any clue where we are now?"

Sukar shakes his head as he draws his gaze back to me. He still has that look from this morning, like he wants to lay his soul bare. My chest tightens with guilt. "The holy text only mentions Ilora by name."

"I don't care if this is Ilora or someplace else," Essnai says. "Arrah, are the tribal people here?"

"Yes." I feel the feather-stroke touch of their magic against my face.

It's the first time since we've been on the trail that I've had more than a memory to guide us. I blink back tears as the tribal people's presence calls to me, but I sense the demons on this side of the gate, too—their insatiable hunger.

I let my awareness go beneath the surface of the demons' magic. When these demons attacked Tribe Zu, they had shed their bodies at will like the gods themselves. They melted into smoke and changed back into physical form to strike. They were impossible to kill. Is this why the orishas hid the truth about the demons from mortal kind? Before Re'Mec and his siblings had trapped the demons' souls in their ancient war, they'd been gods in their own right. But how could that be possible?

You made it possible, the Demon King answers my thoughts.

Some part of me has gotten used to him talking to me as if I'm Dimma. I should ignore him, but I want to know more. *Dimma made the demon people gods?*

You changed our people to protect them from the gods' wrath.

I can't worry about what happened five thousand years ago when I have problems to face now. But I wonder about the cravens, who Re'Mec created to oppose the demons and their magic. The cravens' natural state is always in flux. Fadyi's, Raëke's, and Jahla's skin constantly rearranges itself, working to hold their shape. Did Re'Mec make them so adaptable so they could be formidable against the demons?

The Demon King does not offer an answer to that.

"Lead the way." Essnai snaps me from my thoughts. "We'll fret about how to get home once we free the tribal people."

Essnai's eyes are hard, determined, unwavering. She's right—it doesn't matter where we are. We have to keep going. With the moon bright, we have no trouble picking up the trail. I look to the night sky again, searching, my panic growing more frantic by the moment. I reach my palm up, beckoning for magic to come to me as if it might be hiding. Nothing happens.

"There's no magic here, is there?" Sukar looks at my empty hand. "I don't feel any outside of yours."

I shake my head, dread crawling up my shoulders like cold

fingertips. I have never *not* seen magic. Even when I was little, I used to count the sparks in my room at night to put myself to sleep. The absence of it hits me harder than I expect, like a drought in the middle of a sandstorm. I still feel the chieftains' magic flowing through my veins, but it concerns me that I wouldn't be able to call more if I needed it. Now I'll have to rely on my gifts alone, and I worry that it won't be enough against the demons.

"It does make you question why Heka chose our world to share his magic with and not this one or another," Essnai muses.

"A world without magic," Tyrek remarks as the trail leads into a forest of trees covered in thick vines. "Interesting."

Nothing grows on the ground around the trees, and the soil sinks ever so slightly, leaving molds of our footsteps. Somewhere nearby, a twig cracks. Essnai puts a finger to her lips and jerks her head toward a cluster of bushes. Both Sukar and Tyrek look inclined to fight, but I'm with Essnai on this one. We crouch behind the bushes—the element of surprise on our side.

"Do you smell that?" Tyrek whispers. "It smells like death."

I take a deep breath. The air reeks of sulfur and decay. My stomach twists in knots, but I don't get a good sense of where the smell is coming from. With the wind still, the source must be close. I shift my position and the soil moves beneath me. I frown, almost thinking I imagined it, but the soil adjusts again. The grains fold back on themselves as if pushed from beneath the ground. I pick up a fistful of dark soil speckled with crystals that shine in the moonlight.

"What are you doing?" Essnai asks.

"There's something here." I press my ear to the ground and close my eyes. My senses dive into the soil. Gnarled roots wriggle in the shadows, pushing their way up through the dirt. I go deeper until I reach a wall of bodies with writhing arms and legs and cracked chests filled with dirt. I recoil, but not before a root explodes from the ground and whips around my neck. It jerks me forward, the soil caving in to draw me under. My vision fades in and out. I claw at my throat, but the root curls tighter.

Both Sukar and Essnai spring into action, quick as vipers. Essnai slams her staff into the root, making it loosen, and Sukar cuts it clean in two. My fingers tremble as I fumble to get the dead root from around my neck. When I do, I fling it to the ground.

"Burning gods," Tyrek says, backing away. "What was that?"

"Don't move," I croak out, catching my breath.

Once we stop, the roots go still, too. The forest reminds me of the Gaer tree in the Kingdom, where the first *Ka*-Priest had taken root to cheat death. But this is so much worse. These trees, and the creatures underneath them, hunger for flesh. Why had the demons brought their captives to this world?

I search for the phantom memories of the tribal people, homing in on the moment they reached the forest. A hooded man steps ahead of them and raises his arms to the sky. The thick black vines that hang like ropes against the trees peel away and build a bridge above the ground. The demons force their captives to move forward onto the bridge, and I'm surprised it holds. When they've done crossing the forest, the vines return to the trees. "I know a way across."

As soon as the words are out of my mouth, someone stumbles into the forest. His dark veins stand out against pale brown skin. "Help me!" he screams in the tribal common tongue.

"Stop!" I say in Tamaran—realizing too late that he doesn't understand me.

The ground buckles beneath him and roots lash around his legs and torso, tearing flesh from bone. I start to move, but Essnai grabs my arm and shakes her head. It's too late. It takes everything in me not to bring down a firestorm and burn the trees into withering ashes. Blinking back tears, I call forward the vines and build a new bridge that slopes up from the ground in front of us. It floats above the forest with my magic fortifying it, but as soon as we step onto it, I can feel the vines resisting, writhing to pull themselves apart. The bridge starts to unravel in places, and I weave more of my magic through it.

It takes hours to cross the forest, and the effort to maintain the bridge leaves me exhausted. Every muscle in my body aches, and a sharp pain shoots up the back of my neck. Before, when I called magic from the sky, it was a way to limit the drain on my own reserves. With that option gone, our odds against the demons look less and less favorable.

As we stumble into a valley beyond the forest, I argue that we should keep going, but Tyrek begs for a rest. Somewhere nearby a waterfall roars in the night. The sound is so familiar I convince myself that we'll be okay, that we'll find the tribal people, that we'll all get to go home.

"We could use some help if you're listening, Koré," I pray to the only god that might answer, but even she is silent.

"Who makes a world with underground flesh-eating monsters?" Tyrek takes a swig from his wineskin and tucks it close against his chest. "The gods are cruel."

While Tyrek asks questions that no one answers, I let my awareness extend across the valley. I find a concentration of demons and
the tribal people, a league across the hills. Demons flicker in and out
of my vision, like Familiars in the East Market looking for death and
mayhem. "They're close." I let out a shaky breath.

Tyrek raises the wineskin to his lips and pauses. "We should wait
until morning to attack."

"Do you ever think before you speak?" Sukar grimaces and shifts
on his haunches. "Attacking in broad daylight is a bad idea."

"Attacking while tired is even worse," Essnai says to Sukar, who
grumbles.

Essnai and Tyrek had both been sick on the crossroads, and I'm
tired from building the bridge. I suspect Sukar is exhausted as well,
but he'd never admit it. "We'll scout the area tonight and gather any
information that could help us lay a trap for the demons," I say.

Sukar dramatically bends to one knee and hunches over. "Shall I
carry the three of you since you're so tired?"

Essnai slaps the back of his head, and he winces with a silly grin.

Once rested, we start up the hill. The waterfall drumming against
the rocks masks the sound of our footsteps. I lean close to Essnai, my
voice pitched low. "Don't forget your promise."

Although she shows no outward signs of fear, I know that she's
weighing her options. Instead of answering, she gives me a curt nod
and turns back to her thoughts.

I leave her and Tyrek behind and catch up with Sukar. He's
scouting ahead higher up the hill. He squats along the river, a few
paces from the edge near the head of the waterfall. Moonlight bathes
his dark skin. When I'm nearer, his tattoos begin to glow, and he

relaxes his shoulders. "It wasn't supposed to happen this way." Sukar splashes water on his face. "I had these grand plans. . . . I played it out countless times in my head."

My heart pounds against my chest. With each breath I take, my magic grows in strength again. It rattles in my bones; it warms my blood; it tingles across my skin. The chieftains' *kas* curl around my own, anxious and restless. "What are you talking about, Sukar? What plans?"

When I say his name, he whirls around on me, his eyes brimming with tears. Longing and desire reshape his features into a fine point that pierces my heart. *Gods.* The way he's looking at me, I don't have to guess what he means.

"I'm in love with you," Sukar confesses, his voice quiet. He laughs nervously, shaking his head, almost like he can't believe he actually said it. "I've wanted to tell you for a while." He lets out a deep breath. "I have the worst timing . . . I know."

"I'm sorry, Sukar," I say, and he stops cold, his arms falling to his sides. He glances away, his gaze landing on the water crashing against the rocks below. "I . . ." I stutter as he turns his back to me. I don't know what to say. *Gods.* How could I not know?

"Am I interrupting anything?" Tyrek asks from behind, an unmistakable hint of amusement in his voice.

"No," Sukar snaps, his back still to us.

Tyrek gives me a questioning look, as if to ask what's wrong, but I only glance to my feet, feeling horrible. How long have I felt the shift in our friendship and tried to pretend it away?

"We can't stay here," Sukar says, finally turning around. "We're too exposed."

He avoids looking at me now, and I do the same. We'll talk later—I'll make things right between us. I glance up in time to see a flash of silver. It happens so fast. Moonlight glints off the blade just before it hits Sukar.

I stumble back, gasping for air that won't come. Sukar yanks the blade from his chest, and blood soaks through his tunic; it covers his shaking hands. I can't move—can't breathe.

Sukar looks up at me, his mouth agape, the blade slipping from his hands. Not him—no, no, no. Not Sukar. His tattoos flicker to life, glowing bright, but then they fade one by one until the magic burns out. My screams fall silent the moment my friend slips over the waterfall into a black abyss.

TWENTY-SIX
ARRAH

I thrust my consciousness into the dark, searching for Sukar in the belly of the waterfall. I hit walls of jagged rocks, sharp edges, bits and pieces of torn clothes. I wade through the foam cascading into the pool, taste blood on my tongue. The water's so fast that it would only take a moment for him to wash downstream.

He has to be okay. His tattoos will heal him. The knife missed his heart. He's coming back. I repeat the chorus in my head as my consciousness pushes farther from my body and dives deeper into the river. I keep seeing him on the battlefield, frozen while Efiya raised her shotel over his head. My magic flinging him into the column, and his body sinking to the ground, twisted and broken. The fading glow from his tattoos. I almost killed him then, and now I've gotten him in this situation. How much more proof do I need to accept that I'm a danger to everyone around me?

Tyrek clamps a hand on my shoulder. "He's gone."

I shrug him off, drawing my consciousness back to my body. Green eyes glow in the dark as a horde of demons crests the hill.

Some have Tamaran faces and, to my horror, some have taken the bodies of tribal people. One is tall with ebony skin and high cheekbones like the men from Tribe Aatiri—like my father. Another is a woman with wild curls who could be Mulani. Beyond them, wisps of gray smoke swoop onto the hill and take the shape of the demons from Dimma's memories.

I stumble, not quite believing the sight of them or their size. They are heads taller than the demons in stolen human bodies, with wings of white, black, or brown. Their skin is iridescent, in shades from the deepest purple to silver like Daho's. The moonlight gleams off their sharp teeth. These are the demons that destroyed Tribe Zu.

Essnai is running up the hill toward us when smoke curls around her throat and lifts her from the ground. She strikes, but her staff passes through the demon. More tendrils snake around her body. Her staff hits the ground, and she claws at her neck, gasping for air.

"Argh!" I scream as I fumble down the hill. I don't have time to think or come up with a plan as I draw the wind to me on instinct. It howls in my ears and whips through my braids in a wild rage. Honing it into a sharp knife, I hurl the wind at the demon choking Essnai. It slams into him, and she drops to her knees. The demon shatters into a thousand invisible parts. It'll take time for him to coalesce again, but he's not dead. I hurl more wind, hitting the demons of smoke.

Half out of breath, Essnai snatches up her staff. "Where's Sukar?"

I shake my head, and her eyes fill with tears. I can't say it—he's not gone. I glance over my shoulder and dig my nails into my palms. Moonlight outlines Tyrek's crumpled body, curled up on the ground.

A demon wearing a Tamaran face stands over him. I take a step to go to him and stop. He's so still that I know he's already dead. "The gate . . . we have to go back."

Essnai frowns, but she doesn't hesitate when I pull her arm. There's no time to explain. We run away from the hill toward the forest, and I fling more wind. Each time I do, it drains my magic.

More demons arrive in physical forms and crouch, ready to pounce. They surround us, and there could be only one reason for that. They want to capture me alive. "Go around the forest and find your way back to the gate," I tell Essnai, out of breath. I don't know how much longer I can keep the demons at bay with my wind. "When the demons open it again, you'll be able to get home."

"What will you do?" Essnai asks as we stop short of the forest.

"End this," I answer as my magic shifts the shadows around her so she'll be harder to track in the moonlight. "Find Rudjek and the cravens. We need their help."

"Come with me," Essnai begs, searching my face as if she has some inkling of the desperate plan unraveling in my mind.

"Please, Essnai." I wince. "There's no time."

My friend looks at me, her eyes wild. She knows the promise she made, and we can't win this fight without help, not with how quickly the demons killed Sukar and Tyrek. I won't let them kill her, too. Yet she stands rooted in place, clutching her staff.

I almost think that I'm going to have to repeat myself when she presses her hand to her heart. "I'm sorry," she mouths before backing away from me. Soon she disappears in the night. None of the demons follow her. It's me they want.

I dart into the forest, my chest burning with fury. The soil squirms underneath my feet. I push air in my wake. It should be enough to discourage the demons from turning into smoke and risk getting blown away. If they want me, they'll have to stay corporeal. Something else moves among the roots racing through the soil, coming up fast. Before, I thought that the bodies under the trees had arms and legs, but I was wrong. They're more like tentacles.

The roots burst from the soil behind me, and one of the demons screams. I push the wind down to disturb the soil, and roots burst up one by one, a dozen, too many to count. More screaming, cracked bones, demons' bodies turning into smoke.

A memory claws into my mind—one of *her* memories—and I stop running. I'm standing on a balcony beside Daho as we look upon thousands of demons and thousands more beyond. He wears a gold diadem. It's his first appearance since he slew Yaneki. He is their king now, and the people weep with joy. He saved them.

"Dimma," he says, his eyes finding mine. He looks so small in his white robes, so completely unsure of himself. "I can't do this alone."

"You're not alone." I frown. "I am with you."

Daho bites his lip, his teeth pressing against supple flesh that will never change. A blush rises in his cheeks. "I mean to say that I want you to rule by my side. The elders will tell us to wait until we're older, but we'll never be older, will we?"

"We'll be wiser," I say, but wisdom is yet another thing I don't quite understand.

"Will you be my wife, Dimma?" Daho turns away from his people and takes my hands. "For now, and for when we're wiser?"

"No." I snap out of the memory, even as Dimma's answer drowns out my own. *Yes. Forever and always.*

Sweat stings my eyes as I reach for my magic again. It's sluggish underneath my skin, like when I'm with Rudjek and the cravens, but much worse. I can't stop the demons—I can't save the tribal people. I can't even save myself. I turn to the chieftains' memories, desperately looking for help. They have been quiet all night, like they, too, know that I'm out of options.

I tremble as the roots snake up my feet and legs, tightening around my body. I don't move, so they don't thrash and shred my skin. This is the only way. If I let the roots devour me, then the demons can't use me to bring Daho back.

I can still feel him with me, but his presence is drowned out by my frantic thoughts. I hate that some small part of me longs to see the side of him that Dimma loved. Knowing this only strengthens my resolve to let the roots take me. Better them than him. They wrap around my chest, pinning my arms to my sides, and curve around my throat. I gasp for air, which only makes them squeeze a little harder. I'm already buried to my knees as more appendages wriggle up from the ground. Up close, their translucent skin stretches over a web of veins and pulsing lights.

Accepting my fate, I close my eyes. It has to be this way. I sink deeper, the soil devouring me. I listen to the creaking and hissing of the roots until it all stops. The ground shifts around me and spits me back out. I open my eyes to a horrible scene. All the roots and appendages have frozen in place, and the demons in human bodies are climbing free from their snares.

Someone wades through their ranks, their steps unbothered, and I climb to my feet. A terrible feeling of dread tears through me as I reach to the sky for more magic—as if trying a second time will work. Not even the smallest sparks light on my fingers.

"It's quite cruel, isn't it?" Tyrek steps out of the shadows. "The way the gods have always been selfish and kept magic from mortals."

"Tyrek—" My voice trails off when I see the unnatural glow in his brown eyes. The way the demons move aside for him, the way they cringe, the way my heart lurches in my chest. He runs his hand along a frozen root, and it turns to ashes. "I saw you die," I say, choking on the words.

"Did you?" Tyrek laughs. He stands a little taller, his shoulders drawn back, his eyes eager.

I saw him on the ground with a demon standing over him. I saw what he wanted me to see. When I turn my magic inward, searching for my link with Daho, I find emptiness. I stare at Tyrek and his skin glows iridescent in the moonlight. His mouth twists into a crooked smile. *Gods.* It can't be him. But the truth of the moment cuts me deep. He's been here all along, trekking through the tribal lands and on the crossroads, playing a twisted game. Koré said the Demon King was still imprisoned, but he found a way to trick her.

"If you could see your face," he muses, his expression of mock horror. "Don't look so lost and broken."

"How did you get out of Koré's box?" I ask, my voice breaking.

He stares at me as if the answer should be obvious. It'd all been a game. He'd pretended to be innocent at the coliseum and spun a fake memory that I believed without question. He must have planted the Zu mask at the street fair, knowing that I would follow it in hopes of finding survivors. That night at the tavern, he'd been waiting to make his move. "Efiya freed me," he finally answers after a long pause, his face contemplative. He says my sister's name with such reverence and longing that both jealousy and revulsion tug at my belly.

My gaze roams across the ground like it will fill in the missing parts that make no sense. "You've been free all this time . . . for months."

"You're in shock," he offers with a sympathetic smile. "That's understandable."

The boy with the sharp tongue and the dry sense of humor is gone. Had the real Tyrek been like that, or was that only an impression the Demon King skimmed from eating his soul?

There is only one reason he'd go through such an elaborate ruse to get me here. "I am not Dimma." My words are weak. My legs tremble, and it takes everything inside me to keep standing.

The Demon King steps closer to me, and my heart palpitates. His eyes never leave mine. I am frozen in place—unable to move. He runs his thumb across my lips, and I recoil. "It hardly matters now if you're Dimma or not. I've found a more worthy god to take your place."

I hate that his words make me flinch like someone's twisting a dagger between my ribs. How could I have these feelings of hurt and regret for him—a murderer, a monster, a madman?

"Then why did you help me when the assassin stabbed me with the craven bone?" I snap. "Why not let me die on that mountain? Why this game?"

"Now you're asking the right questions," the Demon King says, the corners of his mouth quivering. He has none of the kindness, warmth, and subtle humor that made Dimma fall in love with him. Instead, he vibrates with manic energy, honed from his millennia in his eternal prison. One of his demons yanks my arms behind my back, and my shoulders burn as they bind my wrists. I'd been too distracted by the Demon King to feel the anti-magic, but now it overwhelms my senses. Several demons force a vest of craven bones across my head, and I wiggle and bite and curse. My magic falls silent. The demons made of smoke scatter as if running away from the anti-magic.

The smile slips from the Demon King's face, and his features sharpen. "I need your help to bring Efiya back."

He opens his cloak and flashes the dagger that holds my sister's soul.

TWENTY-SEVEN
RUDJEK

Two days after Captain Dakte's ill-conceived attack on the demons, I have a mind to drop him into the icy Northern bay. We've lost 172 soldiers, over a third of our rank, all because he moved without my order. For now, I have the misfortune of needing his expertise. The Zeknorian poison nearly ate me alive from the inside, and I walk with a stick to support my weight. The soldier guarding Captain Dakte's tent straightens up when he sees me and peels back the curtain. The rancid smell wafting from inside hits me immediately.

"Thank you," I say to the gendar, and he nods.

"Still pandering to your subordinates, I see," croaks Captain Dakte. He's propped up on a mountain of pillows, a bandage around his throat soaked through with blood and pus. The demons had taken his right eye, and one of the physicians had made him a patch to cover the stitches. He hasn't shaved in days, and gray stubble covers his cheeks. He looks to be at death's door, but he enjoys annoying me too much to die.

"And you're still questioning my actions when I should have you run through with a sword," I bite back.

"We would've won had we known what we were up against," Captain Dakte hisses. His voice strains barely above a whisper. "Our swords were useless against the demons."

"They're stronger than the ones I fought before." I don't like his tone, or that he's insinuating that I hadn't been forthcoming about the demons. "I warned you that we needed the Zeknorians' help, but you didn't listen."

"There's something strange to me, Commandant." Captain Dakte shifts on his pillows. His movement stirs up the sickening smell of festering wounds, and I keep from wrinkling my nose. "Your closest personal guards are quite competent healers for no training. Fadyi and Jahla, the two who we have no record of ever existing before you returned from the tribal lands. What happened to the third? Raëke, wasn't it?"

"Is there a point to this line of questioning?" I rest my hands on my hips. The last thing I need is more dissension from him. He still has support among the gendars.

Captain Dakte breaks into an ugly smile. "I think you and your new friends are keeping secrets."

"Keeping secrets?" I laugh to cover my nerves. Pompous bastard. He's always been too clever for my taste. "Did the demons take your good sense along with your eye, man? I've worked nonstop to forge an alliance with the Zeknorians after you started a war on their soil. I'm not keeping any secrets that would concern you or the Kingdom."

Captain Dakte narrows his eyes at me. "Who are they really?"

"I don't have time for this," I groan. "Do you have the map?" Before Captain Dakte clawed his way up the ranks, he'd been a brilliant mapmaker. The one good thing about him surviving the battle was that he'd seen the layout of the village where the demons have set up camp. With the map, we could mount a better-planned counterattack.

"Yes, Commandant." Captain Dakte's hand trembles as he reaches toward a pile of ink bottles and crumpled paper. "I finished it this morning."

He turns over the scroll, and I take it to one of the tables in his tent and pin it under paperweights. Commander Korr had found a soldier in his camp who'd grown up in the village the demons now occupy. With his help, Captain Dakte has drawn a complete picture. "Best-case scenario, Shezmu is there, but if he isn't with his men, it's still the most strategic place to open the gate when he returns," I conclude.

Captain Dakte grimaces as he presses his fingers against the bandage around his throat. "What makes you think that you can succeed where I failed?"

"I have an advantage over you." I pick up the scroll and turn to leave. "I know what I'm doing."

"We've not always seen eye to eye, Crown Prince," Captain Dakte says, ill humor underlining his words. "Yet I haven't written to your father about the strangeness surrounding you and your friends."

I spin around to face him, my blood boiling. "Are you threatening me? After I've spared your life for what you've done?"

"Not at all," he says, his one eye narrowed. "From everything

I've seen, you have the Kingdom's best interests at heart. You may not have the experience, but I suspect your . . . secrets will help us win the next battle."

I sigh, shaking my head at him. He's a piss-poor excuse for a second-in-command for always challenging me, but he's nobody's fool.

"Glad to know you have so much confidence in my abilities." I leave him to sulk alone. The air outside the tent smells only marginally better, with the wind blowing away some of the foul odors.

I thrust the map into the hands of the guard. "Have copies made of this by midday. As many as you can."

The soldier nods as he sets off to carry out my orders. On the way back to my tent, Majka catches up with me. He brushes leaves out of his thick mane and straightens his mud-smeared uniform. I'm glad that he, Kira, and my guardians made it back from the battle with only minor injuries.

"Is Captain Dakte still giving you a hard time?" he asks.

I grimace. Jahla's scent is all over him, and I know exactly what he's been doing this morning. "We're in the middle of preparing for battle, and you can't keep your pants on for one day?"

"Oh, come on, Rudjek." Majka slaps me on the back. "Jahla is irresistible, and can't a man take some solace in these trying times?"

I stop cold, glaring at him. "We lost a third of our army, and that's all you can think about?"

The smile slips from Majka's face as his shoulders go rigid. "In case you've forgotten, I was on the front line while you were sleeping in your tent."

"I'm sorry I didn't die if that would've made you feel better," I say.

Majka keeps up with me as I cut across the camp. We pass Jahla and Fadyi, along with our physicians, tending to soldiers, most of whom won't be able to go back on the line.

"She isn't just another girl." Majka's gaze lingers on Jahla kneeling to take a pot of water from a campfire. "I really like her."

"I've heard that before." I don't know why, but it bothers me that Majka and Jahla are together. It was one thing when I didn't know his companions, but this feels different. I care about both of them, and I don't want it to end badly as his flings often do. "You better not break her heart."

Majka frowns as I pull back the flap of my tent and gesture for him to enter first. "I think I love her." Before I can discourage this line of conversation, he plops down on the pillows. "You love Arrah, don't you? Even with knowing that the two of you can never be together?"

"Do you really have to ask that question?" I take off my sword belt and drop my shotels on a table.

"Would you like my advice?" Majka asks.

"Your advice on matters of love?" I laugh, wishing he would drop it. "No."

"You should let her go," he offers anyway.

"Excuse me?" I pour myself a cup of water from the pitcher. An attendant left the morning meal on the table hours ago, and I haven't touched it.

"It's just that . . . I see you suffering, Rudjek." Majka looks at his hands. "I bet she's suffering, too. If you can't be together, then maybe it's better to cut the strings now before it hurts more later."

I'm too tired to argue with him. Leave it to Majka to never soften the blow and give it to me straight. I haven't thought about what will happen if Arrah and I can never find a way to counteract her magic and my anti-magic. *Twenty-gods,* I'm in love with a girl that I can't even touch. The gloves, while a temporary solution, will never be enough. With my luck, I'll end like that Delenian tale where the prince becomes a grumpy tyrant living alone in an ice castle. I drop onto the pillows to sulk just as Kira walks into the tent. She looks between the two of us and arches an eyebrow. "Is this a bad time?"

I roll my eyes. "Are you here to give me advice on matters of romance?"

Kira sighs as she kicks off her shoes and joins us. She wraps an arm around my shoulder and squeezes. "I miss my *ama*, too."

"Did you know about Majka and Jahla?" I ask.

She shrugs. "They're not exactly quiet about it."

"Not that it's any of your business." He gives her a scathing look.

Kira laughs. "Since when is your love life private?"

Majka's face hardens, and the barest flush shines underneath his cheeks.

"Lay off, Kira," I warn. Majka really is serious about Jahla. I've never seen him like this. Usually, he'd tell us every single detail of his latest adventure, but right now, he's pissed.

"You tell him," snaps a voice before Re'Mec shimmers into existence in the middle of the tent. His back is to us while he argues with what looks like thin air. "You said that she'd never be able to find the box."

I get to my feet as Koré fades into the tent, wearing blue silks from her headscarf to her slippers. She stands across from her brother, thrusting her finger at him. "You were supposed to keep an eye on the girl!"

Every muscle in my back tenses. *The girl*. "What's happened to Arrah?" I interrupt their squabble.

"She's gone," Koré says, turning on me.

"What do you mean she's gone?" I ask, feeling numb inside.

Kira pushes past me. "What of Essnai?" Re'Mec holds up his hand as if offering peace, but Kira slaps it away. "Where is she?"

"Kira." Majka gently pulls her back from the sun orisha. Her eyes fill with tears as she leans against him for support.

"We felt the gate open this morning," Re'Mec explains after a deep sigh. "Koré believes that Shezmu tricked Arrah and her comrades into going through it, but I'm less sure of that."

"That's not even the worst part," Koré interrupts him. "The Demon King is free."

"Arrah freed him?" I dread the answer. This wouldn't have happened if I'd told her the truth. I should've been there for her.

"Would you have so little faith in her?" Koré asks. "No. The short story is that Efiya freed him before Arrah killed her."

"What . . . ?" My voice grows shrill. "Why would he want Arrah if he's already free?"

"I'd think that would be obvious," Re'Mec says. "He'll want to convince her to switch to his side in the impending war. As I've said before, her magic is dangerous."

One of Koré's braids slips from underneath her scarf and curls around her neck. "I fear we're missing something, brother. Daho is one of my children, and I doubt he'd kidnap Arrah just to turn her to his side. He convinced Arti to help him without lifting a finger, so to speak. There's more to his plans and a reason he took her."

As soon as Koré says the words, it's obvious. The Demon King wants something from her—he wants *her*. The revelation feels like someone's dropped me in a vat of ice to wake me from a deep slumber and thrust me into a living nightmare.

"If Shezmu's already opened the gate," Majka speaks up, "then why haven't more demons invaded our world? That's the plan, right? What's stopping them from attacking?"

There it is. The thought that's been tugging at the back of my mind. I knew something else had to be at play. Shezmu and his demons have been running us in circles. How could I be so dense?

"That's a good question for which I have no answer," says Koré. "For now, the gate still stands in the demon camp."

I laugh, and it comes out bitter and hard. "It was a distraction so that he could take Arrah—all of it." I grab my shotels. "We'll attack the demons today, before Shezmu decides to move his men and the gate. It's the only way we can get her and Essnai back."

TWENTY-EIGHT
ARRAH

The Demon King watches me with an intensity that feels like it could melt my bones. Dimma's memories claw to the surface of my mind, fighting for space, festering like old wounds. A flimsy gossamer separates hers from mine—pulled taut like it's about to tear. I don't know what will happen when it does.

"Despite what you may think, Efiya loved you, and I love her," he says.

A twinge of jealousy twists in my belly again, and I want to rip out this treacherous part of me. Am I responding to the news that he loves my sister, or is it Dimma's reaction? Seeing the Demon King's devotion to Efiya, I'm suddenly less sure that he is the source of these memories. But if he's not the source, that would mean something impossible.

Not impossible.

My father once told me a story about witchdoctors who could cheat death. If a mortal could do it, then it must be a simple matter for a god. No, not a god, I realize, Dimma wouldn't have considered that name for herself. Even that's another detail I shouldn't know about her. None of this makes sense—yet there has to be an answer to why I have her memories.

I lift my chin and give him a look of indifference. "My sister could never truly love someone as pathetic as you."

The Demon King smiles. "I know you're hurting right now, but jealousy doesn't suit you."

I spit on the ground, and he only sighs and starts back in the direction of the hills. The demons shove me forward, and the vest of craven bone rattles and shifts. The heat from the bones seeps through my tunic, and the parts that touch my skin burn.

My friends never liked Tyrek and had seen through his facade from the beginning, but I've been a fool. I've gotten Sukar killed, and now Essnai is alone in a strange world looking for a way home. I've brought nothing but grief upon them.

"There's something I don't understand," I say as the demons march me a few paces behind their master. "Why do you need me to free Efiya when her soul is trapped in *your* dagger?"

He doesn't answer for a moment as we leave the forest behind for the grassy hills under the moonlight. It's only after he lets my question linger in the stretch of silence between us that he finally speaks. "The dagger is finicky. Only the one who took a life can bring it back, and since you killed Efiya, that's you."

I don't miss the hesitation in his voice, like he's not quite sure that we can bring her back. Wielding the blade almost killed me the first time—wait, no, that isn't right. It *did* kill me. Bit by bit fragments of my memories piece together. I stand in a sea of darkness with the orisha of life and death. Fram is magnificence incarnate. They are swathes of light and shadows woven into two symmetrical bodies. Even in my memory, they fade around the edges and bleed across my vision. I want to fall to my knees here and now to behold them forever, but I resist the pull to give in.

I close my eyes and remember the tempered song of their dual voices. They warned me that I must return to the Super Cataclysm to be unmade. Their cooling magic had tugged at me, but I resisted them even then. Fram had taken my memories—just like Daho said. He hadn't lied about that part—not that it makes a difference now.

I died after killing Efiya, and the orisha of life and death came to reap my soul. So why didn't they?

"Are you working with Fram?" I shuffle in my shackles. I hate feeling like someone else's pawn in yet another game. "Did you strike a deal with them?"

"Here's what I will tell you," the Demon King says. "The old gods are petty and selfish. They've kept us all under their thumbs. Efiya wants to remake the world in her image so that mortals are no longer weak." He takes a languid breath like he's reveling in a dream. "Together, we'll destroy the old world to make room for a better one."

I stop cold at that, and two demons grab my arms and push me along. The vest rubs against my neck and sears my skin. I bite back a cry as I stumble over my feet. I don't understand how he could be in love with my sister and think she's some kind of savior for all that she's done.

The rest of the way, I hold my tongue. I have no chance of using my magic, but if he gives me the dagger to bring Efiya back and I'm quick enough, I can kill him first. One strike to the heart to destroy his body and draw his soul into the knife. It doesn't matter what happens to me after that.

In a clearing, an awful scene comes into focus. We pass rows and rows of people on either side, bound and shackled to stakes, curled up on threadbare pallets. Elbows, knees, clavicles, and pelvises jut out under dusty brown and black skin. People from all five tribes stare unseeingly into the dark, eyes hollow, cheeks sunken.

"You bastard," I whisper.

An old Zu man sitting with his head hanging between his shoulders looks up as we pass. His tattoos are dark, and I note the craven bone woven in a collar around his neck. The Demon King has been using anti-magic to keep the tribal people imprisoned. The man's lips tremble as he tries to speak. I crane my neck to watch him, but his words never come.

"What happened to the rest of them?" I spit, my gaze sweeping over the camp. The demons had gathered a few hundred people on the crossroads, but less than half are here.

"They didn't all make it." The Demon King pauses, his back still to me. "Some of them became food."

I growl, my voice a raw ache of frustration and pain. I can sense my magic restoring itself even under the oppressive craven bones, wanting to let loose. I've come all this way, and I can't help them. I can't even help myself.

"Arti, is that you?" someone whispers in the shadows, crawling toward me. The moonlight hits the Mulani woman's face. She has deep wrinkles in her sun-weathered skin and cataracts obscure her amber eyes. Hearing my mother's name turns my blood cold, but the woman peers up at me with so much hope that tears fill my eyes. I turn away to find the Demon King watching me, a conniving smile splitting his face.

"You'll sleep here with the others," he says, thoughtful, "to remind you what's at stake. If you think of disobeying me, I will kill one person on the hour every hour." He flashes me another broad smile. "Rest well, Arrah, for there is much work to do in the morning."

The Demon King leaves at that, heading to a large tent on the edge of the camp. That's when I notice the other tents, the animal stalls, and the piles of half-cut stones. They've been working the tribal people all this time. Two demons force me to one of the stakes in the ground and lock my hands and feet with iron cuffs.

I strain at my chains—pulling, pushing, and picking at the locks without luck. When I start pacing back and forth, one of the demons guarding me threatens to pluck out someone's eye if I don't stop. The tribal people closest to me wince, and I have no doubt the demon will make good on it. I finally force myself to sit. The ground is hard clay and dead grass that pokes against my backside.

"Arrah," says the woman in shackles near me. She sits hunched over with her locs covering her face. "I know that name."

"Do . . . do you know me?" I ask, afraid that she's one of my cousins.

"I know *of* you," she croaks out. "You're the one the chieftains said would save us."

The woman falls silent at that, and a knot settles in my belly. How can I save the tribal people if I can't even save myself? The chieftains made a mistake in thinking that I would be the one to stop my sister and the Demon King. I failed them.

I curl up on the ground, trembling, despite the warm breeze winding through the camp. My body aches from fighting and the sheer horror of everything that's happened. I don't want to sleep, but I weep until I wear myself out and fall into another dream.

People whisper about me at Daho's coronation. It's easy to stay out of mortals' chaotic minds, but it's harder to practice selective hearing in a hall of so many people. Some of them intentionally come near me so that I don't miss their words. *I assure you, she's just a plaything. Once he's more mature, he'll settle down with a girl of his own kind. She should at the very least comb her hair in a more acceptable way. Why didn't he pick someone prettier? Is her name really death?* These are comments from some of the demons, while the endoyans whisper other things. *Who is she? What region is she from? Rumor is that she's a farmer's daughter. He'll never marry her.*

Daho talks to the endoyan emissary who'd been friends with his father. Minister Godanya is much taller than him, with a beard that reaches his chest. His skin is pale with a press of black veins along his temples and forehead. "I've known your father since he was a boy," the man boasts, his eyes warm. "He grew into a good leader and a fierce negotiator. I valued his friendship." The man laughs at that. "It's my hope that we'll renew the strong bond between our people and restore our trade agreements." There is doubt in his voice.

"I'm looking forward to repairing the damage that Yaneki caused, Minister," Daho says. His eyes find mine in the crowd, and there is a gentle tug between our souls. "Would you excuse me for a moment?"

The hem of Daho's white robes sweeps the floor as he crosses the hall, and people move out of his way. Some clear their throats or call his name, but he ignores them. When he reaches me, he lets out a frustrated breath. His hands are shaking as he takes mine. "I have half a mind to strike down every person in this room who's spoken ill of you." His eyes brim with anger.

I frown, knowing that I'm missing some social cue. "Should I be offended by their words?" I ask, unsure. "I'd dismissed them as petty and unimportant."

"They are petty and unimportant," he says, "but I would address them if you don't mind."

I shrug, though I am pleased all the same. "Address them, if you see the need."

Daho raises my hands to his lips and kisses them before leading us to the throne that sits high above the crowd. The room falls silent. "Hear me now, for I will only say this once in my lifetime. You may call me young, immature, or a fool." He looks at each person who had uttered the words, and face after face blushes with shame. "But speak ill of Dimma, your soon-to-be queen, again, and you'll find yourself at the end of my sword."

"Spoken like a true Daneer!" Minister Godanya shouts. The crowd erupts in applause, and the ones who were whispering insults only moments before clap the loudest.

I wake with a start as someone clamps a hand over my mouth. I stare into too-big eyes shining beneath a black hood, relieved at seeing a familiar face. I look around for Rudjek and the others, but they aren't here. Raëke presses a finger to her lips as she lets me go. The two demons on guard lie still in the night.

"Where are the others?" I ask when she releases my mouth and turns to my shackles.

"I'm alone." She rushes her words. "I've been following you since the Barat Mountains."

"What do you mean, following me?" I remember the mysterious archer in the trees at Tribe Zu. "You're the one who helped us fight the assassins?"

"Yes," she whispers. "I'm sorry about your friend Sukar. I looked for him in the river after he fell, but I couldn't find his body."

I shove down my tears, numb. Sukar is gone—he's really gone.

Once Raëke frees my hands, she removes the vest of craven bones from my shoulders. "We'd wondered why the demons had taken our dead after the fight in the Dark Forest. Now I know."

We come to our feet, but I can't stop thinking about what it means that she's been following us. "Did Rudjek send you?" Maybe the question is unimportant given the situation, but I have to know. Rudjek had hidden the news about the demons, now this. *He doesn't trust me.*

"He did—" Raëke cuts off midsentence as a blade pierces through her chest. She doesn't have time to react before the demon pulls out his sword and cleaves her head from her body. Blood splashes on my face, in my eyes, on my tongue. I scream as my magic rushes to the surface. I'm relieved that I can finally call it again after exhausting myself earlier. I strike demon after demon with wind, shredding their souls into ribbons.

A sharp pain catches me in my side, then another in my shoulder. I look down to see arrows stuck in my body. Anti-magic poisons my blood, but I keep shredding until I see an archer nocking another arrow. The next one hits me in the leg, then another in my thigh.

"Bring her to me," the Demon King demands as I fall to my knees, reeling in agony.

THE UNNAMED ORISHA: DIMMA

We're close to the end now. It's not the true end, but those final moments of joy and sadness that plagued the last years of my natural life. Daho and I have a blissful seven centuries together. At first, it's hard for his people and the endoyans to accept that we are immortal. There are uprisings and claims of something called witchcraft.

For generations, no one suffers; no one goes hungry; no one gets their wings clipped. No one comments on my hair. Our rule marks a new era of peace in Jiiek. It could've gone on for many more millennia if I hadn't broken the universe.

Although I've changed Daho, he still clings to mortal needs. Tonight, twin moons pour light through our chamber windows as he sleeps. I miss our mountain, the little cabin, the frozen lake, the clean smell of the air. It's been too long since we've visited. I am thinking of these things when a spark ignites inside me. It's small at first, and I gasp as it draws energy from me, from Daho, and from the universe itself. Daho bolts upright in bed. He looks down at me, his eyes shining bright under the moonlight. "Is this real, or am I dreaming?" he asks, his gaze traveling down the length of my slip. "How is this possible?"

"It shouldn't be"—I stare at my belly—"but it is."

"Dimma," Daho says. I look up at him, and there are tears on his cheeks. His magic intertwines with my own, reaching and searching until he finds his answer. He laughs. "I'm going to be a father!"

My brethren and I can't bear children from our flesh, not like mortals. It's why they're driven by the compulsion to mold the raw material of the universe into some semblance of their own image. This goes against everything that I know about myself. Yet the spark grows inside me.

"Let me be the first to tell our child a story." Daho pulls me into his arms and rests his chin against the top of my head, inhaling my scent. "Once there was a broken boy who fell from the sky, and a goddess, both terrifying and terrifyingly beautiful, saved him from certain death. The goddess had eyes the color of night pearls and a heart bigger than the entirety of the world." I sink against his warm body, listening to our story, and for the first time in my life, fall asleep.

Daho is sleeping when Koré appears in the arboretum on the fourth floor of the palace. I am lying with my head pressed against his back, listening to the rhythm of his heartbeat. Soon there will be another heartbeat—that of our child. Koré must've sensed the change. I could shed my vessel and move more quickly, but the baby is much too fragile. I plant a gentle kiss on Daho's shoulder and slip into a robe before walking to the arboretum.

Koré perches precariously on the edge of a balcony, above a fall that would kill any mortal. I don't approach her. Instead, I weave between the trees and beds of roses. She doesn't speak for a long time as I make my rounds, grass sweeping underneath my bare feet.

"I can't save you this time, Dimma," she finally says. "The Supreme Cataclysm is not an idle creator. It roars in pain at what you've done. You've stolen life from it."

"I haven't stolen anything." I think about how we'd come to this moment. I changed Daho, but he retained his mortal gift—the one to sire children. Not to make them as my brethren had, but have them, flesh and bone, a thing that we could never do together until now.

"You have evolved into something more than intended," Koré says. "Because of this, the Supreme Cataclysm has become unbalanced. It stopped creating the moment you became with child. Now it only destroys. The outer worlds and our children are safe for now, but not forever. Eventually, the destruction will consume the universe."

I wrap a protective arm around my belly. "What will you do with me?"

"For centuries Re'Mec and I debated that very question after you changed Daho," Koré says. "We decided to let you live when we saw that his change had no impact on the greater universe. But your child is different. We asked Iben to travel the threads of time and tell us what this means." Her face twists in anguish. "He would not give up his secrets, of course, but he didn't need to. Your child will be the end of the universe. We can sense it."

"If it's destined for the universe to end, then so be it," I spit out. "Nothing is eternal."

"Tell me, Dimma," Koré asks. "Have you found your nature yet?"

"Perhaps it's to create life in a way that we never have before."

"I bet your nature isn't as benign as that." Koré's soul burns in her eyes, like flickering flames consuming everything. "We have consensus among our brethren. You must give yourself and the child to the Supreme Cataclysm to be unmade." I hear her words, but they don't make sense. She can't think I could ever agree to that. "You were a mistake that must be corrected."

Our kind cannot die. The thought has never crossed my mind that we could be unmade.

"I wish there were another way—you and Daho have achieved something extraordinary." She glances at my belly. "I'm a grandmother, aren't I? Daho and his people are my children."

When I don't answer, Koré stands up, her feet balancing on the thin railing. "Don't force our hand, sister." At that, she steps back and drops over the edge. There is no sound as she changes into a wisp of wind.

Daho wakes in our bedchamber, and I open my mind. My anguish and dread and fear spread to him, and he's at my side in moments, cradling me tight against his chest. "I won't let them take our child," he says. "I will protect both of you until my very last breath."

I know that he means it, but Daho alone can't stop my brethren when they make a decision. They will kill him if he gets in their way, and I can't allow that. I won't take my child to the Supreme Cataclysm, despite Koré's threat.

"I'll raise an army and have them stationed on the palace grounds," Daho says, then his voice falters. His people haven't needed an army for a very long time, and none of them could stand against my brethren.

"An army, whatever for?" asks Minister Godanya—not the first Godanya, one of his descendants. We turn to face the man, who bears little resemblance to his forefather. He frowns, and his fear is palpable. As the ambassador between Endoya and Jiiek, he spends much time at the palace with his staff.

Daho winces in annoyance that the man has interrupted our private moment. But he quickly explains what's happened. "We'll fight alongside you if it comes to it," Minister Godanya offers. "We can't risk losing everything our people have built together."

"I don't care about what we've built together, Godanya," Daho snaps. "I care only about Dimma and our child."

"Of course." The Minister shifts uncomfortably. "That's what I mean."

"No, you meant your precious trade agreements," Daho says.

Minister Godanya lowers his head, sputtering, "My offer still stands should you need it." At that, he excuses himself.

"We'll speak to my brethren," I say. "There may still be time to change their minds."

Daho buries his face against my shoulder, his whole body shaking. He reminds me of that first day on our mountain when he thought that I was *Death*.

If I can't convince my brethren to spare our child, I will not submit to them. I'll fight at Daho's side. I may not know my nature, but that does not make me weak. My brethren will soon discover that it's quite the opposite.

TWENTY-NINE

ARRAH

With the craven bone poisoning my body, I see Dimma's memories for the truth. They pour into my mind like rain flooding the banks of the Serpent River during Su'omi. Most are blurry images of people, conversations, and contraptions that caught her eye. Something ticks in my head, the counting of time, a sound without rhythm or pause. My lip press around the word: *clock*.

I've spent so much time running from her memories, denying them, and now I'm too tired to fight. I resent them, yet I can't deny how right it feels to have her memories. I don't know where mine end and hers begin. I can't push them into a corner like I've done with the chieftains', to recall and forget at will. They make space to live alongside my own. How could it be that my whole life I've been missing a part of myself and didn't know it? I remember dying after killing Efiya and talking to Fram, the orisha of life and death. I spoke to them as Dimma. I *was* Dimma.

I curl up in agony and desperation in the tent. My heart aches for Raëke—another friend dead because of me, just like the twins Tzaric and Ezaric . . . just like Sukar. Morning light filters through the canopy. I'm no longer in shackles and chains. The craven bone inside me tames my magic and keeps me in so much pain that I move as little as possible. Voices echo around me, and hands tear away my clothes. I open my eyes long enough to see two tribal women—one Kes and one Aatiri—peering down at me. The thought crosses my mind that I'm naked in front of strangers, but the pain makes it impossible to care.

The Aatiri woman pushes back my braids from my face and presses a warm rag to my forehead. "Hush now, blessed one," she says in a raspy voice.

I weep, tasting blood in my mouth. Pain blossoms around my wounds, but it's nothing compared to knowing the truth of who I used to be. Dimma didn't want to die and be born again, but Fram trapped her soul in a mortal body. It's hard to accept that I am only a reincarnation of someone else. I am her, yet I am not. She can exist without me, but I can't exist without her. I squeeze my eyes shut again. It'd been love that led her to make Daho immortal, but it was the orishas' punishment that turned him into a monster.

"Don't cry," the Kes woman whispers as they break off the wooden shafts of the arrows. Every break sends a new shock of pain through my wounds. "The sun always shines for those who are willing to look up."

"Well, not in the North, they say," the Aatiri woman remarks begrudgingly. "It shines on this world, though."

The North, where Rudjek is, hunting demons. *Gods.* He'd sent Raëke to keep eyes on me.

"Hurry up and get out," commands the Demon King, his voice

lazy and distant. I imagine him sprawled out on pillows, drinking from a wineskin. It's still hard to believe that it had been him, not Tyrek, all along, taunting Sukar, pretending to be our friend.

The two women flinch and make quick work of cleaning and bandaging my wounds. "The arrows," I groan, feeling the sting of the craven bone still inside me.

"Don't mind that, blessed one." The Aatiri woman has a twinkle in her dark eyes that reminds me of Grandmother. "They're like any wound. Grow a scab over them, and they're easier to bear." She stares at me intently, and through the fog of pain, I know she's trying to tell me something.

The women help me into a coarsely woven shift of thick fabric that itches against my skin. When they're done, two guards drag them out of the tent. The Aatiri dares a glance over her shoulder, giving me a meaningful look.

I'm still lying on my side, struggling to sit up, when the Demon King kneels beside me. He smells clean, like citrus and tree bark. "You're almost as beautiful as she." He brushes his fingers across my forehead. "You don't have her spark, her ambition, her fire." He sits back on his haunches and places the dagger wrapped in red silk between us. The light reflects against the exposed tip, honed to a fine, deadly point. "Unfortunately, since I can't trust you, the craven bone must stay to keep you docile."

"I can't figure out if you're trying to convince yourself or me that you love my sister. Perhaps you're afraid that she'll reject you for someone prettier." I peer down my nose at him, but lying on my side, it doesn't come off half as dignified as I would like. The body he's taken—Tyrek's—is beautiful. Ebony skin, brooding dark eyes, regal jaw, but it's nothing like Dimma's memories of Daho. He'd been tall, like all demons, with eyes that sparkled like starlight, silver skin, and sharp teeth. I gamble that his vanity is as big as his mouth.

The Demon King reaches across the dagger and yanks me upright. With the sudden jerk, pain flares around the arrowheads, and I bite the inside of my cheek hard enough to draw blood. My words apparently hit their mark.

"You have a wicked little mouth, don't you, Arrah?" he says, an eagerness burning in his eyes. He looks exactly like Tyrek did when he sat high above the assembly on the second tier with the royal family. He'd been fervent as he watched his father and my mother's petty bickering. "I would very much like to cut it open from ear to ear to see you bleed some more."

My breaths come out in hiccups from the pain. "Go ahead."

His face turns sour, as the real Tyrek's would've done when things got boring at the assembly. Though it's not long before he breaks into a lazy smile. "Your sister is very impressionable." His words curl around him like a crown upon his brow. "When she told me that you'd hurt her by running off to be with Rudjek, I told her how to hurt you back."

I slap him before I know what I'm doing. My palm stings across his face. I forget myself and the pain. Instead, I feel hot, burning rage. I reach for the dagger, intending to put it through his depraved heart. He slams his hand down on top of mine, pinning me to it. The jeweled hilt digs into my palm through the red silk.

"Think long and hard about your next decision," the Demon King says, his eyes meeting mine. "Perhaps you have some of Efiya's spirit after all, but don't push me too far, or I might take you up on your offer." He nods like there's an unspoken agreement between us. "Now, if you would, please take the dagger and call back her soul. I'll only ask once before I start executing the tribal people."

My hand trembles as I close my fingers around the knife. His admission doesn't absolve Efiya from the vile thing she did to Rudjek, yet he's guilty, too. He pulled her strings like he did with Arti, like he tried to do with me.

If I'm going to kill him, it has to be at the right moment, not when he's expecting an attack. I relax my hand against the dagger and force in a ragged breath. "You win," I say, lowering my eyes. *When I get my strength back, I'm going to carve him up and feed his entrails to birds.*

"On with it." He lets go of me. "The day is young."

I take the dagger and unwrap the silk slowly. Using it killed me once, and I don't doubt that it will again. "Dimma forged this blade for you." I dare myself to look into his cold eyes again. I see nothing of the man that she loved in them. I hate that I keep searching, hoping, wanting him to be the Daho from my memories and not the monster before me.

The Demon King flourishes his hand at the knife. "Stop stalling."

I press one finger to the hilt of the blade, half hoping that it will kill me on the spot. All this time, I worried that I would have to give up my magic so the Demon King wouldn't trick me into freeing him. It's a relief knowing that I can keep the chieftains' gift. I need it now. I still have a chance to stop him.

Power hums in the dagger, vibrating up the length of my fingers to my wrist and forearm. I'm taken back to the last moments in the Temple of Heka, where my sister and I stood out of time. Me plunging the knife into her belly. Her soul seeping from her parted lips.

"Efiya." I run my thumb along the edge of the blade. "Are you there?"

I push my thumb against the blade and pierce my skin. The smell of blood drags me down, down, down, until the world changes into darkness. I am inside the dagger, trapped in a space that is at once as endless as the universe and as confining as a cage. It's empty. Sukar's uncle had told me that the Demon King trapped his enemies in the dagger, so I expected it to be brimming with souls.

"I ate them," drawls a voice as sweet as spoiled milk. "I got bored."

"Efiya." I breathe my sister's name, and my racing heartbeat echoes in my ears. "You should be dead."

"Dead," she muses, the word coming from all around, chilling me to the bone. "I suppose it's all perspective, isn't it? I should be dead, but, then again, you should be, too."

"Tell me how to kill the Demon King."

"I could kill him," she says. "I'd do anything for you, sister. You're all I have left."

"And whose fault is that, Efiya?" I snap. "Do you think I'd be foolish enough to let you out of your prison after everything you've done? I'd rather rot here with you than do that."

"But you're not really here," she whispers close to my ear. "You're only visiting to ask for a favor, not because you miss me." She says it with so much hurt in her voice that I almost feel ashamed, but I push the thought away.

"Sister." I force out the word, yet there's some part of me wanting it to mean more than disgust and anger and pain. "Do something good for once in your life. If you truly know, tell me how to kill him."

Efiya tilts her head to the side. "I am willing to help you, but the price is my freedom."

"You know I can't free you." I back away from her. I remember Arti's warning that Efiya was worse than the Demon King. I pull my consciousness from the dagger. "Goodbye, sister."

I'm back in the tent, staring down as an oily black liquid spreads up my arm. It's as cold as ice. I drop the knife, and the sludge disappears. Beads of my blood soak into the blade.

"Did you find her?" The Demon King grabs my shoulders and shakes me, desperation written all over his face. I realize then that he needs my sister. Is he somehow weaker than he'd been before the orishas imprisoned him? "Did you find Efiya?"

My lips crack and bleed as I open my mouth to speak. I want to lie to spite him, but I'm too afraid that he'll take out his frustration on the tribal people. Instead, I tell him the thing that he wants to hear the most. "Yes."

THIRTY
ARRAH

Efiya won't kill the Demon King. This is just another game for her. My hand feels numb after handling the dagger, and I flex my fingers, hoping to get the blood flowing again. I hunch forward, heaving in air, and do my best to pretend that the dagger has drained my energy. I cough and beg for water, which the Demon King calls for one of his guards to bring me. I can't buy time forever, but I'll do it as long as he allows.

Some things have become clearer now. Efiya brought the Demon King back, but he must be in a weakened state. For all his threats, I haven't seen him use magic since the forest. Why would he go through so much trouble to bind the tribal people with craven bone to block their magic if not out of fear?

I peer up at him from the cup, looking what I hope is docile. Let him think that I'm too broken and afraid to act against him. I squeeze my eyes shut, my lips still pressed to the cup, my wounds throbbing.

The Aatiri woman tried to give me a message about my injuries.

They're like any wound. Grow a scab over them, and they're easier to bear. What does that mean? Scabs don't grow inside your body; scabs grow on cuts.

"What did you see?" the Demon King asks, his voice strung tight with tension like he's about to snap at any moment. "Is she okay?"

"I saw darkness." I open my eyes. "So much darkness."

"Answer me." He pries the cup from my hand, spilling the rest of the water as he shoves it aside. "Is Efiya okay?"

I grimace to hide the smile tugging at my lips. He's desperate to know, and I wish I could say something spiteful to make him sink deeper into despair. "She's right as rain." I answer with the first thing that wells up in my mind. It takes me a moment to realize it's a Jiiek expression from Dimma's memories. The Demon King frowns at me as if he expected a different answer. "She's fine."

His shoulders relax at that, and I don't miss the way he eases out a soft sigh. I'm right about him—he needs her. "She asked for you," I lie. "I was wrong before—when I said that she didn't care about you. I know that now."

"What did she say?" The Demon King leans so close that his cloying scent of citrus and tree bark fills my nose and turns my stomach sour. It's hard not to let my fingers inch toward the knife and use it to cleave his heart in two, but the guards would come at once. "Her exact words."

"'Is Daho safe'?" I lie again, choosing not to push too far, but I realize my mistake almost immediately. The rage in his eyes is visceral, pure, seething, and I glance away. I've made a grave mistake, and I search for the words to appease him. "She says she loves you," I blurt out as though it's painful for me to admit. Let him think that I am jealous, to stroke his ego. "Is that what you want to hear?"

He says nothing, and I chance meeting his terrible gaze again. His whole body is shaking, and for the first time, I know that he's afraid. I don't see the slap coming until the sound thunders in my ears, and my vision blurs into white spots. The impact knocks me to my side, and my teeth tear into my cheek. Blood soaks through my new bandages, my wounds gushing blood, my face burning.

"You lying little twit," the Demon King sneers. "I warned you what would happen if you played games with me." He calls to the guards outside the tent. "Bring the Aatiri woman."

"Please don't," I whisper, dragging myself to sit again. My head spins. "I—I didn't mean to lie, but I did see Efiya. She's eaten the other souls in the dagger."

Two guards bring the Aatiri woman into the tent. She doesn't struggle, as if she's foreseen this moment in a vision. Her cheekbones are too sharp against her skin, her eyes too gaunt in their sockets. Despite that, there's a proud tilt to her chin and the way she stands tall, no stoop in her shoulders. I remember the demons who whispered to me in the desert before I broke my mother's curse. *We should know better than to try to deal with an Aatiri,* one of them had hissed. *They're self-sacrificing to a fault.*

"Take her soul," the Demon King says, his voice cold.

"No," I scream, but the guards don't hesitate. One of them grabs the Aatiri woman's chin and forces her to face him. His eyes are hungry with anticipation as he opens his mouth impossibly wide. The other demon plunges a knife into the woman's back, and her jaw goes slack. I cry silent tears as her soul seeps past her lips, a gray amorphous thing. When they're done, they take her body away.

"Lie to me again, and I'll kill two more, then four, then eight," the Demon King threatens. "Now tell me what she said."

It's my fault that the woman's dead—I messed up. It's my fault that I didn't stop my sister before she killed Grandmother and the other *edam*. Before she hurt Rudjek, destroyed the tribes, and released the Demon King.

"She said that she'd kill you herself if I freed her," I admit, to which he only laughs delightedly.

"Finally, an honest word out of your lying mouth," he says, a sparkle in his eyes again. "Can I tell you a secret, Arrah?"

I glance around the tent, knowing that he's setting me up for a trap. It doesn't matter if I say yes or no; the results will be the same. He takes my shaking hands into his own. His are cool to the touch while sweat beads on my forehead and trickles down my back.

"I'm tired of playing games with you," he adds, not waiting for me to answer. "Call her soul back."

He holds me in a crushing grip, and my fingers scream in pain. If he's weak as I suspect and can't call Efiya, then I have an advantage over him. The tribal people in this camp might die because of me, but if I do as he asks, Efiya will destroy our world, as Heka had warned. With access to Iben's gateway, she will destroy every world in her path. I can't let that happen. When he lets me go, I grab the dagger and shove it against his chest. "Do it yourself."

"Get that thing away from me!" he yells, slapping my hand. The dagger hits the ground between us with a silent thud, and he stares at it in disgust.

I am completely caught off guard by his reaction. I realize then that he hasn't touched the dagger even once, not without silk around it. I look into his eyes again. They glow like the other demons', but they're brown, not green. How did I not notice the significance of that before? All demons have green eyes—it is a mark of their race, Re'Mec had once told me.

"You're not him," I mumble, my mind reeling. He's not the Demon King. He really is Tyrek. Every move he's made has been exactly the sort of pettiness that I would expect from a Sukkara. Boasting, taunting, trying to make me jealous of my sister.

"When I caught you in the forest, you assumed that I was the Demon King, and I decided to play along for a bit," Tyrek says, gleeful. "I do like games."

My first reaction, I'm ashamed to say, is immense, overwhelming relief. He's nothing like Dimma's memories of Daho, his kindness, his love, his strength. My second reaction: How could Tyrek have control over these demons?

"You're trying to puzzle it out." He grins. "Let me fill in the blanks." He inhales a deep breath and I draw back from him. "Your sister came to me while Darnek and I were hunting and made me an offer that sounded quite nice. I could be rid of my father and brother and take the throne for myself."

Of all the questions spinning in my head, I ask, "How did you get magic?"

"I'll spare you the intimate details, but your sister and I grew very close." Tyrek blushes at that. "She was magnificent, the way she caught wandering souls and changed her appearance on a whim."

I recoil at the admiration in his voice. "Here I thought you were sparing me the details."

"Efiya gifted me with a tiny piece of her soul." Tyrek beams with pride. Tyrek—not Daho, not the Demon King. Tyrek. "I was on the battlefield when you killed her, and I stole the Demon King's dagger to bring her back."

The irony of the situation twists in my gut. Dimma had given Daho a part of herself for love, but Efiya would've done it for a pettier reason—or had she done it as a precaution? She'd known there was a chance that she wouldn't make it back from Heka's Temple. Tyrek was her safeguard in case she didn't.

"Enough talk!" He picks up the knife with the silk. "Bring her back now."

I take the knife again, the jewels pressing into my palm. I close my eyes, but I don't let the dagger draw my mind into its depths like before. Instead, I concentrate on the shards of craven bone in the various places inside my body. *Grow a scab over them, and they're easier to bear.* Not over them, I reason, but around them, so the anti-magic can't spread. I wince and open my eyes.

"She's here," I say, my gaze fixed behind Tyrek.

He wrenches himself around to look, and I plunge the dagger toward his chest. My hand seizes up a hair's breadth away. An invisible force keeps me from coming any closer.

"You must've noticed that I have a shadow of Efiya's powers." Tyrek twists his hand, and the shards of craven bones burrow deeper into my body. He's been waiting for this—the chance to hurt me some more. I spit up blood, and the room sways, teetering on some unknowable cliff.

Tyrek can't be as powerful as Efiya, who was impervious to anti-magic. She'd only gifted him a tiny part of her soul—what Dimma did was something else. The craven bone should mute his magic if I'm close enough to him, or at least I convince myself that's true. I launch at him, throwing my body forward. His magic tears into me, but it's no use. Momentum carries me the rest of the way, then I fall into a black abyss.

I'm on my side, wet with my own blood, coughing and choking. I'm gasping for air that never comes. Tyrek lies in front of me—his eyes lifeless, with the Demon King's dagger between us—covered in blood. I don't know how or when, but he's dead. Tears blur my vision as someone pulls me into their arms. I stare up at Sukar, waterlogged and soaked to the bone. His golden-brown skin looks ashen and haggard. I try to speak, but no words come. I smile at him through my tears.

"You're going to be okay." Sukar cradles me against his chest. He's sobbing, and I can't stop thinking that the demons will kill us both if they hear him. "Rest now."

Despite him being wet and cold, I let my body go slack in his arms. He smells like sunlight and cloves—he smells like home. Unlike before, when I wished that it was Rudjek holding me, I'm only glad that Sukar is okay. He's here with me. He's safe. He didn't have to send a spy to keep tabs on me. I want him to tease me, so we can laugh with Essnai about how we almost died in a strange world.

THIRTY-ONE
RUDJEK

I draw a stone along the edge of my blade in furious strokes with no regard for caution. It's less than an hour before we march—the Almighty Army and the cravens. Our alliance is a momentous feat held together by thinly veiled lies and the secrets that Captain Dakte so astutely alluded to. The hour comes too slow as I sit on a stool in the middle of our camp, sharpening my swords. I've promoted Majka and Kira to share Captain Dakte's duties, over the protests of many.

The camp is in an uproar as soldiers pull on armor, adjust helmets, and strap on their scabbards. More than a few gazes roam my way—some not even bothering to hide their doubts. They're scared after Captain Dakte got so many men killed in his charge against the demons only a few days ago.

I've wanted this my whole life. To wear the uniform and make a name for myself climbing up the gendar ranks. But I haven't earned my post, which makes it that much harder to know these soldiers' lives are in my hands.

"Be careful, or you'll cut your thumb off," comes Koré's raspy timbre, low and menacing. I glance up, still keeping pace with my strokes, to see that she's presenting herself as an attendant. She wears an unadorned black tunic with wide yellow pants that sweep around her ankles. Her headscarf is gone, and she's pulled her braids into a ponytail. No one else seems to notice the unnerving way her hair wriggles and crawls over her shoulders. She squats across from me, opposite the dying fire.

I shrug. "I'll just grow a new one."

Koré picks up a discarded stick and pokes at the fire. "You should expect the worst for Arrah."

My hand slips on the stone and the blade slices across my forefinger. I barely feel the prick, and the wound heals before any blood spills. I swallow the raging emotions threatening to get loose. I'm a step ahead of her. I'm already thinking the worst, and the tightness pulling at my insides only grows tauter.

"How is it that you didn't know the Demon King had escaped until now?" I demand, not bothering to humble my voice. Koré is considerably less annoying than her brother, but they're two worms in the same rotten apple.

"Arrogance," the moon orisha answers, staring into the embers. Re'Mec would've never confessed any fault, and her honesty makes me put aside my shotel. "I never expected Efiya to find the box, let alone open it without disturbing the souls of my brethren that bound Daho. She was a clever girl, but, then again, she possessed Heka's power, and he is unlike my kind."

"Where is Heka?" I ask, curious.

"I suspect he's hiding in the mouth of the Supreme Cataclysm, or he's found something else to occupy his time," Koré says. "He's very good at hiding from us."

"Re'Mec told me that the demons are your children." I raise my voice. "Why is it impossible for you to stop them?"

Her wriggling hair falls still at once, and there is a notable change in her expression. Not sadness but a kind of resignation. "Imagine yourself with children one day, Crown Prince."

I blink as blackness bleeds into my eyes, blurring out the camp. I'm in a sunlit salon with toys scattered about my feet. Three children burst through the doors, laughing as they chase each other. The oldest is a boy with golden eyes and smooth brown skin. Twin girls, who look a year or two younger, run after him. They turn circles around me, and I laugh, overcome with joy and pride.

"Now imagine that you must kill them." Koré's voice pierces through the illusion.

The children line up in front of me, and the boy hugs his sisters tight against his sides. "We didn't mean to break the vase, Papa," he says. "It was an accident."

A shotel hangs heavy in my right hand as I stare at my children in horror, knowing what I must do.

"We're sorry, Papa, please," begs one of the twins. Gods, her eyes are exactly like mine.

"You made mistakes when you were little," says her sister.

"Enough!" I scream as the shotel almost drops from my hand. I am back in the camp again with Koré still poking at the fire. "Don't ever do that again," I spit. "Stay out of my head."

"Perhaps you get the point now." Koré leans close to me. "The demons are so very young, with powers that were never meant for them. They are awful, yes, but my brethren and I were awful, too, in the beginning."

I shake my head in disgust. "Are you making excuses for what they've done?"

"No, but you should know what it's like for me to have to hunt and imprison my children," she says. "I have grown to despise them over the millennia, but it hurts no less."

"It's time, Commandant," Majka interrupts us. He's in his full battle armor; his visor pushed back into his helmet. Silver plates over a red elara. "The men are ready—we've got three hundred and thirty-seven who can fight." He quirks an eyebrow. "They're waiting for you."

Three hundred and thirty-seven. We would've had five hundred if not for Captain Dakte. Add to that a hundred cravens to counter the demons' magic. No Zeknorians, though. Commander Korr had answered my last plea to parlay with news that their king had yet to change his mind. I have no clue how they'll react now that we're marching a second time against the demons without their support. But I don't care about the odds. I come to my feet and sheathe my shotels. "Of course, Captain Kelu." I give Majka an incredulous look. We'd always dreamed of becoming officers in the Almighty Army. Now the honor is bittersweet with so many of our comrades dead.

"The title fits me quite nicely." He stands a little taller, his chest out. "It does help that I am by far the most attractive captain in the entire army."

"You are certainly the most egotistical." I look back to where Koré had been sitting. She's already gone. I understand her point about the demons, how hard it might be for her, but we all have to make sacrifices.

"The soldiers will be expecting a speech," Majka says.

"I know," I grumble.

"Did you bother preparing one?" he asks, his voice laced with amusement.

"No." I think of all the times I sweet-talked my scribes into not telling my father how often I skipped lessons. "I'll make it up as I go."

At the edge of the village the demons have taken as their camp, I face the Almighty Army of the Kingdom with Majka and Kira on either side of me. The cravens stand to our right with Fadyi in command by my order. Their white robes and slender blades look deceivingly simple next to the gendars. I've gotten used to how Fadyi and the others never seem quite still. Their skin, hair, and clothes are always in motion. I once likened it to a million fire ants working together to give the illusion of a solid form.

When I asked Fadyi why they're so willing to follow me when I look human, he said, "Don't you understand by now, Rudjek? Appearance is a construct, though I do have to remind Jahla on occasion. What we see when we look at you is the descendant of Caster of the Eldest Clan, and we are yours to command." I clasped his shoulder in solidarity, hoping that their faith in me wouldn't prove to be misplaced.

"Two riders approach from the west!" a gendar calls out.

Commander Korr trots forward on his white steed, armed and cloaked in furs. He has a broadsword across his back and an ax belted against his chest. Another rider follows, bearing the Zeknorian flag—a bear's claw set upon crossed swords. His army marches in his wake. They wear silver and a pale blue that almost blends in with the icy mountains behind them.

"Attention, left flank!" Majka orders, and the gendars turn so that we're facing the Zeknorians. Shezmu had been counting on infighting to divide the Kingdom and Zeknor. I can't let that happen.

Commander Korr stops halfway between our two armies. "You dare march on Zeknorian soil again without our permission."

I don't have time for another confrontation with him. I need to get to the gate and find Arrah and stop the Demon King, in that order. "Here I thought you had come to join the battle against the demons, but if you are content with sitting this one out, by all means."

"You speak boldly for a sickly boy," Commander Korr remarks.

"Yet I'm the most equipped to deal with your demon problem." I gesture at my soldiers. "If you don't want us to fight, we can head back to our ship and leave the demons to you."

"I suggest you do that before you find my sword at your throat," Commander Korr spits.

"As you wish," I say, taking a huge gamble. From what I'd gathered from our brief conversations, he was all for joining forces. But the Zeknorian king has a petty grudge against the Kingdom. Maybe I've been approaching this the wrong way. Before, I asked the Zeknorians to help us, but this is their land and their honor to defend. We would be the ones helping *them*, not the other way around. "Majka, give the order that we are leaving Zeknor."

"Are you sure?" he whispers close to my ear.

"Yes." I don't bother to keep my voice low.

Commander Korr's horse whinnies as he tightens his grip on the reins. "Do my ears deceive me? You, Crown Prince of the Almighty Kingdom, have come to offer your swords to aid my army's attack on the demons." He says it loud enough for his words to spread through the ranks.

"You heard right, Commander Korr," I answer, holding back a smile. Let him keep his pride. "The Kingdom is at your service—if you will allow us to fight by your side."

Commander Korr strokes his beard as if he's thinking on the matter. "We will accept your offer."

Cheers rise across the ranks of both armies. I am relieved, but I don't let it show. I hold my tongue while Commander Korr gives a speech to his soldiers. Their battle cries drown out most of his words.

I stare at gendars thrice my age marked by battle scars and at soldiers no more than a year or two older than me. Soldiers with sweat streaking their brows, their fear evident. I push all doubts from my mind as I look into their eyes. "I won't lie to you: I'm afraid, too, but I'm not afraid of the demons. I'm not afraid to fight, bleed, and die to put down the threat to Zöran and the Kingdom. I'm afraid of what happens to our world if we don't put aside our differences and stand together for a greater good." I pause, letting them soak in my words. "Let us stand with our cousins from the South," I say, my voice rising to a roar, "and our cousins from the North united as one!"

My soldiers break into cheers that rival the Zeknorians'. Not that I'm comparing or anything.

"For the glory of the Almighty Kingdom!" Kira yells.

I wait impatiently as the first wave charges into the heart of the village. Ice-blue uniforms blur with Almighty Kingdom red and craven white. Our forces disappear around dwellings with rough brick walls and slanted roofs. I rotate my wrists, adjusting my shotels until the hilts sink into the curves of my palms. I'm counting down the moments until the war horn blows, and the second wave joins the fight, then it comes at once. Not the horn, but a burst of flames that lights up the sky. Moaning, wailing, screaming, death. I take one step, and Majka grabs my arm. Fadyi, Jahla, and Commander Korr are in the first wave.

"As commandant your place is here," Majka says, his eyes glassy as he tries and fails to keep his face hard. He loves Jahla—I hadn't taken him seriously, but it's written in his stricken features. "With the second wave."

I restrain myself from pulling out of his grasp. The wait is torturous, but when the horn finally blows, I set off at a hard sprint, the rest of the second wave on my heels. Something whizzes past my ear that leaves my cheek burning. Then another and another. The air shifts. I can't believe it. Birds of lightning descend from the sky, advancing upon the demons in a frenzy. Several orishas have joined the fight.

The burning in my cheek sears down to the bone, and I wipe my face with my forearm and find it melted. Charred skin and flesh slosh onto my arm, and I stare in horror. Gods, it hurts.

When I enter the heart of the village, I crouch, my lungs burning, ready to pounce. Bodies litter the ground. No, not bodies, *body parts*. An arm here, a leg there. Hands. Heads. I gag and swallow down my panic. Mostly cravens from the first wave engage the demons in battle alongside the orishas. Very few Kingdom soldiers or Zeknorians are still standing. I am stunned by the sight of some of the demons. They're heads taller than us, with wings dripping blood and sharp teeth. They bear a striking resemblance to the people of the North. Black veins show underneath their skin along their foreheads. These demons must have come through the gate from Ilora.

The cravens' anti-magic counters their magic, evening out the fight. Blood soaked, Korr parries with a woman with long red hair and glowing emerald eyes. He strikes her across the chest with his sword, and she smiles as her wound closes before his eyes.

I no sooner turn away than a demon runs me through with his blade. The man sneers, his eyes triumphant in his stolen Tamaran body. I tighten my grips on my shotels, my anti-magic rolling off me in waves. It assaults the demon—peeling away his flesh. It isn't like before when I killed the demon in the alley and his soul returned to a bodiless state. I'm stronger now. My anti-magic shreds this demon's soul into bits and pieces until there's nothing left. He won't be coming back.

I peer down at the sword still lodged in my gut. The pain is excruciating.

"Need help?" Kira says as her daggers catch two enemies. The knives disappear and reform in the sheaths against her thighs. She yanks the sword from my belly, and I bite down the pain as the wound heals. "We're still protecting you, little runt."

"And doing a poor job of it, too," I say with a wink.

Majka relieves a demon of his head. "Should've left it in there."

Six demons from Ilora surround us. They are tall, broad shouldered, with swords twice the size of our own. "I'll handle this," I say as my eyes adjust, narrowing and honing. My senses heighten to the subtle shifts of space around me. The demons attempt to shed their bodies to become something else, but my skin pulses with anti-magic again. It counters their magic and binds them to their physical forms, making them more vulnerable. "You might want to duck now," I yell to my friends.

Kira grabs Majka's shoulder and pulls him down with her. I search for the threads that bind time and space and yank them. The action pulls me outside time—it'll only last for a moment, but that's all I need. The battle moves in slow motion around me as I cut down demon after demon. There is a tug on my body as I fall back in sync with time. The six demons lie at my feet—their bodies and souls shredded beyond repair.

"What just happened?" Majka says, his eyes wide.

"Rudjek!" Fadyi yells over the commotion. He fights off a dozen demons on the edge of the square. Then I see it: the gate. It shimmers in and out of existence. It's a simple metal arch, towering over us and glowing with strange symbols. Jahla and six other cravens stand beneath it. With their anti-magic so near the gate, Shezmu can't escape through it. It's our only way to find Arrah and the others.

I've taken two steps toward it when Kira screams. It's a blood-curdling sound that cuts through me as I whirl around. I follow her hollow gaze to where Majka lies crumpled on the ground with a wound through his chest. It takes far too long for me to process the horror before my eyes.

"No," I whisper, my body falling still, my arms slack at my sides. I can't move. Majka. I grit my teeth, my mind reeling. The cravens can heal him. It's not too late.

A demon stands over Majka, grinning at me. I've seen those eyes in my nightmares—the eyes of his daughter, Efiya. The demon is tan, compact, and muscular with an angular face. Except for the eyes, they look nothing alike. Efiya's demon father, who she gave a human body. Shezmu. "I've been waiting for you, Rudjek," he says, his voice rough.

Tears blur my vision as I stumble forward. I want to rip out his heart with my bare hands. Kira attacks him, but he lifts one hand to send her hurtling back through the air. She slams into a Zeknorian soldier, and they both go down.

Shezmu blurs before my eyes. He's so much stronger and faster than the six demons I killed, and my anti-magic buckles against him. I stumble, my legs losing strength before I look down to see a gaping hole in my belly. I blink and fall to my knees. I remember Fadyi's lessons—him insisting that I must learn to heal faster. No, he said that I must *be* faster so I could avoid getting injured altogether. The joke's on him now for inheriting such a sorry excuse for a pupil.

Shezmu smiles down at me, unnatural light dancing in his eyes. "I have a gift for you, Rudjek," he says, a gray mist swirling in his hand. I can't move as my body struggles to heal. "Not that you deserve such an honor."

"You . . ." I cough, spitting up blood. "You should've died on the battlefield with that monstrosity of a daughter of yours."

"Is that so?" Shezmu says, his smile still intact.

I open my mouth to tell him what a pompous ass he is, but I never get the chance. The soul flies down my throat. The impact knocks me on my back, and I hit the ground, choking and gasping for air. Every muscle in my body goes rigid. I scream, and two voices rip from my throat—my own and that of the demon inside me.

THIRTY-TWO
ARRAH

I am not dead, but I don't feel alive, either. I am an afterthought in someone's else dream. I am a passing shadow. My eyes flutter closed, and my head slumps forward. Sukar wraps an arm around my shoulders to keep me upright, his touch gentle and steady. Despite my pain, I welcome his embrace, his scent of sunshine and cloves, his cool skin against mine. I am burning up and sitting in a puddle of my blood mixed with Tyrek's. He's dead now, gone to be with my sister. May the both of them rot inside Daho's dagger.

"I thought you were dead." I wince at the pain of talking. "I searched for you."

"I would still be floating in that river if not for my tattoos," Sukar confesses. "That little rat caught me off guard. He's lucky you killed him before I could."

"You and Essnai were right about him all along." I squeeze my eyes shut and tears stream down my cheeks. "I should've listened."

"You have a good, though misguided heart, Arrah," Sukar teases, patting the top of my head like I'm hopeless. "It's not wrong to want to see the best in people until they show you otherwise."

I tell him what I've learned since his fall into the river. "Tyrek commanded the demons to kidnap the last group of tribal people. He was trying to free my sister." I brace myself to tell him the rest—the part about Dimma, how Fram trapped her soul. It comes out in sobs.

Sukar stares at me, half in shock, then he massages his forehead. "So you're saying that you're a reincarnated goddess?"

"Something like that," I concede, grimacing.

"You do have a flair for the dramatic, don't you?"

I almost laugh, but the pain stops me. "Shut it."

Sukar goes still, his voice weak. "I'm sorry that I couldn't protect you and Essnai."

"Where is she?" I'm afraid of his answer. "Did she get away?"

"I don't know." Sukar hesitates. "I thought I'd find the both of you here."

"She went back to the gate," I say, grief-stricken. "We have to search for her."

"We'll go when you're not bleeding to death." He leaves no room for argument. It isn't like I can get up on my own anyway. "Essnai is smart and resourceful—she'll be okay."

"What of the demons?" I pull away from him and peer into his eyes. He looks less haggard. "How did you get past them? What about the tribal people?"

"The tribal people are fine, Arrah," Sukar says, his voice placating. "The demons fled as soon as you killed Tyrek."

The tribal people are safe—that's all that matters for now. "I need to push out these bone shards."

"What can I do to help?" Sukar asks, looking over my wounds.

"Just . . . hold me, please." It comes out so desperate that I'm glad my braids hang in a curtain around my face, so he doesn't see my embarrassment. Hold me because I can't sit up on my own. Hold me because Rudjek can't. "You know what I mean."

"And here I thought you were flirting while bleeding all over me," Sukar says.

"Don't be ridiculous," I grumble, but there's no spirit behind my words, no real bite.

"What would I be if I wasn't your ridiculous friend?" I hear the smile and longing in his voice.

I squeeze his hand, and Dimma's memories draw me into their grasp. The brush of feathers against my lips, the warmth of a mouth, the delight of hands. I shudder, not from disgust but desire. I've had so many glimpses into Dimma's life with Daho that it's hard to see him as the awful person the gods warned about. I don't begrudge them what they had, but I can't forget that Daho's demons have eaten countless souls—he's done it himself.

"I shouldn't have said that," Sukar admits, mistaking my shudder for something else. "I'm a rotten friend."

I let out a frustrated breath. "Considering that I almost killed you once and you almost died a second time on my watch, you get to be rotten once."

"I *am* starting to sense a pattern," Sukar says, his voice laced with his usual air of cynicism. "Whenever you're around, I'm fated to die."

If Essnai were here, she'd thump him on his head, and it would be like old times, the three of us together. But I'm not so sure I want things to go back to the way they were between us. I don't know what I want exactly. I brace myself as I call my magic. It's still sluggish under my skin, but I remember what the Aatiri woman said. *Grow a scab over them, and they're easier to bear.* I resist the impulse to breathe deeply, which only makes the pain worse. The magic inside me rushes to the craven bone, but it stalls and peters out.

"It's not working," I say, frustrated. "I don't know if I can do this."

"I could always try digging out the bone with a knife?" Sukar raises an eyebrow. "At least I won't leave you with some ugly tattoos."

"You really have the nerve to crack a joke right now?" I wince as more pain blossoms around my wounds. "You are absolutely the worst friend there ever was and ever will be."

He cradles me a little tighter against his chest. "And you're truly the most stubborn girl I have ever known."

He's trying to cheer me up, but I can feel his heart racing. He's scared, too. I need his humor right now. I cling to it.

I take another deep breath and try again, nudging the magic closer to the shards. "If I survive this gods' awful mess, I'll conjure up some magic to beautify your new tattoos. How about that?"

"That would be marvelous," Sukar says.

When the magic finally reaches the shards, I close my eyes, exhausted again. Now, the hard part. The Aatiri woman had said to grow a scab over the shards, but what if I surround them with magic? That would lessen their effect on me and the damage they can inflict on the way out. I wrap the shards in a shield of magic, then begin the laborious task of moving them. I bite back a scream as the magic tucks the shards through my flesh. The process goes well into the night. Soon the first shard emerges from my thigh covered in gore. "One down, three to go."

When I'm done with all four, sweat streaks my brow and I can't keep my eyes open. Sukar asks me questions, but when I try to answer, my words jumble in my head. He lifts me into his arms, and I curl against him as he takes me to a cot on the other side of the tent. "Rest now," he says, his voice choked up again. "You need to heal."

I fall into a deep, dreamless sleep. I don't know how long I drift in and out of consciousness. Sometimes Sukar is by my side when I wake, and sometimes I'm alone. Sometimes it's night, sometimes it's day. He presses a cup to my lips, and the water tastes sweet. He talks as he washes my skin with a warm rag, but his voice is too distant to make out his words.

I wake again in the middle of the night, and I'm so cold that my teeth chatter. Sukar sleeps balled up in the corner of the tent, far enough away that two people could fit between us. "Sukar." His name comes out as a croak, and I shouldn't, but I ask, "Can you hold me again?"

I hear his sharp inhale at my words, his trepidation, his need. He doesn't answer as he crosses the tent and pulls me into his arms. His skin is warm against my own, and I sink into him.

"How long have you known?" I ask, hoping he'll know the real question. *How long have you felt this way about me?*

"I've loved you since the first moment I saw you," he admits.

I am so overwhelmed by the emotions that flood into my body that for a moment I can't bring myself to speak. I turn over and lie on my back. I look into his eyes, shining brown gems in the night, and I know it's a mistake I can't take back. I reach up and stroke his cheek, and it's smooth in the way Rudjek's never quite is. He turns his face, and his lips tremble against my palm. *Gods.* They're full and warm and so soft.

"You deserve better, Sukar," I whisper, my words heavy now as his lips light a fire inside me. *You deserve better than to be the second choice of some girl with a treacherous heart.*

"Yet I still want you," he says, his eyes hooded with desire.

This is a line we can't uncross. It's not like when we were children at the Temple when he kissed Essnai and me. That had been pretend, make-believe. This is very real. "Kiss me," I breathe, and he smiles, the moonlight dancing in his eyes. His lips draw close to mine.

I can't explain it. It's irrational. But, gods, I want this so bad. I moan as his lips graze my earlobe. His teeth send a shiver of pleasure through me. I remember another time and sharp teeth that teased and tantalized. Daho's teeth. And a time underneath Heka's Temple with Rudjek's mouth hot against mine.

"Arrah." Sukar sighs. "I can't, not like this." He pulls away from me, looking as flustered and overwhelmed and hungry as I feel. I sag against the cot. I'm breathing hard, too, from his embrace and because it's left me exhausted. Sukar brushes his hand across my cheek, hope filling his eyes. "Rest."

His word is a subtle command, and I'm so very tired. I close my eyes, and this time, I dream about him.

PART V

PART V

THE UNNAMED ORISHA: DIMMA

I become obsessed with clocks. Tracking time is easy enough on my own, though I could never grasp its importance. Clocks add a sense of urgency, the way their song hums of some unknowable future. If I'm to believe them, I will soon see the end of my life.

My brethren have the experience of living before Iben crawled from the womb and fathered time. They've shaped the universe out of the raw material the Supreme Cataclysm gifted them. They've made children, mourned their deaths, and made new ones. They've hidden in the labyrinth of our creator when they needed a reprieve from eternity. I want none of those things. I wish only to see my child born and thrive in his own right.

Daho and I invite my brethren to our summer palace in Zöran to, what he calls "talk some sense into them." I send a message through the threads that bind everyone and everything, even the likes of my kind. It's difficult to say how many of my brethren dwell in the universe, for some hide themselves well.

The palace sits at the top of a mountain in Zöran, bathed in sun-light year-round. As my brethren arrive, the mountain shakes, rocks crack and splinter, and the last of the winter snow melts. They sweep into the palace—cloaked in shadows, bathed in warm light, swathed in flames, awash in rain. They are cinder and stardust and wind—some corporeal, some not. They cling to windowsills, perch on the rooftops, hang from the walls, and sit on divans. I can taste their natures, sweet and bitter, and strange. Many do not speak. They only listen.

Fram, Iben, and Kiva are the oldest in attendance, and they pres-ent themselves in the salon in mortal vessels. I do not know Kiva, but I like him. His appearance reflects his nature. He is a child with wild green curls, brown skin, and golden eyes, who plops down on the floor and plays with his toys. Fram stands in front of the window, staring out at Zöran, their twin bodies, light and dark. Iben, who sits opposite Daho and me on a divan, is a shadow that flickers in and out of our reality. I am disappointed that Re'Mec and Koré did not come, but I expected as much.

Daho hasn't left my side since my brethren started to arrive. He squeezes my hand—and his fear is a flame that wraps his soul in a blanket of doubts. "Thank you for coming," he says after clearing his throat. His words crack on the edges, making him sound so very young. "Dimma and I—"

One of my brethren hisses, and every beast and fowl on the mountain descends into chaos.

"And I thought that I was one to act like a child," Kiva says in a voice as bright and sweet as dove bells. He doesn't look up from the blocks that he's stacking one by one to build a tower.

The hissing drops into a chastened growl, then abruptly stops, and the animals grow calm.

Daho tries again. This time agitation cuts through his words. "We hope that you'll see reason. Our son is a gift, a blessing. How could he not be? Dimma couldn't be with child if the Supreme Cataclysm did not want it."

"A gift," one mocks.

"A blessing," taunts another.

"Silence," Fram says, their voices at once a sharp blade and a warm embrace. "Our sister and our new brother requested our audience with great respect, and we must show the same."

Daho collects his thoughts. "How could you ask us to give up our child?"

Darkness falls over the salon, and desperation crawls across my vessel. For one brief, horrifying moment, Fram's faces lose their balance of light and dark. They become stark white with hollow black eyes. "You wouldn't be the first to give up a child," they say, as their balance returns. "I know that better than most."

Iben pages through a tome with a tan leather binding that Daho left on the divan. He looks up when he feels my gaze upon him and smiles. "I'm only here to bear witness. I will not take sides in our family squabbles."

"It's not enough to bear witness." I feel my child form his first impressions of the world through me. It should be a joyous moment, but the tension in the salon mars it. His thoughts are a tangle of emotions—confusion, curiosity, and wonder. Several of my brethren gasp when they sense the child's newfound awareness. Some hiss, some recoil.

"What *is* it?" someone asks, their voice a low growl. "It is not like us."

"*It* is our end," answers another.

"We're here because you deserve to know why we sided with Re'Mec and Koré." Fram's voices cut through the chatter. "Your child draws strength from the Supreme Cataclysm. We do as well, but unlike ours, his relationship is parasitic. The universe has become unbalanced and unstable because of him."

"They mean to say that the universe is dying," Kiva explains in his high-pitched voice. "In time, the Supreme Cataclysm is going to eat us all, including your little one."

I laugh, the sound a bitter shriek. Iben looks up from the book. Kiva's tower of blocks collapses. Fram raises their eyebrows. Daho and the rest of my brethren go still. "You're afraid." I look at each of them in turn, the corporeal and the incorporeal. "You've lived so long that you fear death. You're willing to sacrifice my child so you don't have to face your end."

"We are eternal!" someone hisses.

"You'd like to think you are." Malice curls around my words. "But you don't know for sure."

"Nor do we intend to find out," replies the hissing voice.

At that, my brethren abandon me. One by one, they retreat from the salon, the palace, and the mountain. Daho pulls me into his arms, his wings trembling at his back. "It's going to be okay, my love," he whispers, his lips brushing my forehead. "We'll fight them."

I nestle my head against his chest. Our path will only lead to suffering and our end. I do not need Iben's gift of traveling the threads of time to know this.

The doors to the salon burst open, and four men storm into the room, drenched in blood and sweat. Yacara, a general in Daho's newly raised army, leads them. They smell of death and desperation and despair.

"Your Highnesses," Yacara breathes, stepping forward. "The endoyans attacked Jiiek."

Daho frowns, not believing what the man is saying. "Attacked? What do you mean? We've been at peace with our familiars for generations upon generations."

"They've killed millions," Yacara explains through sobs, ignoring Daho's question. "We barely got through the gate to warn you."

"We've only been away a month," Daho says, still in shock. "How could this happen?"

"It's the abomination's fault." One of the soldiers points a shaky finger at me. "It was one of her kind that led the endoyans."

Yacara slaps the man hard. "Don't speak of our queen in that tone ever again—she is not her brother's keeper."

The soldier lowers his gaze and whispers an insincere apology.

I cradle my belly, realizing the truth of it. This was the reason Re'Mec and Koré hadn't come today. My brethren attacked the demon people as a warning to me.

THIRTY-THREE
ARRAH

Sukar holds me through the long night like I'm some fragile thing on the verge of breaking. In truth, I've already shattered more times than I can remember. I'll never be the girl I was before, now that I know about Dimma. Most of her mortal lives, after her first death and before me, are vague impressions. They remind me of sitting in the assembly, listening to the mundane grievances of the rich. They don't hold much weight or substance and blend in as background noise.

While Sukar sleeps, his breathing steady, my treacherous heart betrays me. When I let myself think of Daho, he's no longer the Demon King. He's the boy who told me stories, the boy who made me a cake slathered in buttercream. The boy who explored countless worlds at my side. The boy who, after a century, still woke in a cold sweat from nightmares about his parents' death. He's not a monster in Dimma's memories, but I can't forget that he became one after I—after she died. I dig my nails into my palms, anger and frustration turning my blood cold. I hate that one day, when I die, I will only be another faint memory that pales in the shadow of her life with Daho.

I fall asleep with him on my mind, but it's Rudjek in my dreams. He peers at me from behind a curtain of velvety lashes, his obsidian eyes curious. "You didn't know that Sukar was in love with you?"

We're sitting beside the Serpent River with our feet digging in the mud. Crocodiles sunbathe along the banks, watching our every move. A cloud drifts across the sky, blocking out the brunt of the sunlight, but it's still another blazing hot day in Tamar. Our only reprieve is the breeze rustling through the grass that keeps the mosquitoes away.

"How could I know?" I say, annoyed to no end at how unaffected he is about the whole thing. It's like he doesn't care. "Sukar flirts with everyone."

"You *did* look quite comfy with him in the garden at my Coming of Age Ceremony," Rudjek reminds me nonchalantly. "I should've realized then that something was going on between the two of you."

"How could you even think that?" I snap, glaring at him.

"Oh, don't give me that look." Rudjek laughs, and it's a deep rumble in his chest. "I'm not the one kissing other people." He narrows his eyes. "How far would you've gone if he hadn't stopped?"

I cross my arms, my jaw set. Two can play his game. "I don't see how it's any of your business. We can't touch without one of us almost dying."

"I can't change what I am, Arrah." Rudjek turns back to stare at the river. His face is perfect in profile, the curve of his cheek, the tilt of his chin, the smooth skin of his throat, soft as gossamer. "I can't be anything but what I am."

His words shatter the illusion that any of this is real. *I can't be anything but what I am.* He would never be so dismissive about me almost kissing Sukar. That's only wishful thinking.

When I open my eyes, weak sunlight streams into the tent. I'm alone on the cot, and for one brief, blissful moment, I convince myself that it was all a dream. Almost kissing Sukar, him holding me, his body arched against mine. I haven't betrayed Rudjek. But as soon as the sleep fog lifts from my mind, I know the truth. I *did* almost kiss Sukar—I ached to feel his mouth against my own. I ached for more. His scent clings to my skin. I breathe him in, steeling myself for the aftermath of what I've done.

I'm worried about what other nasty surprises my sister has left in her wake, Tyrek being the first. I want to believe that the Demon King is still in his prison, but if he is, then I am back to the same predicament: keep my magic and risk letting him manipulate me, or let go of the chieftains' *kas*. I can't consider the latter, not with the tribal people still somewhere beyond the crossroads and the threat from these new, more powerful demons from Ilora. The chieftains gave up their lives so I could stop Efiya and protect the tribes, and I intend to finish what I started.

My feelings for Daho have become complicated. I haven't heard his voice since the night the demons attacked, but I still sense his presence. It's stronger now that the craven bone is away from me. I don't believe he would've let Tyrek hurt me if he could stop him. As for why he hasn't spoken to me again, that should be obvious. When

I thought he *was* Tyrek, I had every intention of killing him. I have complicated feelings about that, too.

"You're awake," Sukar says from somewhere in the tent, his voice a familiar lullaby.

I want to pretend that I'm still sleeping so I don't have to face him so soon, but it's too late for that now. My head spins as I sit up, and I squint against the morning light. Sukar perches on his haunches in front of a fire, lit where Tyrek had lain dead. The blood and his body are gone. "How long have I been sleeping?"

"Four days," Sukar says.

"Four days?" I struggle to get up. My legs don't cooperate.

"Take it easy," Sukar says, abandoning the fire.

He helps me to my feet, and I sway before collapsing into his arms. His palm is warm against the small of my back as his gaze travels to my lips. All I have to do is lean in and let it happen, take the dangling fruit he's offering. Instead, I force strength into my legs and pull away from him. "Have you found Essnai yet?"

"No." Sukar grimaces. "We've gone out twice already and no sign of her."

"We?" I ask, my eyes going wide.

"Me and some of the tribespeople." Sukar runs his hand across his head. "The ones strong enough. Most are still too weak."

"Did they help you move Tyrek?" I look past him to the fire. A chill crawls across my forearms. How could I have ever mistaken that coward for Daho?

"I'm not helpless, you know." Sukar arches an eyebrow at me. There is so much more behind his expression than I can handle right now. "I did that on my own."

"I want to see them." I realize that I haven't heard a sound outside the tent. An irrational fear overcomes me that this is another dream, that they're all dead. I stumble away from Sukar, my legs awkward and clumsy, but he doesn't try to stop me. I push past the tent flap, and the amber hue of the sun washes out my vision. I gasp, stumbling back.

"I should've warned you." Sukar places a steadying hand on my shoulder. "It's temporary—your vision will adjust. The sun is strange here."

"I still can't believe that we're in another world." I brace myself against him. "Under any other circumstances, it would be exciting."

"Arrah," he breathes my name after a long silence between us. "Whatever you might be feeling after . . . after the other night, know that I don't regret it."

I smile up at him, his face an outline of light and shadows. It's all I can do not to burst into tears. My feelings twist around my heart like thorny vines, and, heavens, they make it hard to think. "What did you do with the dagger?"

"I have it with me." He moves his hand to pat a sheath underneath his tunic. "It didn't feel right to leave it lying around."

I'm relieved as he leads me from the tent, the dirt and prickly grass warm underneath my bare feet. With every step, my body grows stronger. The camp comes into focus, the shape of tents and kettles above fires. Then I see people: stooped, emaciated, hollow eyed. Tattered clothes, dusty faces. I blink back my tears, despite their condition. "They're alive."

"Tyrek and his minions had enough food to hold the tribal people captive for months," Sukar says. "I wouldn't doubt that he'd been planning to get you here for a long time."

I spy a woman crushing grains in a mortar, her withered hands shaking. I kneel beside her, and she looks up at me with suspicion in her golden eyes. The Mulani chieftain stirs inside me, her *ka* a ribbon of silk. She whispers in my head, guiding the way my words glide into a finely spun tapestry. I speak in her native tongue with ease. "Do you know where the others went—the rest of the tribes?"

"Only the *djeli* knew," she says, her voice brittle as paper. The keeper of stories. "She took her own life when the demons and their little prince attacked us. Any *djeli* caught did the same to protect the secret."

Sukar goes rigid, not needing to understand the words to recognize the pain in her voice. "None of them know how to find the other tribal people. I've already tried asking."

"You are truly the one who carries our chieftains' *kas*." The woman's eyes well with tears. "You are blessed."

I can only nod and push back tears as she stops her work to squeeze my hand. I have a responsibility to the tribal people, and I can't fail them again.

"How could Tyrek control Iben's gate to come here?" I wonder aloud, my voice trailing off. Dimma's memories tangle with my own. Iben—the orisha of time. I remember him sitting across from Daho and Dimma. *I'm only here to bear witness. I will not take sides in our family squabbles.* The demons had killed many orishas, including him. "He's dead." The realization knocks against my chest like a hammer cracking stone. Tyrek wanted to bring Efiya back, and Shezmu helped him try. "Shezmu must have Iben's power to control the gate."

Sukar pulls his sickles, his gaze pinned on the hills at my back. I whirl around to see shadows flitting in and out of my line of vision. The demons didn't retreat when I killed Tyrek. They went to get reinforcements.

"Give me Daho's dagger," I say, my voice trembling.

"Maybe we can reason with them." Sukar hesitates. "What if we tell them that you're Dimma—that you *were* Dimma. That has to mean something to them."

"The knife," I say again, and this time he places it in my hand, still wrapped in the red silk and stained with blood. Dimma's love for the demons eats at my courage. She wouldn't want to hurt them. She sacrificed almost everything to give them a chance against the orishas.

But I'm not her.

I close my fingers around the dagger. Now that I have more of Dimma's memories, I understand the full potential of the blade. It melts into a bar of silvery light that lengthens until it becomes a sword.

THIRTY-FOUR
ARRAH

Hundreds of demons swarm the hills in wisps of gray smoke that scorch the land. The grass withers and browns, the life leached from it in great swatches. They're doing this to terrorize us, to show that they mean to take back the dagger, but I won't let them. I can't, not if I want to see the tribal people returned home. My legs feel heavy as dread courses through my body. The demons are a storm cloud promising utter devastation.

I look around, desperate, as the encampment falls into chaos. Hundreds of tribal people take up arms with pots, pans, and the weapons the demons left behind when they fled. They wear tattered, dirty tunics and kaftans caked in grime. Some are so underfed that they can hardly stand. I clench my teeth, wishing that I could bring Tyrek back just to let them exact their revenge. He deserved to suffer; instead, I've delivered his soul into my sister's waiting arms.

Most of the tribal people won't be able to conjure magic in their weakened state. Some have little to no magic to start. Despite having Dimma's memories, I don't have her powers. Only a few dozen tribal people—the ones still strong enough—gather with Sukar and me to defend against the demons. Their eyes burn bright with white light. Some of them reach their hands to the sky to draw in more magic out of reflex, but there's none here. This world is precisely what the orishas intended. Magic*less*. We'll have to rely on our own strength and hope it holds out.

Two Kes women with ice-white eyes and stark white hair kneel and press their hands against the ground. Their magic flickers in sparkles of gold across the grass and stings the bottom of my feet. At first, I don't understand what they're doing until the land between the demons and us blurs and stretches. They're buying time, but it won't work forever. The shift is so subtle that it feels like being on a calm sea. I'm at once fascinated and reminded that I don't know enough about my magic. I want to live and explore the wonders of the chieftains' gifts.

"Are any of you good with controlling the wind?" I shout to the people gathered to fight. "It'll slow down the ones who are incorporeal and force them to take physical form."

Seven people step forward—four from Tribe Litho, two from Tribe Zu, and one Aatiri. The Aatiri's wide-set eyes burn with rage. His magic flares against my skin. He is the strongest of them, and he longs for revenge.

I pick him and three others. "Take up a stance in one of the four corners around the camp and arch your wind to make a barrier. Leave no gaps between or above you." I don't have time to wonder if I'm doing the right thing. I have to act now. The demons are already pushing closer despite the Kes women's efforts. I choose another group for the next task. "You six form a smaller ring around those too weak to fight at the center of the camp." They nod and start to rally others into position. In truth, I hadn't expected them to listen. I'm no one to them, but they keep calling me *blessed one* with reverence in their voices because I carry the chieftains' *kas*.

"Stay with them, Sukar," I say. "Protect them, in case I fail."

As a windstorm whips past me, kicking up loose dirt, Sukar's eyes travel to the sword of light in my hand. A look of uncertainty passes over his face. He doesn't think we can win this time. "I'm not letting you face them alone; I'll be by your side like always." A flame kindles inside me, but I snuff it out. I can't let myself hope, not yet.

"If you find yourself ascending into death again, don't blame me." I shrug, playing at being callous when all I want is to beg him to listen for once in his life. I can't bear to lose him, Essnai, or Rudjek. They're all I have left, and I need them to be okay.

Sukar gives me a sidelong glance, and then he turns to the rest of the witchdoctors ready to fight. "Anyone talented with magic over souls can come with us to the front line," he says. "The rest of you stand between the two wind barriers. If any of them change into physical form, don't let them shed their bodies again."

"How are we supposed to do that, *neké*?" an older Litho man asks, addressing Sukar with the honorific of someone who's not yet come of age. *Neké* wouldn't be a slight in any other situation, but after everything we've been through, it's a slap to our faces.

"You must keep the tether between their souls and bodies intact, *eké*," Sukar says. He uses the title only bestowed upon the head of a family, though this man is not an *eké*. He does not bear the traditional marks on his neck to denote him as such for Tribe Litho. "Do you need me to tell you how to do that?"

The man grimaces, not missing the subtle sarcasm in Sukar's words. "No."

The idea is brilliant in its simplicity, and it could work. The orishas trapped the demons' souls in the veil in Kefu like they were fish flapping in a net. We have to make smaller nets. Seeing my look of surprise, Sukar winks at me. "You didn't think you were the only one with a plan."

In another life, things could've been different between us. "Fight well, my friend."

Sukar searches my face, and I swear he can read my truest feelings. Does he know that I want him to kiss me, that I dread it, that I need it? That if we kiss even once, it will be my unmaking. We could never go back. He glances away, guilt washing over his features. I should say something, but no words will make this easier for either of us.

I inhale a sharp breath, bracing myself for the onslaught. Sukar and I lead three dozen tribal people. The four holding the windstorm open a door for us to leave. Dirt and leaves and grass swirl everywhere, except for beneath the arch.

"He is coming for you, blessed one," whispers one of the tribal people in that dreamy way that only a seer speaks when gripped in a vision. "Soon you must choose."

I hesitate as the others press forward. The words have an air of inevitability. Every inch of me shakes with anticipation and dread. It's an awful feeling that makes me want to scream. Who is coming for me? I want desperately for it to be Rudjek. Maybe he's found a way here. But I can't quell the part of me that hopes it's Daho. Can I convince him to put an end to the war with the orishas and spare my people from further suffering? I need to see him for myself, not through a memory, not as a voice in my head. I need to see the reality of him, not some romanticized myth.

The demons charge toward the camp, a third of them in human bodies. The rest are smoke shaped into echoes of their towering forms with outstretched wings.

My instincts take over. I run, then leap toward the demons, my feet supported by pillars of wind, as I wield the sword of pure light. The edges are sharp enough to destroy worlds, and it slices through souls with ease. I careen through the air, spinning and twisting, my soul aligned with the chieftains'. We are one in a way that I've never experienced before—one body, one soul, one purpose. Dimma is with us: her memories, and a shadow of her magic.

I absorb soul after soul into the blade, pushing through my heart-ache. I remember the day Dimma forged the dagger to protect the very people I'm imprisoning now. Some of the demons try to escape, but I pursue them through the hilltops and the forest, hunting them down one by one. I tell myself that these aren't the demons that Dimma fought to save—those people had been innocent and kind. They wouldn't follow Efiya and Tyrek and do such awful things.

I float in front of a cowering demon in the body of a Zu boy. It's Rassa, the warrior whose mask ended up at the street fair nearly a month ago. Tyrek and the demons really did plant it to lure me onto their trail. Rassa was no older than seventeen. He had his whole life ahead of him—and this demon took his body. I point the sword to his throat, reeling with rage.

"I know that sword," the demon says, his eyes wide with surprise as he scuttles back from me. "Are you the abomination that destroyed my people?" Venom threads through his words, and I welcome the pain that strikes my heart. I deserve every bit of it. I deserve much worse for what Dimma did. Some of the demons had hated her for changing them. They despised her gift of immortality.

"Yes," I hiss before I reap his soul. There is no malice behind my action, only regret.

I turn back to the camp, a hundred souls collected in the dagger and still twice as many to catch. Half the witchdoctors who'd led the attack with me and Sukar are sprawled out in the grass, bleeding to death. The other half fight to hold back the horde of smoke from reaching the tribal people too weak to fight.

I land in the field behind the demons, and their smoke curls around itself as they turn their attention on me. "I have what you want," I say as the sword returns to its dagger form. I hold it up for all to see. The demons only pause for a moment. I can sense their eagerness to take it from me, yet they hesitate. "Know this: if you do not surrender, I will reap every single one of you with it. You will join Efiya and Tyrek in eternal darkness."

"Tell them who you are," Sukar shouts from behind them, his voice pitched high on an unnatural wind. "Tell them the truth."

Unlike Sukar, who hopes the truth will make them see reason, I know it will do the opposite. Already suspecting, the demons whisper among themselves. "I am your queen, returned from the grave," I say, my voice choking with more emotions than I can bear. "I am Dimma."

As the truth sinks in, the demons' shock transforms into pure rage. Good. I need their hatred to give me the strength to finish this. I brace myself for the attack, knowing that it will come swiftly. Before they take one step toward me, Sukar yells, "Now!"

The tribal people wield their magic to slingshot shards of craven bone at the demons. Their aim is true, and the shards hit their marks. I stare in disbelief as the anti-magic sends a ripple of black veins through the demons' smoke. It forces them to take physical form again. Some look like the demons from Dimma's memories with massive wings and sharp teeth. Others revert to their stolen bodies. Tribal people, Tamarans, Estherians. Kefians. Two hundred of them look upon me with anger, fear, and pain written on their faces.

They charge at me headlong. Had I really thought that evoking Dimma's name would change their minds? These demons serve Tyrek and my sister alone, and they've committed themselves to this course. I don't need much time to do what must be done.

Among the carnage, I spot Sukar's grim face, streaked with sweat and blood. He looks miserable as I descend upon the demons like a wraith and reap their souls one by one. When I'm done, I stand in front of their dead bodies, bathed in blood, full of shame, knowing that if given the chance, I'd do it all over again.

THIRTY-FIVE
RUDJEK

Of all the rotten ways to die, a demon devouring one's soul has to be the most undignified. I wallow in the mud, clawing at my armor—snatch off my helmet and my breastplate. Dirt and sweat sting my eyes. I am easy pickings for the demon inside me, like a lamb brought for slaughter with no way to escape.

I grab for someone, for anyone, and my hand closes around a leg. My scream is a roar. *Majka*. I can do little more than clutch on to him as my vision goes black. I convulse, and my teeth tear into the inside of my mouth. I choke on blood and vomit until the demon forces me onto my side. My world is pain as he inhales his first breath in my body. It's a raggedy, hoarse scrape against my lungs, an ancient sound, the first sign of my impending death.

"Get the burning fires out of me!" I demand through gritted teeth.

My anti-magic pushes against the demon as he squeezes my heart. It is a *he*. He makes that known as his presence slams into me like a hammer smashing rocks. I'm losing ground. He's too strong. Fadyi warned me that the demons would exploit my weaknesses. I should've listened.

Let go, Rudjek, says a slippery whisper in my ear. No, not in my ear, in my head. The demon. I am still clutching Majka's leg, wishing that he'd move. Move, damn it. Move. *Your body belongs to me now.*

The demon pries my fingers from Majka's legs, and I fight to regain control. I attempt to expel him as I did with the Zeknorian poison, but he squeezes my heart again. As my anti-magic pushes against his soul, it feels like claws ripping out my guts. He screams in my mind, and I take some grim satisfaction from our joint pain. I won't make this easy for him—I won't stop fighting until one of us concedes.

Majka is heaving in gulps of air, his eyes blank, his lips trembling. Pain bursts through my body, but I grit my teeth. Every breath I take, every move, is agonizing.

"You're going to be okay, Majka." I press my hands against the wound in his chest. Blood gushes around my fingers. It's hot and sticky, and there's so much. He's bathed in gore, his face ashen. "Stay with me!"

Kira crawls to his other side. Tears streak down her cheeks as she glances around wildly. "Can you heal him?"

I want to yell at her for having to ask. Doesn't she know that's what I'm trying to do? I push out my anti-magic, but it bounces off Majka. "It isn't working."

The demon drags me to my feet, my body moving in jerks. Jahla isn't under the gate anymore. She's running toward us—she's coming for Majka. The gate begins to fade. We can't let it close—it's our only way to get Arrah back. I am a bastard for thinking it. Majka is dying, and I'm useless to help him. Three cravens race to the gate to add their anti-magic, and it flickers back into sight.

Jahla pushes me out of the way, and I fall back, staring at my friend. She can save him—like she's done for me so many times. She presses her hands to his torn chest.

"He's going to be okay," I say, and it's a plea to whatever awful god is listening. "Save him."

Jahla closes her eyes, and a ripple of anti-magic sets Majka's body alight at the same time that he closes his eyes. "Please, don't die," she whispers. "Please."

"Where is Shezmu?" demands Re'Mec, a swivel of snow that shifts into a creature out of a nightmare. He is almost a spitting image of his statue in the Hall of Orishas, only a hundred times more terrifying. He has Tam's face, but the similarities end there. His eyes are embers of burning coals as he tilts his head to the side. His black ram's horns curl back and around into daggers that glisten with blood. He is tall, shirtless, bronze. The barbed tail at his back thrashes out and cuts down demon after demon.

The demon wrestles away control of my body, and I stumble toward Re'Mec. The bastard sun orisha is so close. He imprisoned my people—he and his bitch of a sister. Re'Mec's gaze flickers to me, and I reach for my shotels.

"I'm here, old friend," Shezmu says, coalescing behind the orisha. He's got that same nasty grin, and I wrench back control from the demon inside me. I'm going to kill Shezmu myself. Re'Mec is a blur of black and bronze and fur as he closes the space between him and Shezmu. They collide, and the ground cracks. Solders and cravens and demons go down, some falling into a raging fire pit that bursts from the ice. It's madness and chaos.

Shezmu and Re'Mec battle like giants on an anthill, crushing anything or anyone in their path. They fight with no regard for the people around them. They crush buildings and soldiers alike. Re'Mec deals Shezmu a blow that knocks him into the earth, and the ground caves beneath him. A quake tears through the village, bringing down houses already in shambles. Soldiers and demons duck out of the way of debris as they parry each other's blows. No sooner than Re'Mec goes in for the kill, Shezmu strikes back again, a blur of gray smoke that sets the sun god on fire. They are monsters. If we don't stop this war, the orishas and demons will destroy Zöran.

"They're fleeing," someone cheers. "Cowards!"

My legs are unsteady as I turn back to the gate again. It calls to me. Arrah is on the other side. I have to get to her—I have to save her. For once, we're on the offense. Our forces pour into the decimated village as the demons retreat through the gate. I stumble to follow them as the demon in my body drags me forward.

I have a gift for you, Rudjek, Shezmu's words mock me. *Not that you deserve such an honor.*

I remember my conversation with Koré, and I want to double over and vomit. The demon curling around my heart—is it him? Is it the Demon King? Why choose me? He paints a picture of Arrah in my mind. His love and admiration for her are pure and unwavering.

Twenty-gods. This has been the plan all along and why Shezmu left bread crumbs for me to find him. I walked right into their trap. The Demon King wants Arrah, and he's planning to use me to get to her.

"You can't have her," I scream, and both Jahla and Kira startle and look at me, frowning.

"The gate's closing," Fadyi shouts as he cuts through two demons in his path. "We can't hold it much longer."

"I have to find Arrah," I say, but shake my head. No, I can't go anywhere near her. I love. I want. I need her. I have to save her from him, from myself. It's not Arrah who I have to find. It's the girl wearing a diadem with wild hair, rich brown skin that glows, veins that shine across her forehead. *Dimma. My queen.* I pound my fists against my head. *I will do anything to get her back. I will get her back.* The demon has no doubt in his conviction. He thinks he's won, but I won't give up.

"Rudjek!" Fadyi grabs my shoulder. "What's wrong with you?"

He's inside me, I try to scream; instead, the demon twists my tongue. "We need to get to the gate before it closes. Arrah is the only one who can stop Shezmu and the rest of the demons."

You cowardly bastard, get out of me!

You are only prolonging your suffering, boy, he says. *You will fail.*

"Do you know where they've taken Essnai and Arrah?" Kira blinks back tears as she looks between Majka and me.

"The only way to find out is through the gate," the demon answers through me. "We don't have much time."

Jahla holds Majka's head and shoulders on her lap. "I can't leave him."

He's already gone. The demon plants the thought in my mind.

"Stay with him, then," I say, sympathetic, but they aren't my words.

Kira comes to her feet, her face miserable. "Let's go."

"Jahla," Fadyi says, a warning in his voice. "He'll be in good hands with the healers."

I have half a mind to take the craven's head now, but time has taught me patience.

I'll rip out my own heart before I let you touch him, I growl.

Jahla's eyes are hollow as she lets go of Majka. Moments later, four cravens in white robes swarm our position, and I put my hands on my shotels, my eyes narrowing. They kneel to attend to the human boy.

"He has a name," I say out loud, then the demon drops my head to cover my outburst. "His name is Majka."

Fadyi stares into my eyes, his anti-magic brushing against my vessel. He is searching for an answer he won't find. I am too clever. He sees his craven ward when he looks at me, the same dark eyes, the same body, but Rudjek is dying. It won't be long. "We should go." Fadyi grimaces. "We don't have much time."

We step over corpses, debris, and cracks in the land in a rush to the gate. I can't hold back the smile as I glance up at the sky, watching my brethren who've stayed behind to keep the orishas busy. They're playing right into our hands. The gods have always been so predictable. This time we'll win the war and put an end to them once and for all. I've waited for this day for so long, and now I can finally relish the moment.

As soon as we step into the mouth of the gate, I can feel Dimma's lingering presence. She's not in Ilora—she's gone to another world.

"I know where she is," I say. "Follow me."

The gate pulls my vessel apart. It isn't a wholly unpleasant feeling, but it isn't something I would call enjoyable, either. We become pulses that travel one of millions of threads, and I latch on to Dimma's trail. My expectation grows at the thought of seeing her again after all these millennia. The gate spits us out in tall grass underneath a luminescent moon.

"She's close." I turn to look over my shoulder and stop cold when Fadyi thrusts a blade to my throat.

My hands go to my shotels, but this is all wrong. Why is Fadyi attacking me?

Kira has a dagger on Fadyi almost immediately. "What the blazing fires are you doing?"

"Rudjek"—Fadyi's blade bites into my neck—"are you in control?"

A shudder of pain cuts through my chest. "No!" It takes everything out of me to answer, and the demon clamps down on my tongue.

"What's going on?" Kira shouts. "Someone better start talking."

"Rudjek has a demon inside him," Fadyi says, and I want to collapse to my knees with joy. They know. They can stop me. "A very powerful one."

Kira curses as she lowers her knife. She looks conflicted between killing me herself and letting Fadyi take care of it. "How is that possible? He's supposed to be impervious to demon magic."

"Rudjek is only part craven," Jahla says, grief-stricken, "and he's still so very young."

"Take his swords, Jahla," Fadyi says. She doesn't move, her pale eyes hollow. He tells her a second time, raising his voice. "Jahla, his swords."

The craven is careful as she disarms me, and I grin at her. I'd like to cut off her little head and make it a trophy. My stomach turns at the thought. I don't want that. *He* wants it, and I won't let him.

Fadyi stares into my eyes. "You can still fight the demon. You're stronger than you know."

"Don't let"—the words sear my throat as I force them out—"me near . . . Arrah."

"I won't," Fadyi promises. "Bind his hands."

Soon we're walking toward a forest of black trees. I can smell my brethren's deaths lingering in the air, the ones who allied themselves with Efiya and the prince. As far as I'm concerned, they were traitors who deserved to die. I do not pity them.

"Kira, is that you?" someone calls, their voice a whisper.

We're almost at the edge of the forest when a figure rises out of the grass. Rudjek stubbornly pricks at the back of my mind. He is a pest that refuses to die.

"Essnai!" Kira screams with no regard for what may be lurking in the night. She stumbles, then sprints, the grass whipping around her legs.

My heart twists with longing. If Essnai is okay, then Arrah will be, too. Essnai sinks into Kira's arms, and they hold each other, their shoulders shaking with relief.

When they pull apart, Kira cups Essnai's face in a tender embrace and kisses her long and hard. "You're okay, my love," Kira breathes against Essnai's mouth. "I won't leave your side again."

"I tried to get back to the gate, but it took forever to get around the forest." Essnai's voice is frantic. "Sukar is dead. Tyrek took Arrah. I don't know where."

Tyrek, that bastard. He has Arrah. I make another attempt against the demon—my anti-magic surging inside me. I have to put an end to this right now—I have to save Arrah. My body jerks forward as I fight the demon once more. We fall to our knees. I grit my teeth, desperate to purge the demon. He squeezes my heart again. It doesn't matter. I don't stop thrashing him with anti-magic. I retch on the ground so hard that my stomach spasms. One way or another, by the end of the night, one of us will be dead.

THIRTY-SIX
ARRAH

Three hundred broken bodies lie scattered at my feet. I stare at the demons for a long time with the dagger clutched in my palm. I weep for the tribal people, and these wretched souls, too, cursed when Dimma gave them her gift. Sukar takes the blade from me at some point, but the moment is a blur in my mind.

"They gave us no choice." His voice is the gentle coo of summer rain on a scorching hot day. "You did what's best."

He says this like he was the one to cut down three hundred people and reap their souls. I am no better than the orishas who sought to imprison the demons when they became immortal. I am worse. The demons may have been Koré's creation, her children, but Dimma loved them like they were her own.

I am still standing close to the bodies when the surviving witchdoctors set them on fire. Sukar takes my hand and leads me a safe distance from the flames. I watch until the demons are a pile of charred bones and ashes, and the sun sinks in the sky. The Mulani woman from earlier shows me where I can wash in private. She gives me loose-fitting trousers and a tunic to replace my bloody shift.

The Zu tribesmen dance to purify the land and pass the souls of the witchdoctors. I watch as gray mist rises from each body, curling into the sky. Dimma would say they're returning to the Supreme Cataclysm to be unmade and made into something new. That may have been true before she conceived and lost her child. Now the Supreme Cataclysm only destroys. These souls won't be coming back.

When it's full dark, the tribes begin to celebrate our victory over the demons. Some had brought their instruments for the journey before the demons caught up to them. They pull them out now, a shekere with a net of cowries woven around it, an udu, small drums. Bells, clappers. Sukar and I settle cross-legged on the grass as people dance and sing around a great fire. It burns with the same white-and-blue flames as the one at the Blood Moon Festival. They speak tribal common tongue and dialects that melt into a cacophony that sings to my heart.

"It's good to see you smiling," Sukar says as someone passes a wineskin from Tyrek's stash. When I meet his gaze, he glances down at the wine, the warmth in his cheeks luminescent under the moon. He takes a swig, wipes his mouth, and hands it to me. "I haven't seen you smile like that in a long time. I've forgotten how disarming it can be."

"Disarming?" I laugh and take a sip of wine to cover my blush. "That's an interesting way of putting it."

"It's true." He finally meets my eyes again. His soul is bare, his emotions raw. He holds nothing back, and I long to taste his sweet lips. The thought dredges up my guilt. "I'd give anything to see you smile like that all the time."

"Dance with us, *blessed one*," a girl calls, interrupting our conversation. "It's bad luck if the one who carries the *edam*'s *kas* does not honor their sacrifice."

Whatever I want to say to Sukar dies on my tongue as I pass the wineskin on and let the girl pull me to my feet. We dance in a group, twisting, twirling, and shaking to the roar of the drums. It's almost like being in the tribal lands again, but without sparks of magic weaving between people.

I close my eyes and lose myself in the music, letting it drown out my regrets, if only for a little while. I can feel Sukar's presence before I open my eyes again. He gives me a playful smile, his head tilted to the side. An invitation. I grab his arm and pull him close. He switches his hips and shoulders, his hands finding their way to my waist. His touch is so gentle, like he's afraid that I'm a whiff of wind that will blow away. He's usually so flashy with his steps, the center of attention, but tonight we move as one.

I'm breathless by the end of the dance, and I lean against him to stop my head from spinning. "I better call it a night."

"Do you regret almost kissing me?" Sukar asks, his voice streaked with longing.

I search his face for gods know what—a question, an answer, a promise, a reason to say yes. "No." I shake my head, and I take his hand, leading us away from the celebrations. We can't keep going on like this. "Let's talk."

Once we're back in the tent, the fire comes to life on its own.

Only a month ago, I hesitated to start a fire for fear that the Demon King would use my magic against me. I'm not so sure that he ever would, now that I know what I mean to him. Sukar trails behind me, and I brace myself as I turn to face him. He stands very still, his hands at his sides, his breath low and raspy. He's holding himself back, waiting for me to speak first.

I rub my forehead. I'm not ready for this conversation—I could never be ready. "I don't know how to say this without sounding like an ass."

"Use your words," Sukar replies, his eyes dancing with mischief.

"I do love you, Sukar—you're my family," I say, "but I don't love you the way you want." He winces and grabs his chest like I've punched him in the heart and mumbles an *ouch*. I draw on Dimma's, the *edam*'s, and my own memories to give me strength. "As complicated as things are between Rudjek and me, I still want to be with him."

Sukar blinks back tears like water behind a dam, surging to the brink. The tension eases from his shoulders, as if my words have released him from a curse. An echo of his words from the night of the almost kiss comes back to my mind: *I've loved you since the first moment I saw you.* Two voices speak the words, Sukar's and another's. A voice not quite as deep as Rudjek's, but low and rough, accentuated with notes of a song.

"I can't lose you again." His whole body trembles. "I've waited so long."

"You're not going to lose me," I say, putting on a brave face. "We'll always be friends."

"What happened to *our* forever and always?" Sukar blurts out before he can stop himself.

He realizes his mistake immediately and clamps his mouth shut. The muscles in his jaw twitch as his words spin in my mind. *Forever and always*. The memory rushes in like a flood. Dimma and Daho stand on a balcony that overlooks Jiiek at his coronation. He asks her to marry him, and she's so happy. *Forever and always*. I shake my head at the familiar plea in his voice, the cadence of his words.

"Sukar," I whisper as he stares at me with those haunted eyes, eyes that hide his true identity. "How long?" A sob escapes my lips, a whimper. I back away from him. It can't be.

"Your friend died at Heka's Temple," he says, and his words aren't gleeful, they're sad and apologetic.

I relive the moment that Efiya attacked Sukar. She raises a shotel over his head, primed to kill him. I fling my magic out without thinking, and it hits Sukar hard and throws him back. He slams against a pillar. A sickening crack. The crunch of splintered bones. His body slumps to the ground.

"I killed him." My tears blot out the world, and a scream burns in my lungs. Sukar didn't survive the battle. I didn't heal him. He didn't travel with Essnai, Tyrek, and me. He didn't confess his love. My head spins with the truth. "I killed Sukar."

Daho takes one step toward me, and I back away again. He stops in his tracks. "You didn't mean to—I saw it happen. It was an accident."

I glare at him. "You . . . you had no right to take his body."

"Sukar was already dead," Daho says, his shoulders slumping. "It was no use to him."

I say nothing at that—what can I say. My friend is dead, I killed him, and the demon who calls to my heart and soul is inside his body.

I stare at my feet, so I don't make yet another mistake.

Daho had comforted me after I turned the assassin into a *ndzumbi*—not Sukar. He'd climbed the ridge in Tribe Zu and brought me mint tea. Not Sukar. He'd held me when I pushed out the craven bone shards, then again in the middle of the night. He'd helped me kill the demons to protect the tribal people. Daho—not Sukar. I look up from my feet and flinch when I meet his gaze. Daho.

"You must have a lot of questions," he says, keeping his distance. "Efiya released me, and one of my generals took my place in Koré's wretched box so that the gods would not suspect. I couldn't risk outright telling you who I was. If they'd known, they would've killed you. I had to make sure you were safe first. Tyrek was . . . unexpected."

I can hardly process his words—what they mean. "You've been with me all this time."

"When I was in Koré's prison, I could always feel your presence." He smiles, his face earnest and full of hope. "I watched you live countless lives and saw a pattern. You were always born on a third full moon of the year, once for every century. I tried desperately to reach you, but Fram had locked away your gifts." He swallows hard. "When Arti was born, I knew that she'd be the one to give you life again. I . . . I tried to protect her from the *Ka*-Priest, but I couldn't do much from my prison. I lessened the terror he seeded in her mind and filled in the holes, but her hatred for the orishas was her own. Re'Mec knew about her torture and all the women before her and did nothing to stop it."

"She killed children so you could be free. . . . One of them was my friend," I say, seething with anger. "Efiya killed hundreds of people and gave their bodies to your demons. She killed the *edam* and destroyed the tribes."

"I'm sorry," Daho says, tears staining his cheeks. "I could never ask anyone to hurt a child."

I hug my arms around my shoulders, remembering the warm feeling of the light inside Dimma. Their son had made her so happy, but the horrible night at the Almighty Temple with Shezmu spoils the memory. The children had lain so still, their souls captured in jars like fireflies. "What are you saying?" My heart slams against my chest.

"It doesn't matter." Daho grimaces, his gaze flitting away. "You've suffered enough."

I step closer to him. "Tell me the truth."

"Dimma—"

"Don't," I warn through gritted teeth. "Tell me."

After a deep sigh, he explains, "I asked Arti to kill for me, yes. It was the only way to give Shezmu enough strength to father Efiya. Children' souls are strongest, and she chose them for her ritual to guarantee that she would not fail. So you see, I may not have bid her to kill them, but I'm no less at fault. I am so sorry for your friend and the others. Their deaths are my sins to bear."

I can't consider what it means that my mother had chosen to sacrifice children of her own free will. I don't doubt that she would do such a thing if it got her one step closer to striking back at those who wronged her.

"Your sister released the demons in Kefu and started a war with the tribal people against my wishes," Daho says. "She had your mother's fury and ambition and her father's bloodlust. My only concern is to destroy the gods who imprisoned my people, and anyone who would fight for them."

When he falls silent, I realize that the celebration outside has died down. It's quiet, and there is nothing to distract me nor stand between him and my treacherous heart.

"I came back for you, my love." His voice shatters on every word, words that he's waited five thousand years to speak. Words that I didn't know I needed to hear until this moment.

Despite everything that's happened, I close the distance between us. Heka save me, I sink against his chest and let him wrap me in his arms. I give in to his embrace, lost in lifetimes of memories together.

"I've missed you, Dimma," he whispers against my ear, and chills crawl up my spine.

I pull away from him, feeling like a fool. How could I be so dense? He doesn't love me; he doesn't want me. "I'm not Dimma," I say. "She's a part of me, but I am not her."

"No, not yet." Daho shakes his head, his face empathetic. "I will force Fram to release her, so you'll be complete again."

I back away from him. I need to think; I need space. I storm past him and out into the camp, only it's not the camp anymore. We're on a frozen mountain in the early hours of the morning. I gasp, recognizing this place. It's Dimma and Daho's frozen lake, much like Rudjek and I share a spot along the Serpent River. "Dimma loves you"—I blink back tears—"but I love Rudjek."

"He will no longer be a problem for us," Daho says behind me, all warmth suddenly gone from his voice.

I turn back to him, and my heart breaks at the guilt in his eyes.

"What have you done?"

"I had to be sure there was no way he could stand between us."

My magic raises to the surface of my skin, wind whipping through my hair. "What did you do?"

"I gave his body to Yacara, one of my most loyal generals," Daho says, his voice devoid of emotion. "Rudjek is gone."

THE UNNAMED ORISHA: DIMMA

I cannot finish my story without coming to this day. Some memories have sharp edges, and the endoyans' attack on Jiiek cuts deep. Daho and I arrive to burning skyscrapers and rivers red with blood. Demons lie strewn in the streets by the millions.

Daho's wings shudder against his back as he turns in a circle. "How could I let this happen?"

I wrap my arm around my belly, and our child pushes a thousand questions into my mind. He is restless as his shape changes from tiny feet, tiny hands, and tiny wings to energy that hums through my vessel. I haven't the time to answer his questions, and he relents for now. I will remember his curiosity above all else after he's gone. With my hand still on my belly, I stop the endoyans from fighting on every corner of Ilora. I once promised Daho that I would never peer into mortal's minds, but I break my vow. It is the first of many promises I will break.

The endoyans fight out of fear and jealousy. Jiiek is flourishing, people live longer, more children are born. They believe that under Daho and my reign, they will lose their lands. The fear is both rational and irrational. Jiiek has grown, and our borders continue to expand to cover three-fourths of Ilora. What the endoyans do not know is that Daho and I have already made plans to shape a new world for our growing population.

Minister Godanya, who spent many years in our palace, has seeded fear in his people's minds for decades. Their fear grew into hate, and their hatred grew into justification for violence. They bided their time and waited for the right opportunity to strike. They killed the children first—every single one of them—with the help of one of my brethren.

I do not second-guess as I hand out their punishment. I tug the tethers of every endoyan connected to the war—weapons makers, soldiers, politicians. They resist my pull, but it's no use. I snatch them from their bodies. They will become wandering spirits who crave what they can never have again: life.

"You will live this way for eternity as a reminder of your crimes." Shadows cluster in the courtyard where we stand, begging me to release them. "You will be at our mercy until the day my love deems your punishment just. Until then, you will serve the demons when they call upon you."

Fram once told me that they saw something of their nature in me. It tingles in my soul now, the hunger, the need to create and destroy, the need for change. I am not the same as my brethren. I know that now. I am something else, something that will break the universe and remake it again. It is my nature; it is my purpose.

"Have I gotten your attention yet?" hisses a soft voice that echoes in the courtyard. A shadow pulls away from a burning wall and walks toward us, her form shifting to mirror my vessel. She looks exactly like me, but she is an endless black hole, a disease. Her nature is to consume everything in her path and seed chaos in her wake. Her name is Eluua—another one of my brethren who I am meeting for the first time.

Daho steps in front of me, and his beautiful white wings spread wide. "Stay away from my wife, you murdering bitch."

"So testy, aren't you, boy." Eluua flicks her wrist, and Daho falls to his knees. Several dozen demons gather at the edge of the courtyard. They see twins of their queen—two Dimmas, one of destruction and mayhem, and the one they know. Eluua's appearance is not an accident. It will ignite a spark of doubt among the demons that will grow with time. "Where were we, sister? Yes. I remember now. Re'Mec and Koré forbade us from attacking you, but they didn't say anything about the people you cherish. You were taking too long agreeing to die, so I'm here to speed up your decision."

I touch Daho's shoulder, releasing him from Eluua's grasp. He does not yet understand that his body is only a vessel. That he can shake himself loose of it and take a new one at will or no form at all.

"Dimma," he says, his voice riddled with tears. "I can't lose you, too."

"You won't lose me," I promise. "I will take care of my sister."

"Take care of me?" Eluua laughs. "The arrogance of children."

I shed my vessel and bundle my child deep inside me as my true form emerges. I am a windstorm of fury with flecks of ash and gold.

I am smoke; my heart, if I have one, is black and hollow. When I slam into Eluua, her vessel turns into moths that scatter every which way. We are balls of light, tearing each other into pieces only to rejoin again.

"I can do this for centuries," Eluua coos in my ear. "If I'd known you were this easy to upset, I would have come sooner."

I spread my soul into a spiderweb and seep into her cracks. She is empty inside and endless, immense. She gasps, finally understanding that I'm unmaking her bit by bit, stripping her apart.

"No!" Eluua screams. "We are eternal. This can't be possible."

"You will still be eternal, sister," I say, "only in the form of my choosing."

When I'm done, I spin her soul into a dagger with rubies inlaid in its handle. I return to my body and gift it to Daho. "Eluua will only answer to you and me now. She will be a prison for everyone who opposes us and destroy anyone else who attempts to wield her power."

"Bring her back!" screams one of Daho's ministers and his closest friend. He clutches his daughter, Ta'la, in his arm. Her silver skin is ashen, her body limp, her wings broken. "Please. She's my only child."

"Shezmu." Daho stumbles toward his friend. "I'm so sorry, brother."

"All the children are gone." Shezmu stares at my belly. "Give me a chance to avenge my daughter and protect our people."

I offer my gift to every single demon. I speak to them through the threads that bind us. If they want revenge, they must become as powerful as my brethren. Most agree with vengeance in their hearts;

some agree out of fear. Some will grow to regret their decisions and hate me for it. Some do not trust me because of Eluua's vile actions. The ones who refuse will not survive the next attack. I give the ones who want revenge the organ under their tongue that will allow them to eat souls. Then I set to work, splitting myself into endless pieces and bestowing upon them my gift.

I grant them immortality, but I unknowingly give them my hunger, too. I change them forever. In truth, I have prolonged their suffering and sentenced them to eternal damnation.

THIRTY-SEVEN
ARRAH

The mountain air is cold, but my blood runs hot as magic dances underneath my skin. I refuse to believe that Rudjek is gone. He can't be. I shake, the news washing my thoughts blank. Daho stands across from me, his face—Sukar's face—grief-stricken, and I hate that his grief isn't for Rudjek. It's for himself. He's so desperate to get Dimma back that he would do the unspeakable. He already has. The wind flaps against the tent, singing the mountain's song. Dimma loved that sound, and I want to shatter her memories to pieces.

"Dimma is dead, and she's never coming back," I say, striking at his heart. "You're a fool if you don't know that by now." As soon as the words come out, I know they won't convince him. "Take your people and go. Stop fighting this endless war."

He meets my gaze again, and his eyes change from deep brown to green. His skin ripples until it settles into silver flushed with purple undertones. How many people have to die in his quest to punish the gods? How many will be enough to sate his appetite?

"Do you think the gods will ever let my people live in peace?"

Daho asks. "Don't you see what we are? They hate us because we're no different from them."

I watch in shock as my friend's form disappears completely. Wings flutter at Daho's back, their shadows stretching across the tent. He's taller than Sukar, slender with short wavy hair. He's everything I remember, a beautiful storm, a first kiss, a broken boy. My heart pounds against my chest, and I root myself in place. I will not give in to Dimma's memories of him. I can't forget about Kofi and the other children who died so Efiya could be born. The tribal people, the *edam*, hundreds of Tamarans. Rudjek.

"What do you hope to gain now?" I cross my arms, steeling myself for my next strike. "Dimma and your son are long dead."

His eyes flash with pain, and his voice trembles when he speaks again. "Their deaths will not be for nothing. Koré and Re'Mec are afraid of their own mortality, but I will show them what it really means to be mortal."

My hand goes to my belly, remembering the feel of the child, and the emptiness inside me now. I would never exist if Dimma and her child had lived, yet I mourn him. "Let my people be and wage your war on the orishas someplace else. You've already caused so much destruction and death—leave us out of it."

"I will promise you this," he says, his voice crumbling around the edges. "If the tribal people do not side with the Twin Kings, I will order my army to spare their lives."

"When does it end, Daho?" His name is a broken melody on my lips, a discordant song. Desperation weaves between my words like silk unraveling at the seams. "Will you keep fighting the gods until you destroy what's left of yourself and your people?"

"Yes, if it comes to that," he hisses, his eyes wide and terrible like two suns colliding. "It ends the day I tear Re'Mec's soul into pieces and feed him to the Supreme Cataclysm. It ends when I behead Koré and force her to spend five thousand years in a box. It ends when every single one of them is dead."

"Dimma would not want this." I throw up my arms in frustration. "She wouldn't want to see you and her brethren destroy each other."

"You would know," Daho says, his gaze piercing. "You are a part of her."

My fingers ache to trace the curves of his perfectly symmetrical face. His wings shudder as if he can read my thoughts, and I notice the way his left wing sits a little higher than the right. He looks the same as he had earlier when I still thought he was Sukar—like he's holding himself back. The anguish twisting his beautiful face only makes me more anxious and frustrated.

It would be so much easier if I could despise him, but I see the boy who ruled Jiiek with a gentle hand and a kind heart. The boy who never got tired of telling Dimma stories even after seven centuries together. The boy who stood by her side when her brethren condemned her to death. I know that it's hurting him to keep his distance from me after waiting so long to reunite with his *ama*. Yet his patience only makes this that much worse.

I turn and flee into the cold—flecks of snow stinging my face, the wind burning my skin. I wade through blankets of snow that cling to my trousers. I'm freezing, but the cold makes me feel alive; it clears my head. Something shimmers in the rising mist in the middle of the frozen lake.

I slip on ice and pitch backward. Daho is there, a flush of warmth. I land in his arms, my back against his chest, his heart racing to meet mine. "I've got you," he whispers. I resist the urge to lean into him, to close my eyes, to let go. I can't deny that some part of me yearns for him—*needs* him. But he isn't who I want. As soon as I regain my balance, I step away.

The fog peels back from the lake and reveals hundreds of black appendages wiggling up from the ice. They wrap around two bodies, one made of crystal and one obsidian.

"Fram." I wince. They should be the rush of a tide or a cluster of stars, but the appendages have imprisoned them in these limited material forms.

"I warned you," they say, twin voices as beautiful as they are horrible. "But, like Dimma, you never listen."

I shake my head in disbelief. "You tried to kill me."

"You were already dead." Fram's matter-of-fact tone leaves no room for argument. "I only sought to make sure you stayed that way."

I bare my teeth at them. "None of this would be happening if not for you."

"You wouldn't exist, Arrah," Fram says, "if not for me."

Daho's fists clench and unclench at his sides. "Release Dimma."

"To be so clever, child," Fram muses, "you are not that bright. I cannot release Dimma—death is her only release now."

I wrap my arm around my belly. "If I die, Dimma returns to the Supreme Cataclysm."

"Precisely as it should be," Fram says. "The universe will stop dying. It is a noble sacrifice."

"You'll find a way to restore her, or you'll die first," Daho spits through gritted teeth.

"Killing me would be a mistake," Fram warns. There is a thread of fear in their words, not of death but of something worse. "I am all that holds the balance between the living and the dead."

Daho slips the dagger from underneath his sleeve. "Don't force my hand."

I step in front of him, my magic spreading into a swarm of little lights to protect Fram. I am driven by a deep instinct and some forgotten knowledge that they mustn't die.

"What are you doing?" Daho's face twists in shock. "This is the only way. If I kill Fram, then the magic that chains Dimma will break."

"If you take one more step"—I force out every word—"I will kill you myself." It breaks my heart to say it, but I mean to do it.

Daho straightens himself up, his eyes defiant, daring me to make good on my promise. He thrusts the dagger out to me, handle first. "Take it if you want to kill me. I won't stop you."

My hand trembles as his fingers brush against mine. He kneels on the ice with his wings outstretched—his shoulders slumped in submission. There is no doubt in his glowing eyes, and I see the face of the boy he once was, the boy he still is, in all the ways that matter.

"Strike me down if you don't love me anymore," he says, but he isn't talking to me. His words and his heart are for one person alone.

As I squeeze the hilt, the dagger shimmers from blade to light. A hollow hum echoes in my ears, and the knife grows into a sword. I can end this right here. I will end this.

Fram is at my back, silent as night, not encouraging me either way. Death and life are their domains, and even in chains, the prospect of both feeds into their nature. They grow stronger, but more spiny black appendages shoot up from the ice to keep them contained.

When I lift the sword of light, it feels ten times heavier than when I reaped the demons' souls. Daho's eyes pin me in place. They drag up memories of endless nights exploring the wonders of the universe with him. Endless nights exploring his body and him exploring mine. "Dimma loved you," I whisper. For better or worse, she and I are two halves of the same soul. "Always remember that."

I swing the sword, fast and hard, my lives flashing before my eyes. I am lying beside Daho in the cabin as he tells me a story. His lips brush against my ear, and something hot stirs inside me. I am dozens of people who blur into oblivion. I am with Rudjek at the Temple with my back pressed against the wall, waiting for him to kiss me. I scream when the sword is within a breath of Daho, but my arm jerks at the last moment and the cut goes wide.

The sword slams into the ice, and I fall into him for the second time. He grabs my waist, but he doesn't pull me closer. He looks up at me with tears in his eyes, and it's clear he thinks that I couldn't go through with it.

I gasp for air as Dimma stirs inside me, writhing in her chains, pushing against my will. Her consciousness uncoils and a new awareness flickers at the back of my mind. Rather than feel separate and apart from me, she is the whole and I the dim light in her shadow. I squeeze my eyes shut, expecting her to consume me, but her presence fades again. I realize then, and perhaps I should have always known, that she would never let me reap Daho's soul.

"I need to know that Rudjek is really gone," I say, rushing my words before she takes my voice. I fear what will happen if she pulls free of her chains—will I be just another memory in her ancient life?

"If that's what it takes for you to let him go," Daho says, crest-fallen. He flicks his wrist, and the gate appears at the edge of the lake. It looks like floating sparks of magic this time. "Come, and I will show you." Daho flashes a sharp look at Fram. "We'll be back for you soon enough."

"You have Iben's gift?" I ask, surprised. I assumed that Shezmu had it, since he was working with Tyrek.

"Shezmu and I both do," Daho answers as he reaches for my hand. "Iben was very powerful and cunning. It took both of us to kill him, and once we did, we divided his soul in half."

I take Daho's hand, reluctant at first, but my palm fits into his like they've been made for each other. We walk through the gate, him smiling down at me. "Your eyes," he says. "They're changing."

I don't want to know what that means, but I can already guess. *Your eyes are like hers, a deep brown the color of night pearls.* I say nothing as we step back into the camp with the tribal people. Rudjek is there. Essnai, gods, she's okay. She and Kira startle from where they'd been sitting on the ground. Fadyi and Jahla are near Rudjek, but no Majka. I fear the worst. The tribal people scramble to fight. Essnai scoops up her staff, while Kira slips two knives from the sheaths against her thighs. I raise one hand to tell them to hold their attack, and they halt.

"Yacara," Daho says to the demon inside Rudjek. "Your queen requires proof of who you are."

Rudjek doesn't reach for his shotels. His hands remain limp at his sides, his posture relaxed. He looks back and forth between the two of us, from my face to Daho's. His midnight eyes are unreadable—and this is a mask that I cannot see through. *Is it you or the demon? Give me a sign.* He walks closer, leaving the others behind. His gaze flits to our interlaced fingers, and I let go of Daho's hand, my face burning with shame. When Rudjek reaches us, he bends to one knee, his eyes shifting to a brilliant jade. "My king and queen." He bows his head. "I have devoured the boy's soul, and I am yours to command."

THIRTY-EIGHT
ARRAH

Too late. Always too late. I couldn't save Kofi. I couldn't save my father. I couldn't save Sukar. Now Rudjek. I bite the inside of my cheek, the sharp taste of blood filling my mouth. I stare at Rudjek's wild curls, his smooth brown skin, the blood on the hilts of the swords at his sides. I remember the day my sister put a demon's soul into a cat's body, how it writhed in pain and suffered. Had Rudjek suffered, too? All because of me—because he loved a broken girl with a treacherous heart.

"Get out of my sight," I hiss at him, my stomach retching. I am close to throwing up the wine from last night. When the demon looks up with his jade eyes, I flinch as if he'd slapped me across the face. Not Rudjek's eyes, not Rudjek's, not him.

The demon frowns and stands to his full height. "I don't understand."

Where Rudjek, or what used to be Rudjek, is broad shouldered, Daho is lean and two heads taller. Rudjek's curls refuse to stay in place. Daho's dark hair molds to his scalp in waves like the boys in the tribes who wear doreks. Brown skin to silver. Flat teeth to sharp edges. Gods, they are both beautiful. But one is very much dead, and the other should be.

"It's okay, Yacara." Daho pats his general on the shoulder. "Leave us."

As the demon turns to go, I say, "Wait."

He stops with his back to me, but he doesn't turn around. It's better this way. I don't have to look at him as I cross the space between us and whisper my goodbyes to Rudjek. I lean in close to his ear. "I choose you, Rudjek." I know that my declaration will be lost on the demon, but I have to say it out loud for my own sake. "I love you, and I hate you for dying."

The demon's shoulders shudder as he clears his throat. "I don't know what to say to that," he responds in Rudjek's deep timbre. Was that a cackle in his voice, a hint of sarcasm? "Is there anything else, my queen?"

I move away from him. "No."

"Are you satisfied?" Daho asks, impatient, and I'm annoyed that he can still be jealous of Rudjek after what he's done.

"Are you?" I glare up at him, and his cheeks flush purple. "I'll never forgive you for this—not today, not in a thousand years."

"You will in time," he says with so much conviction that I almost believe him.

"Oh, there is one other thing," Yacara says from behind us, his voice a low rumble. I flinch in irritation and glance over my shoulder in time to see flashes of silver. His next words come through gritted teeth, and there's no mistaking whose words they are. My knees go weak. I can hardly stand. "Get away from her, you soul-eating bastard."

Rudjek plunges his swords into Daho, one piercing his chest and the other his belly. I gasp as he pulls back, and blood splatters everywhere. I am torn in two, frozen in place. He's very much alive, but how—his eyes. I can't explain it. I let out something between a snort and a laugh as I blink back tears. Only Rudjek would be foolish enough to antagonize the man who brought the gods to their knees. *He's alive.*

I stare at Daho, bent over, gasping for air. Craven anti-magic brushes against my skin as arrows slam into him. Two, three, four, a dozen. They tear through his wings, his chest, his belly. Blackness spreads from the wounds as the anti-magic poisons his blood. I stumble toward him as he collapses, writhing in pain on the ground. It happens so fast that I am left in shock when he falls still.

"That's for sending your man Yacara to eat my soul." Rudjek shakes the blood from his swords. "You won't be hearing from him again. After I expelled him from my body, I took great pleasure in shredding his soul to pieces."

Fadyi and Jahla are on Daho in a heartbeat, binding him with chains made of craven bones. Dimma roars inside me, her pain slamming against my eardrums. I gather my magic—no, she gathers my magic, her attention on the cravens. She's going to kill them.

"Did he hurt you?" Rudjek asks from behind, and I spin around, back in control again.

"Of course not," I snap, annoyed. "Daho would never hurt me."

"Daho?" Rudjek's face darkens in suspicion as he sheathes his swords. "It would appear that I've missed a lot."

"We don't have much time." The chains won't hold Daho, but for now, they'll keep him from healing. I tell Rudjek almost everything, my mind spinning, the story coming out in the wrong order. I skip the part about the almost kiss. "I share a soul with the Unnamed orisha, with Dimma, his *ama*."

"Hold on." Rudjek rubs his forehead, rocking on his heels. "Are you saying you're the Unnamed orisha—that you and he—" Rudjek grimaces at Daho curled up in a puddle of blood.

"He and *Dimma*," I say. "I'm not his *ama*, nor is he mine. I'm not her."

Rudjek frowns. "And the orisha of life and death did this to you?"

"Yes." I look past him at the tribal people watching us, waiting for trouble. "Raëke is dead." I don't ask the question on the tip of my tongue. I can't when I see the pain in his eyes. First, he lost the craven twins, now her.

"Re'Mec sent her to spy on you and lied about it," Rudjek says, his shoulders sinking, eyes hollow. "I should've known he'd do something so despicable."

"You didn't send her?" I ask, surprised.

"Of course not." Rudjek lets out a long breath. "I trust you with my life."

Dread sinks into my chest. With everything that's happened, it's a foolish thing to say. I hardly know myself now that I have accepted Dimma as part of who I am. I don't tell him what I'm thinking, that he shouldn't trust me, that if he knows what's good for him, he'll run away as fast as he can.

"Where's Majka?" I ask, but Rudjek only glances at Jahla and shakes his head. I don't know what to make of that, but I understand enough to drop the subject for now. It can't be anything good.

I bite my lip as I step closer to him. "Your eyes?"

"I learned some new tricks." His irises fade back to the darkest of nights. "I almost didn't make it. The demon—Yacara—was strong, but my anti-magic bested him in the end."

We stand so close that his familiar scent toys with my senses. "You must get the tribal people as far away from here as possible before Daho wakes again. Where are Koré and Re'Mec? They need to get him back into the box."

"We left them fighting Shezmu and his army." Rudjek glances at Daho's crumpled body again, his expression blank like he's trying to process everything. I can't blame him. This—all of it—Dimma's memories, Daho, the never-ending cycle of death, it's too much. "They're much stronger than any of us could imagine."

"I know," I say. "They intend to destroy the orishas and anyone who gets in our way."

Essnai steps forward with Kira at her side. She's okay except for some scrapes and bruises. I don't know how I'm going to tell her the truth about Sukar. It will break her heart.

"We'll get the tribal people to safety," she tells me. Her face doesn't betray her thoughts, but I wonder if she'll look at me in a different light now that she knows the truth. Once she discovers that I killed Sukar, will she ever forgive me? I don't know if I can forgive myself.

"Thank you," I say quietly.

"Can't leave for a full day without you getting into trouble."

With tears in her eyes, Essnai pulls me into a hug before she and Kira return to where the tribal people are gathered in the camp. They work quickly, organizing the group, and start to move out immediately. The progression is slow, with so many people hurt from fighting the demons or too weak from captivity.

Rudjek lifts a pair of red leather gloves from his pocket. "I've been carrying these around for this moment." He slips them on and brushes his fingers across my cheeks. I lean against his hand, feeling the warmth of him through the glove and the buzz of anti-magic. "I've missed you."

"I've missed you, too," I say, closing my eyes, "but you need to leave with them. I can't help you fight Daho when he wakes. Dimma won't let me."

"You know that I won't—"

We both stumble when the ground moves beneath our feet. I make to push Rudjek away, but it's already too late. Vines shoot up through the dirt and whip around his throat. Rudjek falls to his knees. I pull at the vines, and thorns tear into my hands. His anti-magic burns my fingers, but I don't stop.

"You shouldn't listen to her," Daho says, his voice coming from all around us. There is a husk of a body where Fadyi and Jahla had tied him up, and it blows away on the wind. The cravens sprint to help Rudjek, but more vines shoot up from the ground and thrash around their bodies. Fadyi and Jahla melt into gray masses, letting go of their human forms, to slip through the vines. But Daho is ready for them, and his vines intertwine into a prison to trap Fadyi and Jahla beneath it. The vines start to shrink and burn into their flesh. Their shrill screams pierce through the valley.

"Let them go!" I demand, leaching life from the vines with my magic. They wither and turn brown, only to be replaced by new vines sprouting from their husks.

Essnai, Kira, and the other tribal people stand still—Daho has stopped time for them, but Rudjek and his guardians resist his magic. "Iben's gift is remarkable, but I can't go back in time and save Dimma and my son. I can only watch the moment that Fram killed them. There are gaps in time that I can't explain. Missing pieces." His voice cracks around the edges. "What good is it to see it without being able to do anything to change it?"

Daho materializes behind Rudjek, his silver skin shimmering in the amber sunlight. He looks down his nose at Rudjek clawing at the vines, then he glances at me. "How could you love him—he has traitor blood running through his veins?"

I frown, not understanding, but Dimma's memories slip to the forefront of my mind. She hadn't killed the endoyans who had opposed the slaughter of the demons, but they'd been afraid of her wrath. Some had escaped through the gate to Zöran. The Northern people had dark veins and diaphanous skin because of their endoyan ancestors. Rudjek shares their blood through his mother. *Traitor blood.*

I bite back an irrational sense of anger that curls up inside me. Rudjek isn't responsible for what the endoyans did to the demon people, yet I can feel Dimma's mistrust of him. Knowing she could destroy so many out of revenge makes me think that she was no better than her brethren. But haven't I done the same with the demons whose souls I reaped? And I would again if it means that I could save the tribal people.

"Don't do this," I beg, my voice quiet.

"He had his chance to die the easy way, and he fought it." Daho yanks the vines around Rudjek's throat. "Now it's time to show him why the orishas fear me."

"No!" I shout as something catches around my ankles. I lose my footing and hit the ground on my belly. The craven bone chain that had trapped Daho snakes around my ankles and up my legs. Anti-magic burns against my skin as it drags me close to Fadyi and Jahla.

Daho mouths an apology, but I don't want his *sorry*. He's done this to stop me from helping Rudjek. I struggle against my restraints, screaming, but it's no use. With the cravens so close and the chain around my legs, my magic has fallen asleep underneath my skin. I can't free myself, and I can't stop him. "Please!"

Daho lifts his dagger to Rudjek's throat. "We have some un-finished business."

THIRTY-NINE
RUDJEK

Someone should've warned me how much the Demon King likes the sound of his own voice. I gasp for air, clawing at the vines cutting into my throat. Between the gloves and blood, I can't get a good hold of them, and the pain is almost enough to make me piss my pants.

The Demon King grabs me by the back of my collar and drags me away from Arrah. I'm rather put out that he's making me look like a first-year cadet rather than a commandant with my own army.

Arrah fights to free herself from the craven bone chain Fadyi concocted when we reached the camp. I couldn't have guessed that he would turn our weapon against her. "No!" she screams, her voice hoarse. "Please!"

"We have some unfinished business," the Demon King snarls as he thrusts a dagger to my throat. Not just any dagger—the one Arrah used to kill Efiya.

"For the record," I huff out, "I've beaten Re'Mec several times in the arena, so bragging about the orishas fearing you isn't very impressive."

The Demon King digs the knife into my skin, but my anti-magic resists the blade. "She'll hate you for this, you know," I say, sounding as calm as I can with a blade biting into my throat. "Whatever Arrah feels right now will become a part of Dimma." I lick my lips, tasting blood. "Can you live with that?"

"Your fling with Arrah will be a passing moment in the greater scheme of Dimma's life," he scoffs. "You're nothing to her."

"Are you sure about that?" I say. "She chose me."

My words hang in the air, and his grasp on the dagger slackens a fraction. I've struck a nerve. Now time to twist the knife. "I don't know how things were on Ilora, but here we fight for the ones we love. I challenge you to a battle of strength—no tricks. Let Dimma and Arrah see who will prevail. I warn you, though: I am widely known as the best swordsman in Tamar."

I glance at Arrah, struggling against her restraints. Her golden eyes look like pits of lava. They aren't only her eyes anymore, and she's not the same girl who set off for the tribal lands. I can see that as plain as day. She stares up at the Demon King, and since he hasn't answered my challenge, I assume he's staring back at her. Some silent message passes between them, and a pang of jealousy knots in my gut.

"Fine," the Demon King mumbles, lowering his dagger. "I'm inclined to let you make a fool of yourself."

I pull the vines from around my throat, and they burrow back into the soil. I brush away the dirt and grass from my elara as I glance at the tribal people, Kira, and Essnai. They're still looking toward Arrah, frozen in place. The scene would be jarring if I hadn't stepped outside time when we faced the Zeknorians. I know how endless the space between two moments can seem, how it elongates and stretches.

I toss my gloves aside and unsheathe my shotels in one smooth stroke. The metal sings, and the weight feels good in my hands. "That's better."

The Demon King grins at me, his sharp teeth flashing. Some Yöomi file their teeth to scare their enemies, but I get the feeling his teeth are the least of my concerns. He sheathes his dagger at his waist and flexes his fingers. Two shotels appear in his hands, copies of my blades down to the holy script engraved in the metal. "Shall we begin?"

He's so proper and prim, the way he eyes me from across the field, that I almost don't expect his attack when it comes. He is a blur of silver as he leaps for me, his body spinning, the amber sunlight reflecting off his blades. I parry right, duck, and roll. I'm back on my feet as soon as I hit the ground. I draw in a ragged breath. It takes a moment for me to look down in shock at the deep gash across my side. I stumble as my anti-magic stitches the wound back together.

The Demon King is strong and nimble as our swords collide. I grit my teeth as I pivot right, aiming my shotel for a vital organ. He lurches back, flipping his wrists so that even as he dodges my attack, he's in control of his next strike. His sword cuts into my shoulder—a little higher, and he would've taken my head. "You're pretty good for being so ancient," I say, spitting on the ground.

"You're the best that the Kingdom and the cravens have to offer?" He laughs. Good to see he's enjoying the part where he gets to cut me into tiny ribbons. "That's highly disappointing."

Ignoring the sweat stinging my eyes, I press the attack. I strike, metal clashing against metal. Again. Again. My arms shake. The Demon King goes for another killing blow, and I drop to my knees, thrusting both shotels up. One pierces his belly and the other jabs between two ribs, shy of my target—his heart.

He growls in pain as I draw my shotels back, and I catch a knee to the face. Several bones shatter, and I fall on my backside. He bears down on my position, and I roll out of the way in time. His momentum pitches him forward, and he stumbles, almost losing his balance. There. My opportunity. While he's distracted, I slice clean through his wrist and sever his hand. I allow myself a grin as blood blurs my vision.

"I seem to be holding my own, old man." I want nothing more than to press the attack again, but I'm still struggling to heal from too many cuts. Is this the future Caster of the Eldest Clan—my craven ancestor—saw for me? Unite the cravens and humans and kill this pompous ass?

"You fight like a man who wants to live, Rudjek," the Demon King says, shaking his head as light glows where his hand had been. When it fades, he has a new hand in its place, identical to the old one. "To fight well, you must be willing to die."

"Are you lecturing me in the middle of trying to kill me?" I cock my head to the side. "You really are an arrogant bastard."

"Your insults won't win you my mercy," he replies as he circles me again.

Arrah is still thrashing against the craven bone chain near Fadyi and Jahla, who are both in their amorphous state. Her skin is smoking where the bone burns into her flesh. The Demon King keeps an eye on her, too, and has the nerve to look grief-stricken. "You say that you loved Dimma, yet you can do that to Arrah." I spit on the ground. "You're pathetic."

"I . . . I don't want to hurt her." The Demon King hesitates, his voice wavering. "I have no choice. Dimma doesn't know what she's doing."

"She's not Dimma," I say through gritted teeth. "That is Arrah—get that through your thick head."

Jahla—I can still tell them apart in their natural forms—bends the space between Arrah and them. Now they're closer to her, which only makes it harder for her to escape. Fadyi manages to slip through a crack in the vines to reach an elongated, slender appendage toward Arrah. It hooks around the edge of the craven bone chain and yanks it off her. When she is free, Arrah stumbles to her feet, dazed, then races toward me. First she is flesh and bone, then she is fire and wind. I try to call to her to stay away, but something's wrong.

I choke on blood that bubbles in my throat and my chest is on fire. The Demon King towers over me, breathing hard, his eyes glowing embers. I clutch my fingers around empty air. My shotels are gone, but I don't remember dropping them. I'm on my knees.

I look down at my chest, the torn skin and muscle, the splintered bone. I gasp for air that doesn't come—I'm not healing. The Demon King raises his sword once more. The last time. I've got no fight left in me, but I lift my chin to stare up at him as he brings it down. I will die with honor—let him remember the face of Rudjek Omari. Arrah materializes between us, her arms outstretched. He comes within a breath of striking her.

"Dimma," he gasps, stumbling back, as if suddenly aware of the brutality of the moment. "You're only prolonging the inevitable."

"I won't let you kill him," she says, but it's too late for that. I'm already dying.

"Ah, this explains a lot," drawls Re'Mec as he flows from the sky on a beam of sunlight. He has two wicked swords in his hands, made of white light almost too bright to look at. Two other orishas stand at his back in shifting shadows. "It seems that my dead sister has come back from her grave, only to die by my sword." He gives Arrah a look of pure disgust. "I always knew there was a reason I didn't like you."

Arrah's magic pushes me away from them—away from her. I blink once, and I land near Fadyi and Jahla, still tangled in the vines. I reach a bloody hand out for them, and I snap the vines with the little strength I have left. Good. They deserve better than dying by that bastard's hand. I close my eyes, succumbing to the pain. When I open them again, Fadyi and Jahla are kneeling over me, back in human form. Jahla presses her hand to my chest to add her anti-magic to mine.

Gasping for air, I glance over my shoulder back to where Arrah and the Demon King stand side by side. Her back is to me. He looks down at her with so much yearning in his eyes that it's a knife to my heart. She should kill him now while his guard is down, but she only stares up at him. I'm glad that I can't see her face. Is she looking at him with the same longing? Two phantom swords appear in her hands. As magic sets her skin aglow, I know that she isn't just Arrah anymore. She is something very ancient and very dangerous. Re'Mec feared that she'd help the Demon King, but this is much worse than I could ever imagine.

I squeeze my eyes shut, sinking into darkness, my mind going blank. It occurs to me, as I'm taking my last breath, that when I die this time, I won't come back.

FORTY
ARRAH

Dimma roars inside me, thrashing against the chains that bind her. Her fury and rage bleed into my mind, planting seeds that grow into writhing shadows. Her thoughts are incoherent and threaten to eclipse my own. She doesn't care if Daho kills Rudjek, and I hate her for it.

I want to go to him now, seeing him so still on the ground. Fadyi and Jahla lean over him with matching grim faces. I have to believe that he'll be okay. Our story can't end like this. He's my best friend; even if we can never be more, I'll always love him.

"Fram lied to us all," Re'Mec says with a bitter laugh. "We thought you were dead. We mourned you before we erased your name from history." He shudders as if shaking off a bad memory. "You were better off dead."

Dimma snatches control of my tongue, and two voices come from my throat. One that is my own and another that sounds menacingly sweet. "Nice to see you, too, brother."

Re'Mec flinches and covers it by pacing back and forth in front of Mouran and Sisi. Mouran, the master of the sea, is tall and dark skinned with ocean eyes, his hair cropped short. His barbed tail curls around his waist. This is the first time Dimma has seen him in mortal form. He's taken the shape of one of his children. Sisi, the fire god, makes no pretenses. She is an ever-changing spiral of flames consuming itself.

Daho attacks first. He's a flash of silver light, his swords slicing, cutting, impaling, but the orishas are just as fast. They streak across the field and through the sky like comets. I sweep my swords to block a blow, then another. Daho and I are back to back. Fighting with him feels right—like it would've been if I hadn't let Fram take my soul.

I push against Dimma's thoughts. As I do, Mouran lassos his barbed tail around my waist and brings me to my knees. Pain shoots through my body, and I scream.

Daho turns his attention to Mouran. When he does, Re'Mec takes advantage. He'd known that I would be a distraction. The sun orisha runs Daho through with his sword, and Sisi joins in the attack, her fire marring his flesh. Daho stumbles, but he keeps fighting, swinging his swords wide, until he drops to his knees, too.

Re'Mec breaks away from Daho and lifts my chin with his sword. The light burns against my skin, and I bite back another scream.

"You kill her, and none of you will make it from this world in one piece," Daho says, his voice even. I can almost hear him strategizing the best way out.

"I'll take my chances." Re'Mec aims his sword for my head, but the space around us shifts. His sword clashes with another. Sparks of light scatter across my vision until they coalesce into a familiar face. Koré stands in front of me, blocking Re'Mec's blow.

The sun orisha stares at his twin in grim horror. "You would defend her after everything we've been through together . . . after Dimma corrupted your people."

"Yes," Koré hisses at her brother, her eyes two blazing orbs. "I would."

Re'Mec splutters to get out his next word, his face twisted in indignation. "Why?"

"I owe Arrah a debt," Koré says, her hair wiggling down her back. "I'm repaying it now. That should be obvious."

"Can't you see that she's our sister hiding in plain sight?" Re'Mec pulls back his sword and paces again. "And you still defend her?"

"Thanks for stating the obvious, brother," Koré says, her voice wary. "I know who she is now, but we've already tried killing her once, and it's led to nothing but turmoil for five thousand years. Let's not make the same mistake."

"Am I to believe that you've grown a conscience?" Re'Mec spits, as the light from the sun intensifies around Koré. Amber rays bounce off her dark skin.

"Brother, don't," she warns, but Re'Mec sets his jaw, his eyes hard.

Koré pushes against the light and fails to break free of it. I'd never expected the Twin Kings to go against each other. I had my doubts about Koré, but she's changed over the years, which is no small feat for one of Dimma's brethren. Change is not in their nature.

"Again, I must show you why I was born first," Re'Mec says with a deep sigh. "You mean well, sister, but your mistakes have cost us twice."

Iben's gate opens behind Daho. It's a wall of fog as he backs through it. He meets my eyes before he disappears. Re'Mec laughs. He thinks that Daho has run away, but I know better. He would never leave Dimma—not after everything he's done to get her back.

Another gate opens on the edge of the field, and the orishas grow brighter—their power immense, crushing, all-consuming. Re'Mec releases his sister from her prison, and she moves to his side, her swords ready. They complement each other in every way—light and dark, mercy and vengeance. Demons stalk through a pool of golden light. Black, brown, and white winged, skin from the deepest purple to near colorless. Still more demons pour into the field behind them—ones in human vessels. The tribal people stand between the demons and the orishas.

It's my worst nightmare come true. The orishas and demons will destroy everything and everyone in their path. I can't stop them—it's happening all over again. History repeating itself. Dimma died so that Daho and his people could live—she killed to save him, but it was for nothing. Her brethren and the demons will fight until the end of time if left to their own devices, and I'm helpless to stop them.

Shezmu leads the demons' army, but they don't attack. Instead, they form a circle around us. Re'Mec hisses at Shezmu, who blows him a kiss. "Squabbling with your sister again, I see," Shezmu says. "The two of you are so predictable."

"It beats being a puppet on the Demon King's string," Re'Mec snaps.

I come to my feet, and for a brief moment Shezmu turns his attention to me. His greedy gaze feels like a thousand ants burrowing underneath my skin. I expect him to want revenge for me killing Efiya, but he only gives me a sheepish smile. The gesture catches me off guard, and I don't trust it. Daho may have objected to Arti's ritual, but Shezmu had no qualms about eating the children's souls.

Fog appears again where Daho had opened his gate. Snow and wind flutter from the vortex as Fram floats out of it still in chains. Now the black appendages leave nothing exposed below their shoulders. They thrash across Fram's bodies, twisting in a sea of darkness that threatens to swallow the orisha. Daho is behind Fram with his blade pressed into their back.

"You don't want to be doing that, boy," Re'Mec warns.

An uncontrollable fear sinks in my chest. Fram killed Dimma, and I should feel no sympathy for them. Yet I'm terrified. Fram is the balance between life and death, chaos and order. What will these things be without them?

"Daho," Dimma and I say together, twin voices. "Let them go."

"Fram is the key to freeing you," Daho says through gritted teeth, his voice choked with grief. He lowers the dagger and it grows into a sword of pure light. I don't move—I am frozen in place as the horror of the moment unfolds. His sword is a blur as Koré, Re'Mec, Mouran, and Sisi descend upon him. He sweeps the blade wide and takes both of Fram's heads.

I stumble back as the orisha of life and death slumps to the ground. Their bodies twitch before bursting into light that spreads across the field. Their cooling magic brings me a sense of peace. It calms Dimma, but it does not free her.

"What have you done?" Koré says, her face grim. "Fram was holding *them* back."

Them.

Her children.

The calming light from only a moment ago stretches into shadows that bleed across the sky, swallowing the sun. Darkness settles over the land. The shadows leach the life from everything they touch. The grass turns to ash, and the air grows cold. A sense of dread overwhelms me—it overwhelms everyone. Some of the tribal people and the demons begin to weep. Fram told Dimma that their children were too dangerous for the world. All this time, the orisha of life and death had held their children inside them. Now they are free and devouring everything in their path.

You wouldn't be the first to give up a child, Fram had told Dimma. *I know that better than most.*

"The reapers," Koré whispers. "The destroyers of worlds."

"Mortal kind is doomed," Re'Mec adds, resigned.

Without them saying more, I understand. Only Fram could control their children. Daho opens Iben's gate again, and Shezmu and his army melt into gray smoke as they flee through it. "We have to go, Dimma." Daho clutches my arm, suddenly at my side. "Come with me. I can protect you."

"I can't." I look up into his glowing eyes. *I won't.* An unspoken understanding passes between us, and he lets go of me. He isn't giving up forever, but he relents for now. "Help us," I beg. "Open another gate, so my people can return home."

"This isn't the end of our story," Daho says, as he concedes to my request.

I back away from him. "I know."

The orishas slow down the reapers with shields of bright light as the tribal people run through the gate to Zöran, but the orishas can't stop them. Everything Fram's children touch dies, and soon the light begins to fade, too. Fadyi and Jahla carry Rudjek through the gate. His body is limp, his face gray. Kira and Essnai bring up the rear, urging me to hurry up. Re'Mec and Koré disappear last.

Daho and I are the only two left now. He backs into his gate, and I step into the one that will take me home. He mouths "I love you" to Dimma, and she says it back to him—*I* say it. His beautiful face is the last thing I see before the gate pulls me into a stream of light. I land on my feet on the other side, my eyes trained on the gate until it disappears.

I don't doubt that I will see Daho again, but I push him out of my mind as I look for Rudjek. There are so many people here. Kingdom soldiers in red. Guardians in white. Another army in blue and silver. Zeknorians? It's cold and snowing, but I keep pushing through the crowd. Soldiers offer aid to the tribal people, who are underdressed for this weather.

"Arrah, here!" Essnai calls from across the crowd. I push my way to meet her and Kira in front of a tent. Kira's face is pale, and her eyes hollow. "He's inside with the cravens."

"It's too late." Fadyi pulls back the flap of the tent, shaking his head. "He's too far gone."

Jahla looks as hollow as Kira, wrapping her arms around herself.

I don't ask if I can see him—I barge into the tent, my legs heavy. Rudjek is on a cot, his brown skin pallid. I kneel at his side and stroke his face. He is so cold, and I can barely sense his anti-magic. "Wake up," I say, swallowing my tears.

I expect him to give me a crooked grin, but he doesn't move. I curl up next to him. "Come back to me."

I close my eyes, and I am in a dark place. Dimma stands across from me. She is taller than I expected, almost as tall as Daho, with eyes as dark as Rudjek's. Her wild curls stand up every which way and frame her long lashes and a forehead lined with slender veins.

"Is what Fram said true?" I bite my lip. "The only way to separate us is through my death."

"Yes," Dimma answers.

"That's not fair!" I shout, seething with anger. "You had your chance at life. You had seven hundred years with Daho. Why can't I save Rudjek—why can't I be with him?"

"I can save him for a price."

How could Daho love her when she's so . . . *cold*. No, not cold; that isn't right. Tired, weary, defeated. Her emotions wrap around me in slivers of fire and ice. "Name it," I say without thinking. "I'll pay it."

"You're too powerful with the chieftains' magic, and you'll use it to hurt Daho if given a chance," Dimma says. "I can't allow that."

"What are you saying?" I look up at her, seeing the girl who helped the Demon King bring the gods to their knees. Dimma: god, girl, wife, mother, traitor, monster.

"Your magic in exchange for his life," she says as if it's a simple matter. "If you agree, I will save your *ama* and return to my slumber until your death. Daho can wait for me a little longer. All you have to do is release the chieftains' *kas*."

I can hardly process what she's asking, no, not asking—what she is demanding. I can't give up my magic with the demons threatening our world. How can I protect the tribal people—how can I protect myself? The chieftains' memories have become a comfort—their magic my savior and my curse. I tell myself that I've used their gift to do more good than bad, but I can't forget the awful things that I've done, too. I've killed so many, and given the chance, I *will* kill Daho to save Rudjek. Dimma knows my mind better than I know hers.

"You would leave me helpless against the demons?" I ask, my voice small.

She would have me give up my only connection left to the tribal people—*my magic.*

"Daho would never hurt you," Dimma says without doubt.

"Daho would never hurt me?" I shake my head. "He knows that I must die to free you."

"While you decide, Rudjek grows closer to death," Dimma says, ignoring my words. "Soon I will not be able to stop his soul from ascending. If he reaches the Supreme Cataclysm, he will be unmade."

In the end, she and I are more alike than we are different. She's counting on that. She knew that I could never say no. She's risked everything to save Daho, and I'd do the same for Rudjek.

"I'll do it," I whisper through choked tears.

I call up the chieftains' memories one last time. Grandmother, Beka, and the others bid me a silent farewell. I speak the words to unbind them, and the chieftains' *kas* shake loose from my soul. It feels like I'm shattering into a million pieces, and I can't help but wonder if Dimma felt the same way when she split her soul to make the demons immortal.

When it's done, I am left with an immense sense of emptiness. I am a *ben'ik* again—almost magicless—but Rudjek will live.

FORTY-ONE
ARRAH

Rudjek and I stand on the ridge where the crossroads starts. The refugees from the camp have settled in Tribe Zu's lands for now, but we must keep going. Last night we held a funeral for Sukar, Majka, and Raëke. Jahla was stone-faced as she stared into the fire. Rudjek told me that she and Majka had become more than friends. Essnai and I hummed a burial song for Sukar. We've mourned him twice, and I know that I will mourn him for the rest of my life.

Rudjek pulls me into his arms. I inhale him, savoring his scent of woodsmoke and lilac. I can still sense his anti-magic. It moves across his skin like invisible ants marching to the beat of their own drum. Now that I'm back to my old self—the almost magicless girl—his anti-magic doesn't act against me. It is only an impression of warmth and awareness that pricks down my back.

"Are you sure you're up for this?" Rudjek asks, cocking one crooked eyebrow. He's healed from his injuries except for a few tender spots. "We could wait a few more days."

"We're already on borrowed time," I say, running my fingers along his jaw. I've become obsessed with the feel of his stubble. The way it bristles against my skin, how it pricks and teases and tickles my face when we kiss. It won't be long before Daho learns how to control the reapers and comes for his enemies—before he comes for me.

"I can think of several ways to make good use of that borrowed time." Rudjek's voice is heavy as he brushes a finger across my lips. I want more of him, but that must wait for now.

"Watch yourself with that one." Re'Mec shimmers out of thin air in front of us. He is in white robes trimmed in gold—the Almighty One's colors. It's a not-so-subtle reminder of Rudjek's place in the war to come. "She is truly a viper in disguise. She'll poison your heart if you let her."

Rudjek rests his hands on his shotels. "Why are you here, Re'Mec?"

"Oh, you know, waiting for the Demon King to open Iben's gate and destroy this world." Re'Mec flourishes his hand like it's no consequence to him, but I know him better than that. "Or maybe he won't bother to come himself and just send the reapers."

I shudder, remembering the sense of dread and sadness that had overcome me when Daho killed Fram. Dimma had shared a kinship with them—closer than she had with any of her other siblings. Through her, I understand the reapers' hunger, their need to destroy. She had passed along a similar craving to the demons when she made them immortal. "I can't believe Fram is really gone."

"I don't know about that." Re'Mec shrugs. "Only time will tell."

I inhale a sharp breath. "What are you saying?"

"Dimma's still alive within you, so Fram may yet resurface," Re'Mec answers.

"What about the reapers?" Rudjek asks. "Can you stop them?"

"No." Re'Mec grimaces. "The Demon King is the only one who can control them now."

Rudjek frowns like he's in deep thought. "What is he waiting for?"

"That's a good question," Koré drawls, appearing next to her brother. She wears red, the color of the Blood Moon. It takes a little getting used to, seeing her without her box, and she doesn't seem to know what to do with her idle hands.

"Perhaps he's waiting for Dimma to call to him?" Re'Mec says, raising an eyebrow.

Rudjek shifts uncomfortably beside me, and I glance at the ground, my cheeks burning with shame. Dimma kept her end of our bargain. She manipulated the chieftains' magic to draw Rudjek back from the brink of death. All this time, I thought my magic and his anti-magic would keep us apart, but Dimma had found a way around it.

"Dimma is asleep." I swallow hard. I remember every moment she spent with Daho, the child growing in her belly, the day she made the demons immortal. It's all there. But since I let go of the chieftains' *kas*, I can only glean faint impressions of them. They did leave me with one parting gift. I know hundreds, if not thousands, of rituals by heart now. Little good it does me without magic of my own. To use any of the rituals, I would have to go back to trading my years in exchange for magic.

"She won't always be asleep," Koré warns. "You know that."

I don't take her words lightly, or what's left unsaid. Dimma won't always be asleep, and when she wakes, she'll side with the Demon King against her brethren. When she wakes, it will mean my death. "We'll worry about that day when it comes," I say. "For now, I'd like to see the tribal people one last time."

I don't know why Daho hasn't come through the gate to Zöran, but I won't squander what time I have left. I interlace my fingers with Rudjek's and lean into him. I will never get used to the feel of his skin against mine.

Essnai, Kira, and Fadyi join us at the head of the crossroads as the sun and moon orishas quietly disappear. I've grown used to their impromptu visits and idle conversation. Though they'll never admit to it, they want to be close to Dimma. They miss her. Maybe they even regret the choices that they've made. She misses them, too.

Without the chieftains, the outline of the crossroads isn't as bright, but I can still see the sparks clinging to the path. A white cat saunters past me, and then jumps into Fadyi's arms. Jahla hasn't taken human form since we left the North. We're all grieving in our own way. Fadyi smiles down at her, stroking her back, then he cradles her against his chest. She lets out a gentle purr and closes her eyes.

As I step onto the crossroads, I don't know what tomorrow holds. Dimma may have taken away my magic to fight against Daho, but I don't need magic when I have her as leverage. Whether she knows it or not, she is my hostage, my unwilling accomplice, my coconspirator. When the time comes, I will wield her memories like a newly forged blade and put an end to the Demon King.

THE UNNAMED ORISHA: DIMMA

Of my brethren's creations, time has always been the most difficult for me to accept. All these years, it's been slippery on my fingertips. Now time is running out for me. It ticks down to the moment of my first death and the day the war between my brethren and Daho began in earnest.

The palace rings with the clash of swords, the sizzle of magic, the taste of blood. The battle is growing closer now—it echoes in the halls. I sit upon a throne of polished bone inlaid with gold and jewels that is at once grotesque and beautiful. I am high above the floor, at the top of the stairs that Daho built for me to watch the heavens. At this hour, when my brother Re'Mec rules, I am bathed in his sunlight through the amethyst sky dome above.

"You must leave this place, my son," I say, cradling my belly. "Do not return or visit any of the continuum of worlds that my brethren have created, and they will not seek you out. Stay hidden, and one day, you will find your purpose." I smile as tears wet my cheeks, listening to his protests. "I know that none of this makes sense, and I am sorry that we will not watch you grow up. My son, you are the beginning of the end. I know that now. That is why my brethren are afraid." I stroke my belly as the child makes a single declaration. He wants to save us. "You already have. We will live through you."

I reach into my vessel, my hand passing through my flesh like a phantom, and take the child. He is a tiny beam of light. He has my true form and Daho's kind heart. I sense it pulsing in him—he is stronger than my brethren, stronger than Daho or me. He is more like the Supreme Cataclysm than I could've ever imagined. I don't know how this is possible, and I would like to understand if there was time. But my brethren are moments from breaking through my shield around the throne. "Go, Heka," I say. "You must live."

He floats up from my hand and hovers in front of my face, right between my eyes. His presence is warm against my skin as he pulses with love. He touches my nose in an embrace and then rises through the sky dome. Fram is almost through my defenses, but I have time for one final act. I collect my memories from this moment, like catching fireflies in a jar; I crush them in my hand. The only way to protect my son is not to remember that I sent him away. I squeeze my eyes shut, shuddering.

A cloak of darkness bleeds into the chamber, swallowing the sunshine and the sounds of the battle. One of my siblings has slipped past Daho and his army and broken through my defenses. I let out a deep, tired sigh.

So many will die because of my decisions. My sister Koré once told me that a god's love is a dangerous thing. I know that now. I don't want to die, but I deserve my fate.

"Oh, Dimma." Fram's anguished dual voices cut through me. "What have you done?"

When I open my eyes, Fram stands before me in their two forms, twins of light and dark, life and death, chaos and calm. I realize almost immediately that I have lost a slice of time—there is a hole in my memories, a piece cut out. I look down at my clenched fist, the hand that only a moment ago held my child. My fingers tremble as they unfold, one by one, and reveal an empty palm.

The amethyst ceiling cracks with my rage and rains down in shards that tear into my flesh. The walls weep my tears. "Where is he?" I demand. "Where is my son?"

"I am sorry, sister," Fram says as their shadows cup my face. They brush away my tears, and I am flooded with relief that it is Fram who came to steal my life, not Koré or Re'Mec. Of all my siblings, Fram understands me best. "You shouldn't have been the one to do it. That is cruelty that I do not wish upon anyone."

"I killed him?" I ask, drawing the only possible conclusion. I shrink against the throne, gutted and hollow. I've done something unforgivable. "I killed my son."

I remember every single moment of my first life, except this one. I'd cradled my child in my hands and then . . . he was gone. Some acts are too horrible to remember—some deeds too painful to keep.

Tears spill from Fram's eyes, too. "Re'Mec and Koré will end the war only when both you and the child are dead. They will spare Daho and his people if you agree to our terms."

I stare down at my hands again. I can't live with what I've done—I can't face Daho. I cannot tell him that I've killed our son. "Do it," I say. "Before I change my mind."

Fram strikes me with ribbons of light. They cut into my chest and rip out the part of me connected to the Supreme Cataclysm—my immortality. My soul withers as their shadows brush away the last of the tears on my empty vessel's face. Even I cannot free myself from the clutches of the god of life and death. But as I've said, this is not the end of my story.

It is also the beginning.

EPILOGUE: DAHO

I rake my fingers through the soil. It's lifeless. Nothing grows in Ilora. Imagine spending five thousand years on a world with no trees, no grass, no flowers. The gods turned our world into purgatory and trapped my people here. They've been in a box of their own—and some of them are shell-shocked and combative.

My mission in life is to destroy the gods, and now that I have Fram's children, it will be easy. I can feel them seeping into the edges of my mind—their hunger, their yearning to devour.

I glance up at the wasteland around me. There are so many faces in the gloomy half light of our dying sun. I know that we can't stay here, not forever, but it will do for now. My people have been separated for so long. They need a moment of rest, and I need to collect my thoughts.

This is only a minor setback. I won't give up. Dimma is so close to being whole again. I thought that Arrah would understand—that once Dimma woke, everything would be like before. That was only a fantasy born out of a lethal cocktail of hope and desperation. There is no way to reclaim the past. It's time to look to the future—to what will be.

Fram did more damage than I thought possible. I will find a way to release Dimma from her prison, but it means nothing with the boy still alive. Rudjek. His name sends a wave of ice down my spine. I can't kill him myself. That would be another mistake. It would only push Dimma farther away, which leaves me in a very difficult predicament.

There's laughter among the people scattered around me, and celebration. Some are getting used to having bodies again for the first time in five thousand years. Some are finding long-lost friends and family from before the gods closed the gate.

"When do you plan to release my daughter?" Shezmu asks from behind me. He has a sharp edge to his voice, like when he's preparing to argue his point. It's been so long since I debated him over strategy of war and, before that, over a game board after evening meals. "Haven't you punished her enough?"

He's reshaped his human vessel to look like his old self. Silver skin, sea-green eyes, and long hair as white as snow pulled back over his shoulders. In his posture, I see his wariness, his strength, his hunger for revenge. I see his sadness for Ta'la, the daughter he lost so long ago. I remember that day in the courtyard after Eluua and the endoyans attacked.

That was the day that Dimma gave our people her gift of immortality, but it came with a curse. None of them can bear children of their own anymore. Efiya was the first child in over five thousand years, and it took Heka's power to make it possible. He keeps himself separate from the orishas, but I shall pay him a visit soon. He is the key. Once I consume his soul and possess his power, along with that of the reapers, I will finally end this war and get Dimma back.

"Efiya went against my orders and attacked the tribal people." I come to my feet. I sympathize with Shezmu, but he must understand why I have left Efiya imprisoned for months. "She's proved herself time and time again to be unpredictable and untrustworthy."

"If there are character flaws in my daughter, then I am the one to blame." Shezmu's wings quake against his back like they always do when he's worried. "I poured everything that is me into her soul—good and bad. Punish me for her mistakes, for she did not have her parents to guide her in the way that a child should have. Let me make up for that now."

"What will you do if she steps out of line again?" I ask after a deep sigh. "What happens the next time she doesn't obey my orders?"

"If it's all the same to you, I'd like my daughter to stay out of your war with the gods." Shezmu crosses his arms and takes a wide stance like he's been thinking about this for some time. "There's no reason for her to fight. She's done enough by freeing you."

"You have a point there, although I did not miss how you avoided answering my questions." I brush the dirt from my hands and remove the dagger from the sheath at my waist. "Try to keep her out of trouble, will you?"

"Of course, my king." Shezmu gives me a sarcastic bow. We haven't been formal since before Koré imprisoned me in her box. It's good that he has his sense of humor back.

His face is full of hope and anticipation, like I'd been the day I found out that Dimma was with child. I so enjoyed listening to the sounds our son made growing in her belly. She always said that he was talking to her, but theirs was a language only knowable through their bond. Fram told me that Dimma killed our child before they reaped her soul. I don't believe that—I know my wife, and she could never do something so unspeakable. Only she knows what happened to our son, and I must find out the truth.

I run my finger across the blade with the intent of drawing Efiya to the surface. I can sense her almost immediately. Her soul feels like trying to hold water and watching it slip between my fingers. When she emerges from the blade, she is mist that settles into the shape of a girl. She looks the same. Human. Green eyes like her father's, wild hair, her mother's beauty. Shezmu weeps at the sight of her and pulls her into an embrace.

"I've missed you so much, daughter," he says, his eyes squeezed shut.

Efiya stands with her arms limp at her sides until he lets her go. Then she turns around to face me. "Well," she puts her hands on her hips, "it's about time."

ACKNOWLEDGMENTS

In *Reaper of Souls*, our heroine is surrounded by a cast of players that drive the plot to its inevitable crescendo. By that same token, I couldn't have written Arrah's story without the support, love, and encouragement from my very own cast of players. Always thankful to my mother, who bought my first electric typewriter and read my first manuscript. Those early days of encouragement helped me through the doubt and rejection that every writer faces. To my brothers, I will always be grateful for your support and thankful for our many chats.

To Cyril, so thankful for your patience and our mutual love of K-dramas. You're there for the good writing days and the bad ones. Your dedication to your passion inspires me to never give up.

To my literary agent, Suzie Townsend, you are a tireless advocate and cheerleader, and I am thankful to have you on my team. Thanks to Joanna Volpe, New Leaf Literary Agency's fearless leader and mastermind. Pouya Shahbazian, the best film agent in the known world and my go-to person for movie news. Veronica Grijalva and Victoria Henderson for shopping *Reaper* in the international markets. Meredith Barnes, for your wealth of advice and witty sense of humor. To Dani, you're a rock star. To Hilary, Joe, Madhuri, Cassandra, and Kelsey, thank you for your support.

To my amazing editors, Stephanie Stein at HarperTeen and Vicky Leech at HarperVoyager UK. I am thankful for your thoughtfulness, sharp eyes, and our brainstorming sessions. Always appreciate that you support my incessant need to never make things easy for my characters.

To the team behind Stephanie at HarperTeen—Louisa Currigan, Jon Howard, Martha Schwartz, and Monique Vescia—I couldn't do it without your expertise. Many thanks. To Sam Benson for publicity, Valerie Wong for marketing, and Allison Brown for production, thank you for supporting *Reaper*. I'm so grateful for the school and library team: Patty Rosati, Mimi Rankin, and Katie Dutton. Another round of applause for Jenna Stempel-Lobell for design.

Much respect to cover artist Adeyemi Adegbesan. You did it again, and, Keisha, you channeled Arrah brilliantly.

Natasha Bardon, thank you for being a champion of this book at HarperVoyager UK. To the marketing team, Rachel Quin, Fleur Clarke, and Hannah O'Brien, thank you. Jaime Frost, thank you for publicity. To the design team, you created a magical cover for the UK market. Thanks to Robyn Watts for working tirelessly on production and organizing the special edition.

To my friend Ronni Davis, you are amazing. I adore your energy, kindness, friendship, and humor. Thanks for being there for all the ups and downs, and the fun news.

To my ride-or-die friend Alexis Henderson, one of these days when we're not on endless deadlines we're going to finish that secret project, I promise. Thank you for your unrivaled support, which has been a lifeline.

My writing family: Samira, Gloria, Lizzie, Ronni (Hi again!), Ebony, Cathy, Nancy, Irene, Nevien, and honorable members Anna and Kat. Reese, Mia, Lane, Rosaria, and Jeff, who left us for warmer weather. To the Speculators who adopted me: David S, Antra, Axie, David M, Nikki, Liz, Erin, Alex, Helen, Amanda.

Thank you to the countless others who have offered me encouragement and support throughout the years.

The biggest thanks go to the booksellers and librarians for championing *Reaper of Souls*. And to the readers who've championed my books and sent me nice messages, thank you for everything.

ONE
ARRAH

I dream of a different life. I dream of kissing Rudjek in our secret place by the Serpent River underneath a shade tree, magic alighting on my skin and glowing inside me. Grinding herbs at my father's side in his shop while he tells me another story of his tribe. Watching my mother paint dancers on the wall outside my bedchamber. I dream of holding my sister's hand as we traverse the crowds of haggling patrons and eager merchants in the East Market.

This Efiya is a little girl admiring all the trinkets with wide-eyed innocence. She's not the monster who killed our parents and so many others—the monster who freed the Demon King. And my mother isn't the woman who fed children's souls to a demon in a bid to destroy the gods. My father is still alive. Sukar. Grandmother. All the others. But these dreams will never come true—they're only wishful thinking to calm the ghosts that haunt my memories.

I've sacrificed so much already. I don't doubt that I will sacrifice much more before the end.

I wish that I could bury my thoughts as easily as I push back the branches of saplings that cut across our path. We're deep in a forest on the crossroads in search of what's left of the five tribes of Heka. Sweat softens our grime-stiff clothes, and mosquitoes the size of horseflies buzz about our faces. Under different circumstances, I might close my eyes and listen to the birdsong or watch the lizards scurry across tree trunks or admire the wildflowers nestled in the underbrush. But all I can think about is Dimma.

I tell myself that I will be better than her. That I won't make her mistakes. That I will turn away from the temptation that ruined her . . . but I am very good at pretending. I am good at killing, too, or I was before she stripped me of the chieftains' magic to protect her *ama*. In a way, the Demon King was my *ama*, too, for she is a part of me. *Twenty-gods, I was her.* That much, I will concede. I was once a ruthless god who loved the Demon King. Let me clarify: Dimma still loves him despite the horrible things that he's done. I sigh at the memories of his touch, his lips against hers, the calming timbre of his voice. I am not her, but I can't deny the longing stirring inside me.

"Dare I ask what's on your mind?" Rudjek asks as the still morning air gives way to the lash of the hot sun. He's keeping his distance as he walks alongside me.

I curse under my breath when we pass a familiar wizened tree stump. I can't bring myself to meet his gaze, so I stare intently at the path. "I think we've been here before."

"We should stop for a bit," Rudjek suggests, though he sounds like he has enough energy to go on for days.

His craven guardians have shifted into hawks that circle the sky, their wings occasionally offering slivers of respite from the sun.

Essnai clings to her *ama*'s arm and whispers something that draws a coy smile from Kira. I try not to think about the absence of Majka, Raëke, Sukar, but a hollow ache rises in my throat nonetheless. With it comes the bitter taste of shame. I killed Sukar while trying to protect him, and then the Demon King stole his body.

"I would rather keep moving," I finally answer.

After a month on the crossroads, we're no closer to finding the tribal people. Without the chieftains' magic, it's been nearly impossible. Ahead of us, the path splits into forks that double back and cross over themselves in every direction. I sigh when I see a circle of white ash against the bark of a tree. Kira drew it just this morning. She's been tracking our path through the crossroads. Somewhere I've made another wrong turn.

"We knew this wouldn't be easy," Essnai offers, her voice a soft coo. "We expected detours, but we can't give up hope. We'll find the tribes."

"It would help if I weren't leading us in circles half the time," I mutter, annoyed.

I have to believe the tribes made it to safety after Efiya and the demons attacked their lands, but my hope is beginning to dim. We've found no fresh footprints. No smoldering ashes of campfires, no bones from roasted meat, not so much as a branch crushed under a passing foot that wasn't our own. I think of Dimma again and my plan. She'd used my borrowed magic to heal Rudjek; maybe it was possible to use *her* magic to stop the Demon King. There must be someone left in the tribes who could help me unlock it while keeping her asleep. I can't stand by and let the Demon King hurt anyone else—not if I can do something to stop him.

I wish that I could trust Koré and Re'Mec, but I've seen firsthand through my own eyes and secondhand through Dimma's that things only get worse when the gods are involved.

"We've been walking for hours," Rudjek says suddenly; then he leans in close to me, knowing full well what will happen. "You look like you could use some rest."

I brace myself for the effect of his anti-magic, and it comes at once. The faint lines of the trail suddenly disappear. I bite my lip, pushing back my frustration. I don't regret making the deal with Dimma to give up the chieftains' gift to save Rudjek's life, but I hate that his anti-magic completely washes out my ability to see magic when he's this close. "I'm fine," I say, insisting on pushing ahead.

Rudjek squints and glances at me sideways. A look meant to bait me. "You're not a very good liar."

It works.

I press my hand to his cheek, tracing the bristle of the beard that has only recently appeared. I suspect it will be as thick and curly as the hair on his head in a few years. Touching him, now that we *can* touch, always helps me not to feel so lost. Rudjek, Essnai, Kira, and even Fadyi and Jahla are my anchors. They are all I have left. I shiver when Rudjek kisses my palm—Dimma liked when Daho did that.

"You always get that dreamy look when. . . ," Rudjek murmurs, his gaze searching. He lets his words trail off, but I know what he started to say. *"When you're thinking about him."* "At least when I kiss you, I won't puncture your lips."

The joke is about Daho's pointed teeth, of course. Teeth that spent countless hours delicately grazing Dimma's wrists, her neck, the hollows of her collarbone. Other places that I try not to remember.

"Are you so insecure that you think I'd waste my time fantasizing about the Demon King?"

"Yes." Rudjek looks down at me, rubbing the back of his neck. "He's taller than me, I'll give him that—and then there are those wings and glowing eyes. Oh, and that wicked blade for trapping souls."

I frown. "Now that you mention it . . ."

Rudjek pretends to stagger back, clutching his heart. Then he bats his long dark lashes and poses. "I happen to be very pretty, too, you know."

I raise an eyebrow, delighting in this playful banter. It reminds me of the way we were before things became so complicated. "I hadn't noticed."

But pretty is an understatement. Rudjek is also tall, with golden brown skin, eyes as black as a moonless night, dark, lush eyebrows, and an irresistible smile. His curls have grown long and unruly while we've been on the road. I like it. He looks less like the Crown Prince and more like the boy I used to sneak away to meet by the river, the boy with a spark of adventure in his eyes, who couldn't have cared less what his demanding father thought of him.

Essnai laughs. I glance over my shoulder and get the feeling that she and Kira are gossiping about us. Sometimes I think it's a mistake to let my friends come with me, but I don't know how to do this alone.

"See?" Rudjek scoffs. "Even Kira and Essnai think I'm pretty."

"You wish," Kira says, making a face.

"Must you always be so insufferable, Rudjek?" Essnai asks.

"You finally see how much work it was to serve as his attendant!

And then again under his command." Kira pretends to be exasperated. "He is so tiring."

"Hey!" Rudjek protests.

Kira picks up a small stone and pitches it at him, and he dodges it with ease.

I'm grateful for these moments of levity, but they don't last nearly long enough. "Now, if you don't mind, I need to get back to tracking the crossroads," I say, gesturing for Rudjek to give me more space.

He frowns, but he doesn't object when Kira hooks her arm underneath his and pulls him away. "There'll be plenty of time for frolicking later. Stop distracting her."

"I am not distracting her," he mumbles. "As usual, she's being stubborn."

Once the sting of his anti-magic fades, I seek out the lines of the crossroads again, my gaze searching over rocks and crooked tree roots and vines. I'm convinced that one day even this gift will be stripped away, leaving me with nothing. Since I was a child, it'd been my one true talent, and I couldn't imagine losing it.

I stare so long I have to blink back tears gathering in the corners of my eyes. It helps the burning, but not by much. My vision isn't what it used to be—yet another not-so-subtle side effect of trading my years in exchange for magic. Another consequence I must live with to the end of my days. I let out a soft sigh when the lines of the crossroads finally shimmer underneath the sun. The tightness eases in my chest.

Rudjek's guardians perch high in a tree, waiting for us. One is iridescent brown, the other snow white. Before I lost the chieftains' gift, I could see the way the cravens worked to hold their physical shape—their skin always moving like water washing over the hull of a ship.

My friends don't question our route as we pick up the trail again, though it loops, circles, and takes random turns through thorned bushes that sting our ankles. We cross into a thick part of the forest that offers relief from the sun. In the shadows, the magic is much more pronounced. It clings to the trees like silky moss and drifts lazily between the branches. It makes me ache for the nights that it came to me willingly.

After everything that's happened, I should be repulsed by it, but I still feel a sense of wonder like when I was a child during Imebyé in Tribe Aatiri and tried to pluck it from the air. I swallow my bitterness. If I can't tap into Dimma's gifts, the only way I can possess magic again is to trade my years. That could lead to nothing good. If recent events have taught me anything, it's that I want the chance to live my life on my own terms, for however much time I have left.

"There's something strange about the magic here," Rudjek says almost to himself. He stops in the middle of the path and slowly turns, frowning at a single sapling in a clearing bathed in the amber of the afternoon light.

I stop, too. I don't sense anything amiss, but I trust his instincts. The sun orisha made cravens to hunt down magic, so his perception of it is much stronger than mine. I look ahead at a tangle of lines on the crossroads that intersect near a tree. They pulse and writhe, but that isn't unusual. It's by design; the entire crossroads is a maze meant to keep anyone from finding the tribal people.

"What is it?" Kira asks.

Rudjek rests his hands on his hips, near the hilts of his swords. "I don't know. All I can say is that it feels *strange*."

"Maybe it's best if we keep going and not stay here." I point to the lines as if my friends can see them. "I just need some time to study the intersection."

"I think I'll scout ahead," Rudjek says, but it's an excuse to give me more distance from his anti-magic. His guardians, Fadyi and Jahla, land nearby, and their shapes stretch from feathers and wings into arms and legs. Their human forms look much like the hawks': Fadyi with rich brown skin and dark hair; Jahla with paler skin, light eyes, and snow-white hair.

Essnai thrusts a waterskin in my hand. "Drink this before you pass out from the heat."

I take it from her, but I hesitate, my hand shaking. The supple leather reminds me of the night when she, Sukar, Tyrek, and I sat around a campfire, sharing a wineskin and playing the drum. Sukar had danced with Essnai, the two of them ethereal underneath the moonlight.

Only it wasn't Sukar.

Essnai's eyes meet mine as if she knows what I am thinking. Her touch is gentle as she guides the waterskin to my lips. "Drink."

Always so bossy, Sukar used to tease her. And he was always cynical but warm and funny.

"Fine." I sigh. After taking a swig, I turn back to the path. The magic of the crossroads is clever. Sometimes it pulses like a heartbeat; sometimes it flows like water over smooth stone. I kneel and run my hand along the tangle of lines, feeling the throb of the magic.

It takes a moment, but one of the lines shimmers, suddenly

standing out from the others, revealing the right path. I get to my feet. "I've found the next leg of our journey."

"Time to go," Essnai calls to the others.

Rudjek returns to the clearing with his guardians. They stay back while Kira and Essnai keep me company, chattering away. Now that we're following the shimmering line, I see the strangeness that Rudjek sensed earlier. The magic is disjointed, as though it's held together by a fraying rope.

As the sun sinks low in the sky and then finally slips below the horizon, I take a fork on the path and immediately know that I've made another mistake. I'm hit with a blast of rank air that twists my belly in knots. The stink is of death and decay, things that I have become intimately familiar with.

Shadows pass in front of the flickering lines of the crossroads. *Familiars*, I tell myself. Until recently, they'd been harmless— shapeless wandering souls trapped between life and death by Dimma's hand. But when Efiya released Daho, he commanded them to attack Rudjek. Another rush of rank air sweeps across my path, and I see staring, hollow eyes in the dark. Dozens of them, faintly glowing.

Familiars don't have eyes.

I stumble back and collide with Rudjek, and he catches me in his arms. The crossroads blink out, blocked by his anti-magic. "I take it we took a wrong turn . . . ," he says as he pulls away from me and draws his swords. His guardians flank him, searching the darkness unfolding in front of us. Essnai readies her staff.

"Demons?" Kira asks as she retrieves two of the many daggers strapped to her body.

"No," Rudjek murmurs, and Fadyi nods in agreement.

Magic swells in the forest. Sparks fly from the trees to join with the shadows, swarming like wasps, until they illuminate the faces of decaying carcasses. Dread crawls across my skin at the realization: before us stand a dozen *akkaye*.

"So much for looking forward to a moment's rest," Rudjek says as he and the cravens move between the *akkaye* and me.

"Burning fire," Kira curses. "What kind of perversion is this?"

I swallow down my horror as the *akkaye* shudder. Their long spindly arms quake, and their skeletal fingers stretch and flex as they fully awaken. Ghastly shrieks tear into the night as, one by one, the creatures lurch forward, each step smoother and faster than the last. The *akkaye* are almost inconceivably thin, with pocked, grayish skin stretched tight over protruding ribs and clavicles. They heave in gulps of air, gasping before their hollow, unblinking eyes seem to find us all at once.

"We have to go." I back away from Rudjek so his anti-magic doesn't keep me from finding the path again. I frantically search. I should see something, a glimmer, a stray spark of magic, but the crossroads have gone dark.

Too late I realize that I've led my friends into a trap meant for the demons. The *akkaye* have only one instinct: to kill. And we've been caught in their snare.